CAST THE FIRST STONE

ALSO BY JAMES W. ZISKIN

Styx & Stone

No Stone Unturned

Stone Cold Dead

Heart of Stone

CAST THE FIRST STONE

An Ellie Stone Mystery

JAMES W. ZISKIN

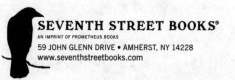

SEVENTH STREET BOOKS®
AN IMPRINT OF PROMETHEUS BOOKS
59 JOHN GLENN DRIVE • AMHERST, NY 14228
www.seventhstreetbooks.com

Published 2017 by Seventh Street Books®, an imprint of Prometheus Books

Cover design by Jacqueline Nasso Cooke
Cover image © jakkapan/Shutterstock
Cover design © Prometheus Books

This is a work of fiction. Characters, organizations, products, locales, and events portrayed in this novel either are products of the author's imagination or are used fictitiously.

Inquiries should be addressed to
Seventh Street Books
59 John Glenn Drive
Amherst, New York 14228
VOICE: 716–691–0133
FAX: 716–691–0137
WWW.SEVENTHSTREETBOOKS.COM

21 20 19 18 17   5 4 3 2 1

Library of Congress Cataloging-in-Publication Data

Names: Ziskin, James W., 1960-, author.
Title: Cast the first stone : an Ellie Stone mystery / James W. Ziskin.
Description: Amherst, NY : Seventh Street Books, an imprint of Prometheus Books, 2017.
Identifiers: LCCN 2017000967 (print) | LCCN 2017006058 (ebook) | ISBN 9781633882812 (paperback) | ISBN 9781633882829 (ebook)
Subjects: LCSH: Women journalists—Fiction. | Murder—Investigation—Fiction | Nineteen sixties—Fiction. | BISAC: FICTION / Mystery & Detective / Women Sleuths. | FICTION / Mystery & Detective / Historical. | GSAFD: Mystery fiction.
Classification: LCC PS3626.I83 C37 2017 (print) | LCC PS3626.I83 (ebook) | DDC 813/.6—dc23
LC record available at https://lccn.loc.gov/2017000967

Printed in the United States of America

*I dedicate this book to all those who have suffered
fear, humiliation, and violence for the crime of being themselves.*

All the world loves a hero. We worship fame and accomplishment, and reward with our devotion and reverence those who rise to the rarified heights of success. We marvel at the virtuosity of prodigies, admire the radiance of the beautiful, and applaud the gifts of the talented. With open hearts, we heap praise and affection on those remarkable individuals. And why? Without even knowing them, we accept an inexplicable shared acknowledgement that these people are our betters. Perhaps we are more generous than we believe ourselves to be. Or perhaps, well aware of our own shortcomings, we revel in the thrill of glimpsing a perfection that we will never approach in our own lives. Perhaps. But idolatry bestows its adoration only for as long as it will. It exists barely a hair's breadth away from envy and animus. And from there, it passes to judgment and resentment in the blink of an eye. A hero walks a fickle path. And woe to him should he misstep. All the world loves to see a hero fall.

CHAPTER ONE

MONDAY, FEBRUARY 5, 1962

Sitting at the head of runway 31R at Idlewild, the jet hummed patiently, its four turbines spinning, almost whining. The captain's voice crackled over the public-address system to inform us that we were next in line for takeoff. I'd noticed him earlier leaning against the doorframe of the cockpit, greeting passengers as we boarded the plane. He'd given me a thorough once-over—a hungry leer I know all too well—and I averted my gaze like the good girl that I'm not.

"Welcome aboard, miss," he'd said, compelling me to look him in the eye. He winked and flashed me a bright smile. "I hope to give you a comfortable ride."

I surely blushed.

Now, just moments after the handsome pilot had assured us of our imminent departure, the engines roared to life, and the aircraft lurched forward from its standstill. Juddering at first as it began to move, the plane rumbled down the runway, gathering speed as it barreled toward takeoff. I craned my neck to see better through the window, holding my breath as I gripped the armrest of my seat and grinned like a fool. I sensed the man seated next to me was rolling his eyes, but I didn't care. Of course I'd flown before—a regional flight from LaGuardia to Albany on Mohawk Airlines, and a couple of quick hops in a single-engine Cessna with a man who was trying to impress me with his derring-do. Alas, his derring-didn't. But this was my first-ever flight on a jet plane.

Just forty-eight hours earlier, I'd had no travel plans at all, let alone a transcontinental trip to Los Angeles aboard a TWA 707 Jetliner. Late Saturday night, I'd been sitting as usual at the counter at Fiorello's Home of the Hot Fudge, swiveling back and forth on the stool, as I chatted with Fadge Fiorello, my dearest friend in the world. The evening crush of teenagers had subsided, and things were quiet. Fadge was staring at the floor. I could almost hear the pitched battle raging in his head: to sweep or not to sweep? I usually could tell what he was thinking, at least when work, food, or sex was on his mind. Work, put it off. Food, shovel it in. And sex, if only. Once he'd decided the floor could wait another day to be swept, he asked where I'd like to go for our late-night pizza, Tedesco's or Scafitti's? I said it didn't matter as long as there was something strong to wash it down. Then the front door jingled, and my editor, Charlie Reese, stepped inside.

"Hiya, pops," I said.

Charlie removed his hat and gloves. Then, pulling off his overcoat, he frowned at me. He didn't like me calling him "pops." Made him feel old. He motioned to an empty booth in the back. I slid off the stool and led the way.

"How soon can you be ready to leave for Los Angeles?" he asked without preamble once we were seated across from each other.

I cocked my head. "Are you inviting me or sending me?" That surely made him feel young. He smiled.

"Sending."

"When do you need me to go?"

"Tomorrow."

I sat up straight in my seat. "Tomorrow? Wait a minute. Is this the Tony Eberle story? I thought Georgie Porgie was all set to leave tomorrow. What happened?"

Charlie drew a deep breath and looked away. He rubbed his arthritic left pinky finger as he sometimes did when searching for the right words. And other times when it was paining him.

"George can't go."

"Why not? This is his big chance to go to Hollywood and get discovered at Schwab's."

Though he didn't approve, Charlie knew I enjoyed a good chuckle at my colleague George Walsh's expense whenever the opportunity presented itself, which was often. If Charlie's discomfort was any indication, the reason for George's change in plans was a doozy.

Georgie Porgie fancied himself the top reporter at the *New Holland Republic*, on an equal footing with the likes of Edward R. Murrow. But in reality, he was ill-suited to working at a newspaper. Folding one into a tricorne hat, perhaps, but not writing for one. He thought Eisenhower's warning about the rise of the military-industrial complex referred to an army factory that was being built outside Washington, DC. But since his father-in-law, Artie Short, was the publisher, George Walsh always landed the best assignments, all the jobs that were deemed too important for a "girl reporter." Artie Short hated me anyway and would probably have preferred it if I walked into a propeller. For my part, I made a habit of beating his son-in-law to the punch on the biggest stories, including a couple of recent high-profile murders in town. But the Tony Eberle story was the juiciest assignment to come down the pike in a long time: a chance to travel all expenses paid to California to interview the young New Holland native on the set of his first Hollywood movie.

"What happened?" I repeated. "Why can't Georgie Porgie go?"

Charlie frowned and warned me not to laugh, which only succeeded in eliciting a ticklish smile on my lips. He warned me again, and I tamped down the urge.

"His wife had a dream," he said finally. "A dream that the plane crashed. She's a superstitious sort. Believes in that kind of thing. She told George he couldn't go."

"What did Artie say?" I asked, now grinning ear to ear. "Surely he doesn't believe such nonsense."

Charlie shrugged. "He told me his daughter has always had an uncanny knack for premonitions."

"So Artie doesn't care if the plane goes down with me aboard?" I asked, summoning some indignation despite the absurdity of his daughter's dream.

Charlie dismissed my concerns, assuring me that nothing bad was going to happen to the plane. As the editor in chief, he didn't often write news stories anymore, except for those he enjoyed, specifically scientific pieces. And so, sitting in a booth in the back of Fiorello's on a frigid Saturday night, he treated me to a catalogue of statistics on the safety of modern air travel. I wasn't listening. I was already planning my wardrobe for the trip.

"You'll take the train down to New York tomorrow, then fly from Idlewild Monday. We've booked you a hotel in Hollywood. Artie says it's a nice place. He stayed there a couple of nights during the war before he shipped out to the Pacific."

"I thought the Battle of the Bulge was in Europe."

Charlie stared me down. He didn't need to say anything. Artie Short had seen action in the navy in the Pacific, and I shouldn't have mocked his service. Still, he was carrying a spare tire around his waist, which had inspired my little joke.

"Why doesn't Artie just send George by train?" I asked, steering my derision back to the nebbish. "It'll take a couple of days longer, but that'll give him time to memorize the alphabet."

Charlie ignored my crack. "No time for a train. Artie's worried that the *Gazette* is going to send someone out to Los Angeles to scoop us on this. They've been eating into our circulation for the past year and a half. Artie's become obsessed with them."

"Who are they going to send, Harvey Dunnolt?" I asked. "He doesn't even get out of his car to cover city council meetings. Barely rolls down the window as he drives by."

"Look, Ellie. Do you want this assignment or not?"

I smiled sweetly at my boss. "Sure, pops. I'll bail you out on this one."

Against all odds and George Walsh's wife's dream of a fiery plane crash, TWA Flight 7 arrived without incident at Los Angeles Airport at 2:50 p.m. on Monday, February 5. In fact, it was an incredibly pleasant experience, with fine food, plenty of drink, and smooth sailing. As I disembarked, the friendly captain smiled at me again.

"Welcome home, miss," he said, his gaze darting from my eyes to linger on my bust before he remembered himself and his good manners.

"I'm not from Los Angeles."

He arched a brow and cocked his head just so as if to flirt. "Perhaps I could show you around town," he said. "Where are you staying?"

It took no small measure of self-control, but I managed to keep the name of my hotel to myself. I thanked him for a fine flight and stepped through the door and down the airstairs.

On the ground, I was greeted by a cool, gray day. About sixty degrees. It was still an improvement over the cold New York winter I'd left behind. I retrieved my luggage and made my way to the taxi stand. My driver, a chatty fellow who kept pulling off his cap to scratch his balding head, called me "sweetie" for the forty minutes it took to reach Hollywood. As we motored up La Brea Avenue, he pointed out various landmarks and places of interest, including the Perry Mason Studio near Sunset Boulevard. I nearly squealed with delight and asked him if he'd ever seen William

Hopper around town. I'd had a big crush on "Paul Drake" for years. Something about that shock of white hair and the checked jackets he wore.

"Never seen him," said the driver. "But I dropped Raymond Burr at Musso and Frank once about a year ago." He performed a feathery hand gesture as he pronounced the name, presumably an indication of the actor's predilections. Was he suggesting that Perry Mason was queer? I said nothing for fear of coming off as a rube unfamiliar with what seemed to be common knowledge.

We drove to my hotel on McCadden Place, just north of Hollywood Boulevard. Before the brakes had even stopped squeaking, I asked the cabbie if he hadn't perhaps made a mistake. Peering out the window, I saw a dingy brick building with a torn awning and a faded sign announcing the McCadden Hotel. Two shady-looking men were pitching pennies against the stoop. One of them was the bellhop.

"I'm afraid this is it, sweetie," said the driver.

"But my boss assured me this was a nice hotel. He stayed here during the war."

"Which war?"

I paid the fare and climbed out of the cab. The driver fetched my bag from the trunk and wished me luck. Upon seeing me, the bellhop reluctantly tore himself away from his game, but not before his opponent had gathered up his winnings. The bellhop frowned, undoubtedly mourning the loss of his penny. Then, putting on a brave face, he straightened the little drummer-boy cap on his head, welcomed me to the McCadden, and grabbed my suitcase. I followed him up the stairs and into the dark lobby.

The McCadden had been built when heavy velvet curtains, oriental rugs, and flocked wallpaper were all the rage. Probably before 1920. And no one had thought to remodel since. Or clean. The odor of cigar ashes gave the place much of its dry-cough charm, and you could scarcely ignore the vague smell of sulfur lurking underneath. I figured the dusty old gentleman manning the reception desk had recently polished off a luncheon of hard-boiled eggs.

"Your room's been paid up for the week," he said, straining to read from a note he'd retrieved from a cubbyhole behind the desk.

He handed the key to the bellhop, who by now must have considered himself my friend because he introduced himself as Marty. He lugged my bag up the stairs to a room on the second floor. Once inside, he gave me the grand tour, pointing out the bed, a Philco radio on the scratched desk, and the radiator valve against the wall. Finally, he threw open the curtains to present the view: a brick wall painted over with faded letters spelling out "Selma Hardware."

I considered my new friend, Marty, in the quiet of my room. He looked to be in his late twenties, tall and lanky, and in need of a shave. His uniform was a sea of wrinkles, except where the fabric showed shiny patches, the result of too many scalding ironings. The sleeves of his jacket fell three inches short of the finish line of his bony wrists. I could see now that his hat had lost most of its shape, as a sweaty pillow might during a particularly hot spell, and I figured he'd probably slept or sat on it one too many times. Marty told me it was going to rain.

"I heard it was always sunny in California," I said, feeling cheated on my first trip to Los Angeles.

"When it rains it pours. And the weatherman is calling for 'pours' day after tomorrow and all week after that. I'll leave a newspaper for you in the mornings so you can check the forecast."

Looking around the grim room, I wondered where I might find better accommodations. I tipped Marty a quarter. That ought to keep him in pennies for a while.

⚭

TUESDAY, FEBRUARY 6, 1962

I managed to sleep through the night none the worse for wear, with no bites from bedbugs. And the door to my room had dispatched its duties, keeping any and all marauders, junkies, and thieves on the other side. At 6:00 a.m. I was wide awake, thanks to the time difference and my excitement at the prospect of meeting Tony Eberle on the set of his movie. The bathtub proved to be a pleasant surprise, dispensing plenty of hot water and good pressure. By seven, I was ready for the day.

Having skipped dinner the night before, I felt hollow and needed something to eat. The McCadden provided no food service, but the same dusty desk clerk from the previous day steered me to Hody's Coffee Shop a couple of blocks away on the corner of Hollywood and Vine. I almost gave it a miss when I saw the giant creepy clown on the sign atop the roof. I swear the eyes were following me. But my appetite won out. Inside, a friendly waitress poured me a cup of piping hot coffee before I'd had the chance to ask, and the vulcanized eggs were edible if rubbery. The English muffin was perfectly charred, and the butter soft. I studied my notes as I picked over the remains of my breakfast.

Tony Eberle had grown up on Clizbe Avenue in the Rockton district of New Holland. His mother, Louise, a Hagaman girl, kept house for her family, which included a daughter three years older than Tony. Joe Eberle, Tony's father, had delivered milk and eggs for Stadler's Dairy for more than twenty years.

From what I could gather, Tony was the most talented actor to come out of New Holland in recent memory. He'd starred in every drama club musical production during his years at New Holland's Walter T. Finch High School. From *Forty-Second Street* to *Show Boat* to *Kiss Me Kate*, Tony Eberle had set the standard for local theater. According to the newspaper clippings my assistant, Norma Geary, had prepared for me, he could sing and dance as well as act. One review, written by none other than George Walsh in 1956, predicted great things for the high schooler after his stunning success as Curly in *Oklahoma!*

"A modern-day Thespis, a Barrymore on the Mohawk, young Eberle steals the show, his voice ringing through the hall like the clarion call of a distant trumpet on a heroic battlefield. His gay dancing delights old and young as he glides light-footed, even in cowboy boots, across the stage."

That—believe it—was from George's notice. And, yes, that was how he wrote his stories: odd turns of phrase weighed down by healthy doses of hyperbole, which he slathered atop his inadvertent double entendres as if with a trowel. His mangled metaphors lay bleeding on the page, begging to be put out of their misery. His sports stories were even worse, but that's a topic for another day. In a codicil to his review, George declared the show a success, but he lamented the bad grammar and low moral values of some of the characters, Ado Annie and Aunt Eller in particular.

Norma had also managed to secure a copy of Tony's high school yearbook for my research, and I retrieved it from my bag. His portrait showed a tall, well-built young man with straight teeth and handsome features. But, ultimately, he lacked any of the charm I'd expected. I chalked that up to the photographer, not the good-looking Tony Eberle. Studying the portrait, I sensed that somewhere in his deep dark eyes lurked fear and loneliness, perhaps even self-doubt. His only activities involved the drama club and the marching band, where he'd served for three years as the drum major. I was sure he'd taken some lumps for that from the other boys in school.

As far as I could tell, Tony hadn't gone to college. Probably a luxury his family couldn't afford on a milkman's salary. I wished I'd had the opportunity to interview his parents and sister for the story before leaving for Hollywood, but, of course, the assignment had come as a last-minute surprise. I resolved to follow up with the family upon my return to New Holland.

I read on. Tony had spent a couple of years in Massachusetts and Vermont doing summer stock. O'Neill, Chekhov, Tennessee Williams, Strindberg, and Shakespeare. And now he was about to make the leap from the boards to the world of Hollywood stardom as the beach bum best friend of a teenaged Casanova on a surfboard—to wit, the ageless Bobby Renfro, who had to be thirty-five years old if he was a day.

I took a bite of my English muffin and drew a sip of hot coffee. It was exciting to be in California for the first time, about to meet a real movie actor at a major film studio. Not even Marty's prediction of the impending deluge dampened my enthusiasm. The waitress dropped my bill on the table and asked what was so interesting that I was reading. I told her it was a fairy tale.

Outside, temperatures had risen only into the upper fifties—chilly, I was told, for Los Angeles—but no rain yet. I raised my collar to the wind and hailed a cab. Soon I was cruising down Highland Avenue toward Paramount Studios. My driver treated me to endless tidbits about the movie business, starting with the stars who'd attended Hollywood High, which we'd just passed. He catalogued a list of alumni that included Lon Chaney Jr., Gloria Grahame, John Huston, Joel McCrea, Mickey Rooney, and Judy Garland. Oh, and James Garner. I kind of had a thing for him.

The cabbie dropped me at the studio's Bronson Gate, where I'd been instructed to check in. I approached the guard booth with no small measure of trepidation. This was a storied movie studio, after all, and I felt like a starstruck small-town hick. I drew a deep breath as I arrived at the arch with its wrought-iron gate and majestic columns. Norma Desmond had driven through the very same portal in *Sunset Boulevard*.

"I have an appointment to see Tony Eberle," I told the uniformed man on duty. "He's shooting *Twistin' on the Beach* today."

The officious guard checked my name against a list on his clipboard. Then he double-checked, an operation aided by scratching his chin. Finally, satisfied that the only Eleonora Stone on the list must be me, he handed me a pass and dispensed directions to soundstage 5.

"Go straight on Avenue P then turn left on Seventh Street. Keep quiet on set, please. Welcome to Paramount Studios, Miss Stone."

I walked briskly along the narrow alleys that ran between the soundstages, bungalows, and offices. The studio lot was a city in miniature. It reminded me of those O Gauge train sets; everything looked quite real only smaller. The world was an illusion inside the gates of the studio. This was Hollywood, after all.

It was nearly eight, and I didn't want to be late for my interview with hometown hero Tony Eberle. He was about to embark on what everyone back in New Holland hoped would be a long, successful career as a movie star. The news that Tony had landed a big role in a real Hollywood movie had generated a swell of pride throughout the city, as if all the frustrations and disappointments of a mill town in decline could be put right by the accomplishments of one favorite son. Tony Eberle provided an answer to the snide whispers and condescending mockery of neighboring cities, particularly Schenectady, which looked on New Holland as the punch line to a joke. People laughed at the schools, where students excelled more in wood and metal shop than in math. They mocked the elected officials, who, they maintained, wouldn't qualify for dogcatcher anywhere else. And they ridiculed New Holland's ethnic mix, dubbing the city New San Juanland, after the Puerto Ricans who now populated the city's East End. The hopes and dreams of New Holland rested on young Tony Eberle's shoulders. And, thanks to George Walsh's wife, I got to travel across the country to document his success for the world to see. In effect, to rub New Holland's neighbors' noses in our hometown boy's triumph.

Following the guard's instructions to the letter, I rounded the corner of Avenue P and joined Seventh Street. Ahead I could see a host of people, perhaps thirty or so, milling about. A line of long tables loaded with Danish and coffee and fruit on one side, audio and camera gear and a couple of equipment trucks on the other. And in the middle of it all, a tall, thin man of about fifty was screaming, seemingly at everyone in general and no one in particular. He tore the newsboy cap off his bald head—red and wet with perspiration despite the cool air—and threw it at a young man holding a clipboard. Then he overturned one of the catering tables, sending a percolator crashing to the pavement where it vomited its contents in a hissing, brown wave that crested over the shoes of two slow-to-react crew members. They hopped and swore and glared at the guy who'd doused them with scalding coffee.

"What's going on?" I asked a stocky man who was leaning on the fender of one of the trucks.

"That's the director, Archie Stemple," he said in a drone, eyes half-shut as if from boredom. "He does this kind of thing all the time."

"What's got him riled up today?"

"One of the actors didn't show. Stemple's got a foul temper and hates actors to boot."

A smartly dressed woman in her forties appeared and took charge of the situation. She managed to stop Stemple from smashing a spotlight he'd grabbed from an equipment truck, but he continued to seethe. She led him gently by the elbow off to one side where she spoke to him alone. At length her words calmed him. He wasn't quite serene, but at least he wasn't hurling tables or dumping coffee on unsuspecting Teamsters.

"I swear to God, Dorothy, that kid will never work on this picture," said Stemple loud enough for me to hear. "Or any other of my pictures!"

The woman, whose back was turned to me, nodded and answered in a low voice that I couldn't make out. That seemed to mollify the director, and the worst appeared to have passed. The young man with the clipboard—the one who'd been on the receiving end of Stemple's flying cap— approached him tentatively with, of all things, a mug of steaming coffee. The director huffed, wiped his brow, and accepted the peace offering.

"So who's the poor sap who didn't show up for work today?" I asked my world-weary friend.

The man looked straight ahead, eyes still at half-mast. "Some kid named Tony Eberle."

CHAPTER TWO

To say that Tony Eberle's disappearance put a wrinkle in my day would be to understate the case. I had traveled across the continent at great expense to my publisher in order to interview the rising star. And though I'd had nothing to do with his disappearance, I was certain Artie Short would find some way to blame it on me. Or, at the very least, the debacle would forever be associated with my name. Furthermore, I had spent a couple of hours on the plane dreaming of how much sand to kick in George Walsh's face once I had my big story. And finally, the assignment truly interested me and would make for a fine feather in my cap. But now, standing in the chill on the lot at Paramount Studios, with no subject to interview and no idea how to find him, I wondered if it was already too late to salvage my assignment, not to mention young Tony's acting career. Because, if he was, in fact, finished, so too was my story.

"Do you know where this Tony Eberle lives?" I asked the man who'd been leaning on the truck.

He was lighting a cigarette and looking up at the gray sky as if searching for patience or perhaps a revelation. Smoke oozed from his nose as he considered his response.

"Sorry," he said. "I never even seen the guy. But why don't you ask Dorothy over there? She'll know. She handles everything."

With the absence of the second lead and with an apoplectic director, shooting was scrubbed for the day, a delay that surely would cost the studio a bundle. In a matter of minutes, the throng of production assistants, union gorillas, and various crew had all decamped. I chased after Dorothy as she hurried down Seventh Street in her navy wool jacket and matching skirt. She was probably off to defuse another bomb somewhere on the lot. I called out to her. She stopped, turned, and looked me up and down as if trying to place me. I introduced myself, but my name meant nothing to her. Still, she was polite enough to ask how she might help me.

"I'm looking for Tony Eberle," I said.

Dorothy scoffed. "Aren't we all?"

"I was scheduled to interview him this morning for my paper. Do you have any idea where he is?"

"I do not. And at this point, I'm afraid I no longer care. He's been fired from the picture. I've got to get someone else in so that we can resume shooting tomorrow. If you'll excuse me."

She gazed expectantly at me, as if waiting for me to grant her leave. I wasn't about to slink away empty-handed, not after I'd come so far. I must have looked determined since she didn't move.

"Tell you what, Miss Stone," she said finally. "Come with me, and I'll see if we can't find a telephone number or an address for your Mr. Eberle."

Dorothy Fetterman, as I learned her name was, led me through the narrow lanes to a bungalow on the corner of Avenue L and Twelfth Street. We climbed the stairs to the second floor, where she let me into her office.

"What exactly do you do here at the studio?" I asked as she removed her jacket and hung it carefully on a stand near the door.

"My official position is advisor to Mr. Balaban."

"Who's Mr. Balaban?"

She blinked. "He's the president of Paramount Studios."

I'm pretty sure I blushed. "You say 'official' as if it's actually something else that you do."

"I fix things," she said, taking a seat on the corner of her desk.

She retrieved a cigarette from a silver case and slipped it between her lips. In one motion, she grabbed a lighter from the desk and lit her cigarette. Her thick, ruby-red lipstick had the shiny, hardened look of a brand-new crayon. Perfectly drawn, even, without a smudge or a flake. Not like when I rolled on my lipstick. Closer to Emmett Kelly than to Grace.

"Where are my manners?" she said. "Would you like one?"

"Your job sounds interesting." I took the cigarette she'd offered and thanked her, wishing I could question her more closely about her work. But I was there to find Tony Eberle.

"It is," she said. "But there's a lot of babysitting and hand-holding. And soothing of bruised egos. Mostly male egos, though there are some actresses I'd like to strangle."

"So how do you fix a problem like Archie Stemple?"

"Archie's problem is easy. This Tony Eberle is a nobody. We'll simply replace him and continue shooting the picture tomorrow."

"That rather ruins my story," I said.

"Does it? Now you've got a mystery. Or a tragedy. You can always sell newspapers with that."

"That won't do."

"I suppose not. But it can't be helped. He should have shown up for work."

I had no answer to that.

"Let me see if I have his number or an address," she said, resting her cigarette in the ashtray on her desk. She leaned back and opened a drawer on the opposite side to retrieve a file. "Eberle was the producer's choice, I think. Said he was perfect for the role. Our casting director didn't know him."

"Who's the producer?" I asked. "Perhaps he'll know where to find Tony."

"Bertram Wallis. Now there's a man a little harder to satisfy than Archie Stemple."

"How so?"

"He's difficult. But I don't have time to go into that. I have to fix Mr. Stemple's problem, and your Tony Eberle is standing in the way of my doing that."

She held a pair of glasses in front of her eyes with one hand while turning pages in a folder with the other. "Here it is," she announced, extracting an eight-by-ten headshot and handing it to me. She folded the glasses neatly and slipped them into her purse.

I set my cigarette down in the ashtray and examined the photograph. It was Tony Eberle, looking relaxed and casual in a cardigan sweater and open-collar shirt. His teeth shone bright white from a half smile, and his hair was silky brown, a little long on the top to give him that youthful boy-next-door look. His eyes sparkled at the camera, and I thought he was terrifically handsome. What a difference a decent photographer makes. Tony had the look of a star, all right. I just wondered if he'd ever get a second chance now that he'd blown his first. Reading from the back of the photograph, I scribbled his address and telephone number in my pad. Then I jotted down his agent's contact information: Irving Greenberg, with a Sunset Boulevard address.

"Is there any chance you'd give me Mr. Wallis's number?" I asked, sure I was pushing my luck.

Dorothy regarded me for a long moment. Hers was a stern but attractive face. Not a beauty, but stylish and impeccably turned out. She picked up her cigarette and took a short drag.

"Why do you want Mr. Wallis's number?"

I smiled sheepishly. "I thought I might prevail upon him to give Tony Eberle his job back. Assuming I can find him, of course."

"I'm afraid not, Miss Stone," said Dorothy, and I felt a chill from my hostess. "Mr. Eberle is finished here. And we do not give out producers' telephone numbers to reporters."

Settled into a phone booth just outside the studio, I swallowed hard and made a person-to-person collect call to Charlie Reese back in New Holland. I was sure my news would be as welcome as a pimple on prom night. I'd only just arrived, after all, and already I was spending company money to phone home with bad tidings. Charlie was surprised to hear from me so soon.

"How's your first day going?" he asked over the crackly line.

I struggled with how to answer that. I could lie and say that Tony had been busy and couldn't accommodate me. Or I might say that the shooting had been canceled due to bad weather. But those lies would only put off the inevitable. Better to tell the truth, I thought. And maybe to put a humorous spin on it to lighten the mood.

"I had a good breakfast," I said. Silence down the line. "And I was punctual." Perhaps humor wasn't the right tack.

"What aren't you telling me, Ellie?" he asked after an uncomfortable pause.

I chewed my lip. "Tony Eberle is AWOL."

"AWOL? In what sense AWOL?"

"AWOL. He's not here. No one knows where he is."

More silence from Charlie. This was going worse than I'd anticipated. Finally he cleared his throat.

"Tell me the whole story."

I gave Charlie the abridged version. In truth, there really was no long version to tell. I explained how my morning had been ruined by the missing actor, who'd been summarily fired from the picture by the director.

"Things aren't looking good for Tony Eberle's Hollywood career," I said in summation.

"Damn it," muttered Charlie down the line from three thousand miles away. "What's your plan, Ellie?"

"I've already tried to phone him at home and got no answer. Then I tried his agent, but the line was busy. He's probably fielding enraged calls from the studio as we speak. I'll chase him down after I hang up with you."

"Good. At the very least, we still might have a story here. Not sure if we'll end up running it, though. It all depends on what actually happened to our hometown hero."

I nodded in agreement even though Charlie couldn't see me. "Yeah, if he's on a bender, there's no story." I recalled Dorothy Fetterman's advice. "But if something bad has happened . . . Well, there are lots of newspapers to be sold."

"Precisely. You know what you've got to do. In the meantime, do you need anything from me?"

I had some notes. I asked him to contact Tony's family to find out if they knew anything.

"How do they feel about Tony's choice of career? Have they spoken to him recently? That kind of stuff. And does he still have friends in New Holland? Maybe he's in touch with them."

Charlie said he'd take care of it and signed off with an admonition to keep him informed of my progress.

$$\mathcal{D}$$

Irving Greenberg's office was on the top floor of a three-story, plain-brick building on the corner of Sunset and Hayworth. A most unimpressive-looking place. For some reason I had expected one of those shiny new high rises like you see in New York, all glass and steel, with pretty secretaries and powerful men making big deals. Instead, the air smelled close and dusty when I reached the landing. I considered the wooden door and its frosted glass. The words "Greenberg Talent Agency" stretched across the window in black letters. I could hear typing through the open transom above.

I knocked, dislodging some flakes of paint from the door. A voice called out for me to enter. Inside I was greeted by a middle-aged woman at a desk in the dark reception area. Her hands rested on an old typewriter. A simple black phone sat on the desk next to a nameplate that read *Mrs. Zelda Weitz.*

"Yes?" she asked, looking me up and down.

"I called earlier. I'm here to see Mr. Greenberg."

She pursed her lips and continued to study me top to bottom. "Sweetheart, you're a pretty girl," she said at length, shaking her head. "But you're not Hollywood pretty."

"I-I beg your pardon?"

She assumed a softer expression. "It's tough to make it in this town. A girl's got to have something really special to catch the eye of a casting director or a producer. You're cute, no doubt. But you've got to manage your expectations, dear."

I must have looked crestfallen. As a point of fact, I was insulted.

"Now don't despair. You seem like a nice girl," she continued. "You might be good for a plain-Jane secretary. A school teacher, perhaps. Or the mousy best friend. Maybe Mr. Greenberg can find something for you."

I finally found the breath to explain that I wasn't an actress, that I was a reporter wanting to speak to Mr. Greenberg about Tony Eberle.

"Well, thank God for that," she said, a little too relieved for my taste. "I was afraid you were going to have your heart broken and dreams shattered."

"Nice of you to let me down easy," I said. "Now, is Mr. Greenberg free?"

"I'm afraid I can't help you, miss," said Irving Greenberg from behind a huge, cluttered mahogany desk.

His inner office had two sash windows for light and air, but they did little to brighten the general atmosphere of sadness and decay that blanketed the room. Framed clippings on the wall proclaimed successes, hits, deals, and even some weddings. All had been torn from the trades or *Life* magazine or one of the Los Angeles papers, and few bore names or movies that I recognized. The same was true for the dozens of headshots that shared space on the wall with the clippings. They were decades old, and the only stars I knew were Janet Gaynor, Ramon Navarro, a very young Judy Garland, and Louise Brooks.

I couldn't say for sure how old Irving Greenberg was, but if he had ten years left in the tank, he was playing with house money. He sat low in his chair, a little lopsided too, making him appear shorter than he was. He spoke in a voice that was a mite too loud for the close confines of his office, probably due to his failing hearing. That, along with his poor eyesight, gave the impression of decrepitude. He insisted that I call him Irv.

"Hedy Lamar called me Irv," he said. "And Dick Powell and little Judy Garland. I once represented them, you know. Before they made it big."

"I didn't know that."

"So you can call me Irv, too, young lady."

"Thank you," I said. "And you can call me Ellie."

In truth, I don't believe he heard me or gave a hang what I wanted him to call me. He stuck with "miss" and "young lady" for the balance of our interview.

"As I was saying before," he continued, "I can't help you find Tony because I don't know where he is myself."

"But isn't it strange that he would disappear just as he landed his first break?"

He cupped a hand to his ear, and I repeated the question louder. Then a third time, louder still.

Irv nodded. "Very strange. He always seemed like a nice boy. He was going to go places. I was sure he could help me with my comeback."

"So what do you think happened?" (Practically yelling.)

He shrugged. "Who knows? I got a call this morning at seven thirty from a production assistant at Paramount asking where he was. Then some secretary a few minutes later. I was in the toilet." He huffed his indignation. "Ten minutes after that, the director, Archie Stemple, was screaming at me over the phone. I told them I didn't have any idea where Tony was. But I said I had an actor who could fill in for him if they needed someone."

"And what did he say?"

"I can't repeat it in polite company, young lady. That Archie Stemple is an unpleasant man. You'd think I was the one who didn't show up."

"Did you try to reach Tony?"

"Of course. But there was no answer at his place."

"It's too bad," I said, thinking of my story and Tony's career.

Irv agreed. He shook his head in woe. "He was perfect for the role, too. So perfect the producer himself wanted him for the part."

"Bertram Wallis?"

"His name is Bertram Wallis," said Irv, who'd clearly not heard me despite my best efforts. "A real *kelev she-beklovim*, pardon my French."

I asked how Wallis had come to know Tony. Irv wasn't sure.

"I've met him a few times," he said. "A schmuck. And a pervert. People want to give him a free pass because he's British and has a posh accent. I've got an accent, and no one thinks I'm fancy. They say he's some kind of genius. But I can tell you that he's never made anything but rotten beach pictures and lightweight teenage *opfal*. A genius, my foot. Yech!"

"Did you negotiate the contract with Wallis?"

Irv waved a hand. "He sent over the contract. No negotiations. Said he'd find someone else if we didn't take it as is. To tell the truth, I was just glad to get the commission. Things have been a little slow recently."

"Has Mr. Wallis contacted you since Tony disappeared?"

"No. And I won't take his call if he does. Let him try to get his money back." He laughed himself into a coughing fit.

I asked him for Bertram Wallis's phone number and address, and he bellowed to Mrs. Weitz in the next room to look up the information for me.

"What else can you tell me about Tony Eberle?" I boomed.

"Like I said, a nice boy," he muttered, his drooping face and hunched shoulders betraying a crushing disappointment. "He reminded me of our Shabbos goy when I was a kid in Brooklyn." He allowed himself a moment of fond recollection before returning to the subject at hand. "Tony was going to go far. But now? Feh! He's finished."

CHAPTER THREE

The cab rolled to a stop opposite 1859 North Wilton. It was a modest, five-story apartment building with a fire-escape ladder zigzagging down the front, ending just above the entrance to the underground garage. In the doorway, a sign advertised a bachelor apartment for rent. This was the address on the back of the headshot that Dorothy Fetterman had given me. This was Tony Eberle's apartment.

I asked the cabbie to wait. He leaned against the steering wheel, puffing on his cigarette, and nodded. I retrieved my Leica from my purse and snapped three shots of the exterior of the building before crossing the street and approaching the door. Scanning the directory in the entrance, I located Eberle/Harper in apartment 101 on the ground floor. A roommate. Maybe this Harper person could tell me where to find Tony.

The front door was ajar, so I let myself in. Apartment 101 was the first door on the right. I knocked three times to no effect. Then the door to apartment 102 cracked open, and a woman peered into the corridor. Somewhere in her mid-thirties, she was decked out in a pair of what looked like men's wool trousers and an Arrow shirt unbuttoned at the neck. A cigarette, fastened to the end of a long ebony holder, dangled from her right hand. Her hair was dyed black and cut short in a bob, the way Louise Brooks used to wear it back in the twenties.

"They're not home," she said, eyeing me with suspicion. Or perhaps with interest.

I cleared my throat and asked if she knew where they'd gone. She shook her head.

"Have you seen Mr. Eberle recently? Tony Eberle?"

"Who wants to know?"

I showed her my press card from a few feet away and explained that I was a reporter from New Holland, New York. She said she couldn't see it without her eyeglasses. When I offered to bring it closer, she waved me off, saying she'd take my word on it.

"I don't suppose anyone would lie about being a reporter from New Belgium, New York," she said.

"New Holland."

She took a drag of her cigarette and, clenching the end of the holder between her teeth in a playful manner, told me she was just having some fun with me. "You should get yourself a sense of humor, angel."

She introduced herself as the super, Evelyn Maynard, and offered her hand for me to shake. The formalities concluded, she said that her two neighbors seemed like nice, quiet boys. She didn't know them well enough to give a character reference, but she volunteered that they were often behind in the rent. In fact, Mickey Harper had just paid up six weeks' of arrears a day earlier. I wondered why she was telling me this. She seemed to like to talk.

"They've been late before, but they always manage to come up with the money. That's the way it is for these young actors. They all have big dreams and empty pocketbooks. It's a constant struggle to make ends meet."

"Have you seen Tony Eberle recently?" I repeated.

She tapped her ash onto the floor in the hallway. I must have made a face of some kind because she told me not to worry; she'd sweep it up later.

"I saw him yesterday morning as he was heading out somewhere. Told me he had a part in a movie with Bobby Renfro. Bobby Renfro, if you can believe it." She shook her head and grunted a short laugh. "I thought he was dead."

"What about the other fellow? Harper."

"He's quiet. Pretty much keeps to himself. Not sure where he got the money for the rent. Some of these actors work as waiters. Or figure models."

"Is Harper an actor too?"

Evelyn Maynard shrugged and took another drag of her cigarette. "I assume so."

I churned through my purse, looking for a calling card. I scribbled the address and phone number of the McCadden Hotel on the back.

"If you see either one of them, please give me a call. I'm in room two-F," I said, handing it to her.

She stashed it in the breast pocket of her shirt and considered me from the corner of her eye.

"If I didn't know better," she said, "and I do—I'd swear you were making a pass at me."

I suppose I should have suspected something like that, but I'd become quite provincial in New Belgium, unable to recognize sarcasm when it smacked me on the forehead or a lesbian when she was flirting with me. I stammered an inadequate response.

"Don't sweat it, angel. I won't bite." She paused, studying my face as I tried to hide my discomfort. "Unless you want me to."

"That won't be necessary," I said.

I can't know for certain what reaction my face betrayed, but it must have crushed her. There was no other explanation for the sudden gloom that enveloped her. She attempted one last smile, but it collapsed before it had a chance to shine. Her heart was no longer in it. She excused herself, disappeared inside, and closed the door softly behind her.

I drifted back out to the street where, disquieted, I reflected on what had just happened. Of course I knew there were people like Evelyn Maynard in the world. A girl in my study group at Barnard had been that way. But I hadn't had much direct contact with any lesbians since. And I couldn't recall a woman ever having flirted with me. The situation left me feeling uncomfortable. Sophisticate that I considered myself to be, I wanted to brush it off, flick it off my sleeve like a piece of lint. But somehow I couldn't let it go. I wasn't one to cast stones for what people did behind closed doors—my own behavior in that regard wouldn't have won me any comportment prizes—but the idea of turning sex on its head, questioning every urge I'd ever felt for a man, every impulse that had ever caused me to lust or love, struck me as queer. Yes, queer. Perhaps that's where the term had originated. But at the same time, I felt like a fake, all too aware of my own hypocrisy and close-mindedness. I had always prided myself on my enlightened, generous views of the world. Try as I might to push it out of my mind, the image of Evelyn Maynard's embarrassment wouldn't leave me. I'd seen pain in her eyes, and I was the one who'd provoked it.

My cab driver was still waiting across the street. He'd thrown his head back and looked to be snoring while the meter ran. As I paced on the stoop, smoking a bitter cigarette, I considered my options and debated whether to go back inside and knock on 102 to apologize. But before I could make up my mind, a small young man in a lightweight jacket, checked shirt, and brown trousers approached the building at a brisk pace. He clutched a green paper bag of groceries under his left arm and a folded umbrella in his right hand. Nose to the ground, he made straight for the front door, lifting his eyes to regard me only after he'd seen my shoes—and by extension me—blocking the way. His eyes caught mine, and I stepped aside, muttering an apology.

He was a striking creature, truly remarkable-looking. Not handsome. Not even cute, as an adolescent might be. This young man was pretty. No mistaking him for a girl, of course, but he was attractive in the way girls are. Fine features, graceful lines, and delicate, hairless hands. Nothing rugged or coarse in his face, no beard or lantern jaw. Barely an Adam's apple visible above his open collar. With his long eyelashes, smooth skin, and soft black hair, he looked fresh out of high school. He stepped around me, diverted his eyes again, and let himself into the building. I watched him through the glass as he fumbled for his keys just inside the door. Then he opened 101. Harper.

I tossed my cigarette, pushed my way into the lobby, and called out to him before he could close the apartment door. Startled, he turned to face me. I could see now that his right cheek showed a bluish bruise under the eye. His upper lip, too, betrayed the barest hint of swelling and a scratch that he'd tried to conceal with makeup or pimple cream.

"Excuse me. I'm looking for Tony Eberle."

"He's not here," he said. "I haven't seen him since yesterday. What do you want with him anyway?"

"Are you Mr. Harper?" I asked, avoiding his question for the moment.

He hesitated, probably wary of strangers approaching him and asking for his name, even innocent-looking young women like me. I might have been there to serve a summons, after all. Maybe I was a religious nut or a fresh-faced thief with a gun in my purse. At length he must have concluded I posed no threat because he nodded and said he was Mickey Harper. Then he asked again what I wanted with Tony.

"My name is Eleonora Stone. Ellie Stone," I explained. Why did I insist on introducing myself as Eleonora in such situations? I hated that name. "I'm a reporter from Tony's hometown newspaper," I continued. "I was supposed to interview him this morning at the studio, but he never showed up. Do you have any idea where I might find him?"

He shook his head. "I told you I haven't seen him since yesterday. I was at a party with friends last night. I didn't get home until after one. He must have been asleep. Or out."

I could see over Mickey Harper's shoulder. The apartment looked like a bachelor to me, what we called a studio in New York, and I doubted there were any bedrooms.

"So you're not sure if he was here or not when you got in last night?"

"Might have been. I didn't see him."

Still holding his bag of groceries tight to his chest, Mickey gazed at me with deep, brown, inscrutable eyes. No more than five feet three, slim and timid, he was—as already noted—a beautiful boy. And, standing before me, he was shrinking with each passing moment. I didn't quite tower over him, but in my heels, I had an inch or two advantage.

I had loads of questions for him, including how he and Tony had met. Were they close friends now? I certainly hadn't formed that impression from speaking to Mickey. And why didn't he seem concerned that his roommate was missing? I also wondered if he was an actor like Tony. Not many roles for men his size, no matter how beautiful. Perhaps he could play a part in one of Bertram Wallis's teenage movies. The ones Irv Greenberg had disparaged as *opfal*.

"If I may say, you don't seem surprised that Tony's missing."

"He's a big boy. He can take care of himself."

"He lost his role in the picture they're shooting. Any reaction to that?"

He shrugged. "He'll find another, I guess."

"I suppose you two aren't that close," I offered, trying to get some kind of rise out of him.

"Not really."

"Would you mind if I quoted you for my article?" I asked.

That got his attention. Mickey nearly dropped his groceries.

"No, you can't quote me. And don't use my name. This has nothing to do with me. I told you I don't know where he is."

"All right. I won't mention you. But may I ask you a couple of more questions?"

He shook his head and reached for the door, intending to close it in my face.

"You must be concerned for Tony," I said, blocking the door with my left foot and forearm. "Even if you're not close. He pays half the rent, doesn't he?"

"He'll be fine."

"He might be in trouble. Just two questions. Please."

Mickey relented but wasn't about to invite me in for a cup of tea.

"Does Tony have any friends you know of? People who might know where he's gone?"

"He has a girlfriend. April something. She might know."

"Do you have her address or phone number?"

Mickey shook his head again. "They've only been going together for a short while. She moved to Los Angeles recently. He spends time at her place, so I don't see them much. You should check with her."

"I'd love to, but I don't have her name or address."

Mickey remained in the doorway and shrugged. "Sorry."

"May I come in?" I asked. "Maybe Tony wrote her number down somewhere among his things."

"That's Tony's private business. I can't let some stranger paw through his stuff."

I sighed. This wasn't going well.

"Okay, one last question," I said. "Is Tony's car in the garage downstairs?"

"He doesn't have a car."

"What about April?"

Mickey said that she did, but he didn't know the make or model or year.

"I think it's cream colored," he offered.

I jotted the McCadden Hotel's number into my pad, tore out the sheet, and handed it to him.

"If you hear from Tony, will you contact me?"

He said he would, but I wasn't buying it. Then, eyeing me guardedly, he slowly closed the door without another word, leaving me with more questions than when I'd arrived. Fat lot of help he'd been. I didn't believe anything he'd told me, and I was sure he didn't trust me. This kid was scared or hiding something. I wanted a look inside that apartment, but beautiful little Mickey Harper wasn't about to allow that.

I turned to leave, and my eye fell on the brass numbers 102 across the hall. I'd almost forgotten about Evelyn Maynard, and the reminder stung. I put my head down and pushed back through the front door to the street.

Outside on Wilton, as I climbed back into my cab, the first drops of rain began to fall. Just a sprinkling for now, but, according to my driver, more was on the way. He drove me back across Hollywood, passing under the Hollywood Freeway, to my hotel on McCadden.

It was just past five o'clock. The sky had gone dark with clouds and the setting sun, and I was hungry. I'd missed lunch. The McCadden offered no meals, but Marty the bellhop assured me that he could scavenge something for me from a nearby restaurant. He said Miceli's was around the corner. I gave him three dollars and asked for a bowl of spaghetti and meatballs and a bottle of Chianti, if that wasn't too much trouble.

I treated myself to a hot shower in the claw-foot tub in the bathroom, then slipped into a robe and phoned Charlie Reese back in New Holland. The call was going to be expensive, even station-to-station, but I would have had to wait another two hours for the rates to drop, and Charlie would have been fast asleep by then. As I feared, his wife, Edith, answered the phone. She sounded put out, as always, whenever I called. It was past nine on the East Coast.

"What's the update?" asked Charlie, once Edith had handed him the receiver.

"I spoke to Tony's agent. He wasn't much help. But he did give me the phone number and address of the producer who hired Tony for the picture. Apparently this Bertram Wallis handpicked Tony for the role. I'll try the number in a few minutes."

"Anything else?"

"I found Tony's apartment and met his roommate. An odd young man. I felt he was holding back something. Maybe he's spooked by Tony's disappearance, but he sure wasn't in a chatty mood."

"He didn't provide anything useful?"

"Just that Tony has a girlfriend named April. The roommate doesn't know anything else about her. Says he doesn't know where she lives or even what her last name is."

Charlie grunted. "Any chance of getting him to open up?"

"Maybe with an oyster shucker."

"You could unleash your feminine charms on him."

I clicked my tongue. "Don't you think I'd try that if I thought it would work? This kid doesn't strike me as the type to go for my charms."

"Are you saying he's a queer?"

"Could be," I said, recalling the super, Evelyn Maynard.

"Well we can't put that in our story. This is a family newspaper, after all."

"Let's find Tony Eberle, then we'll decide what we can write. Did you manage to reach his parents?"

Charlie said he had indeed seen them. They'd had no idea he'd missed his first day of the shoot. His mother turned white, the father red.

"I got the distinct impression that Mr. Eberle doesn't approve of his son's vocation. He kept saying 'I told you so' to his wife, who was in tears. The father said Tony should have taken that city job he was offered."

"Doing what?" I asked.

"Filling potholes."

"Poor kid. What about the sister?"

"She's married. Lives in Pennsylvania now. I didn't speak to her."

"Did his parents know of any friends Tony might still have in New Holland?"

"They said he didn't have many friends. His closest buddy moved away after high school. I'll try a couple of kids from the drama club, and we'll share notes tomorrow."

I dialed the number Zelda Weitz had given me that morning for Bertram Wallis. It rang five times before his answering service picked up. The young lady on the line didn't know where Mr. Wallis was, but she took my name and number with a promise that he would get the message.

Marty the bellhop returned just after I'd hung up the phone. He waited in the corridor outside my door. I stood inside, safely wrapped in my robe. Marty seemed harmless, but I preferred to keep him on the far side of familiarity just the same. I cracked the door and stuck my head out. In fairness to him, he maintained an indifferent attitude toward me and my state of dress. What he wanted from me was more money.

"The total came to three fifty-eight," he said, holding out a paper bag. "Because of the wine, you know."

I fished another dollar out of my purse, wondering again if Artie Short would begrudge me a meal and a little wine at the end of a long, frustrating day. And, of course, Marty had brought no bill for me to present as evidence of the expense. Figuring I'd have to swallow the cost along with the meal, I tipped him a quarter then devoured the soggy spaghetti as I listened to the radio on the bed.

An hour and a half after dinner, I'd drunk half the bottle of wine and sat pondering the untimely disappearance of Tony Eberle. Where had he gotten to? Some banal, possibly comical, explanation was most likely, but

still I fretted. Had he run off for some better prospect? What that might
be, I couldn't imagine. Or maybe he was on a bender and had simply forgotten his big day. Perhaps he'd followed his girlfriend, April, to the local
mountains for a skiing jaunt. I couldn't possibly know in that moment.
But lurking in my thoughts was the possibility that something else had
happened to our local boy. Something sinister. I tried but failed to shake
the image of Mickey Harper's bruises from my mind. Someone had beaten
him up recently. Maybe Tony Eberle. Had they fought over the rent?
A dirty hot plate? Clothes on the floor, or even April? I doubted that.
Mickey didn't strike me as a ladies' man.

Of course I suspected Mickey was holding out on me. But did I have
any real evidence that he was lying? Sure I'd rattled him, but maybe he
was the nervous type. Even though I hadn't inspected the apartment for
myself, I was convinced there was one room and one room only. So why
might beautiful little Mickey tell me he didn't know if Tony had been
sleeping or out somewhere in parts unknown? And, if he'd wanted to lie,
why hadn't he come up with a simpler one? Why not just say that Tony
wasn't in when he'd arrived home?

The last thing I remembered thinking before nodding off to sleep was
that finding Tony Eberle was not going to be easy.

CHAPTER FOUR

WEDNESDAY, FEBRUARY 7, 1962

At Hody's, I ordered an English muffin, dark, and a coffee, black. After just one day, the big diner, with its freakishly spooky clown's face on the sign, had become my morning stop. The same waitress from the day before asked me how my fairy tale had worked out. I shook my head and said it had turned grim.

I dialed Tony Eberle's phone again from a booth near the door, but got no answer. Where might Mickey Harper be at 8:00 a.m. on a rainy Wednesday morning? Probably lying low, hiding under the covers and refusing to answer the phone or the door. I decided to make a second visit to the apartment on Wilton Place, but not before I'd tried to speak to Archie Stemple.

⬥

This taxi thing was inconvenient. Especially with rain now in the picture for the next week. I liked having my own transportation, even if my company car back home in New Holland did suffer occasional electrical problems caused by a dunk in Lake Winandauga a year and a half before. Fred Blaylock, the associate publisher of the paper, had mistaken a boat launch for the highway after too many drinks to drown his sorrows. He'd taken a bath at the races in Saratoga that day, and his car did the same in the lake after his dinner. Once it had dried out, I inherited the Dodge because Artie Short—the same man who considered me expendable in the event of a plane crash—didn't believe girls should be allowed to drive. At least not good cars. Fred Blaylock was rewarded with a shiny new Chrysler New Yorker.

While I was sure that taxicabs served an essential purpose, particularly in cities like New York, I was less convinced of their practicality in Los

Angeles. It was a huge, sprawling metropolis, with vast distances to cover. I needed a car of my own. Would the cheapskate Artie Short ever approve such an expenditure? I doubted it, but was willing to give it a try. I was through hunting for taxi stands.

I found a car rental on Vine Street, just next to the Capitol Records Building. At a little past nine, I was behind the wheel of a seven-year-old blue Chevy 150 two-door. It wasn't luxury, but it started right up. And at $6.90 a day, I figured it would end up costing less than taxis.

The car agency sold me a dog-eared copy of the 1954 Thomas Brothers street guide for seventy-five cents. Highway robbery, but I needed it. I later discovered that quite a few things had changed in Los Angeles since 1954, especially downtown. And of course the Hollywood Freeway. But the guide proved useful on the whole.

Traffic was painfully slow due to the rain, and I wondered how the locals would react to snow on their streets. Outside the studio, I parked on the street, and, armed with a ragged umbrella I'd borrowed from Marty the bellhop, I approached the front gate.

"I'd like to see Mr. Stemple," I told the guard.

"Do you have an appointment?" he asked.

I assured him I did, even though I didn't. He let me wait inside, safe from the rain, while he made up my pass. I read a magazine. Ten minutes later, just as I was wondering what was taking so long, the door flew open, and a woman in full rain gear—hat, rain slicker, boots, and umbrella— pushed her way inside. It was Dorothy Fetterman.

"Good morning, Miss Stone," she announced, collapsing her perfect umbrella without looking at me. "I wasn't expecting to see you today."

And I surely hadn't wanted to see her.

"I was hoping to speak to Mr. Stemple," I said.

"Do you have an appointment?"

"No."

She removed her hat and coat and hung them on a hook against the wall before taking a seat across from me. Her lipstick was still faultless, and not a hair was out of place.

"That's not what you told the guard," she said.

I offered a sheepish apology.

"Miss Stone, you must understand that Tony Eberle no longer works for Paramount Studios. There's really no point in your speaking to Archie

Stemple or anyone else here for that matter. And though I sympathize with your predicament, I cannot allow you to interrupt our business of making movies."

"If I could just speak to Mr. Stemple for five minutes."

"I promise you he doesn't know where Tony Eberle is."

"I'm not here to ask him where Tony is," I blurted out. "I've already found him."

That was a lie, of course. An improvised one. I doubted it would work and, in fact, wondered if it might not come back to haunt me later on. But now I'd said it.

Over the next several minutes, I tried to convince her to let me see Archie Stemple. She was patient but firm, determined to block all access to anyone at the studio, starting with the ill-tempered director. I was sure someone on the crew must have spoken with Tony before his disappearance, and the director was as good a place as any to start.

"If you know where Tony Eberle is, what do you want with Mr. Stemple? Don't tell me you're an actress."

I shook my head.

"That's a relief. You're a pretty young lady," she continued. "But not Hollywood pretty."

All right, that was twice I'd been insulted in that manner in twenty-four hours. If this continued, I was going to develop a complex. She must have noticed my expression because she offered an apology of sorts.

"Don't take it the wrong way. I'm not pretty enough for Hollywood either. Never was. Not even when I was a daisy-fresh girl of eighteen." She smiled at me. "Very few girls are. And that's a blessing. This town chews up pretty girls and spits them out. Handsome boys, too."

"I assure you that I am not looking to be discovered," I said. "I'd like to speak to Mr. Stemple to ask for Tony's job back."

My indignation and pleading aside, Dorothy still wasn't biting. She crossed her right leg over the left, her stockings brushing against each other. She leaned forward and fixed me with a captive stare.

"You say you've located Tony Eberle?" she asked. "Where is he?"

"He asked me not to say."

She digested that for a full ten seconds, her eyes still studying me. I felt like a pinned-down frog in science class.

"At least not yet," I added.

She made me nervous. I urged myself to get a grip. These were the same tactics I liked to use when interviewing subjects. Let them fill the gaps in the conversation. Stare at them, make them squirm as you prepare to dissect them alive.

At length she uncrossed her legs and smoothed her skirt over her knees. She pursed her red lips then told me Archie Stemple was unavailable to meet me.

"He's making a movie," she said. "He's already lost one day of production thanks to your Mr. Eberle. And this isn't helping. I'm sure you understand."

"Might I speak to some of the cast and crew?" I asked. "Carole Haven, perhaps? Isn't she the female lead?"

"Miss Haven has been shooting a film in Mexico for the past three weeks. She won't be back for another ten days. As far as I know, she's never met Tony Eberle."

"What about Bobby Renfro?"

"Bobby Renfro? You want a private interview with a movie star?"

I hardly thought of Bobby Renfro as a movie star but figured I would only lose points with Dorothy if I quibbled.

"What about Mr. Wallis?" I asked. "Is he on the lot today?"

"Mr. Wallis rarely comes here. That's not how producers work."

She was a tough nut to crack.

"I'd really like to speak to him."

"So would I," she mumbled half to herself. Then to me, "He's an eccentric. A very difficult man. I haven't spoken to him yet about Tony Eberle. As far as I know, no one has."

I thought that odd. Bertram Wallis was the producer of *Twistin' on the Beach*. If your second lead is a no-show on the first day of production, wouldn't you want to know about it right away? Before the director took matters into his own hands and replaced him?

"Are you saying he's missing?" I asked.

"No, nothing like that." She paused a moment to reflect. "As I said, he's an eccentric."

"I've heard him described otherwise."

"You're a clever girl, aren't you?" she said. "But we're not here to discuss Bertram Wallis. He's my problem, not yours. And you've found your Tony Eberle. You should be happy."

"Please. Just five minutes with Mr. Stemple?"

She eyed me for several beats, inscrutable, then rose and picked up the receiver of a house phone on a nearby table. She dialed four numbers and waited.

"Archie, it's Dot," she said at length. "Do you have a sec? I'm coming over to see you."

For a moment I thought I'd broken through her intransigence. It appeared I was about to get my interview with Archie Stemple after all. Except I wasn't.

"Good-bye, Miss Stone," said Dorothy as she donned her coat and hat. "Please excuse me. I have work to do."

On her way out the door, she instructed the guard to see me off the lot.

The Writers Guild building was located on Beverly Boulevard. I'd phoned ahead to ask for some information on Bertram Wallis. The nice woman who answered—I believe her name was Blanche—told me she wasn't the time and temperature lady, and I'd have to come in and do my own research.

According to the biographical sketch on record, Bertram Wallis was born in 1926 in Aberdeen, Scotland, into a prominent military family. His maternal grandfather, Andrew Gilchrist, received the Distinguished Service Order medal for his service in the Second Boer War, before serving on the personal staff of the earl of Minto, viceroy of India. He died in 1909 in Simla, following a fall from a horse in a polo match, leaving behind a widow and young daughter—Wallis's mother. Bertram's father, Brian Alvin Wallis, held the rank of lieutenant in the Fourth Army of the British Expeditionary Force and fought and was wounded in France in the First World War. He worked under Home Secretary Herbert Morrison during the Second World War. Young Bertram was in his first year at boarding school when the Battle of Britain began. Like so many children, little Bertie Wallis was evacuated out of the UK. His parents dispatched him to Simla to be safe with his maternal grandmother, who had remained in India after her husband's death.

After the war, Bertram returned to Britain and university at Aberdeen. He never finished, deciding instead that he wanted to be a writer.

I could find no references to any books or stories he might have published. But in 1953, at the age of twenty-seven, he served as a script assistant on *Demetrius and the Gladiators*. There was no indication of how he'd landed the job. From that moment forward, he worked on several pictures each year, before eventually graduating to producer. *Lenny Goes to College* (1957), starring Bobby Renfro; *Drag Race Friday Night* (1958), with Blake Wheeler and Vicky Shay, the pretty blonde who died tragically in a car accident a year later; *Varsity Letterman* (1959), with Bobby Renfro, again, and Carole Haven; and *Beach Bash '61* (1961), with—once more— Bobby Renfro. *Twistin' on the Beach*, Tony Eberle's star-crossed debut, was next in Wallis's filmography. I noticed that Bobby Renfro had appeared in three of Bertram Wallis's films, and I made a note to track him down. His thoughts on Tony might come in handy.

Wallis's movie career looked pretty dismal to me. Imagine making teen romp after teen romp with little concern for how long in the tooth your main actor was growing. Bobby Renfro? He had to be thirty-five or thirty-six. But just as I was ready to close the file on Wallis, I noticed that he'd registered a screenplay with the guild for his next movie, *The Colonel's Widow*. A précis didn't provide much in the way of details other than a simple categorization as "historical art film."

Outside the rain continued to fall, perhaps a little harder than before, and the wind nearly finished off my pathetic umbrella. I wrestled my way into a phone booth on the corner in front of the Writers Guild, dialed Wallis's number, and got no answer. Next I tried Mickey Harper, also without success. Afraid I was getting nowhere, I drove past Tony and Mickey's apartment on Wilton Place to see if maybe there was a light on inside. All was dark, and no one answered when I knocked.

Back at the McCadden Hotel, I changed out of my soggy shoes and clothes. Marty the bellhop knocked on my door just as I pulled a warm sweater over my head. He had a message from the front desk:

Are you available to meet Mr. Stemple and me at eight at Dino's Lodge? We'd like to discuss Tony Eberle with you. Call my office at HO5-4202 to confirm.

Cordially,
Dorothy Fetterman

I'd seen Dino's Lodge on the opening of *77 Sunset Strip* many times. And now I was standing in the entrance, just like Efrem Zimbalist Jr. I wanted to savor the moment, light a cigarette or run a comb through my hair like Kookie Kookson III, but the rain chased me inside.

I took a seat at the bar, ordered a drink, and cooled my heels for nearly twenty minutes before I spotted Dorothy and Archie Stemple at the coat check. Stemple wandered off to a table somewhere inside while Dorothy came to collect me in the bar.

"I see you found the place," she said once we were seated in a booth.

She and Stemple sat on one side of the table, and I took the other. The setup felt like a police interrogation. I tried to break the ice and my own jitters by asking if Dean Martin and his friends might stop in. The two exchanged a glance. Archie Stemple snorted through his nose.

"Oh, no, Miss Stone," said Dorothy, shaking her head in a most condescending manner. "Dean Martin wouldn't be caught dead in here."

My face flushed hot. "But it's his place, isn't it?"

"He sold his name to these people," said Stemple, oozing even more arrogance than Dorothy had done. At least she'd appeared to pity me. "He had a disagreement with the owners and stopped coming here. In fact, no one comes here anymore."

"That's why we chose this place," added Dorothy. "We didn't want to be seen."

I gulped, trying to swallow my embarrassment. "Is that because of me, or are you two having an affair?" I asked in a cheeky attempt to win back my own self-respect.

"Neither," said Dorothy, unfazed. "But we want to keep this matter as quiet as possible."

"Tony Eberle?"

They shared another knowing look, and I fancied they were deciding who would take the lead. Dorothy turned back to face me and leaned in ever so slightly to speak.

"Not Tony Eberle," she said, almost in a whisper. "Bertram Wallis."

I must have looked puzzled because she explained.

"We haven't been able to locate Mr. Wallis for a couple of days."

"I don't understand. Why would you want to talk to me about Bertram Wallis? I'd never heard of him before yesterday."

"All right, enough of this," said Stemple, practically spitting his words at me. "Tell us where Eberle is."

Dorothy put a gentle hand on Stemple's arm. She didn't utter a word to him. Didn't even look at him. He parked his tongue and sat back in his seat. I knew who was in charge.

"We think Tony might be able to tell us something about Mr. Wallis's whereabouts," she said in a softer voice. "Can you share your information with us? Where is he hiding?"

I was holding nothing in my hand and was already regretting my lie earlier in the day. I still had no clue where Tony was and even less of an idea of how to find him. Of course there was his roommate, Mickey Harper, but I was having trouble corralling him as well. And if he knew anything, he wasn't telling. Then there was the mysterious girlfriend. April something or other. I sensed that if I could locate her, I'd find Tony too. I didn't dare tell Dorothy and Stemple any of this. I stalled instead.

"What makes you think Tony knows where Wallis is?"

"Bertie hired him," said Dorothy. "He seems to have some kind of connection with him."

"And you're worried about Mr. Wallis. What exactly do you think happened?"

"Of course we're concerned. A man disappears for two days without a word."

"But you're not so concerned for Tony Eberle."

"Bertie Wallis is an important man," said Dorothy. "Tony Eberle is a nobody. Now less than a nobody."

"Except that he may know something about your Mr. Wallis. Not entirely a nobody yet."

"You're avoiding my question."

"I can reach him," I said. "But I'll need a day or two."

Dorothy stared deep into my eyes, trying to read my thoughts. I have a pretty good poker face, but she was testing my resolve.

"I suppose we have no choice," she said finally. "You'll keep me apprised of your progress."

She slipped out of the booth, and Stemple followed. She stopped at the bar and settled my bill. I watched them collect their things from the coat-check girl and disappear through the door.

The window was dark at the Wilton Place apartment. I knocked anyway, but no one answered. I hadn't eaten, so I drove off to a nearby deli and grabbed a sandwich to go. It was just about ten, and I wasn't sleepy. I needed to catch a break if I was going to locate Tony Eberle in the couple of days I'd promised Dorothy Fetterman. Dinner in hand, I returned to Wilton Place to wait. It didn't take long.

CHAPTER FIVE

I nibbled on my sandwich as the rain drummed on the roof of my rented car. The radio kept me company as I sat in the dark. For once, I didn't even mind the selections coming over the airwaves. Bobby Vee, the Shirelles, Ray Charles. Not so bad. But when "Bristol Stomp" came on, I drew the line. I switched off the radio and looked just as the window of apartment 101 lit up. I nearly choked on my sandwich, which I promptly dropped on the floor at my feet.

There were a couple of shapes moving around in the room, but I couldn't make out than that. I was parked about fifty or sixty feet from the window. There was no way to tell who was inside, but I assumed whoever it was had arrived while I was at the deli ordering my dinner. Or maybe I'd been concentrating on the radio when Mickey or Tony had come home. Or was it someone else inside? Perhaps someone who wanted to find Tony Eberle as much as I did. That was a frightening thought. I watched for ten minutes, waiting for the perfect moment to go and knock at the door.

Glancing at my watch, I saw that it was just about ten thirty when the light blinked off. I reached for the door handle, ready to get out and investigate, but I held off, figuring Mickey or Tony would be safely tucked into bed by the time I rapped on the door. I rehearsed what I would say when I finally made contact with whoever was inside. If it was Tony, I'd ask why he'd decided to run off and blow his one big chance. And I'd ask about Bertram Wallis. If it was Mickey on the other side of the door, I'd make him show me Tony's possessions one way or another so I might locate April. Three minutes later, as I contemplated my next move, a soft glow appeared in the maw of the garage exit to the right of the darkened window. The throw of two headlights, growing ever brighter, lit the wet pavement. Then a car, a light-colored wagon, emerged from the underground garage onto the street, pausing at the entrance as if to check that the coast was clear. I shrank into my seat, trying to melt into the dark, rainy night until the car had made its decision. When it finally pushed its way out and turned left onto Wilton, I reached for the key in the ignition and held it fast between my right forefinger and thumb. The wagon waited for a moment at the traffic light, then made a left when it changed. I turned the key, shifted into gear, and followed.

From behind, the car looked like an early fifties Rambler station wagon. Through the driving rain it was hard to be sure, but I thought I could make out the shapes of three heads inside. The Rambler continued west along Franklin Avenue, crossing La Brea where it zigzagged down to Hollywood Boulevard. I marked the car some thirty yards back, keeping my distance so as not to raise suspicion. Only when we reached a red light did I pull to a stop directly behind it. Hoping the passengers wouldn't notice me among the other cars, I wondered if the street lamp was bright enough for me to get a clear shot of the license plate. I pulled my Leica from my purse and popped off the lens cover. The light changed, but I snapped one frame before the Rambler had moved. I would have to develop the film to see if I'd managed to focus on the license plate in my haste.

I gave the car in front of me some space. A short time later, it turned right off Hollywood onto Nichols Canyon Road. I stepped on the gas to keep pace.

The road narrowed as it twisted its way slowly up a hill. We climbed for about three minutes, leaving the city behind in short order. I marveled at how lonely and remote the hills were, just a couple of hundred yards from Hollywood Boulevard. Matching their every turn, I sloshed through the runoff rainwater that was rushing down the hill. Three times, the Rambler steered around fallen branches or some creeping mud that had slid down the sides of the canyon into the road, and I did the same. I worried that the passengers might notice a car following them, but I didn't dare fall too far behind and lose them.

The Rambler stopped at an intersection. I cringed as I came nearer, knowing full well that I couldn't pull up short without arousing suspicion. So I did the only thing I could. I forged on ahead and stopped right behind them. Now, as my wipers beat back and forth across the windshield, throwing waves of the pouring rain off to either side, I could clearly discern three heads inside the car in front of me. Surely they'd noticed me by now. My headlights were shining directly into their car, and the road was deserted besides us. The Rambler sat stubbornly at the stop sign. What were they doing?

Fifteen seconds ticked by. I wanted to pick up my camera and risk another photo, but my courage didn't go that far. Yet I had to do something before they climbed out of the car to investigate who was tailing them. I decided it was better to blow my horn than to idle silently behind them. I gave them a short blast and watched, hoping they'd take me for just another motorist eager to get home. My gambit worked. The brake lights blinked off, and the car continued up Nichols Canyon Road. I exhaled, clutching the steering wheel as the Rambler receded into the distance up the hill. In for a penny in for a pound, I set off after them.

My targets picked up speed, and I let them. The rain flooded the road now, and, unfamiliar with the area, I drove carefully, slowly, not wanting to risk a crash. They rounded a curve about a hundred yards ahead, and I lost sight of them for about twenty seconds. Once I'd reached the turn, they'd already disappeared around another bend in the road. I accelerated. But a quarter of a mile later, they were still nowhere in sight.

My headlights peered through the driving rain. I leaned forward and wiped the foggy windshield with my right hand to see better. Something loomed ahead. My eyes grew as I watched. I'd never witnessed anything like it before. A muddy mountain of slop was crawling across the road directly in my path. It looked alive, and it took me a moment to realize that this was a mudslide. A living blob of earth tumbled across the pavement, piling up upon itself, blocking the way. I stamped on the brakes and skidded to a stop. All was silent except my heavy breathing and the humming of the windshield wipers, sloshing back and forth across the glass. The mound of mud and branches stood before me, stretching right to left across Nichols Canyon Road. There was no room for me to maneuver around it. I'd have needed a shovel, a snowplow, or an earthmover to push the mud out of the way. I cursed my luck as I imagined the Rambler and its three passengers snaking up the hill. I'd lost them and any chance of finding Tony Eberle.

CHAPTER SIX

THURSDAY, FEBRUARY 8, 1962

I'd expected Southern California to provide a warm, sunny respite from the East Coast winter. But Thursday morning brought the wettest day of all. A deluge. I switched on the radio for the news. All Los Angeles schools were canceled due to the rain. Wow, I thought. New Holland refused to close schools even for a blizzard. Besides the weather, the top stories of the day were the state of emergency in France and the Cuban embargo announced by President Kennedy. I was preparing to brush my teeth in the bathroom when the local news came on. I rushed back into the bedroom, mouth full of toothpaste, to catch the end of the report.

"Repeating our top story, producer Bertram Wallis has been found dead in a ravine below his Hollywood Hills mansion. Police have not yet given a time or cause of death, but the lead investigator on the scene described the circumstances as suspicious. More as this story develops."

❧

"No luck yet," I told Charlie over the phone. "I almost got him last night. At least I think it was him. But there was a mudslide on the road, and I lost him."

"A mudslide?" he asked, and I could tell he wished he could write a story about that. "Did you take any pictures?"

I explained that I'd had little interest in photographing a mound of slop in the dead of night.

"Besides, I've got to follow up on some big news I just heard on the radio. Do you remember I mentioned the name Bertram Wallis the other day? Well, last night that woman from the studio told me he was missing. She thought Tony Eberle might know where he was. But this morning Wallis was found dead in a ravine below his home in the Hollywood Hills."

Charlie whistled down the line.

"Doesn't look good for our friend Tony," I said. "Not as long he remains on the lam."

"Yeah, he's going to have some explaining to do when he turns up. Assuming he's not lying at the bottom of another ravine somewhere."

"I've got Wallis's address. I'm heading up there right now."

"Keep track of your carfare. Artie will want to account for every last penny."

I gulped. This wasn't the moment to break the news about the rented car, so I kept my mouth shut.

"Any progress with Tony's family and friends?" I asked instead.

"Afraid not. The father won't talk any more to the press until he's spoken to Tony."

"Can't say I blame him," I said. "What about his old drama club chums?"

"I spoke to three of them. They said Tony was a great talent, polite enough, but no one ever got close to him. And none have heard from him since high school. Apparently, he had few friends back then."

"Quite mysterious for a milkman's son from Rockton."

Charlie wished me luck, and I hung up.

Sitting on the edge of the bed, I scribbled some notes to myself. I thought about Tony's childhood friends. Surely he had more than one, and I wanted to speak to them. Eberle Sr. had to know their names, but Charlie had failed to get him to talk. I had another idea. I picked up the receiver and asked for the operator. Taking into account Fadge's laziness and overall unreliability, I still figured he'd be in the store at that hour. I placed a station-to-station call to Fiorello's, and my dear friend answered on the seventh ring.

"I need a favor," I said after I'd completed the niceties and given him the short version of my California adventure. "But you've got to promise me you won't breathe a word to anybody. At least not yet."

He made another in a series of childish jokes that I was going to owe him for this. "And not some lousy Hollywood knickknack from a souvenir shop. I'm talking sex."

"You'll get a Dodgers pennant and a Hollywood snow globe, but only if you're good."

"At least some heavy petting."

"Let's see the results, then we'll talk about payback. Here's the sitch. Tony Eberle never showed up for his close-up. If anyone knows where he is, they're not talking. And get this: the producer who hired him turned up dead this morning."

"Trouble seems to follow you around lately," he said. "So how can I help and make you beholden to me at the same time?"

"I need you to go see Tony's father and get the names of some of Tony's childhood friends. Then you can let Charlie Reese know. He'll take it from there."

"That doesn't sound too hard. Why can't Charlie get the names for you?"

"The father doesn't want to talk to the press. So I thought you might persuade him. Lean on him a little."

"You want me to rough him up?"

"No, I want you to lean on him till he tells you what you want to know. Literally lean on him. He'll talk or suffocate."

Fadge uttered a mirthless laugh from three thousand miles away. "You want a favor and you start in with the fat jokes?"

"I'm batting my eyelashes as I ask please."

Reluctantly Fadge agreed to take on the job. I gave him the address, and he promised he'd try to get me something before the end of the day. Joking aside, he was my favorite guy in the world.

I dropped my film off at Thelan's Camera Center on Hollywood Boulevard and begged the man behind the counter to develop the film as quickly as he could. He took pity on me and said he'd have it ready by six. But it was going to cost me. Maybe no heavy petting, but five dollars extra.

The car idled at the curb, wipers laboring to keep up with the rain, as I dug into my purse for the scrap of paper Zelda Weitz had given me: Bertram Wallis's address and phone number. Solar Drive. I flipped through the Thomas guide and located it. Then, plotting my route, I ran my finger down the map and gave a little start. Solar Drive was at the rim of a canyon high in the Hollywood Hills. And it was reachable only from Nichols Canyon Road, the very place I'd followed the Rambler wagon the night before.

CHAPTER SEVEN

Hollywood Boulevard was flooded, but not so much that I couldn't navigate my way west. I made the same turn up Nichols Canyon as I had the night before, hoping crews had cleared away the mudslide. They hadn't, but some industrious drivers and the heavy rain had worn down the mound of earth and made the way passable if messy.

Near the top of Nichols Canyon Road, I turned right onto Solar Drive and saw police cars and a gaggle of onlookers ahead. I parked about fifty yards away, grabbed my camera, and set out on foot. I braved the weather, pointing my borrowed umbrella into the driving wind and rain. Despite all odds and appearances to the contrary, the distressed ribs of Marty the bellhop's umbrella managed to hold onto the shredded fabric and provide a small measure of shelter from the storm. As I approached the house, I saw several more cars, some with radio and television call letters on the doors, and a gang of waterlogged souls milling about in slickers and rubber boots. I sidled up to a tall fellow holding a camera under his open raincoat. It was hard to say for sure, what with his rain hat and wet face, but I figured him to be about thirty, of large build, like a football player, with a friendly face. He flashed me an aw-shucks smile and told me his name was Andy Blaine. I introduced myself and asked which paper he was with.

"I used to shoot for the *Examiner*," he said. "But since the merger last month, I peddle my photos to the highest bidder."

A man huddling in a rain poncho beside Andy snorted a laugh and remarked in a dry, tired voice that the papers weren't exactly breaking down doors to pay for pictures.

"It's not as bad as all that," Andy said to him. "I still sell my pictures if they're good."

"Good for you," the other man said. "I lost my job last month when they announced the merger. Gene Duerson, by the way." He extended a dry hand to me. "I have to scramble now to cover stories in the hopes of selling something to the dailies or scandal sheets."

Gene was a wiry man of about forty-five or fifty, with horn-rimmed glasses and a long nose. I couldn't see his hair thanks to the yellow rain hat he was wearing, but his face was open and genuine, if a little world weary. He looked frail. Or perhaps bored.

"Do you live around here, Miss Stone?" asked Andy, stepping between Gene and me.

"No, I'm from back East. Actually I'm a reporter, too. I write for a small daily in upstate New York."

"No kidding? You're a reporter?"

"You'll have to excuse young Andy, here," said Duerson, scribbling something into a pad of paper. "He's from Iowa and never heard of a woman reporter."

Andy grinned at me and apologized. "I'm still getting used to Los Angeles. It's an education for a Midwest boy."

"So what brings a girl from New York out here to a dead Hollywood producer's house?" asked Duerson.

Unless George Walsh is involved, I'm not miserly when it comes to chatting with colleagues about my stories. Still, I've learned the hard way not to be too loose-lipped. I wasn't sure where the Tony Eberle story might lead or even if he was involved in this latest development. But Bertram Wallis had handpicked him for his role in *Twistin' on the Beach*, after all, and Tony was missing in action somewhere. And then there was Dorothy Fetterman, unsettling, competent, and powerful, wanting to know where the hometown hero was holed up. Who was to say that Tony Eberle wasn't in this up to his ears? I wanted to be friendly with my new pals, but not at the expense of losing my story. I decided to give them the abbreviated version and leave out anything that might give away my advantage.

"I'm here to write a piece on a local boy who has a bit part in the movie Mr. Wallis was making. I heard about Mr. Wallis on the radio and couldn't ignore a story like this."

They both nodded politely, surely glad they didn't have to do a profile on a small-town nobody, to echo Dorothy Fetterman's words. Andy asked me for the actor's name. I dodged his question.

"Nobody you've heard of," I said. "Not much more than an extra, really."

I chatted with the two men for about ten minutes. They told me that the police were inside the house, scouring the place for clues. A sergeant had given them and the other reporters an update about an hour and a half earlier, but they were still waiting for more information.

I asked what Andy and Gene knew of Bertram Wallis. Gene had met him a couple of times through Andy.

"Wallis sometimes needs a photographer for his parties," said Andy. "Other times he's just hoping to get some publicity. These producers are always looking to get their names or pictures in the papers."

"Not always," said Gene.

"How so?" I asked.

He balked, insisting he didn't like to say such things in mixed company, especially with someone as young and innocent as I. Finally, after assurances that I didn't offend easily, Andy chimed in and told me that Wallis often threw parties, including one Monday night.

"And some of the parties were indecent."

"You mean like orgies?"

"The Romans had nothing on Bertie Wallis," he said.

"Was it one of those orgies on Monday night?"

"I don't think so. More of a respectable gathering that night. As respectable as Wallis ever got. I was here outside with some other photographers and reporters, waiting to see if anyone famous showed up. And sometimes Wallis invites us in to take a couple of photos. He likes the publicity so long as it's not one of his indecent parties."

"Did he invite any photographers inside that night?"

Andy shook his head. "No. I took a few pictures outside, though. Just people arriving in their cars."

"Maybe you could show me sometime," I said. "I'd like to see who attends these parties."

Gene leaned against the fender of a news van and popped a cigarette into his mouth. He produced one of those old-fashioned strike lighters and scratched it three times before managing to generate a flame in the wet. He replaced the wand and tucked the contraption into his trouser pocket.

"I'll tell you who attends. Men, girls, boys, you name it," continued Andy. "Of course I was never asked to shoot photographs at those private affairs, but we've all heard about them."

Gene just squinted off into the distance at the next ridge, watching the rain as cigarette smoke trailed out of his nostrils and disappeared on the wind.

"Boys?" I asked. "That can't be. It's illegal."

"Well, by boys I mean young men. Actors and models, most of them. Of course every now and then there's a rumor about a kid with some movie star. Fourteen, fifteen, or sixteen. That kind of thing."

"Bertram Wallis liked young boys?"

"I never said that about Wallis," said Andy, holding up his hands as if putting on the brakes. "I was talking about actors. Famous actors. Some of them swing that way. There's folks who'll scare up whatever perverts want in this town."

"Really? And you say this is common knowledge? About famous actors?"

"You must've heard rumors about Rock Hudson."

I told him I had but didn't believe them.

"He's just so manly," I said. "I can't picture it."

"He's not the only manly man who likes men. Not by a long shot. All the newspapermen and reporters know it, but we can't print it. Wouldn't be decent."

"Nothing to do with decency," Gene added in a near whisper. "The studios pay off the scandal sheets. If they didn't, the whole country would know about Rock Hudson and Tony Perkins. And others. The list goes on and on."

I swallowed a dry gulp. I hardly considered myself a Pollyanna, but my illusions were being smashed and drowned in the rain of a gray Hollywood morning.

A commotion coming from the house interrupted our palaver. Andy picked up his tripod and hustled over to the driveway. Gene followed, a little less frantically, but all he was carrying was a pad and pencil. I sloshed through the rain after them. The throng of about twenty reporters closed ranks in seconds, surrounding a plainclothes policeman who'd just emerged from the house. The cop was a beefy man of about thirty-five with black hair slicked down on his head, perhaps with pomade, perhaps from the rain. The circle of reporters crowded around him, leaving no room for me to squeeze in. In fact, I was shut out. I held my camera at the ready, but the huddle was too tall for me to get a shot of the cop. The press fired questions at him, and I was thankful to be close enough to hear if not see the briefing.

"Come on, Millard, throw us a bone. Give us something we can write," said one voice.

"Hold your horses, fellas," answered the cop. "You'll get your stories once we have some more information."

"Can't you tell us anything new?" asked another reporter.

"All I can say for now is that the deceased, one Bertram Wallis, age thirty-six, was discovered in the ravine below his terrace this morning."

"Who discovered the body?" I yelled from my position on the periphery.

The crowd turned to see who was the owner of the pixie voice. A crack opened in the wall of raincoats, and I got my first clear view of the policeman. And he got his first glimpse of me. He grinned one of those toothy, wolfish grins in my direction.

"What do we got here?" he said, taking a step toward me, shoving a couple of reporters out the way as he did. "You must be lost, young lady."

I straightened my back, trying to summon a couple of extra inches of height beneath my umbrella, but, in truth, without much success. The cop stood before me, wearing nothing to protect himself from the rain. Just a wool overcoat and the aforementioned pomade, which resisted water like a duck's oily feathers. He wasn't bad-looking in a five-o'clock-shadow kind of way, but I found him off-putting just the same. A bully, I thought right off the bat. But then his grizzled features softened just a bit, and his smile went from threatening to welcoming in an instant. Maybe I'd misjudged him.

"Are you with a magazine or a newspaper, miss?" he asked.

"Newspaper," I said.

"Which one?"

How to answer? If I told him the truth, he'd surely want to know why I was there. I'd have to tell him about Tony Eberle, which couldn't be good for Tony. Still, I had no other affiliation and no choice.

"The *Republic*," I said, hoping it would end there. It didn't. "The *New Holland Republic*," I clarified after he'd asked.

The cop, Sergeant John L. Millard, as he later told me for my article, nodded and dropped the matter, at least for the time being.

"The cleaning lady spotted him," he said, finally answering my question. "That is she saw him in the mud and brush from the terrace above."

"What was she doing on the terrace?" I asked. "I mean it was pouring this morning. Why would she be standing out in the rain?"

"You hear that, fellas?" he said to the other reporters. "You mugs should learn to ask questions like that." Then turning back to me, he answered that she'd gone looking for the dog. "She got here at seven this morning and didn't see Wallis or his dog. Then she heard the little guy barking out on the terrace. He was locked outside. Been out there at least two days."

"How did she know that?" called one of the reporters.

Millard smirked. "You believe this guy?" he asked me but not expecting an answer. Then he turned back to the circle of reporters and explained that the dog had "done his business, big and small" all over the terrace.

"What kind of dog is it? And what's his name?" I asked.

Millard regarded me queerly. Then he attempted to show me a friendly smile. "You really want to know what kind of dog it is? Do you write for *Doggy Daily* or something?"

I repeated my affiliation, and he told me Bertram Wallis's dog was a Chinese pug named Leon. I noticed some of my brethren of the press corps writing furiously on their pads.

"The cleaning lady's been off since Monday night," continued Millard. "So the little dog was pretty cold and hungry when she found him."

"Then do you suspect the body had been in the ravine for at least as long as Leon was locked out on the terrace?" I asked.

"Another excellent question, boys. I hope you're all paying attention." He turned back to me. "To answer your question, we're not sure about the time of death, but judging by the condition of the body, it looks like the guy was down there for a day or two."

"How's the dog doing now?" asked an earnest reporter. Millard rolled his eyes. "It's not for the paper," the reporter said in his defense. "I love dogs, is all."

Millard waved a hand at him. "He's fine. Had his breakfast and is sleeping in his warm bed."

Then he asked me if the little lady had any more questions. I did. Many. I wondered, for instance, when Wallis had last been seen alive? Did the police suspect foul play and, if so, did they have anyone in mind? What was the name of the housekeeper? Were there any witnesses besides the housekeeper? Did Mr. Wallis have any next of kin? I was trying to decide which question to ask first when Gene Duerson piped up in his strongest voice from behind the policeman.

"Was this an accident? Or do you suspect murder or suicide?"

Millard shrugged at me as if to say "You lost your chance, sister," and turned to answer Gene.

"We haven't determined anything yet. As I said before, it appears Mr. Wallis has been dead for a day or two. Possibly three. The coroner's office will have a better estimate later today or tomorrow."

"Excuse me," I said, pushing my way into the scrum of reporters. "Can you tell us what the deceased was wearing?"

"What he was wearing?" asked Millard. I nodded. "He was dressed in slacks and a shirt. Nothing unusual there."

"And did he have anything on his person?"

Millard took a step toward me. Gone was the friendly demeanor he'd been wielding. "What do you mean by anything on his person?"

I gulped. "Just that. Was he carrying anything that might help you determine what happened to him?"

For a long moment, Sergeant Millard stared me down, cocking his head and aiming his squinting right eye at me.

"Have you been talking to one of my boys?"

"No, I just got here five minutes ago."

"I hope not, because if I find out someone blabbed to you, I'll have his badge."

"Honest. I haven't spoken to any cops. I just got here."

He glared a little more, unsettling me, before finally clearing his throat. "I suppose it will come out later," he began. "Wallis had his wallet on him. His driver's license, a Diner's Club card, house key, and twenty-two dollars. Nothing appears to be missing."

He shuffled in the mud. Then he nodded, almost as if he'd made up his mind. "We found a telephone number in his right front trouser pocket. We've established who the subscriber is and have dispatched a patrol car to the address to investigate."

The crush of reporters tightened the circle around the cop, bombarding him with questions as they scribbled in their pads. Whose phone number was it? What was the address? Was he a suspect? Sergeant Millard didn't appreciate the mob's advance, cursing and shoving reporters out of his way as he cleared a path for himself. Once he'd separated himself from the boys of the press, he wiped some rain off his forehead with the back of his hand and warned them all that he'd throw every last one of them in jail if they ever surrounded him like that again.

"I don't like being crowded, is all," he yelled at them. Us. "Keep your distance."

Once he'd cooled off, Millard made his last remarks to the reporters. No, he wasn't going to release the information on the phone number. Not until the police had had a chance to interview the fellow.

"Then it was a man," said Gene Duerson, practically risking arrest.

Millard fumed. He stared him down for about ten seconds before admitting—grudgingly—that, yes, the telephone number belonged to a man. With that last statement, he stomped off back to the house and shelter.

"So we have to stand out here and wait some more," said Andy, who rejoined me under a nearby tree that offered a small measure of protection from the rain.

"I'm not waiting here," I said. "I've got an idea."

CHAPTER EIGHT

I wasn't sure if I was making a mistake letting Andy Blaine and Gene Duerson in on my hunch, but I did it anyway. They could certainly help me in some way later on, perhaps get me permission to send a wirephoto back to New Holland or give me advice on where to eat. They were locals, after all. I invited them to take a ride with me, and we drove down the hill into Hollywood toward Wilton Place. I wasn't too worried that they would scoop me if my hunch was right. After all, I didn't care about losing the story to any Los Angeles reporters. My focus was on the New Holland audience.

We chatted along the way, getting to know each other. Andy told me he'd taken up photography in high school in Davenport. He landed in Los Angeles after his tour in the navy ended. He'd been stationed in Long Beach, liked the Southern California weather, and never left. I became aware of a lingering smile on his part, and it was stuck on me. Sure, he seemed sweet, but I wasn't looking for love in the front seat of my rented car. Gene sat in the back, staring out the window and listening to Andy's prattling.

"What about you, Gene?" I asked. "What's your story?"

Glancing in the rearview mirror, I saw him shrug. He told me in his languid fashion that he had come from Dallas. Served in the army in the Second World War, wrote for *Stars and Stripes*, then drifted from job to job before landing at the *Herald-Express*.

"And now, at age forty-nine, I'm looking for a steady position," he concluded. "Thanks to Mr. Hearst."

"Maybe you'll sell one of your scripts to the movies," Andy chimed in.

Gene grunted. "Yeah. I'll hold my breath. Everybody in LA has a script, you know, but mine are the best anyone's ever seen," he said for my benefit.

"What's your script about?" I asked.

Andy hooted a laugh. "Don't ask him that. He won't tell. So paranoid that someone will steal his idea."

"Ideas are the only things writers have," said Gene dryly.

"At least tell me the title."

"He told me once," said Andy. "*Twilight in the Summer Capital.*"

Gene shook his head as he gazed out the window. "There's nothing lower than stealing a writer's work. I don't tell anyone what I'm writing until I have a contract and cash on the barrelhead."

Andy ribbed Gene, asking if he was the one who'd written *Gone with the Wind* and *Ben Hur*. Gene chuckled but said nothing.

As I made the turn onto Wilton, Andy practically broke into "For She's a Jolly Good Fellow." Three patrol cars sat parked in front of Tony and Mickey's apartment. A couple of cops huddled in the entrance of the building, while another one looked to be radioing someone from inside one of the cars. The window to apartment 101 seemed to indicate that the police had found someone at home. I hadn't had much luck on that score lately. I assumed there was a detective or two inside grilling Mickey, if not Tony, as we parked a few yards past the last patrol car.

"How did you know there'd be police here?" asked Gene.

"To tell the truth, I was hoping I was wrong," I said as we turned to look back at the scene through the rear window. "My local-boy-makes-good angle is going down the drain."

"How do you mean? This must be juicier than your sweet little profile of a bit actor."

"You'd think so. But my paper will never print this kind of salacious story. At least not unless our boy is arrested for murder. Then it's a tragedy and an embarrassment for the whole town of New Holland."

"But I still don't get how you figured it was your guy," said Andy from the seat next to me. "Millard only said there was a phone number in Bertie's pocket."

"I figured it would be just my luck if it was Tony. Both men disappeared around the same time. And I knew that Wallis had handpicked Tony for his part."

"I thought you said it was just an extra role," said Andy.

"Sorry. That was a lie," I offered. "I didn't know if I should share what I knew with you two. But Tony Eberle was slated to play the second male lead in *Twistin' on the Beach*. Until Archie Stemple fired him for not showing up on the first day of shooting."

"No harm," said Gene from the backseat. "I would have done the same in your shoes. In fact, if this had been my hunch, you wouldn't be here right now." His lips betrayed no hint of a smile, but I knew it was his sense of humor again. Sardonic, biting, and as dry as a bone despite the weather. "Shall we get a statement from the boys in blue?"

"They'll never let us near the place," said Andy.

I grabbed my purse and popped open the door. "Wait here. I think I can get inside."

The three cops in the doorway stiffened as I reached the top of the stoop, and the tall, thin one asked if I lived in the building. I told him no, but I was there to visit my friend, Evelyn Maynard, in apartment 102. He thought it over for a moment then asked for my name.

"Price, go ask the super if she knows anyone named Ellie Stone, will you?" he said to the younger of his two fellow officers.

Officer Price ducked inside and rapped on 102. A short time later, he reemerged with a bemused Evelyn Maynard on his heels. She said nothing at first, but stared at me doubtfully, almost as if she expected this to be a practical joke of some kind.

"Do you know this lady?" asked the first cop.

"Yes," answered Evelyn.

"All right, you can go in," he told me, and I squeezed past, but not without Price "inadvertently" brushing an arm against my bust as I did.

"What's this all about?" asked Evelyn once we were inside her apartment.

"I wanted to apologize for the other day."

She cocked her head to the side and fired a skeptical eye at me. "Apologize for what? For not wanting to spend a romantic evening with me? Not necessary. You don't owe me anything."

"But I do. I wanted to apologize that day, but I didn't know what to say."

"Don't flatter yourself. I make passes at lots of girls. Get shot down all the time. It comes with the territory."

And in that moment I realized I couldn't go through with my plan to use her to gain access to the police.

"I confess that I actually came here to see if the police had found Tony Eberle or Mickey Harper next door," I said. "A man was found dead in a ravine over in Nichols Canyon. He was a producer and he knew Tony. In fact he handpicked him for a role in his picture. I thought maybe the police would come here to find him."

"Why are you telling me this?" she asked.

"Because I'm truly sorry for the other day. I wanted to be honest with you. I'll go now."

She watched me open the door and step into the hallway. Then she followed after me.

"Wait a minute," she called. "Come back inside. The cops said they want to talk to me once they're finished across the hall. Tony's not here. They're questioning Mickey Harper in there."

❧

The police didn't haul Mickey off to the station, confirming my suspicions that they were after Tony Eberle. When they knocked on Evelyn's door, I said good-bye and excused myself. I waited until the cops had shut the door before I rapped on 101. Mickey opened up almost immediately, as if he'd been expecting me. In truth, he probably thought it was the police who'd forgotten to ask him something because he looked surprised to find me in the corridor.

"What do you want?" he asked. "I already told them everything I know."

"May I come in? I need to speak to you about Tony."

"I don't know where he is. Can't you leave me alone?"

"Just five minutes, Mickey."

He thought it over, probably wondering what he'd done to deserve a roommate such as Tony Eberle. Then he let the door fall open ever so slightly, and I slipped past him.

The apartment was indeed a bachelor as I'd suspected. No bedrooms. Just a Murphy bed against the wall and a rollaway folded up in the corner. The place smelled of canned beans. There was a kitchenette on one side: a hot plate next to a small sink filled with a couple of dishes and dirty glasses. The only other furniture in the room was an aluminum table with a red laminate surface, two wooden chairs, and a large dresser with a telephone on top. No television, no radio, no pictures on the walls. Through a half-open door on the opposite wall, I could see a toilet and a bathtub. The place screamed desperate straits. Hollywood, how glamorous.

Mickey located his manners and motioned to one of the wooden chairs for my comfort. I sensed he had nothing to offer me to eat or drink. We sat down. He stared at the floor and waited for me to begin. I reached for the cigarette case in my purse and asked Mickey if he'd like a smoke. He declined.

"It's poison, you know," he said.

I put the case back and resigned myself to wait until I was outside to light up.

"I want you to know that I'm trying to help Tony," I began. "I might even be able to get him his job back on the picture. But I need to find him. Right away."

"Really?" he said. It was more of a challenge than a question. "The cops think Tony murdered that producer, but you're going to get him his job back?"

"Did he have anything to do with Bertram Wallis's death?"

Mickey frowned. Winced. "How would I know?"

I stared long and hard into his eyes. After a moment he looked away.

"Why did you lie to me the other day?" I asked finally.

"Lied? I didn't lie to you."

"You told me you weren't sure if Tony was here the night before he disappeared."

"That's the truth," he said, coming to life. "I didn't see him."

"There's only one room here. How could you have failed to see him?"

Mickey stammered a poor excuse that he didn't switch on the lights when he came in. "I didn't want to wake him. I knew he had to be on set early the next morning."

I must have looked skeptical because he repeated his story, more forcefully the second time.

"Mickey, you've got to tell me where Tony is," I said. "I won't share what you tell me with anyone. No police."

"Why do you want to help? You don't even know Tony. You're just a reporter for some hick-town newspaper."

Ouch. I patted down my annoyance and told him that my job as a reporter was precisely why I wanted to help Tony. "I have no story without him," I said. "Every other reporter in Los Angeles will soon have exactly the same information as I do now. Tony is a person of interest in the death of Bertram Wallis. He's on the run, which only makes him look guilty. If I can find him, he'll have a chance to tell his side of things. And, if he had nothing to do with Wallis's death, I think I can convince the studio to take him back."

Mickey repeated that he didn't have any idea where Tony was.

"I saw you leave here with him last night," I said, causing him to start. "It was about ten thirty. You and Tony and April left in a Rambler wagon. You turned off Hollywood Boulevard and climbed into the hills. Nichols Canyon."

I watched him turn white. He licked his upper lip, as a nervous cat might, just on the spot where the scratch had been two days before. The bruise under his eye had faded and was nearly invisible. I caught myself admiring his beauty and shook my thoughts back to the matter at hand.

"You're making this up," he said. "I didn't go anywhere."

"Do you remember a car behind you on Nichols Canyon Road? A car that sounded the horn when you stopped?"

Mickey Harper was stubborn. I was sure he and Tony and April had been in the Rambler I'd followed, but he refused to admit it. He just kept insisting I must have followed someone else, because he hadn't left his apartment. I challenged him again and again over the next two minutes, insisting that I had knocked several times on his door, and he hadn't answered. But he swore he'd been in, had heard me, but pretended to be out.

"What do you think the cops would think if I told them about last night?"

That got him. His big brown eyes grew and filled with what I read as terror. He was about to cry; I was sure of it.

"Tell me why, Mickey. Why are you holding out on me?"

He pushed back in his chair and stood up to pace the room, wiping his eyes as he did. I gave him some time to think, to collect himself. He shuffled over to the window, his back to me, and stared out at the three patrol cars and the rain that was still coming down in sheets. His narrow shoulders rose and fell as he stood there, drawing deep breaths or weeping. I couldn't tell which. Finally, after a full minute had passed, he turned to face me again.

"I can't tell you where Tony is," he said in a steady voice. "Because I don't know."

In the car, my new friends, Andy and Gene, had switched on the radio and were listening to the latest dispatches on the Bertram Wallis investigation. Reports that the police were searching for a person of interest was the only update.

"So was the kid there?" asked Gene.

"Not Tony Eberle," I said. "Just the roommate who swears he doesn't know where Tony is."

"We've still got a head start on everyone. We're the only ones who know who the cops are looking for."

"A fat lot of good that does us," I said. "I need to find the name of Tony's girlfriend. The roommate still won't give it to me."

"How do you plan on finding her?" asked Andy.

"The only thing I know about her is that her name is April and she drives a Rambler station wagon."

Short of going through the entire Los Angeles telephone directory name by name to find all the Aprils, I had no ideas. And even that strategy was unlikely to produce results. There must have been hundreds of Aprils in the city. Furthermore, Mickey had said she'd only recently come to Los Angeles. She might not even be in the book. And what if she was listed by her first initial only?

My friends had no ideas to offer. Finding April depended on Mickey Harper, and that only if he actually knew her last name or where she lived. But then I remembered something.

"Wait a minute," I said. "Do either of you two know anyone at Motor Vehicles?"

It was after two when we reached the top of Nichols Canyon and Bertram Wallis's mansion. I climbed out of the car, retrieved my camera, and took some establishing shots for my story, if I ever got to write it. Then I focused on the house itself. Of recent construction, the steel-and-glass affair sat at the end of a short drive, hanging over the edge of the hill. From the side of the building, I could see the stilts that held the place up. I don't normally suffer from heights, but the drop was precipitous. My stomach performed a somersault, and I stepped back. The house's stilts plunged down the hill some forty feet before planting themselves in the muddy brush. The canyon continued to fall away on a steep grade below. It gave me the willies to think of living in such a place. And what about earthquakes? California was famous for them. How could a few poles hold a huge house up in a temblor? I snapped some more frames, finishing off the roll, as I thought that Charlie Reese could—and would—surely explain the science to me.

I returned to the car. My pals were still inside. Gene was lounging in the back, and Andy was fiddling with his camera. I rewound the film and stashed it in its canister.

We watched the gang of reporters outside, huddling under their umbrellas, and talked about Bertram Wallis. If indeed this had been no accident, who would want to dump him over the railing of his terrace?

Andy shrugged. "I suppose any number of young actors and actresses he used. I've heard rumors that he rented beautiful girls and handsome boys. Had his way with them and shared them with other producers and actors."

"You mean prostitution?" I asked.

"Sort of. These young actors are all so desperate to make it in the movies. And they have to eat, too. Some of them earn a little extra by . . ." Andy was blushing. "Well, you can imagine how they earn it."

"But where did he find these desperate young actors?"

"There are people who arrange things. I've heard of one guy in particular. Skip something or other. He's been fixing up the perverts for years."

I looked to Gene for his contribution. He blinked slowly and shrugged.

"'Love for Sale,'" he drawled, staring off into space.

"In addition to his orgies and other activities, Bertie was a fair hand with a camera," continued Andy, not sure what to make of Gene's tribute to Cole Porter. "It's well known that he liked to take pictures and shoot eight-millimeter films."

"If everyone knew about his orgies, how come Wallis never got raided by the cops?"

"They bust in every now and then. But guys like Bertie Wallis just pay them off."

I suspected my face had gone ash white. This was a lot to digest on my fourth day in Hollywood. I asked myself if Tony Eberle—New Holland's golden boy—could possibly be mixed up in such sordid behavior. I had no evidence that he frequented Bertram Wallis's parties, but the producer had selected him personally for his beach picture, after all. Still, I didn't want to believe it. For one thing, if it were true, I had no story. The paper would never print such a thing. The success of my trip to California depended on Tony getting back into the beach picture. At least I believed it did. And if he was somehow involved in orgies and prostitution, I might just as well head to Marineland of the Pacific for a couple of days for all the good my journey would do for my career.

"Anyone else dislike Wallis?" I asked, trying to take my mind off the portrait of the hometown hero that was coming into focus.

"Sure," said Andy. "Lots of people hated him. He was an unpleasant guy. There were directors, actors, producers, and studio honchos to start with. And maybe the fathers or brothers of some of the starlets he spoiled."

My head was beginning to spin. "Wait, I thought he liked boys."

"He was omnivorous when it came to sex." This was Gene from the backseat. "Ellie, you seem like a woman of the world. Surely you know how things work out here. Wallis liked 'em all. Boys, girls, men, women. He was, in a word, a pig."

"And he didn't pay his debts," added Andy with a smile.

"And he was a plagiarist," concluded Gene.

"Wow. And no one ever wrote about this stuff?" I asked.

"Like we said, the studios pay off the cops and the scandal sheets," said Andy.

Gene popped the door and jumped out. "Millard's back," he said and set off toward the house and the crowd of reporters.

The police sergeant had new information. He provided the name of the cleaning lady, Patricia Gormley. She lived in East Hollywood and worked three days a week for Wallis. He also told us that based on the condition of the body, the coroner believed Wallis had likely died in the small hours of Tuesday morning, somewhere between two and ten. Finally, he said there had been a party Monday night, attended by as many as fifty people. The police were working on identifying everyone who'd been present.

"Can you tell us whose phone number you found in his pocket?" This was Gene Duerson asking the question.

"We're not divulging that information yet," he answered. "When it's time, we'll share that with all you boys." Then his gaze fell on me. He made a show of correcting himself. "Sorry. We'll share it with all you boys and girl."

The group of reporters broke up and, mumbling among themselves, wandered off to scribble their notes or find a phone to call their editors. I smiled at Gene and congratulated him on his question.

He shrugged it off. "Just making sure we still have our advantage."

"Who's that man over there?" interrupted Andy. "The one with the dog. He's been staring at you for the last five minutes."

I followed Andy's gaze and located a solitary figure holding a leash. A brownish terrier of some kind was sitting obediently at his heel, water-logged and quite unhappy to be there. The man was tall and thin, hard to gauge his age under his rain hat, but I figured him to be in his late forties. Even from a distance, I thought I recognized the profile. I excused myself and made my way over to him.

"I thought it might be you," he said with a broad smile of protruding teeth a size or two too large for his mouth. "But then I thought it was impossible."

Memory is a complex faculty. We remember information that we need, storing it in handy little bins that we can access in an instant. Other, older memories are also within reach. Proust made a name for himself with that stuff. But it's the rest of the disposable data we process that can prove tricky. I remember our family telephone number from when I was a child, but the license number of my first car in New Holland escapes me. I don't need it anymore, and its importance doesn't qualify it for space in my memory. And so the sudden appearance of a man I'd met in the Adirondacks the previous summer should have presented a challenge. But I knew him instantly. It didn't hurt that he and his beautiful consort, notorious wife-swappers, had wanted to share with me activities that I normally enjoy *à deux*.

"Oh, my," I uttered. "Nelson Blanchard."

"What on earth are you doing here, Ellie?"

I recalled that he and his wife, Lucia, had a home in the Hollywood Hills, but this meeting was a coincidence.

"I'm in Los Angeles to interview a hometown boy who's landed a role in a movie."

"And you thought you'd look in on Bertram Wallis?"

"He was the producer of the film," I told him. "And now my subject's run off somewhere. No one knows where."

"I heard the reports about Wallis on the radio this morning. What a terrible story."

"Did you know him?"

Nelson Blanchard shook his head. "Not well. I saw him from time to time at a party or on a studio lot. And walking his dog, too. His little pug, Leon, and our Pablito are friends." He tugged on the leash to indicate the dog.

We chatted for a while under the rain about Wallis, then Blanchard's wife, Lucia. He told me she was well, prepping to star in his *chef-d'œuvre*, *The Scarlett Lady*. Yes, two Ts. And he used the word *chef-d'œuvre*, too. He'd told me all about it the previous summer. Nelson Blanchard had bragged that Brigitte Bardot wanted the part of Scarlett, but that role was reserved for his beautiful Lucia. I had my doubts that the picture would ever get made, but Nelson assured me it was going to happen.

"Why don't you join us for dinner this evening?" he said once we'd hit a lull in the conversation. "We live just over there." He pointed farther up the canyon to the next road. "Astral Drive. It's actually quite close. Just a five minutes' walk from here."

I thought about begging off, but, in the end, I didn't have any other plans for the evening. I didn't know anyone in Los Angeles besides my new friends Andy and Gene, and I wasn't quite ready to chum up with them yet. And though the Blanchards and I had locked horns the previous summer—I'd briefly suspected them of pushing two men off a cliff—all had ended well. Shared experiences like murder tend to forge a bond among people.

Struggling with the wind to hold my umbrella in place over my head, I jotted down the address. The rain nearly washed it away as soon as I'd written it in my pad. We agreed that I'd join them at eight.

No sooner had I made the date with Nelson, Andy invited me to join him and Gene for supper. I explained the situation and made a date with them for breakfast in the morning instead.

"Hody's? Really?" asked Gene.

"Is that not a good place?"

"It's fine," said Andy. "A nice family restaurant."

"I hope you reserved weeks in advance," said Gene.

"I'll have the photos by then," I said, feeling like a rube. "If the picture of the license plate comes out, Gene, you can ask your pal at Motor Vehicles to trace it."

I climbed into my car and wrote a list of things I needed to do before dinner with the Blanchards. One, check in with Charlie Reese at the paper; two, call Fadge to see if he'd had any success with Tony Eberle's father; and three, pick up my prints at Thelan's Camera Center. I was just considering my options for the headline to my first story when a tap came on the window. I looked up to see Sergeant Millard smiling at me.

CHAPTER NINE

What he wanted was a date. It took me a few minutes to figure out that his offer to answer my questions was no more than a ploy to worm his way into my car. With me a captive audience, he turned on the charm. After a fashion. He made me uncomfortable, even as he was trying to be nice. He never quite crossed the limits of propriety, but he toed it, like a bowler flirting with the foul line. It was the predatory look. The smiling crocodile or a tiger. Yes, I might have been wrong about him. Sometimes we misjudge or prejudge people, after all. But more often than not, my first instincts proved correct down the road. I give everyone a fair chance. Character emerges, seeps through the veneers and out from under the closed doors people use to hide their true nature. I don't ignore the signs.

"So what do you say about dinner tonight?" he asked. "I'll pick you up at your hotel."

"I'd love to, of course," I said. "But I have plans this evening with some old friends."

Millard frowned. But more than that, he seemed annoyed. As if he'd wasted perfectly good breath on a failed proposition. I'd spurned really nice guys. I'd turned down cads and curs. And most of them took rejection on the chin with magnanimity or, at least, with some dignity. But Sergeant John Millard resented me for having said no. His pique simmered just below the surface. I could sense it, smell it in the close confines of my rented Chevy 150. At length he managed to force a smile onto his lips. I thought he might be able to provide useful information on the investigation, so, despite my better judgment, I told him I'd be free the following evening.

His wolfish smile returned, along with my regrets. He told me he'd call for me at my hotel around five thirty.

"I'll take you to a real nice place," he said.

I returned to the McCadden and greeted my pal Marty, who was matching wits with the ancient desk clerk, Mr. Cromartie, in a pitched battle of Chinese checkers. I watched them for a moment.

"Is there anything you'd like me to get for you, Miss Stone?" asked Marty after a triple jump over his somnolent opponent's pieces.

I thanked him and said no, then made my way upstairs to make my long-distance calls. I dictated a story to Norma Geary over the phone, but not before scolding her for being in the office after seven. She insisted that her neighbor was happy to look after her son, Toby, a sweet little boy who suffered from a form of severe mental retardation.

I wasn't sure Charlie would publish my story anyway. How would the locals respond to my report that golden boy Tony Eberle had thrown away his big chance at stardom by missing the first day of shooting and getting himself fired from the picture? I left the conclusions vague enough to give the kid the benefit of the doubt, but there was no way to bury the crushing revelation that, at the eleventh hour, just as success was at hand, Tony Eberle had seen his chance of being a Hollywood heartthrob vanish as quickly and as mysteriously as had he. Norma expressed her disappointment at how the story was playing out. I told her I didn't make the stuff up. I merely reported it.

Fadge was next on my list. I gave the operator the number, cringing at the bill I would have to present to Artie Short. If he didn't accept it, I would be responsible for the transcontinental chitchat with my dear friend.

"You know I have a business to run," he said when I asked if he'd managed to pressure Joe Eberle into talking about his son's childhood friends. "You owe me, El."

He wasn't helping his case. "El" was what my late brother used to call me. I'd grown used to Fadge's usurping it. But his using that nickname only made him feel more of a brother to me.

"Just tell me what you've got," I said. "I'll stand you to a pizza when I get home."

"Pizza?" he scoffed. "You owe me a steak dinner at least. That or a ride on the Big Bus of Love."

"Big Bus of Love?" I asked. "Steak dinner it is. Now what did Tony's dad say?"

Fadge sighed. "I tracked him down at the Bigelow-Shaw Weavers Club. He was drinking at two in the afternoon."

"So what did he have to say?"

"I made friendly with him for a while then asked him the sixty-four-thousand-dollar question. Did his son have any friends when he was in New Holland."

"And what did he say?"

"I can't repeat it. But I don't give up so easily. I poked him in the chest a couple of times and breathed raw onions into his face. I had a burger for lunch. Suddenly he was happy to tell me what I wanted to know."

"And that is?"

"Tony didn't have a lot of friends in school. His father said the drama club and band didn't exactly make his boy Mr. Popularity."

"So does Tony still have friends or not?" I asked.

"Seems like no. His dad said Tony was kind of a loner. Only had one close friend in school. From kindergarten through senior year. Some kid who moved away after high school. Said his name was Harper. Mickey Harper."

CHAPTER TEN

Nelson Blanchard met me at the door with a toothy kiss on the cheek and a warm hug that nibbled at, but didn't quite surpass, the edge of acceptable behavior. He took my wet coat and fractured umbrella, stashed them in a closet, and escorted me inside. A large sunken living room opened before us, with floor-to-ceiling plate glass windows providing spectacular views of the canyon below, the ridges on the other side to the west, and the twinkling lights of the city to the south. The floor was smooth hardwood painted black. A giant pastel-pink-and-blue Chinese rug anchored the center of the room, where a cream-colored leather sofa and matching chairs had been positioned to afford maximum advantage of the views.

Lucia Blanchard lounged recumbent on the sofa, back to us, facing the windows, her lithe, tanned arms draped across the cushions like two foulards. Across the room, a fire burned in a modern, clean-lined, sandstone hearth. A lazy terrier—Pablito—lay flat in front of the fire. His eyes shifted to see me, but he never moved his head. Then he went back to soaking in all the heat he could manage.

Nelson squired me around the furniture to present me to his bride. Eyes shut and decked out in a white silk cheongsam dress with red embroidery, Lucia leaned back against the cushions, motionless, as if in a trance or experiencing some kind of rapture. Or, I suppose, even dead. Her dress was slit up both legs, baring three quarters of each thigh and drawing the attention of whosoever beheld her. In this case, me. Lucia Blanchard understood sexy, that much was obvious. Nelson emitted a feathery cough to rouse her, and she opened her eyes.

"Ellie," she purred in her soft Spanish accent. "*Qué hermosa que eres.* I'm so happy you wandered into Nelson's web this afternoon. You look lovely."

I knew I wasn't as lovely as she. Not only because the rain had worked its magic on my unruly hair but—let's face it—mostly because Nature had outdone herself on Lucia in the first place.

Once Nelson had fixed us all drinks—sake—we sat admiring the stormy evening through the bank of windows.

"If the rain keeps up like this, Ellie will have to spend the night, isn't that right, *querida*?" said Nelson with an eager grin.

Lucia sighed. "Don't beg, *mi amor*. Too desperate. You'll scare her away."

"Is that Bertram Wallis's house over there?" I asked, rising and crossing to the window to indicate the next hill. Anything to get the subject off Nelson Blanchard's designs on me.

He joined me, sipping his glass of sake, and nodded. That was when I noticed for the first time a telescope on a tripod outside on the terrace.

"Are you two stargazers?"

"I beg your pardon?"

"The telescope. Are you an amateur astronomer?"

Nelson chuckled, exchanged a knowing glance with his wife, and told me that, yes, he did enjoy viewing heavenly bodies.

"I see. And your neighbors don't mind having an audience?"

"Some of them invite it," said Nelson. "At least they leave their curtains open at the most inopportune times."

"And have you ever aimed your telescope at Bertram Wallis's place?"

Neither Nelson nor Lucia answered my question. Then I asked them if Wallis had been in the habit of closing his blinds. Nelson just smiled and looked away.

"I met him once a couple of years ago," said Lucia from the sofa.

"What was he like?"

She shrugged and pouted. "He was a pervert. But there are so many perverts in this town. Nothing unusual about that. I remember he liked to take pictures. And movies sometimes. Especially of the beautiful young boys."

"What kind of photos?" I asked.

"Nudes, pairs, trios. Everything."

"Blue movies?" I asked.

"Pornography. Why not call it what it is?"

"At night sometimes we would see flashbulbs going off through his window," added Nelson. "That's when we knew he was taking pictures. Too dark to see anything from here, though."

Not even with your telescope? I thought, throwing Nelson a naughty grin. He actually had the nerve to blush.

"Have you seen anything going on over there recently?" I asked. "Say, in the past few days?"

"There was that party he threw the other night. Monday, I think," said Nelson.

"Who throws parties on a Monday night?"

Nelson gave me a knowing look. "Every day was a holiday for Bertram Wallis."

"You know," said Lucia, finally pushing herself off the sofa to join us at the window, "the canyon is intimate enough that we can often hear what's going on, even from the other side. Sounds bounce off the hills if the wind is right. Not when it's raining, of course."

"What kind of sounds have you heard?"

"You can imagine," said Nelson. "Laughter, music, shouting, and the occasional achievement of ecstasy. . . ."

"You know there was angry shouting the other night," added Lucia. "You were fast asleep, *mi amor*. But there was a loud argument."

"Was that Monday? The night of the party?" I asked.

Lucia nodded. "More like Tuesday morning. Probably around three."

I put some thoughts in order. The police believed Wallis died sometime between two and ten Tuesday morning. Now Lucia was telling me she'd heard an argument of some kind from across the canyon at about 3:00 a.m. And what did all that mean in light of the late-night trip up Nichols Canyon taken by Mickey and—I assumed—Tony and April? That had occurred Wednesday night after ten, at least forty hours after the loud argument Lucia had heard coming from Wallis's house. Did that bode well for Tony's innocence? Not necessarily, I thought. The three friends might have been heading back to Wallis's place to retrieve or cover up some bit of damning evidence. Perhaps even to throw his already dead body over the terrace. Such a theory was premature. I had to remind myself to take things slowly. Still, the Rambler's presence so close to Wallis's house troubled me. I could think of no reason for the three to be in that neighborhood at that hour if not to visit Bertram Wallis's house.

"If you really want to know what goes on over there, you should talk to our neighbor Trudy Hirshland," said Nelson, rousing me from my thoughts. "I'm merely a hobbyist. She's a true voyeur. A pro. Watches day and night, old pervert."

Pot calling the kettle black, I thought. And inside a glass house, to boot.

"She's a widow of about sixty. You can see her place over there," he said, pointing to the north. "Just below us on Nichols Canyon Road."

The road descended the ridge, twisting and turning around curves on its journey down the hill. I had to squeeze against the window to see the house, given the angles and orientation of the Blanchard place. Wallis's house was in between, and the three houses formed a crooked triangle on the side of the hill.

"Do you think she might have seen or heard something that night?" I asked. "Or some other night?"

"I don't know about that. But she's your best bet. She spends her nights watching. An insomniac. Or she's nocturnal and sleeps during the day. A vampire."

"Why don't you pay her a visit and find out for yourself?" said Lucia. "She loves to gossip. She'll tell you everything she knows. About us, too."

Lucia gazed at her husband, grinning like a coquette, as she informed me that they didn't have any blinds on their windows.

She turned back to face me. "I'm afraid of the dark, you see. And Nelson is a very naughty boy."

The evening continued without too much discomfort on my part. The subject turned to the events of the previous August, to the deaths of two men who'd fallen from a cliff above a dangerous diving pool. And we reminisced about other friends from that eventful week in the Adirondack Mountains.

Once we'd enjoyed two rounds of cocktails, dinner, consisting of beef and cheese fondues, was served, accompanied by a bottle of Bordeaux. Lucia bragged that Nelson was a gourmet chef who'd trained at the Cordon Bleu in Paris.

"That was many years ago," he said, blushing. "After the war when I spent two years discovering myself in Paris."

I would have thought he'd discovered himself around the age of twelve or thirteen and had been enjoying himself ever since, but I kept that thought to myself.

After a demitasse and a smoke in front of the warm fire, I bade the

Blanchards good night. Nelson pouted that it was only ten o'clock, but I told him it had been a long, wet day. He made one last suggestive remark about showing me some etchings in the bedroom. I kissed him on the cheek, thanked them both for their hospitality, and skipped out the door and through the slop to my car.

The rain was lighter now as I wound my way down Nichols Canyon back into Hollywood. With the fun of the evening behind me, I concentrated on the great revelation of the day. Not only was Mickey Harper a New Holland boy, but he was Tony Eberle's oldest and dearest friend. Why had he lied to me? Why had he claimed to know Tony only casually? Or had he said that? I thought back to my meetings with him. I'd told him clearly who I was and where I was from, yet he showed no sign of recognition, made no attempt to share that he, too, was from New Holland. He'd remained tight-lipped and never said how well he knew Tony. That was my fault; I should have pressed him.

So what else had he hidden from me? For one, he'd claimed he never saw Tony in the darkened room when he returned home in the wee-small hours of Tuesday morning. That strained credulity. The room was barely eighteen feet across. If nothing else, he would have heard Tony's breathing or snoring. Yes, I was certain he'd lied about that. And I thought about what else he'd told me. First, that he didn't know April or her family name. Another hard-to-believe story, especially in light of Mickey's close relationship with Tony. Then there was the question of his own activities. Had he attended a party with friends Monday night as he'd said? And the biggest doubt in my mind concerned Mickey's adamant denials that he knew anything about Tony's current whereabouts.

I turned onto Hollywood Boulevard and made up my mind to get some better answers from Mickey Harper. But first, I knew, I'd have to find him. And that might prove to be a tall order if the recent past was any indication.

The other significant development of the day was the roll of film I'd picked up from Thelan's earlier in the evening. I was pleased to see that the one frame I'd shot of the Rambler indeed showed the rear of the car in good focus. The black numbers on the orange plate stood out clearly: J26 582. I hoped Gene Duerson's friend at Motor Vehicles would come through for us. If so, I might be able to track down the mysterious April and, I was sure, Tony Eberle.

⁊◯

The day may have been long and wet, but I wasn't quite finished for the night. While I'd appreciated Nelson Blanchard's offer of a nightcap, I wanted to be alone to think. And I wanted another drink.

I parked my car across from the hotel and set out on foot down Hollywood Boulevard. Musso and Frank Grill was located just a short distance away. I recalled the cabbie who'd driven me into Hollywood from the airport a couple of days before. He'd once dropped Raymond Burr at Musso and Frank. And while it might have been fun to spot Perry Mason in the wild, that wasn't my motivation that night.

The joint wasn't exactly jumping. At ten thirty, diners filled only a few of the booths and tables; the rain had chased away most of the patrons. I found a seat at the empty end of the long mahogany bar. Within seconds, the friendly bartender in a red waiter's jacket, complete with epaulettes and brass buttons, poured me a healthy two fingers of Scotch, winked at me, and called me sweetheart. I sipped my drink, savoring the sting on my tongue and in my nose. The first bite of whiskey. I felt I deserved it after my disappointing day. In fact, I felt I deserved the second drink as well, which I ordered a few minutes later.

"Is this seat taken?"

I turned to see who'd interrupted my thoughts, and my gaze came to rest on a tall, handsome, athletic man with thick black eyebrows and a strong chin. He stood above me in a blue suit and silver tie, his eyes trying to draw me in as if with a rope. He had a cigarette wedged between the fore- and middle finger of his right hand, and he wore a gold Omega watch on his left wrist.

I shrugged. "It's a free country. But I must warn you I'm not looking for company."

"I'll take that as your opening offer. We can negotiate from there," he said, appropriating the chair next to me.

He signaled to the barkeep, who seemed to recognize him and know what he was drinking.

"Chuck Porter," he said to me, holding out a hand.

I took it, debating whether to give him my real name or not. I figured there was no harm. Mr. Chuck Porter probably trolled this place nightly, tossing out his net to see what he might snare. A pretty actress on the make for a steak dinner and a couple of drinks. Maybe a girl looking for a rich friend to help with the rent in exchange for the occasional evening of thrills. Or even a naive out-of-towner. Well, I wasn't in the market for steak or a roll in the hay, and I could certainly buy my own drinks. Ultimately, though, I found him just charming enough to bear, and I resisted the urge to tell him to push off.

"A pretty girl like you should smile," he said. "Come on. I'll bet you've got a beautiful smile."

"I smile when someone says something funny."

"Good one," he said with a chuckle. "So, does Ellen come here often?"

"I don't know about Ellen, but Ellie doesn't. First time."

The bartender slid a Manhattan under his nose.

"There you go, Mr. Alden."

My new friend blushed and cleared his throat. He took a drag of his cigarette then stubbed it out in the ashtray on the bar.

"I use a different name here," he said in a low voice, almost a whisper, by way of an explanation. "Just for business purposes, you understand."

"Are you a spy, Mr. Porter?"

He cracked a toothy smile. "No, nothing like that. I'm in the music business. Capitol Records. I'm sure you've seen our headquarters on Vine."

I took a sip of my drink and nodded, unclear why anyone in the music business would need to use an alias. He wore no wedding ring, but I was sure of one thing. This guy was married and a cheater on the prowl.

"Yes, I've seen it," I said. "It looks like a great big layer cake."

"We like to think it's more like a stack of records. I could give you a tour if you like. Tonight."

"I told you I'm not looking for company."

He shrugged and took a swig of his Manhattan. "You're not waiting for someone, are you? If so, say the word, and I'll withdraw to lick my wounds at the other end of the bar."

"Actually, I was hoping William Hopper might drop in and sweep me off my feet."

"William . . . William Hopper the actor? Paul Drake?" Chuck couldn't tell if I was joking or not. A strike against him in my book.

I giggled. "Wishful thinking. I'm not meeting anyone, Mr. Porter. I came in from the rain for a drink."

"That's your second drink," he said. "And please call me Chuck. We're old friends by now."

I retrieved a cigarette from my purse and lit it.

"You should know that I have a horror of men who keep track of how much I drink," I said. "Or who watch me secretly from across the room. Perhaps you're a spy after all."

"Duly noted. Apologies, Ellie."

"Ellen."

"Sorry, Ellen. It's just that you caught my eye," he continued without missing a beat. "You can't blame a fellow for appreciating a pretty girl."

We sat quietly for a minute. I didn't mind chatting with him, but he was mistaken if he thought he was striking gold this evening.

"Do you know Ray Charles?" he asked, breaking the silence.

"The singer?" I asked. "I've never met him, if that's what you mean."

"Would you like to?"

"Tonight? At Capitol Records?"

Chuck smiled and said no. "Next week he'll be in town to record his new LP. Not with Capitol, but he's a friend of mine. I could pull some strings."

I thanked him but said that while I appreciated Ray Charles, I was more of a Sam Cooke kind of gal.

"You wouldn't know him, by any chance?" I asked.

He didn't. Strike two. But over the course of the next twenty minutes, Chuck treated me to war stories about the music business. He was a producer, so he said, and knew almost anyone who'd ever strummed a guitar, tickled a piano, or banged a drum. For fun, I asked if he'd ever met Fritz Wunderlich. He shook his head. Then he told me he worked in the movies, too. Rather some of the singers he handled did. What is it that makes some men fall in love with the sound of their own voices?

"Have you ever heard of Rockin' Johnny Bristol?" he asked.

Strike three. Johnny Bristol was exactly the type of teen idol that I couldn't stomach. All teeth and hair and muscles, with a pedestrian voice and a stringless guitar for a prop.

"Not my speed," I said, nodding to the bartender for one more drink. Chuck tried to pay for it, but I refused. I might have enjoyed passing some time chatting with the big side of beef, but I wanted there to be no confusion in his mind as to my intentions. He took it like a man.

"What brings you to Los Angeles?" he asked, changing the subject.

"What makes you think I don't live here?"

He smiled indulgently.

"Is it that obvious?"

"You're quite a looker. Not at all provincial. But once you've spent some time in LA, you can spot the interlopers pretty easily."

"I'm in LA to meet someone," I said cryptically.

"A man?"

"As a matter of fact, yes."

"A love affair?"

"Nothing like that. I'm a reporter, here to interview an actor."

"Let me guess," he said. "Rock Hudson?"

I shook my head.

"Tony Curtis?"

"No one as famous as that."

He thought hard, scratching his head and squinting at the light. "Then it must be Ed Wynn."

"You've never heard of this fellow," I said, trying to sip my drink with a huge grin on my lips. Chuck Porter was cleverer than I'd thought. "He's just a young actor from a small town."

"Try me. I know a lot of people."

This Chuck Porter refused to take a hint. I asked him if he knew Paul Newman to get him off my back.

"Afraid not," he said. "But I once spilled a drink on Joanne Woodward in the Beverly Hills Hotel bar. She was quite gracious, considering it was a bloody Mary and she was wearing a white silk dress."

I'd had my fill. While it was mildly amusing to listen to Chuck Porter/ Alden talk about himself, I'd originally intended to enjoy a quiet drink by myself as I tried to sort out what I might do to find Tony Eberle. Now, three whiskeys in, I felt my faculties punching out for the day. Suddenly I was annoyed at this man who'd deprived me of my own time.

"I doubt I would have been as magnanimous," I said. "And before you spill your Manhattan on me, I'll say good night."

My words seemed to sting him, like alcohol in the eye. He straightened up and cleared his throat. He put on a brave face, trying to mask the affront with bravado before managing to fashion a counterfeit smile out of his pursed lips. He fished into his breast pocket and produced a business card.

"If you change your mind, Ellie, let me know." His curled lip told me he knew I'd been pulling his leg about my name.

I pointed out that the number and address were in New York.

"I live in New York but spend most of my time out here. I'm staying at the Roosevelt Hotel, room 135." His eyes offered one last invitation.

CHAPTER ELEVEN

FRIDAY, FEBRUARY 9, 1962

Arhythmic banging invaded my dreams. The "Anvil Chorus" from *Il Trovatore*, I thought, but realized that wasn't right. No, it wasn't Verdi. It sounded more like someone pounding on wood than iron. Then I awoke with a start, lost in one of those terrifying moments when you don't know where you are. I found my bearings soon enough, but the disorientation was an unpleasant way to greet the day.

The knocking on my door resumed, this time with an accompanying baritone.

"Miss Stone, it's Marty. The bellhop," came the voice from the other side.

"Just a minute," I called out, leaping out of bed.

Marty must have heard "Come in," because the doorknob rattled back and forth. Standing there stark naked, trapped in no-man's-land halfway between the bed and bathroom, I screamed at him to stop. The lock held, and the knob returned to its resting position. My modesty safe by a whisker, I wrapped myself in a robe.

"What is it?" I asked through the door.

"You got a telegram," said Marty from the corridor. "It's marked urgent."

I opened the door a crack. "At six a.m.?" I asked, eyes half shut. "Since when does Western Union deliver so early?"

"Yeah, about that. This came in last night around a quarter to seven. You had just went out."

I swung open the door and grabbed the wire from him. "Why didn't anyone give this to me last night when I came back?"

Marty shrugged halfheartedly as if to apologize and explained that Mr. Cromartie at the front desk had lost it and didn't find it till about fifteen minutes ago. "He was sitting on it."

I examined the wrinkled telegram in the low light, my sour face surely betraying what I thought of the news. "You mean he sat on it for twelve hours?"

Marty pshawed. "Of course not. He got up to use the bathroom three or four times in the night."

I thanked Marty and tipped him a quarter.

Safely behind my locked door again, I tore open the wire and read. It was from Charlie Reese.

ELLIE,

SITUATION TENSE. SHORT WANTS YOU TO FIND EBERLE IMMED. SAYS GAZETTE SENDING DUNNOLT TO GET STORY. SHORT THREATENS TO SEND GEORGE IF NO RESULTS SOON.
　　　FRIENDLY ENCOURAGEMENT FROM ME. FIND HIM AND REPORT BACK.

CHARLIE

I rolled my eyes. So easy for folks on the sidelines to demand a touchdown pass like ordering a beer. It was another matter altogether to throw a perfect spiral while being chased by a pack of pituitary cases in tights and plastic helmets. I might have been more concerned if I hadn't had April's license number in my possession and a new pal with contacts at the DMV. In fact, I was due to meet Gene and Andy at Hody's coffee shop at eight.

At 7:45 a.m., armed with my trusty, busted umbrella, I hurried down the stairs to the street. Mr. Cromartie called to me from the front desk. Did he work twenty-four-hour shifts?

"Telegram, Miss Stone," he said.

I told him that Marty had already given me the "rump-led" wire. But Cromartie said there was a second one that had just arrived. I hoped he hadn't had time to sit on this one, which was from none other than Artie Short, owner and publisher of the *New Holland Republic*. I read.

STONE,

FIND EBERLE. URGENT. DON'T UNDERSTAND DELAY.
NO SUN BATHING ON MY DIME. REPORT BACK THIS PM
WITH INFO.

A. SHORT

This second telegram upset me more than the first. I hated being told I was failing by people who had no idea of the challenge, the job, or the rain. Through no fault of my own, I had arrived in Los Angeles to find my subject vanished without a trace. His only friend was lying to all and sundry about his whereabouts, and the studio executives were asking for my help. Through sheer stubbornness and persistence, I'd managed to follow Tony Eberle up a deserted canyon road that led to a dead man's home. A dead man who'd hired young Tony himself for his picture. And now, thanks to my ingenuity and quick thinking, I had what I believed was the license plate number of his girlfriend's car. Striding through the light rain on Hollywood Boulevard toward breakfast at Hody's, I bit my lip and swore I would locate Tony Eberle that very day. And when I did, I'd wire Artie Short to tell him that my tan was coming along just fine.

❧

"Did you get it?" Andy asked me as I sat down at the table next to Gene, opposite him.

I dug into my purse and produced the photo envelope from Thelan's as if pulling a rabbit from a silk hat. Slapping the pictures on the table, I put on my best poker face and stared Andy down.

"She got it," he said, a grin mushrooming into a huge smile. "I told you she had it."

"Let's see." Gene reached for the envelope and then pulled out the print. Andy burst into laughter, as Gene examined the photo. He, too, smiled.

"Excuse me," he said, rising from the booth. "I'm going to call my friend at Motor Vehicles right now."

While Gene was in the phone booth, Andy congratulated me for the fine job I'd done. Then he asked if he could see my camera. Turning it over in his hands, treating it like a fragile work of art, he cooed like a dove.

"This is a swell camera, Ellie. I'd like to get a Leica someday. They're pricey, though, aren't they?"

"It was a gift," I said simply, as I fell into a distant memory.

On the eve of my eighteenth birthday, I'd slipped out of our apartment on lower Fifth Avenue and joined my girlfriend Janey Silverman in Union Square at half past eleven. We boarded an uptown Lexington train and jumped off at Sixty-Eighth Street. From there, Janey led the way to an apartment on Seventy-Fifth and Third where five recent law school grads were throwing a party. At least we'd been told it was a party. But when we arrived, there was no music, no food, and no other guests. There was, however, plenty of alcohol. I got a bad feeling right off the bat, but Janey told me to relax. She knew these fellows. On closer questioning, she admitted that she'd only met one of them, and he wasn't even there.

At first the boys were nice if fresh. Then after a couple of drinks, they got a little pushy. I was taking things easy given my unease. In fact, I hadn't even taken a sip of the two drinks the tall blond named Larry poured for me. I was seated next to a large potted plant and was doing my part to make sure it didn't die of dehydration in the June heat. Janey, on the other hand, was a lightweight when it came to alcohol. One and a half cocktails were about her limit, and after that you could find her either with a lampshade on her head or passed out on the couch, depending on the breaks. Now, with five leering men standing by, Janey slouched into her chair catatonic. I was sure they were waiting for me to follow my friend into the arms of Morpheus, but I had other plans.

"Will one of you kindly call a cab for us?" I asked. "I think we should go now."

"Come on," said Larry, putting an arm around my waist, "the night's young. Let your friend sleep it off. We'll make sure you get home later."

I had to play this carefully. Even if I could scratch my way past five grown men and reach the door, there was no way I'd be able to lug an unconscious Janey with me. So making a break for it was off the table.

"Pour me another?" I asked, tapping my glass with my right index finger. He snatched my drink to oblige. "Where's the powder room?"

One of the other gents showed me the way into the bedroom down the hall. Once inside, I used the phone to dial my brother, Elijah, who was staying with a friend in Murray Hill that summer. When I returned to the living room, Larry asked what had taken me so long. I told him that was an indelicate thing to ask a lady.

"Lady?" he scoffed. "Let's drop the act. Come on, we want to have some fun."

He placed my new drink on the table and slipped an arm around my waist again.

"Actually, what took me so long was the switchboard," I said as he nuzzled my neck.

"Switchboard? What are you talking about?"

"The switchboard at the Nineteenth Precinct."

Larry let go of my waist. His lips relinquished their claim to the nape of my neck. "You called the police?"

"Janey's father," I lied. "He's the duty sergeant at the Nineteenth. What took me so long was that the switchboard operator couldn't find him at first."

"What? Why would you call the cops?"

"I called Janey's father because she's not feeling well. You wouldn't want her father to think you didn't take care of his little girl, would you?"

Larry stammered something incoherent then looked to his buddies for assistance. Two of them shrugged, while the other two were already pulling on their jackets and straightening their ties.

Three minutes later, Larry and Hank—I believe his name was—were helping Janey down the stairs, each with one of her arms over their strong shoulders. Once outside in the warm evening air, they bolted, leaving us leaning against a lamppost. Janey crumpled to the ground and vomited in the gutter, but at least she was safe. Five minutes later a taxi screeched to a halt in front of us, and Elijah and three of his beefiest friends poured out.

"Where are they?" asked Elijah, and I saw a tire iron under his arm. His companions were similarly prepared with baseball bats.

"They've run off," I said. "We're all right. Janey's out. I think they slipped her a Mickey."

"How did you get out of there?" asked the largest of Elijah's friends, Sammy.

"I told them I'd called the police. I said Janey's father was a cop and gave them the chance to do the right thing before he showed up. They were quite eager to help after that."

Elijah was furious with me. He lectured me as we rode home together in a taxi, swore I was going to get myself killed someday if I didn't change my ways. I was sure he would rat me out to Dad as soon as we got home, but he didn't. He said instead that we'd had a good time with some of his friends.

The following morning, my birthday, my parents presented me with a brand-new Leica M3 camera. I'd shown some interest in photography, though the sum total of my photographic experience consisted of snapping pictures at Coney Island with my father's Brownie.

It was a beautiful and expensive gift. And as I struggled to find the words to thank them, my father told me that it would have a positive influence on me. Create a healthy activity that I could enjoy for the rest of my life.

"We hope you won't abandon it as you did the piano. So much potential wasted."

That put a damper on my enthusiasm for the gift. But my father hadn't finished.

"Now we all know about your occasional bouts with whiskey," he continued, and I groaned inside. "And now that you're eighteen, you have the legal right to drink. But that doesn't mean you have to overdo it. My hope is that you'll spend more time with this camera than you will with the bottle."

That did it. I remember promising myself in that very moment that I would go out and buy myself my first legal bottle of whiskey later that day.

"Thank you, Dad," I said, giving him a hug. "Thank you, Mom. I'll treasure this camera always. And, Dad, I'll never forget what you said."

Andy's voice called me back from my memory. I smiled, not having heard a word of what he'd said. Then Gene returned. I glanced at my watch. God knows what Andy had been going on about, but four full minutes had passed since Gene left the table.

"Well?" I asked.

"Got it," he said with a broad smile.

CHAPTER TWELVE

We parked alongside the curb in front of a squat three-story apartment building on North Edgemont. The surrounding residences, mostly modest family homes and bungalows, seemed to want no part of the box of grayish bricks, as if they were holding their noses and shrinking away from the ugly neighbor. Andy, Gene, and I climbed out of my car, braving a light rain, and approached the front door. Reading from the list of tenants—there were eleven names and one vacant apartment—I found A. Kincaid in 2B. Inside the door, a red notice informed us that 3B, a furnished bachelor, was for rent.

No one answered when we knocked on 2B. The door was locked, and neither Andy nor Gene would entertain my suggestion that they put a sturdy shoulder or two into the door, just to see what happened. We trudged back down the stairs to the entrance. I examined the list of tenants again, and, remembering Evelyn Maynard, I buzzed the super. Andy asked what I was hoping to accomplish.

"I'm going to get him to let us into April's room," I said.

Gene chuckled. "You're going to convince him to kick the door down? I doubt it."

"Buy me a drink if we get in?" I asked. "Each?"

Gene and Andy exchanged a glance. "Deal," said Gene. "But drinks are on you if he calls the cops."

A crooked little man peered out of a door down the hall. Then he shuffled out to see what we wanted. He was shorter than I—in part due to his posture, part due to his height—with salt-and-pepper hair and a long, tangled gray mustache.

"What you want?" he asked. His accent was hard to identify, but I narrowed it down to something between Spanish and Polish.

He squinted as he spoke, looking up at his interlocutor from his stooped position.

"I'd like to see the room you're renting," I said. "Three-B."

The gray man took a step back, almost as if I'd staggered him with an uppercut. "You?" he asked. "I don't think this is the right place for a fancy girl like you."

"Nevertheless, I am interested in renting the apartment. Is it weekly or monthly?"

He stared up at me, his loose lower lip hanging a little limp to the left side, following the gravity of his cocked head.

"Either. Who are these guys?" he asked with a halfhearted gesture to indicate Andy and Gene.

"Them? My brother and my father."

Andy smiled dumbly. Gene looked positively insulted.

"They don't look much like you."

"Thanks," I said, confusing him and slighting my friends at the same time. I threw them a high sign to indicate that it was all part of my plan.

Mr. Szolosi, as I soon found out his name was, showed us to the third floor. As we climbed the stairs, Andy asked me what I had up my sleeve. I whispered that he should watch and follow my lead. Once we reached the top, the super stopped on the landing to catch his breath, threw a resentful glare my way, then fished some keys from his pocket and let us into apartment 3B.

"This might do," I said, surveying the dim room.

There was, of course, nothing acceptable about the empty place. The smell of dusty old paint and crumbling plaster filled the air. Light barely managed to penetrate the grimy windows, whose dark-green roll-up shades were faded and looked brittle from years of baking in the sun. I noticed the wallpaper above the window was peeling like the skin of an overripe banana. The floors had been worn bare, warped and scratched, and were in need of a master carpenter to sand, refinish, and—in the end—throw down his tools in disgust and declare defeat. They were beyond all hope of salvage.

"You like this place?" asked Szolosi.

"I'm not so sure," said Gene, surprising me. He wandered around the room, wiping a finger over the dust on the windowsill and assuming an expression intended to communicate indifference or disappointment. "That place we saw in Silver Lake was a sight nicer than this one."

"But that one wasn't furnished," I said, playing along.

Then, turning to the super, I asked why there was no furniture in the apartment.

"We threw out everything. The guy who died here— Sorry, the guy who lived here left it a mess. The landlord will put a bed, a table, chair, and some drawers in here."

"See?" I said to Gene. "New furniture."

"Not new, but clean," said Szolosi. "Kind of."

I strolled around the room, pretending to be considering the pros of this white-glove residence versus Gene's imaginary palace in Silver Lake.

"Now I'm not sure," I said at length. "What if I don't like the furniture he picks? Perhaps you could show me a different apartment to give me an idea of what it might look like?"

The super frowned. "Lady, this is the only room for rent."

"I understand that. I just want to see what this apartment would look with furniture. Couldn't you show me the one below? It must be the same layout."

Mr. Szolosi drew a sigh and wiped an itch off his face. After a moment's reflection, he agreed.

"You don't touch nothing," he cautioned as we made our way down to the second floor. "Just a quick look. That's all."

April's apartment matched the one directly above perfectly. With the exception of the meager furnishings and some personal effects strewn here and there, the place was empty. But it had the look of a temporary solution, as if the tenant had no intention of staying. No pictures on the walls, no television or radio, no telephone. Only a couple of chipped plates and glasses and simple flatware for one lonely person. In fact, I would have bet dollars to doughnuts that April had never even cooked a meal there.

Standing a few feet inside the room, with Andy, Gene, and Mr. Szolosi behind me, I struck a pensive pose, chin in hand, as if I were struggling to decide. But in reality, I was scanning the room, furiously searching for something, anything, that might provide a clue of where April Kincaid had gone. There was nothing. No personal touches anywhere.

"Who lives here?" I asked the super.

"Why you ask?"

"Because I'd like to know who my neighbors will be. I don't want to live above someone who makes a lot of noise or throws wild parties."

"A girl lives here. Very quiet. No worries."

"Do you know if she has a boyfriend?" I asked, worried it was one question too many.

It was. Szolosi glared at me and said I'd seen enough. I apologized and asked for just another minute to decide. He stewed but didn't say no.

I returned to my intense examination of the room. There had to be something of hers to steer me in the right direction. But I wasn't finding it. I was at the point of surrender when I saw it. There, on a mullion of the window, a small black-and-white snapshot, pinned to the wood by a thumbtack. I wandered into the room, still feigning interest, and got close enough to see the photo. I reached out and lifted it slightly to see better. The super shuffled over and told me not to touch anything.

"I was just admiring this photograph," I said. "She's pretty. Is she the girl who lives here?"

"That's not your business. Come on. Out. Let's go."

Mr. Szolosi griped and scolded me all the way down to the street. At the front door I broke the news to him that I had decided to go with the other place. He said good riddance, or something approaching that, and slammed the door.

"Well, that was a waste of time," said Andy. "What do we do now?"

Gene hushed him and fixed me with a stare. "Wait a minute. What did you get in there, Ellie? Was there something in the snapshot?"

I smiled and nodded.

CHAPTER THIRTEEN

The three-and-a-half-by-five photograph was wrinkled and scratched, but I had seen the pretty young woman without any trouble. Dressed in a dark waitress uniform, she looked to be relaxing after a long shift in a restaurant. Reclining in a chair, holding a cigarette in one hand, she'd planted the other in her mussed hair and propped her shoeless feet up on an ottoman of some kind. An impish smile curled her lips as she stared at the birdie. And stitched into the left breast of her uniform was the name Charlie Horse Diner.

I drove Andy and Gene back to Hollywood where they took their own cars to do some research. We agreed that they would check out the Charlie Horse while I sent off a wire to my editor about my progress. We would then meet after lunch to discuss the results at the snack bar at Hollywood Ranch Market on Vine Street.

CHARLIE,

TONY STILL AWOL. HAVE LOCATED GIRLFRIEND'S APT. SHE IS ALSO MISSING. HAVE FOUND IMPORTANT LEAD TO FOLLOW. WILL INFORM YOU AT EARLIEST.

NOT EASY TO FIND SOMEONE WHO DOESN'T WANT TO BE FOUND.

IF I SEE WALSH IN LA, BOYS WILL COME OUT TO PLAY, AND GEORGIE PORGIE WILL RUN AWAY.

ELLIE

I sent the cable and spent ninety minutes in my hotel room, scribbling out a follow-up to my first article, concentrating on the death of producer Bertram Wallis. While not implicating Tony in so many words, I dutifully reported that the police wanted to question him. I wasn't sure if Charlie would publish it, but I was determined to give him the full story, including that Tony's phone number had been found on the dead man. I held back the revelation that his roommate was, in fact, a son of New Holland as well. That might have to come out later, but for now, I wanted to keep that information as an ace up my sleeve. More likely than not, Tony and Mickey's living arrangements were a well-guarded secret. I couldn't believe Tony's father knew anything about it, or he wouldn't have given Fadge Mickey's name.

But why hide the friendship at all? So what if two young men were sharing a modest apartment in a big city far from home? They wouldn't have been the first to do so. My brother, Elijah, had done the same after college. And those memories of Elijah prompted me to circle back to one question that continued to nag me: was hometown golden boy Tony Eberle queer?

⊛

The Hollywood Ranch Market on Fountain and Vine covered almost an entire city block. Open twenty-four hours a day, the market offered everything a housewife needed to feed her family and clean her house. There was also a snack bar in front where the famous and not-so-famous alike were often spotted sipping coffee or stuffing a hot dog into their mouths. I ordered a Coke and waited for my pals to show up. When they did a few minutes later, I was treated to two stony faces.

"What happened?" I asked.

"No luck on the Charlie Horse Diner," said Andy. "Nothing in the phone book under that name."

"So then what?" I pushed.

"Huh?"

"What did you do next?"

"There's no Charlie Horse in Los Angeles," explained Andy. "It must be somewhere else."

"Exactly," I said. "Where?"

"Who knows? Must've been an old snapshot. Impossible to say where April came from."

I was just a reporter for a small afternoon daily in a mill town in upstate New York, and yet I knew I'd be looking for a new job if I told my editor what they'd just told me.

"Can't you dig a little deeper?" I asked. "Maybe check some phone books from surrounding cities?"

Gene lit a cigarette and shook his head. "We checked the valley, too. Look, Ellie. This is a needle in a haystack. It's a big country. She could have come here from anywhere. Back East, the Midwest. James M. Cain said most Californians came from Iowa. Isn't that right, Andy?"

"How helpful. Then what do you think we should do?"

"Watch her place," said Andy. "She's bound to go back there eventually."

I had my doubts on that score. We'd all seen the apartment. There was nothing she might need inside. Why would she return there at this point? Perhaps once Tony had resurfaced, but not before. No, I was sure April Kincaid had gone to ground with her boyfriend and wouldn't come back until the all clear sounded. I shared this opinion with my friends.

Gene drew a sigh, then a deep drag on his cigarette. "If you can find her with an old photograph from God knows when or where, I salute you. But I don't have a steady job anymore. I've got to land a scoop or I'm going to starve to death one of these days."

"But that's precisely why you can't sit on your duff waiting for April to come back," I said. "You've got to go out and find her, Gene."

My words fell on deaf ears. Andy was eager enough to come with me, but in the end I didn't want a sidekick. I wanted to divide and conquer the leads. I wanted to split the legwork with these two, but they were decided.

"We'll let you know if she shows," said Gene. "And if you find anything, you'll clue us in?"

I frowned but agreed all the same. "This doesn't change anything about the drinks you two owe me."

I needed to find a collection of phone directories and wasn't sure any of the local library branches would fit the bill. Refusing to let my new friends' lack of initiative stand in my way, I consulted my trusty Thomas guide and took Beverly Boulevard all the way to downtown Los Angeles. I found out later that the freeway would have saved me a little time, but my guide was a few years out of date. I managed to find parking a few blocks away from the library. Striding through the drizzle, holding my coat tight around my neck, I endured catcalls from hungry, wet construction workers. All around me, as far as I could see, old buildings were being demolished to make way for future development. The library, however, intended to stay. It loomed before me like an Egyptian Art Deco castle, capped by a magnificent mosaic-tiled pyramid.

A librarian on the main floor directed me to some carrels opposite a bank of telephone booths. There I settled in with a map of Southern California at a long table. One by one, I pulled phone directories off the shelves and searched for the Charlie Horse Diner. Working in a clockwise direction starting in Santa Barbara, I pored over dozens of phone books, any city or town I could recognize on my map. Each directory took several minutes, depending on how many municipalities were included. I felt my eyes begin to cross after two hours. Then the librarian told me the place was going to close in fifteen minutes. I hadn't seen one Charlie Horse, if you didn't count a subscriber in Oxnard named Chas. Horce. I needed to change my strategy or be kicked out no closer to finding April Kincaid and Tony Eberle.

I stared at my map, looking for the larger cities in the area that I hadn't yet searched. Ventura, Bakersfield, and Barstow. I fetched the phone books and dumped them on the table. Nothing in Ventura, nothing in Bakersfield. To tell the truth, I expected nothing in Barstow either. That was why the librarian shushed me when I let out a yelp as my finger ran down the page and hit pay dirt on "Charlie Horse Diner, Route 15." I jotted down the number just as the lights overhead dimmed.

"Time to go, miss," said the librarian. "Did you find what you were looking for?"

I beamed a bright smile at her. "Yes, thank you."

I don't believe she noticed the Barstow telephone directory stuffed in my purse as I walked out.

�🌀

"We've been expecting to hear from you, Miss Stone."

Dorothy Fetterman and Archie Stemple were waiting for me in the darkened lobby of the McCadden Hotel. It was after six.

"You gave me a start," I said.

"Where's Eberle?" demanded Stemple.

"Is there someplace private where we can talk?" asked Dorothy, ignoring her companion. "In your room, perhaps?"

I wasn't at all sure I liked that idea. Dorothy seemed harmless enough, but who knew? She did throw off a spooky air, after all. And Stemple might well douse me with scalding-hot coffee, throw his sweaty cap at me, or simply punch me in the face if the mood struck him.

"Are these people bothering you, Miss Stone?" The bellhop.

"It's all right, Marty," I said. "They're friends."

Pushing my doubts aside, I tipped Marty a quarter for his trouble and invited my visitors to follow me to the second floor.

"Can't we take the elevator?" asked Stemple as we started up the stairs.

"There is no elevator, Archie," said Dorothy. "You can wait in the lobby if you like."

Stemple closed his trap and climbed to the second floor without another word.

"I can't tell you where Tony is yet," I said once we were inside my room with the door locked.

"You don't know where he is, do you?" asked Dorothy.

"Yes, I do. I'm planning on seeing him tomorrow."

She studied me for a long moment in the low light of my warm room. Then she slipped a hand into her purse and retrieved a cigarette. Leaning against the nearby desk, Stemple sprung into action, almost tripping over the wastepaper basket to offer her a light. Dorothy inhaled, sat down in the chair, the only one in the room—I was seated on the edge of the bed—and stared me in the eye.

"I like you, Miss Stone. And I want to believe you. But you've had two days to bring us Mr. Eberle. I'm growing impatient."

Their interest in Tony's whereabouts might have made sense while Bertram Wallis was still missing. But now he'd been found dead. Why would a "studio fixer" and a contract director from the far end of the dugout care where he was now? I lit a cigarette of my own as I screwed up the nerve to find out.

"Tell me again why I should help you."

That took her by surprise, and I fancied I could hear Archie Stemple grinding his teeth. Dorothy moistened her lips and tapped her cigarette ash into the tray on the desk.

"I thought you wanted to help us," she said.

"But why?"

She had no answer.

"I'm more concerned with Tony's wellbeing right now," I continued. "Especially after what happened to Bertram Wallis."

"Are you saying there was foul play in his death? Are the police saying that?"

"I'll tell you what the police think in a couple of hours. I'm having dinner with the lead investigator this evening."

She smiled and gave the subtlest nod of approval. "You're quite the gal reporter, aren't you? I may have underestimated you, Miss Stone."

"Quit stalling and tell us where Eberle is," barked Stemple, startling both Dorothy and me.

Dorothy turned in her seat and aimed some kind of a look at him. I couldn't see her face. But he backed off and assumed a position against the window. Dorothy swiveled back to me.

"You asked me why you should want to help us. What do you want?"

"For starters, you could tell me why you need Tony. Wallis has been found, so Tony can't help you there."

Dorothy exchanged a glance with Stemple, drew a sigh, and smoothed her skirt over her knees.

"Tony Eberle visited Bertram Wallis shortly before he died," she began in a slow, measured tone. "We've spoken to witnesses who saw him at the party there. And they tell us that Tony and Bertie argued over something. What exactly, they didn't know. So we are trying to locate Mr. Eberle to find out what happened and if, somehow, it had something to do with Bertie's death."

I took a drag from my cigarette. "You're still underestimating me. You don't appear to suspect anything untoward about Wallis's fall. And if that's the case, why would you want to find Tony? He's just a nobody you fired from your picture. You said so yourself. There's something else you're not telling me."

She stubbed out her cigarette, rose from her chair, and approached the window. Stemple sidled away to give her wide berth. Her back to me, Dorothy peered through the glass at the Selma Hardware ad. I waited.

"We're worried that something was stolen from Bertie's home that night," she said, still gazing out the window. "And we think Tony may know something about that."

"What was it?" I asked. Dorothy turned back to face me.

"A script."

Now I rose and snuffed out my cigarette. I circled around the desk to look out the window. Dorothy followed my lead, and, shoulder to shoulder, we both stared at a brick wall.

"If I bring Tony Eberle to you, and if it turns out he's innocent of stealing this script you say is missing, will you give him his job back on *Twistin' on the Beach*?"

"Never," said Stemple.

"Yes, of course," said Dorothy.

Stemple fumed in silence.

"What can you tell me about this script?" I asked.

Dorothy explained that Bertram Wallis had been planning a new project at the time of his death. I asked what was so important about another beach bash movie, and she said that this was no teenage romp. It was a serious film, and the studio was prepared to invest a million dollars to make it.

"Don't tell me Wallis ran out of carbon paper and there's no copy," I said.

Dorothy cracked a sardonic smile. "Funny. Perhaps you should write dialogue for our movies."

"What was it about?"

"Nothing that would interest you. Or me for that matter."

"Try me," I said.

She drew a sigh before continuing, as if the subject were so dull it pained her to discuss it. Or maybe she was stalling for time while she thought up another lie.

"It's an art picture. Mr. Balaban believes it's one that will finally show what a misunderstood genius Bertram Wallis is. Was."

"And maybe the studio is counting on the murder to sell more tickets."

Dorothy stared straight ahead into the window's glass. "You might be better suited to the publicity department. But back to Bertie's script, it's the story of an old widow, the last of her line, slowly losing her wits as she reminisces about her long life and the world that she used to know. A world that's long since disappeared."

"That actually sounds interesting," I said. "Is that *The Colonel's Widow*?"

Dorothy's right eyebrow inched up her forehead ever so slightly. "You know about *The Colonel's Widow*?"

"I do my research."

"Well, that's the script we're trying to find. Mr. Balaban is quite keen on making the movie. That's why we must find Tony Eberle. And why I would appreciate your help."

"And there really is no other copy of the script?"

"None that we can find."

It all rang false to me. Her story made no sense. For starters, did she not realize that a copy of the script was registered with the Writers Guild? And if the project had been signed with Wallis, why did the studio not have its own copy?

I wanted to get to the bottom of their interest in Tony, which was why I didn't mention the Writers Guild. Dorothy Fetterman was a sharp woman. I was sure she knew how to get her hands on that script. And so I figured she was after something else altogether.

CHAPTER FOURTEEN

"**Y**ou look real nice," said Sergeant John L. Millard.

He took his time ogling me in the lobby of the McCadden Hotel as I wriggled into my coat. I couldn't tell if he was trying to decide which article of my clothing he would like to remove first or whether there was a loose thread that, if pulled, would cause every stitch I was wearing to fall magically to the ground. Christmas morning for him, and I was the present under the tree.

"Where are we dining this evening?" I asked, trying to ignore his unabashed stare.

"Norm's," he said. "It's a regular haunt of mine."

I wasn't familiar with the place, but fifteen minutes later, when we pulled into the parking lot of a space-age diner on La Cienega Boulevard, the penny dropped. Fine with me, I thought. I liked simple fare, and I wasn't a snob about fancy restaurants. Still, if I were trying to impress a young lady, I wouldn't treat her to all-you-can-eat spare ribs and onion rings.

"Order anything you want," he told me once we were seated in a booth with red Naugahyde bench seats.

A middle-aged waitress in a uniform arrived to take our order. Millard acted as if he knew her and addressed her as Myrna. She corrected him, Moira. He brushed off his gaffe and unloaded a couple of stale jokes on her. Then he tried to engage her in some banter that was as uncomfortable and unwelcome as a sneeze on your neck. Every so often, he threw a glance at me to make sure I wasn't missing any of his performance. At length, Moira said she had other tables to attend to if we weren't ready to order. Millard cleared his throat, his smile hanging on by its fingernails, and ordered the Surf and Turf special. I selected the Norm's cheeseburger and asked the wine steward for a glass of Coke to wash it down.

Millard smiled at me from the other side of the table. He'd taken care to shave, and his wiry black hair had been oiled up and pasted down onto his flat head. I'd nearly choked on his cloying musky cologne, as thick as soup, on the drive over. He continued to stare at me, his lips stretched tight and thin over his white teeth. The skin around his dry eyes wrinkled into a squint, but I didn't detect mirth or amity in his gaze. Rather I saw a hunger, a wolfish desire hiding behind a rapacious smile.

"Tell me about yourself," he said.

"I'm my least favorite topic. I'm much more interested in what you do. Why did you want to become a cop?"

That bought me ten minutes as he treated me to his life story. I thought he should have become a pearl diver instead, since he didn't stop to take a breath as he regaled me with his feats of bravery and tales of his successes.

"What about the Wallis case?" I asked when our drinks arrived. "Have you determined how he managed to fall off the terrace?"

"Oh, he didn't fall," he said. "We knew that the moment we found him."

"How so?"

"Easy. The railing is too high to fall over by accident. It's forty-eight inches. Wallis probably built it that high for just that reason. We found the body about three hundred feet down in the ravine. It's a long way to the bottom."

"Then you're saying he was pushed."

Millard took a swig of his Coke and nodded. "Can't see any other explanation."

That was news he hadn't shared with the boys of the press. I wondered what else he might tell me.

"Then you must have some suspects," I said, trying to flatter him.

"We've got some ideas. What you have to realize about these degenerates is that there's no shortage of lowlifes who'll rat them out for a pint of rye or a hot meal."

"So what have you learned so far?"

"First, Wallis was known for his wild lifestyle. We knew all about his limp-wristed pajama parties and broke them up regularly."

Andy had mentioned that the police often extracted bribes to leave people like Wallis in peace. I wondered how much black money Millard had stuffed into his own pockets.

"Was Wallis ever arrested for his parties?" I asked.

"No. He had smart lawyers. As long as you're rich, you'll never go to jail. But back to your question. We're putting together a list of people who were seen at the party that night. If I told you some of the names who attended his flings, you'd spit your Coke in my face and call me a liar."

I wanted to ask, of course, but I was pacing myself with this cop. His ego needed constant stroking, and I didn't want him to think I was only interested in him for his information.

"You seem to be quite well known around here," I said, referring to his familiarity with the waitress and the lukewarm wave he'd received from the manager when we entered. "You must be a big deal."

Lucky for me his buttons didn't burst off his shirt and ping off my forehead. He glowed and aw-shucked for about thirty seconds before brushing aside my observation with the humble excuse that he was a regular.

Okay, I thought. That ought to hold him for a while. I prepared to ask some questions.

"You must know what kind of things went on at those parties," I said. "Can you tell me?"

He joked that I was awfully curious about the perversions Bertram Wallis had been up to. Not much I could say to that except that I wanted to know for my story.

"You can't quote me on that," he said, suddenly serious. "This is off the record. I'm only telling you this because you're my favorite reporter."

"Off the record, then." How would he ever know if I quoted him in the *New Holland Republic* three thousand miles away?

"This Wallis fellow and his friends were deviants. Real pervs. Sorry. The chief wants us to say homosexuals when we talk to the press. Fag, fairy, fruit, pansy. Call 'em what you want. They turn my stomach."

"I heard he took photos of young men in compromising positions."

"You're going to ruin my supper with this talk," he said with a grin. "If we ever found dirty pictures or movies, he'd have gone up for obscenity."

"What about indecency or sodomy? You couldn't arrest him for that?"

"I suppose we'd have to catch him in the act. Anyway, he was always careful not to cross certain lines. We'd break up his parties if we got a tip or if the neighbors complained about the noise. Not much more than harassment, really. We never had anything we could make stick."

He then reflected for a few minutes on the variety of perversions people got up to, and I asked him if he could tell me the name that would make me spit my Coke in his face and call him a liar. He balked, saying he could get in trouble for naming names.

"In this town there are some people you can't cross," he explained. "The studios, the big stars, and, of course, the Jews. They run everything."

I wanted to throw—not spit—my Coke in his face, but I held back.

"You know I'm Jewish," I said.

Millard took the information in stride. "I didn't mean anything by it, hon. I got nothing against Jews myself. And certainly nothing against you."

"On the record," I said, swallowing my disgust, "can you tell me anything about the condition of the body when you found it in the ravine?"

"About what you'd expect after tumbling down three hundred feet of rough canyon. There's all kinds of trees, brush, and sharp rocks on the way down. He was pretty beat up by the time he stopped rolling. Vomit on his shirt, and all muddy and waterlogged, too. Remember it started raining on Tuesday, and he wasn't found till Thursday morning."

"Vomit on his shirt?"

"Yeah. The cleaning lady said he puked in the parlor at some point after the party. She found it Thursday morning and had to clean it up."

"Anything else you can tell me?"

He thought about it for a moment then added that the body had been bloated and was turning a greenish blue.

"Smelled awful, too," he concluded.

"How was he dressed?"

"Just regular clothes. Trousers and a shirt. And one of those froufrou scarves around his neck. You know like Europeans wear."

"An ascot?"

"That's it. One of those. He looked like a beaten-up fairy covered with mud."

"Was there any indication that he might have died before going over the railing?"

Millard shook his head. "No way for me to say if he was already dead when he went down the hill."

Moira the waitress returned with our dinners. She overhead the last snatch of our conversation and made a face. Millard laughed and told her it was police business.

I took a break from our conversation to pick at my dinner. Millard dug in with relish, alternatively stuffing his face with steak then lobster. Once he'd polished off his food and wiped the plate clean with bread, he sat back and slapped his stomach with satisfaction.

"How about some dessert?"

"I'm not very hungry," I said.

"You hardly ate anything. You sure are a cheap date."

Oh, no. Not that. Not a date, not a date.

I wanted to push that thought aside as quickly as possible, so I resumed my questioning. "Can you tell me about the phone number you found in Wallis's pocket? Off the record if you like."

He thought about it for a long moment, passing the time by probing his teeth with his tongue in attempts—I can only surmise—to dislodge the last scraps of his dinner and send them down the hatch.

"I can't tell you that," he said after a long moment.

"What if I give you a name? Can you confirm it if I'm right?"

He laughed. "You're funny, you know that? How would you know whose number it is?"

"Was it an actor named Tony Eberle?" I asked, and he stopped laughing.

Millard went all serious and leaned across the table. "How did you get that name?" he whispered. "I want to know who leaked it to you."

"No one leaked it to me," I said. "I've been asking questions at the studio, and I learned that Bertram Wallis hired Tony Eberle personally for his picture. Then when Tony disappeared and Wallis turned up dead at the same time, I thought it just might be his number."

Millard sat back in his seat, his sweaty posterior producing a rude-sounding noise against the Naugahyde.

"I don't think we should be discussing this," he said.

"Can you confirm that Tony Eberle is a suspect in the murder?"

He squirmed in his seat. "Well, I can't very well say he isn't. Not after we found his number on Wallis. And after a couple of witnesses claimed they saw him at the party that night. And that he had words with Wallis."

"Do you have any idea of where he might be hiding?"

He pursed his lips and shook his head.

Moira the waitress presented the bill, which Millard snatched up.

"No, this is on me," he said, smiling broadly, even though I'd made no move to grab the check.

I waited at the table while he made his way to the register. I watched as he spoke in a low voice to the cashier. When he'd finished, she pushed off her stool and set out in search of the manager, who returned with her moments later. The pained expression on his face was hard to ignore. He tried to smile at the cop, who whispered something short and sweet into his ear, but gave up the pretense once Millard handed him the bill.

"That's awfully nice of you, Gary," said Millard in a voice meant to be heard. "But next time you've got to let me pay. This is embarrassing."

In the car, I calculated how many minutes it would take to reach the hotel. Fifteen? Twelve if I was lucky? I just wanted to get away from Millard and never lay eyes on his greasy head again. As I retraced in my mind the route we'd taken to get to Norm's, I became aware of something touching my left hand. Oh, God, it was Millard. Without thinking, I yanked it away.

"Did I startle you?" he asked.

"Yes," I said, inching across the seat toward the door. "You should keep both hands on the wheel, ten and two o'clock. You're a cop. You should know that."

I watched his smile dim and his fingers tighten on the steering wheel. He grew quiet after that. Had I led him on? Been too friendly? I didn't think so, but there was the flattery and ego stroking from earlier. Perhaps I never should have accepted his invitation in the first place. I certainly hadn't wanted to dine with him. And the information I'd wrung out of him wasn't all that helpful either. But whatever I should or shouldn't have done, I was stuck now.

The ride back to the McCadden took exactly seventeen minutes. I checked my watch. The Friday night traffic, made worse by the rain, had slowed us and marooned me in the passenger seat next to Sergeant Millard for longer than I'd promised myself.

At the curb in front of the hotel, he leaned over and tried to put an arm around me. I was trapped against the door and feared the worst. But then the door opened, and I nearly tumbled into the street.

"So sorry, Miss Stone," said Marty as he caught me in his arms.

"What the hell are you doing?" demanded Millard.

"Just opening the car door," stammered Marty. "It's my job."

"I'm all right," I said, righting myself on the curb. "Thank you again for dinner. It was lovely."

Like a child gaping in disbelief as the scoop of ice cream falls from his cone to the ground, Millard watched me climb the stoop and disappear inside with Marty on my heels.

∞

I phoned Andy and Gene to tell them about Barstow. They both liked my plan and were eager to accompany me the following morning, Andy in particular. I think he'd had a few drinks, judging from the slurred speech and the overly familiar tone he took with me. He asked me to come over to his place, and when I told him that wasn't a good idea, he reminded me of the photographs he'd taken Monday night outside Wallis's party.

"I'm not going out at this hour," I said.

"I can come over to your hotel, then."

Reluctantly I agreed, but made sure to meet him in the lobby. He'd been drinking all right. His skin was red, lips chapped, and eyes bloodshot. Completing the tableau, he was oozing the stale odor of alcohol as if he'd been soaking in a tub of gin. He was genuinely disappointed that we weren't going to review the photographs in my room, but I managed to steer him into one of the lobby armchairs.

Andy produced a large envelope with a dozen three-and-a-half-by-five black-and-white prints. He handed them to me and drew a drunken sigh. I shuffled through the pictures quickly. There wasn't much to see. Except one man who resembled Tony Eberle. I groaned as I looked more closely. Yes, it might just have been him. Hard to tell, as he only appeared in one shot and he was partially obscured by another man. The rest of the attendees were nondescript, handsome young men climbing out of taxis, roadsters, and other vehicles. Then there was the odd female arriving, dressed to the nines, always on the arm of an older gentleman whose shifting glances made clear he was acutely aware of the scrutiny a young lovely invites when accompanied by someone's wealthy grandfather. He held the cash; she had the beauty. A shame, I thought. For now, she's getting what she needs. Later that night, he'll get what he wants. In the morning, he'll move on to the next aspiring starlet. Excelsior. And she, poor thing, will be that much less desirable, on the make for another patron, probably not as rich or handsome. Eventually she'll hit bottom and give up on her dream of stardom. She'll settle for a kindhearted Joe who'll marry her despite her past and take her away to Bakersfield or Palmdale or Fresno, wherever failed beauties go to wither.

I glanced at the last few photos, thinking what a wasted trip Andy had made, when I noticed one person I knew.

"Isn't that Gene?" I asked.

He leaned closer to see, and I got a snootful of his eighty-proof breath. Risking an explosion, I lit a cigarette to counter the effects.

"Yeah. He was there," he said, staring at the figure in the background. "He's always on the prowl for a story."

I'd seen all I needed to see, and the hour was late. I yawned and tried to excuse myself for bed, but Andy wasn't ready to throw in the towel. He jumped to his feet and made an awkward pass at me, reaching with both arms as he tried to plant a wet kiss on my face. When it rains it pours, I thought. Why couldn't some handsome Hollywood star blow in my ear instead of a surly cop and a drunken photographer? And both in the same evening. Where was William Hopper when I needed him?

I loosed a minor scream, and Marty arrived to investigate.

"Is everything all right, Miss Stone?" he asked, glaring at Andy.

"I'm fine, Marty. Just going to bed."

"Sorry. Sorry," slurred Andy, holding his hands up as if to surrender.

Marty showed him to the door, and I tipped him another quarter.

CHAPTER FIFTEEN

SATURDAY, FEBRUARY 10, 1962

I rose early Saturday, bathed and dressed, before skipping down the stairs and out the door by seven. Marty called after me as I opened my bent umbrella against the rain. Did he ever take a day off?

"Another wire for you," he said, extending an envelope to me on the stoop.

I dug into my purse but came up empty-handed. No more quarters. Reluctantly I slipped him a dollar.

"Thanks," he said. "I was wondering if you'd ever pull something more than a quarter out of there."

After his double heroics of the night before, I couldn't very well hold his nerve against him. And I was growing fond of the rumpled bellhop. I told him he could expect nothing but nickels from now on.

He smiled. "You have a nice day, Miss Stone."

I hurried around the corner and down the block to Hody's, where I sat in a booth and ordered an English muffin and coffee. I opened the telegram and groaned.

ELLIE,

SHORT WORRIED. SAYS YOU HAVE THE WEEKEND TO FIND EBERLE OR WILL SEND WALSH TO LA. ADVISE AT EARLIEST.

CHARLIE

I thought of how I'd have liked to answer Charlie's wire, but I doubted Western Union would deliver such explicit instructions. There was no time to send a response anyway. I was on a tight schedule. I intended to drive out to Barstow, nearly a hundred miles east of Los Angeles, and make it back to Hollywood in time to talk to Mickey. At fifty miles an hour, I might reach my destination in two hours. But I had no idea what I would find when I got there. I knew April Kincaid had once worked at the Charlie Horse, but when I phoned the diner from the hotel the previous night, they said she'd left five months earlier. Lucky for me I wasn't in the habit of being thwarted by shushing librarians. I'd pinched the Barstow phone directory from the Central Library, and in it I found a listing for "Kincaid, Gordon" on Bradshaw Drive. When I dialed it, an operator informed me it had been disconnected several months earlier. I was playing a hunch, but if I was right, Gordon Kincaid was April's father. And he was deceased.

I unfolded a road map I'd found in the glove compartment of my rental, and spread it out on the table before me, anchoring it with my coffee mug, the milk pitcher, and my plate. I plotted the best route to Barstow.

Gene Duerson slipped into the booth. He told me Andy had phoned him that morning to beg off the journey.

"What happened? Hung over?"

"Possibly. But he got an assignment today to cover some of the rain damage for the *Times*. They're sending him to Griffith Park to take pictures of mud."

"It's just you and me, then," I said, breathing a sigh of relief. "Want some coffee?"

"I'll take it for the road."

We took my car. He said his would never make it to Barstow and back.

"It's an old DeSoto," he explained as we made our way east on Route 66. "I've been meaning to get the transmission fixed, but since I got laid off I can't swing it."

He told me his life's story. Born in 1912, he'd grown up the second of four children on a small farm outside Dallas. When his father died in a harvester accident, Gene left school and went to work. He was fifteen. He supported his three sisters and mother until the girls were married off, none older than eighteen. His mother remarried after that. Gene enlisted in the army in 1933 and served for six years, finally leaving to work as a copyboy for the *Fort Worth Star-Telegram* at the ripe age of twenty-seven.

"It was the Depression, and the pay was lousy," he said as he gazed out the window into the rain and desolate landscape of the desert. "Then they let me go. I did various jobs for a few years, trying to keep my head above water. And I was writing, too. I loved to tell stories, even as a kid. I used to make up wild yarns about the Texas Rangers and Mexican bandits in 1915. Scared the heck out of my sisters."

"Why did you give it up?" I asked.

He made a face. "No money in stories about bloody border wars. I worked for a while on an oil rig in Oklahoma. Then the Japs attacked Pearl Harbor, and I got called up again."

"I see."

"It was a steady paycheck," he said. "And I landed a job with *Stars and Stripes*. They taught me how to be a newspaperman."

I smiled, clutching the steering wheel. "Then it all worked out for the best. The war, I mean."

He chuckled. "Yeah, the war was good to me." His mien darkened. "Not so good for some of my pals, though."

"Were you in Europe or the Pacific?" I asked.

"Neither. CBI. China Burma India Theater. Burma mostly. It was quite an education for a Texas boy, I can tell you. But I made a lot of great friends. Yanks, Brits, even Indians and Burmese. You might not think it, but they're good guys under the brown skin and sweat and smell. Real good guys."

I threw a glance his way, but he didn't notice. He was still looking out the window at the rain.

"It used to rain like this only worse in Burma," he said. "Monsoons. It felt like you were taking a shower for three months straight. Or a steam bath. And despite the heat, you were cold. Rain does that to you."

At length, Gene left his past behind, and we discussed the details of our collaboration. We'd agreed the night before to share all information and write the story together for the Los Angeles news market, that was if the story panned out at all. Gene left New Holland to me. We also decided to share the credit if the national press picked up on the news of Bertram Wallis's murder.

"What about Andy?" I asked.

Gene shrugged. "If you want to let him take the pictures, I'm okay with it. But you've got your own camera. And you're a sight better shooter than he is, too."

"Let's see how it goes," I said.

Gene sniffed and looked off into the gray. "Fine by me. But we might finish this today, and Andy's shooting mud in Griffith Park."

We drove on through the rain for a couple of miles without speaking. Then I asked him if he'd been at Bertram Wallis's house for the party on Monday night.

"Yeah, I was there," he said. "I've been working on a scandal piece about him. I hang around outside whenever he throws a party just in case something happens or someone famous shows up."

"Anything interesting that night?"

"Not really. Just a lot of waiting."

"Anyone famous?"

"Only if you consider Bobby Renfro famous."

"Bobby Renfro was there that night?"

"Yeah. I've seen him there before, too. He's a regular."

"Are you saying he's queer?"

Gene shook his head. "Not Bobby Renfro. He's always with a pretty young thing who thinks her ship's just come in. Some fellows have all the luck. Good looks, money, and disposable girls."

"Disposable girls?"

"I didn't mean anything by it," he said by way of an apology. "These boys and girls are hired for a night or two. Sometimes just for an hour."

"Andy mentioned someone the other day."

"Skip Barnes. He's a procurer. He finds handsome young actors and beautiful actresses for people like Wallis. Then he hires them out to his friends."

"Is that the scandalous story you were writing on Wallis?"

"It was easier than finding something else."

"I thought the studios paid off the scandal sheets to keep those stories out of the papers."

"Exactly," he said without even the hint of a smile.

※

We arrived in Barstow a little after ten thirty. My map didn't show Bradshaw Drive, but a waterlogged man waiting at a lonely bus stop pointed the way. We followed his directions and located the street in short order. Meandering alongside the railroad tracks on the north side of Barstow, Bradshaw Drive was a muddy stretch of road, home to dilapidated ranch houses, wheelless wrecks on blocks in the drive, and empty fields of scrub plants.

"This is high desert," said Gene as we pulled to a stop in front of a small house near the intersection with Santa Fe Drive. "Normally this would all be dry and dusty. Now it's a swamp."

I gazed out the windshield. "Kind of a sad place. Has that end-of-the-earth feel to it, don't you think?"

"Not at all. It's more like the back of beyond."

I smiled. He didn't. He rarely did, especially when he was being funny.

"Come on," he said, reaching for the door handle. "Let's see if your hunch was right."

"It was right."

"How do you know?"

"See that car parked in front?" I asked. Gene grunted yes. "That's the Rambler I followed up Nichols Canyon Road Wednesday night."

Gene nodded knowingly and popped open the door.

We approached the house, a single story affair, probably hammered together in the thirties by a do-it-yourselfer. No frills. Just wooden slats whose paint had been sand-blasted off by harsh winds and a baking sun. The roof was wooden shingles with a tarp stretched over the eastern half, probably to cover a leak. The porch was all two-by-fours, warped and weathered, with a couple of old chairs and a retired boiler full of dents for patio furniture.

"You want me to knock?" asked Gene. "In case we're not welcome."

I shook my head, already soaking wet from the walk from the car. "They won't try any rough stuff with a girl."

Gene extended a gentlemanly hand to cede me the right of way. I knocked on the wooden frame of the screen door to no effect. I rapped again a few moments later. The sound of the rain made it hard to hear anything from inside, but finally, after about twenty seconds, the inner door opened partway, and a pair of eyes peered out.

"Yes?" came a woman's voice. "What do you want?"

"Are you April Kincaid?" I asked, already recognizing her from the photograph I'd seen in her apartment.

"Who are you?"

She was thin. Too thin. A pretty brunette with shoulder-length hair held back by a plastic hairband. Dressed in a wrinkled white blouse and a dark skirt, she was wearing socks and no shoes. She stared us down through the screen.

"My name is Eleonora Stone. Ellie Stone. And this is Gene Duerson."

"Yeah, what do you want?"

"We're reporters. We'd like to ask you a few questions, if that's all right."

"Questions? About what?"

I played my card. "We're looking for Tony Eberle."

She positioned the door firmly between herself and us, as if preparing to slam it shut.

"I don't know anyone named Tony Eberle," she said.

"We know he's here. We're not going to cause any trouble. We want to help."

"What about your friends?" she asked.

"What's that?"

"Out there. The car down the street."

Gene and I turned as one to look. There, about forty yards down the unpaved road, a late-model sedan crouched, huffing exhaust into the air. I tried to remember if I'd seen any cars on the street when we arrived. I doubted it. At least nothing as new and fancy as this one. It looked to be a big Chrysler or something similar. Not a pickup truck or an old junker like the rest of the cars in the neighborhood.

I glanced at Gene to check his reaction. He shook his head slowly.

"You'd better let us in," I said. "We have no idea who's in that car, but they must have followed us."

She stood to one side. "You've ruined everything. Now you've brought the police with you."

Gene and I ducked inside, and the girl locked the door behind us. Her eyes showed fear. She told us Tony wasn't there.

"Where is he?" I asked.

"Out. He went to the market."

"That means he'll be coming back soon. We need to get word to him and warn him to stay away."

"Taylor's Market is on Route Fifteen," she said. "He went to get some beans and milk and bread."

I turned to Gene. "I know it's raining hard, but if those are cops in that car, we all lose. Can you sneak out the back way and try to find Tony?"

"I've seen worse rain."

"Burma?"

He nodded.

April explained how to find the market, and Gene slipped out the back door. We watched him pick through the scrub, working his way around a house about a hundred yards away and regain Bradshaw Drive to the east. Moving to the front of the house, I pulled back the sheer white curtains—worn thin and yellow by the years and the wind—and peeked out to see if the dark sedan had moved. It was still there.

"How did you find us?" asked April.

"It wasn't easy," I said.

"That doesn't answer my question."

I told her I'd found a snapshot of her in her old waitress uniform. A little research and voilà. The Charlie Horse in Barstow.

"Where did you find a picture of me?" she demanded.

I coughed. "Your apartment."

"You broke into my place?"

"No. Nothing like that. The super let me in. Mr. Szolosi."

April took a step back, regarding me with renewed distrust. She might have wanted to run, but where would she have gone? She certainly regretted having let me inside. And I was sure she was wishing she hadn't left that snapshot behind in her apartment.

"What do you want with Tony?" she asked.

"I work for the newspaper in his hometown. They sent me out here to interview him. He was supposed to meet me Tuesday morning on set, but he didn't show."

She frowned and took a seat on an old couch. "So you've really got a good story to tell. Tony washed out as an actor, and now he's suspected of murder."

"I don't want to write that story. I want to tell the folks back home that he made it. I'm trying to get him his job back on the picture."

She sniggered, sad and bitter. "How are you going to manage that?"

"Is Tony mixed up in this murder of Bertram Wallis?" I asked.

She glared at me, her eyes sharp and restive, as if she were challenging me to accuse him. Then she looked away and shook her head.

"Tony didn't kill that awful man, but who's going to believe that? He's nobody. He'll be a convenient scapegoat for the police. Everyone will be happy."

I sat down next to her on the couch and let her think for a moment. Then I asked if she had any ideas of who might have wanted to toss Bertram Wallis over the railing of his terrace.

She shook her head and went quiet.

☙

Forty minutes later, Gene reappeared at the back door, soaked to the skin. He was alone.

"No sign of Tony at the market," he said. "But there's a special on round steak."

CHAPTER SIXTEEN

The dark sedan was still waiting down the street when we checked again a little after noon. Tony must have been spooked by the two strange cars on the street, because he hadn't returned.

"He can't call. The phone's been disconnected," said April, sitting on the sofa in the dark room.

"Where do you think he might have gone?" I asked. "Do you have any friends or family in Barstow?"

April shook her head. "My dad passed away a year ago. Mom ran off when I was little. There's no one else."

Gene had shown the wherewithal to pick up some hot dogs and soup at the market on his failed mission to find Tony. I asked April if she was hungry.

"Sure," she said, looking half starved. "The stove is out of commission, but there's the fireplace."

"Maybe I can fix it," said Gene. "I worked as an electrician's assistant for a while."

"Power's cut off. I didn't pay the bill."

Gene made a small fire with some kindling and a few pieces of broken furniture. We warmed the soup and cooked the hot dogs in the hearth then ate in silence. I didn't have much of an appetite, but Gene and April looked as if they wanted more. I asked her how she and Tony had been managing the past few days without any money.

"Tony has a couple of bucks," she said. "Got it from Mickey."

"What will you do when that runs out?"

She shrugged and peered miserably into her empty soup bowl.

"Okay," I said, reaching for my purse. "I've got a ten-dollar bill here. It's yours on one condition."

April argued with me for the better part of an hour. She didn't like the idea of driving back to Los Angeles with Gene. And she liked even less the plan of leaving Tony behind in Barstow.

"We wait until dark," I explained. "Then you and Gene will stroll out to my car, climb in, and drive away. Gene will take you back to your place. No one knows who you are. They'll never trace you there."

"What if that car follows us?" she asked.

"It won't. Whoever's out there isn't interested in me. Or you, for that matter. They're looking for Tony. So when they see you two leave, they'll assume you're me."

"What happens to you, then? Won't they barge in here as soon as we leave?"

"Maybe," I said. "But they won't find Tony."

Gene was conspicuously quiet throughout our discussion. He sat in a chair near the fireplace, chipped plate balanced on his knee. He watched April the entire time, studying her. Or maybe he was writing his story in his head. Finally he piped up.

"Whoever followed us here knows who Ellie is. I doubt they want to harm her. They could have done that in Los Angeles."

"What happens if Tony comes back when we leave?" asked April.

"First of all," said Gene, "we don't even know what those people want. Maybe their intentions are friendly. Or maybe not. Second, Tony's a smart guy. He knew enough to make himself scarce once he saw the unfamiliar cars in the street. He won't come back if that one's still out there."

"I don't like it," she said. "If it's not the cops, whoever it is probably killed Wallis. Now they're after Tony."

"It's Ellie's way, or you don't get the money."

April mulled it over for another minute before she caved. She held out her hand for the ten-dollar bill I'd been offering as a carrot since the conversation began. I gave it to her, and she tucked it into the pocket of her skirt.

※

We sat in the darkened room for hours, at turns talking and keeping quiet. During one of her more loquacious spells, April told us how she and Tony had met. She'd moved to Los Angeles in late August and found work as a waitress in the tearoom at Bullock's department store on Wilshire. The job wasn't going well, according to April. Her supervisor was a shrew who demanded perfection from her staff. And April was often late or poorly turned out.

"She told me I wasn't pretty enough to make it on my looks alone," she said. "She was always picking on me for my uniform, my hair, and my makeup. Finally I had enough and I quit. Tore off my apron and threw it at her in front of a table of lavender-haired ladies in fox stoles." April smiled at the memory. "And I called her a dirty c—"

"Let's put that to one side, shall we?" I said.

"Anyway," she continued, "I ran out of the tearoom smack into Tony, who was just coming in with some rich guy in a suit. I hit the floor, and Tony helped me up. It was love at first sight."

"How long ago was that?" I asked, making mental notes for my story.

"October fourteenth. He asked me out on a date, and we've been together ever since. We're going to get married as soon as this mess blows over."

"Married? What are you going to live on?"

"Tony's going to be a star," she said, practically breathless. "And I can wait tables and take acting classes until I get my big break. Tony's not the only one who's going to make it in the movies."

I resisted the urge to remind her what that shrew of a supervisor had said about her looks. And Tony's career wasn't looking all that promising just then, either. I concentrated instead on what she knew of Bertram Wallis.

"Tony had nothing to do with that," she insisted.

"There are witnesses who can place Tony at Wallis's place the night he died."

April swore he'd never been to Bertram Wallis's house. The witnesses were lying. "Fag liars," she said. Every last one of them.

"And you've never been there either?"

"Of course not. Like I said, the cops will find people to lie and say whatever suits their story. They'll swear Tony was there and that he killed that pervert."

"I saw you drive up Nichols Canyon Road Wednesday night," I said. "Wallis's house is at the top of Nichols Canyon on Solar Drive."

"What? No you didn't. I've never been up there."

"I followed you," I repeated, then produced the print of her license plate. "You drove from Tony's apartment on Wilton Place around ten thirty Wednesday. I tracked you across Hollywood Boulevard and up Nichols Canyon Road. Do you remember a car blowing the horn behind you at a stop sign?"

She did. At least her trapped expression suggested as much.

"April, if I wanted to turn you in, I would have done it last night. I had dinner with the cop investigating Wallis's murder. You've got to trust me. Tell me the truth."

"I might have driven up Nichols Canyon, I don't remember. But I was alone."

My head dropped into my hands. "There were three people in the car," I said. "Take a look at the photograph before you lie to me. You can clearly see three heads through the rear window."

She clammed up, refusing to say anything more. I begged her to level with me, but she said she had a headache.

The rain continued to fall on the shingled roof and roll down the grimy windows. The dark sedan still waited outside in the street. And Gene and I slouched in our chairs waiting for April to open up or for Tony to return.

Another hour passed. With April reluctant to talk, I chatted some more with Gene about his life. And he asked me about mine. I don't normally like to discuss my personal affairs, and that day was no different. I divulged what I felt like sharing and held back what I didn't.

"How is it you never married?" I asked.

He took a drag from a cigarette he'd lit and scowled in his practiced way. He wasn't as grouchy as he liked to pretend. "I've never been lucky in love," he said in a low, gruff voice. "There was a girl or two along the way, but the sentiment was never returned."

"You loved, she didn't?"

"Something like that. What about you? Pretty girl. No offers?"

I laughed. "Something like that. I'm not in the market for a husband. Most men end up disappointing me. They belch or they have dirty fingernails. Or bad grammar. And I'm afraid they see plenty of faults in me, too."

"Some folks aren't meant to find love," he said, stubbing out his cigarette. "Not everyone finds love at first sight." He threw a glance at April.

I turned to our hostess. "Tell me something, April. Is Tony in the habit of lying as much as you and Mickey?"

By five thirty all was dark outside. April had a few candle stumps left from some long-forgotten blackout or perhaps a distant romantic evening. It was chilly in the house, even for an easterner like me. There wasn't enough wood to build a proper fire, so we huddled in the dark, wrapped in wool blankets. April nodded off.

Gene and I plotted out the story we intended to write together. Starting with the discovery of the body on Thursday morning, we worked backward to the party at Wallis's place on Monday night. Then we wove Tony Eberle into the narrative, starting with the presence of his phone number in the victim's pocket. With practice, I'd become a fast writer, at least when all my ducks were in a row. I worked the small-town-boy, big-city angle, trying to create an element of mystery at the same time. Who was Tony Eberle really? And how had he gotten mixed up with an enfant terrible producer like Bertram Wallis? While I toiled away on the opening and middle, Gene worked on the Barstow portion of the article.

I read his stuff. It was good. Tight and muscular, with the occasional gem of simplicity. Referring to the broken dreams of aspiring actors, actresses, and writers, he called Hollywood "the last depot before oblivion." I glanced up at him in the candlelight after reading that line. He was puzzling over some turn of phrase or another, face twisted in concentration. I thought what a shame he'd never landed somewhere permanently. He'd had a rough row to hoe.

We reviewed each other's work and reread the whole thing, exchanging notes and corrections. Barely an hour and a half after we'd started, we had a pretty good story. Now the only thing left to decide was when to go to the papers or wire services with it.

"It's time," I said, rising from the couch and crossing to the window where I pulled back the curtains to see. The sedan was still there. "April, leave me your keys and take my coat and umbrella. Keep your head down as you walk to the car. You should drive, at least until you're out of sight. Then you can let Gene take the wheel."

"I know how to drive," she said to protest.

"Suit yourself. It's a rental. If you wreck it, can you pay for it?"

She seemed to reconsider.

I watched them slip out the door. Gene turned to wave to me, making a good show of his departure. I hung back in the shadows of the threshold, hoping our watchers wouldn't notice the switch. Gene and April made their way through the mud to my car and climbed in. April started the engine and shifted into gear. Then she pulled away, heading directly toward the dark sedan. This was the moment. Would the car follow her or stay put?

My rented Chevy receded down Bradshaw Drive and turned onto Santa Fe. I strained to see it until it disappeared from view. Then I turned my attention back to the sedan parked down the street. It hadn't budged.

∂◯

Perhaps I'd been too cavalier about trading places with April. I began to question the wisdom of my plan. Who was going to help me if the people in the sedan decided to get rough? And what if Tony came back at the wrong moment? I might end up the inconvenient remainder in the equation. I lit a cigarette and puffed away in the dark.

I dozed off sometime later. Asleep on the lumpy sofa, neck crooked into an uncomfortable angle, I dreamt that George Walsh had arrived in Los Angeles. He was staying at the McCadden Hotel, sharing the room next to mine with Harvey Dunnolt, the reporter from the *Schenectady Gazette*. George and Harvey had won over Marty the bellhop, who wouldn't even accept my quarters anymore. He called me Eleonora. And Tony was having dinner with my rivals, telling jokes and posing for pictures. I got a wire from Charlie Reese informing me that Artie Short had fired me. Then Sergeant John Millard grabbed me around the waist from behind.

∂◯

I lay there in the dark of April Kincaid's broken-down house in Barstow, California, staring at the ceiling, stomach growling, and wondered where my next meal was coming from. The closest thing to food in the house was the rusty water from the pump out back. A train clattered along the tracks outside for several minutes before passing into the night. I smelled smoke.

"Awake?" came a voice from across the room.

The candles had all burned down and extinguished themselves. Suicide by wax. I could see nothing but a faint red glow several feet away. It looked like a tiny star in a cloudy sky. Then it moved and brightened for a moment before returning, retrograde, to its earlier position.

"Are you awake, Miss Stone?" the voice repeated.

A flashlight sparked to life and illuminated the room. I sat bolt upright and struggled to focus.

The first thing I saw was a beefy figure in a fedora and an overcoat holding the light, which he was aiming at the floor. Then I saw the pair of legs. Silk stockings, crossed, their owner reclining in the same chair Gene had used earlier. I couldn't see more than her mud-splattered heels in the low light, but I recognized the voice. It was Dorothy Fetterman.

"Where is Tony Eberle?" she asked.

"You're trespassing," I answered. That didn't impress her. "I remember when you had me kicked off the lot at the studio. Tell me why I shouldn't return the favor."

"You're welcome to try," she said. "But my visit is a friendly one. Why spoil it with threats?"

"Is that why you brought Grendel along?" I asked, motioning to the man holding the flashlight.

Dorothy rose out of the chair and crossed the room into the light. Standing above me, she smiled.

"You're very clever, Miss Stone. I could use someone like you at the studio."

"I have a job." My eyes shifted back and forth between her and her companion. "Where's your pal Stemple?"

"Archie? He's in Ventura. He has a picture to shoot, though with this weather, that's going to be a challenge. Still, I'd rather be there than here. Driving to Barstow in the pouring rain was not how I thought I'd be spending my Saturday."

"Nobody asked you to follow me."

"Actually, somebody did."

"I don't know where Tony is. Your car scared him off."

"So that was his girlfriend who left here earlier with Mr. Duerson?"

I said nothing.

"If you sent her away, that means you stayed behind to wait for Tony Eberle."

"Not necessarily. We didn't know who was lurking in the sedan out on the street. I thought it might be wise to smuggle her out of here just in case your intentions weren't friendly."

"What's the girl's name?" she asked, taking a seat on the arm of the sofa.

Again I said nothing.

"You know we can get the name off the mailbox."

"There is no mailbox."

Dorothy's nose twitched. "Are you really going to force me to search property records to get the name?"

"All I know is that her first name is April. You'll have to find the rest."

"Dennis, would you mind waiting for me in the car?" she asked her man. Dennis nodded, handed her the flashlight, and left without a word. "Eleonora. May I call you Eleonora?"

"I prefer Ellie."

"That's fine. Ellie. You may call me Dot."

"I don't know where Tony is," I said, anticipating her question. "He was smart enough to run when he saw our cars in the street."

She drew a deep sigh. "Ellie, you've got to believe me. I'm not the enemy. True, I have no particular interest in Tony except for the missing script. But I gave you my word he can have his job back if he's not involved in Bertie's death."

She corrected herself, explaining that his role in *Twistin' on the Beach* was gone. But she would make sure he'd get another role as soon as feasible on another picture.

"Seems fair enough," I said. "But I still don't know where he is."

⁂

My watch read 9:00 p.m. Dorothy Fetterman finally gave up. She'd done her best to win me over, assuring me that she meant no harm to Tony Eberle or April. Or me. I was skeptical, of course. Dorothy was no fool. She could smell my distrust. But there was nothing more she could accomplish that Saturday night. There was nothing to eat, nothing to drink in the ramshackle house. In the end, she pursed her lips and announced that she was returning to Los Angeles. She instructed me to keep her informed of any news of Tony's whereabouts. That was her way; she needed my help but still spoke to me as if to a plebe.

She left. Walked out the door of the tumble-down shack and climbed into the sleek dark sedan. The engine turned over, and the headlights sparked to life, flooding the windows of the house, nearly blinding me. Then the car was gone.

∞

I knew Dorothy would have April's full name by Monday morning at the latest. That meant I needed to get April out of her apartment before then. I wanted to phone Gene to fill him in on the visit and decide where to stash her, but there was no phone in the house. It was past nine, and I had to eat something or faint. Reluctantly I grabbed April's keys and slipped into her car.

The fuel needle was pointing to E. That figured. I'd have to fill up before anything else. And I worried that Tony would choose the precise moment I was away to return to the house. It couldn't be helped, I thought, as I turned the key and shifted into reverse.

I found a Richfield station on Route 15, where a sleepy kid topped off the tank and checked the oil, wiping the dipstick on his coveralls. He was about to wash the windshield with a rag but caught himself. We shared a silent smile over that.

The Charlie Horse Diner seemed as good an option for food as any in the area, so I pulled up at the curb and climbed out. I took a seat on a stool and ordered a BLT and a coffee from the man in a spattered apron behind the counter. He was about fifty, sturdily built, with a faded-blue anchor tattooed on each of his hairy forearms. He wiped the Formica in front of me and remarked that I was a stranger in these parts.

"Los Angeles?" he asked.

"Not exactly."

"Is it a state secret?"

"New York," I said to cut the explanations short.

"What brings you out here?"

"I'm looking for someone. You wouldn't know a fellow named Tony Eberle, by any chance?"

He shook his head and pushed a mug of steaming coffee across the counter.

"What about April Kincaid?"

That name he knew. He cocked his head and took a long look at me before asking what I wanted with April.

"She used to work here, didn't she?"

"Yeah. Left a while ago to move to LA. Is she in trouble?"

"A little bit," I said. "Maybe things will work out all right. If I can find her boyfriend."

"That Tony fellow you mentioned?"

"That's right. The police want to talk to him about a movie producer who took a long tumble down a ravine last Monday."

"Dead?"

I nodded and sipped my coffee. "Tell me about April. Why did she go to LA?"

"You're cute, you know that?" He flashed a smile at me. "I don't even know who you are or what you want with April, and you think I'll tell you anything you ask. I know you're not a cop. Don't tell me you're a PI. I won't believe it."

"I'm a reporter," I said. "Working on a story on Tony Eberle, but he's been hard to find since the producer was murdered. He was here in Barstow earlier today and might still be around."

"Good luck on that."

"Can you tell me a little about her? I won't print anything I can't corroborate."

"Save your breath, hon," he said with a smile. "I got no love lost for April Kincaid."

"So why did she quit?"

"She wanted to be a star in Hollywood. She's a pretty girl, all right, but no more than any cheerleader in a thousand towns across the country. And I'm not sure she's got any talent. Wouldn't bet on it. But that didn't stop her from reading movie magazines and talking nineteen to the dozen about becoming a star. Some of the girls here made fun of her. Called her Shirley Temple."

I glanced at a couple of the waitresses across the room. In their fifties. That explained the Shirley Temple crack.

"Anything else you can tell me about her?"

He wiped his hands on his apron. "Yeah. That girl's rotten to the core. And she'll do anything to get what she wants." He leaned in and fixed me with a dark, dead serious stare. "Anything."

I returned to the ranch house in hopes of finding Tony there. But the place was empty. No one had been there since I'd left. I wanted a drink. It was after ten, and I calculated how long it would take me to get back to Hollywood and pour myself into a glass of whiskey. Two hours later, I was seated at the bar in a place called the Frolic Room on Hollywood Boulevard. A couple of fellows traveling stag tried to buy me drinks, but I ignored them. I was too busy worrying about where I was going to hide April Kincaid.

CHAPTER SEVENTEEN

SUNDAY, FEBRUARY 11, 1962

S till raining. Still chilly. I was ready to go home to upstate New York to enjoy some dry weather. This California sunshine was not delivering as advertised.

By nine o'clock that morning, I'd made some phone calls and driven April's Rambler back over to her place on North Edgemont. I roused her from bed, bundled her into my car, which Gene had left parked downstairs the night before, and transported her up to Nichols Canyon.

"Thank you for agreeing to help," I said to Nelson Blanchard.

Lucia was nowhere in sight so early in the day. But Nelson, who positively glowed when he caught sight of April, said not to worry. She could stay in their small guest house for the time being.

"She's a pretty young thing," he whispered to me. "A little underfed, perhaps, but we can remedy that."

"Please behave," I said. "She needs a hand, Nelson. And not up her skirt."

"Clever you," he replied. "You say the funniest things."

With April safe for the time being, I concentrated on my next task: talk to Bobby Renfro. A tall order on a Sunday. The Screen Actors Guild offices were closed, so there was no way to find his agent's contact information until Monday. I checked with Gene on the off chance he might know how to find him. No luck. Then I screwed up my nerve—and *chutzpah*—and dialed the Roosevelt Hotel.

"Room 135, please," I said.

"May I have the guest's name?"

"Mr. Porter."

There was a pause. "I'm sorry, miss. There's no Mr. Porter registered in that room."

Damn. Had he gone back to New York? He'd said he spent most of his time in Los Angeles.

"Could you check if he's in another room?" I asked.

"I'm afraid there's no one in the hotel under that name. Can I help you with something else today?"

"Yes, as a matter of fact. By any chance, is there a Mr. Alden in room 135?"

"This is a pleasant surprise," said Chuck Porter.

We were seated outside his poolside cabana watching the rain fall. An overhang kept us dry as we sipped our drinks. He'd wrapped himself in a robe, under which he was wearing tan slacks and an open-collar shirt with a paisley ascot.

"I was thinking what a dreary Sunday this was going to be," he said, baring his white teeth at me. "Now here we are, enjoying cocktails around the pool."

"But it's pouring buckets."

"Still. It's a pool, and we're enjoying drinks."

"Life's funny that way," I said, aiming for mordantly philosophical but probably achieving staggeringly banal instead.

"And here I thought that you weren't interested in my company."

"Let's not get ahead of ourselves, Chuck. I need a favor from you."

"You scratch my back . . ."

"Let's not ruin this nice afternoon with talk of quid pro quo. I need to locate an actor. And I thought of you. You told me, after all, that you knew lots of people in the film business."

"I'm happy to help if I can."

But his expression betrayed doubt. Perhaps he wasn't as well connected as he wanted young women in restaurant bars to believe.

"Is it your hometown actor you're looking for? Your Tony what's-his-name?"

"No, not him. Do you know Bobby Renfro?" I asked.

Relief spread over Chuck Porter's face. Of the dozen or so celebrities he might have known, eternal teenager Bobby Renfro could count himself among the lucky.

"Of course I know Bobby. He's working on a picture with one of my acts."

"You don't mean Rockin' Johnny Bristol," I said, recalling that Chuck had mentioned him when we met a few days before.

"That's right. He's got two songs in *Twistin' on the Beach*."

"And you know Bobby Renfro?"

"Well, not exactly. But Johnny pals around with him. He can put me in touch."

"Can he do it today?" I asked.

⁂

For all his flirting and persistence, Chuck Porter turned out to be a decent sort. Sure he probably would have loved to exact a price for his help, preferably with payment on delivery inside his conveniently located cabana, but not at the expense of my good opinion of him. In my experience, some men didn't care either way what you thought of them as long as they got theirs. I once asked a fellow I knew in college how he could patronize prostitutes. Didn't he realize that they were only interested in him for his money? That they wouldn't give him the time of day if he weren't paying them? He laughed and told me he didn't mind at all. After all he had absolutely no interest in them beyond what he was renting them for.

But then there were men like Chuck who seemed to care about what people thought of them. He wore a leer on his chops for sure. But he seemed more a sheep in wolf's clothing than the other way around.

⁂

Rockin' Johnny came through for Chuck. He agreed to meet me at four with Bobby Renfro at a place called Barney's Beanery in West Hollywood. A sign on the wall behind the bar declared "Fagots [sic] Stay Out," and I nearly choked. I wanted to leave, but this was my only chance to speak to

Bobby Renfro, so I held my nose and took a seat in a booth where I could see the front and side doors. The heartthrob wasn't going to recognize me, but I would know him from the lousy movies he'd made.

The atmosphere was dark, and the place smelled of chili and spilled beer. I ordered a Scotch to keep the afternoon chill at bay. It was Sunday, after all, and I'd already joined the battle, having tucked a couple of cocktails under my belt at the Roosevelt pool with Chuck Porter.

I retrieved a cigarette from my purse but couldn't find my lighter. The waitress gave me a book of matches, red with large black lettering: Again "Fagots Stay Out." I hated the idea of patronizing the troglodyte who owned that place. I lit my cigarette, then the entire matchbook, which I threw into the ashtray to watch it burn.

When Bobby Renfro and Rockin' Johnny Bristol arrived ten minutes later, they paused at the door, perhaps waiting for a welcoming cheer from the three old men nursing their beers at the counter. If so, they were disappointed. No one took notice.

I waved to attract their attention, and, at length, Rockin' Johnny spotted me. The two "stars" slid into my booth opposite me. I introduced myself.

"I wasn't expecting a young chick," said Johnny, and he winked at me.

"Yes, hello," I replied. "But actually I'm here to talk to Mr. Renfro."

Johnny's enthusiasm wilted. Wasn't he used to chicks fawning over his more famous friend? Of course I wouldn't exactly characterize my attitude toward Bobby Renfro as fawning, but he was the object of my current professional interest. I took pity on Rockin' Johnny and explained that this was business and had nothing to do with his charm.

"You can call me Bobby," announced Renfro on cue. He was incredibly pleased with himself, if the twenty-tooth smile meant what I thought it did. "I have a rule: all cute girls get to call me Bobby."

"I thought that was your name," I said, and his grin dimmed a couple of lumens.

A waitress arrived and took orders from the two idols. They studied the menu for the better part of thirty seconds. I took advantage of their distraction to consider the only two famous people I'd come across during my week in Hollywood.

Bobby Renfro had put on a couple pounds since I'd last seen him in a picture. On the other hand, the hair on the top of his head had lost some weight. The *Twistin' on the Beach* hair-and-makeup folks had their work cut out for them, I thought. Would they be able to engineer a tonsorial solution that could resist strong beach breezes and spraying surf? I exaggerate, of course. But only a little. Bobby Renfro still had a lot of charm and good looks, but the boy next door was looking more and more like the boy next door's dad.

Rockin' Johnny, on the other hand, was easily ten or twelve years younger than his pal. He sported a full head of thick, black hair, swept back behind the ears. And I could scarcely ignore his broad shoulders, chiseled chin, and bright white teeth. Yes, he was awfully good-looking, even in street clothes without makeup. It made sense in the order of the universe; he had to be handsome because he sure couldn't play the guitar or sing worth a lick.

Bobby finished reading the menu but had a doubt. Who exactly was paying?

"Oh," I said, thinking what a gentleman he was, "yes, of course, this is on me."

His worries behind him, he ordered a couple of beers and some chili fries for himself and Rockin' Johnny. I asked for a second whiskey.

"Scotch drinker," observed Bobby. No point that I could discern. Just stating the obvious. Next I assumed he would start reading off the numbers on the license plates nailed to the wall.

"Hey, look over there," he said as if on cue. "A Tennessee license plate. I'm from Tennessee." He squinted across the room and read, "MB 546."

"I'm from California," said Rockin' Johnny, disappointed to miss out on the thrill of discovery of a piece of home on the walls of Barney's Beanery.

We made some more small talk. I gathered that Johnny Bristol and Bobby Renfro had only just met on the set of *Twistin' on the Beach*, but they were already fast friends. Bobby was a fan of Rockin' Johnny's songs, he said. And Johnny liked cruising for chicks on the Sunset Strip with a Hollywood star like Bobby Renfro. The wants-to-be and the hardly-was.

"So, young lady, what did you want to know about Tony?" asked Bobby.

He'd forgotten my name already.

"As Johnny might have told you, I work for a newspaper in Tony Eberle's hometown of New Holland, New York, and I'd like to ask you a few questions for my story."

"Shoot."

"How well do you know him?"

"A little bit. We met a few times during casting and rehearsals. The producer and director wanted to see if we had good on-screen chemistry."

"Did you?"

"Sure. Tony's a good guy. I like him. Good actor, too."

"Did you ever see him away from the set?"

"Twice, I think. We went out for lunch one day after a cast meeting. I had a club sandwich. Don't remember what Tony had."

"We can come back to that later," I said. Right over his head. "Did Tony talk to you about himself? Anything personal?"

Bobby frowned. "How do you mean?"

"Did he confide in you about any problems or worries? Private stuff."

"Heck, no. He just had soup or a sandwich. Damn. Wish I could remember."

"Never mind what he had for lunch," I said. "I'm more interested in his state of mind."

"I'm afraid I can't help you there. We just talked about my movies."

The waitress returned with two mugs of beer and my Scotch. She said the fries would be out soon.

"What about the second time you and Tony met off set?" I asked.

"Wait a minute." He paused and considered me across the table. "What are you planning to write about him? What are you planning to write about me?"

I'd rushed in too quickly. Backing off, I reassured Bobby that my intentions were good. In fact, I told him, the article would probably never even see the light of day, depending on how it ended.

"You know we can't print certain things," I said. "I work for a family paper in a town that worships Tony Eberle. I wouldn't smear him in any way." Then I steeled myself and added, "And I'm such a big fan of yours. I would never write anything to make you look bad."

Bobby seemed to like that. I launched into a twenty-five-minute, three-beer discussion of what I loved about Bobby Renfro and his movies. I cited his adorable smile in *Varsity Letterman*, the movie that had inspired my huge "crush" on him.

"Really? No kidding?"

"And don't get me started on your muscles in *Lenny Goes to College*.

I cut pictures of you out of *Movie Teen Magazine* and pasted them into a collage."

"Wow. That's so cool of you . . ." He stumbled over my name.

To spare his ego, I interrupted to gush some more. "I told myself, 'Ellie, you're too old to have crushes on heartthrobs.' But I've always had a thing for cute guys with wavy hair."

"You're not too old, Ellie," he said, picking up on my cue. He gulped the last of his beer and signaled to the waitress for another.

An hour later, with five beers under his belt—now I could see where the extra pounds were coming from—Bobby excused himself to go to the restroom. He promised me he'd tell me about his next film as soon as he returned. I said I couldn't wait.

Alone with Rockin' Johnny, I smiled awkwardly at him. A couple of young girls at the counter—recent arrivals—were giggling moon-eyed over him, but he didn't care. Those two were on the line. What he wanted was what he didn't have. Poor thing hadn't said a word in nearly thirty minutes, and even that was in response to Bobby's giddy question of which Bobby Renfro picture was his favorite. And I hadn't even looked at him during my long, humiliating gush.

"You're a pretty girl, Ellie," he said with a crooked smile, the kind I like. "Can I ask you something?"

Uh-oh, I thought. Here it comes.

Johnny wet his lips, screwed up his nerve, and leaned in to pose his question. His voice a hoarse whisper, he asked if I'd ever listened to any of his records.

Johnny was quite sweet, actually. But like so many people blessed with fame, he'd lost all perspective of what real people thought, wanted, or liked. Everything had to be about him, or his head would explode. I patted his hand and told him I'd seen him on *American Bandstand* three times. I loved his honey voice and thick head of hair. My God, what was I getting myself into with these two narcissists?

Bobby returned from the men's room, eager to resume the discussion of his career with me. I encouraged him to have another drink. The alcohol loosened his tongue. Finally I had him talking freely about Tony Eberle.

"What about the second time you and Tony went out together?" I asked.

"He was going to a party and invited me along," he said, swigging his beer. "In the hills somewhere."

"Was it Bertram Wallis's place?"

Maybe Bobby had drunk enough beer to lower his defenses. Or maybe he'd forgotten that Wallis was dead. But he answered yes without hesitation.

"Why did Tony take you there?" I asked.

"I'm not sure. He said it would be a rocking party with lots of pretty girls, so I was game. I didn't even pay attention to where we were going at first. But when we got there I knew I had to leave."

"Why's that?"

"Because it was Bertie's house."

"And?"

He paused to consider his answer. "Well, I didn't want to be seen by him. He was producing my picture, after all."

"Would he have objected to your being there?"

"No, of course not."

"So you thought he might make an unwelcome pass at you?"

"Well, sure. I mean why wouldn't he want to try?" Bobby Renfro was humble to a fault. "I didn't know him well and didn't want him getting the wrong idea about me. When I saw him across the room, I told Tony we had to get out of there."

"Does that kind of thing bother you? Men going with other men?"

"Look, there were lots of pretty boys and lavender lads there. I've been around the block. That kind of thing doesn't bother me, so long as nobody tries to kiss me." He twisted his lip at the thought.

I took a sip of whiskey. Bobby gulped his beer. Rockin' Johnny just sat there, surely wishing we would talk about him.

"You say you didn't know Wallis well, yet you've starred in three of his pictures. Four if you count *Twistin' on the Beach*."

"That doesn't mean anything. He was the producer. I was the actor. I only saw him at the studio or in meetings. So that night at the party, I wanted to get away from there before something happened that could harm my career."

"So a lot of people knew about Wallis's peccadilloes?"

"Shoot," he said, bursting into nervous laughter. "Everyone in town knew about him. And he's not the only one, either. The list is longer than my arm, and the last thing I wanted was to be on that list."

"Why did Tony want to go to that party?"

Bobby shook his head. "Damned if I know. He might've said he had to meet someone there. I don't remember."

Rockin' Johnny could contain himself no more. He just had to join in on the conversation.

"That happens all the time here. Young actors and actresses trying to make some connections. Some of them'll do whatever it takes to get a leg up, if you get my drift."

I got his drift. But I still didn't understand why Tony would drag a third-rate star to one of Bertram Wallis's parties.

"When was this party?" I asked Bobby.

"I think it was a Saturday," he said, trying to recall. "About three weeks ago. Probably the third week of January."

"The twentieth?"

Bobby nodded just as the waitress set down a double cheeseburger that he'd ordered after his fifth beer.

"Any ideas why Tony would light out and miss the first day of filming?" I asked.

"I was surprised to hear it," said Bobby, and he tore into his burger with his white teeth. "He was really excited about the part. And with the great script we had, he was going places."

"Did you ever meet him, Johnny?"

His face lit up at having heard his name. He said he'd seen Tony a couple of times, but they'd never been introduced.

"So, was Tony Eberle on *that* list?" I asked both of them.

Bobby was mid-bite. He lowered his burger and, mouth full, asked me what list.

"The one that's longer than your arm. The one you don't want to be on."

He resumed chewing. "I don't know anything about that. He seemed like a normal guy to me."

I returned to the hotel a little past eight. My meeting with Bobby Renfro produced one interesting piece of new information: Tony Eberle had attended another party at Bertram Wallis's house on January 20, perhaps with the intention of meeting someone there. Probably not Wallis, I figured. He would have had ample opportunity to speak to him any day of the week. At least his phone number in the dead producer's pocket would indicate as much. I figured Tony had gone to the party to meet someone else. Who and why eluded me. Only Tony himself could tell me that.

It was too late to phone Charlie to fill him in. I didn't have much to tell him anyway. But I thought a telegram was necessary, if for no reason but to acknowledge his message of the previous day. I scribbled down an update and asked Marty to send it off first thing next morning. I tipped him a quarter and climbed the stairs to my room.

It was still raining outside. Cold and wet. A perfect night to stay dry under the covers. I had just scrubbed my face and brushed my teeth, ready to slip into bed, when a knock came at the door. Damn Marty, I thought, wrapping myself in a robe and crossing the room to answer. But it wasn't the bellhop waiting in the hallway.

CHAPTER EIGHTEEN

"Mickey."

He stood in the penumbra outside my door. I asked him how he'd manage to get past the desk clerk, though, in truth, I knew the answer. A marching band could have filed by the reception desk without attracting Mr. Cromartie's attention. Mickey said nothing. He simply stared at me with vacant eyes and a miserable expression. And his nose was broken.

I pulled him inside, sat him down on the bed, and gave him a glass of water. Then, reconsidering his vacant stare, I dug out the bottle of White Label I'd been hoarding in my suitcase.

"What happened to you?" I asked.

He didn't answer.

"Take a sip of this," I said, pouring him a finger of whiskey.

He took it without a murmur and threw it back. His face twisted into a grimace, and he nearly gagged. But then he licked his lips and swallowed a couple of times before holding out the glass for another. I obliged. He sipped his second drink slowly, still silent, as he tried to calm his respiration. I thought he was searching for the right words to say to me. Why else would he have slogged through a driving rainstorm to knock on my door on a Sunday night?

I took a seat beside him on the edge of the bed. Did he want another drink? Something to eat? A hug? I surely didn't know and had no intention of asking. I waited.

His lips moved, and I saw that he'd also taken a punch to the mouth. The tissue was broken and swollen. I couldn't make out what he'd said, but he repeated it, just as a heavy tear escaped his eye and ran down his cheek.

"What happened?" I asked. "Who hit you?"

More tears fell. His lower lip trembled, and he clenched his eyes shut as if closing the lid on a casket. The regrets of a lifetime, perhaps two, would not have weighed so heavily on a body. Whatever sorrow he was feeling, something utterly desperate and hopeless had crushed his spirits. This was a lost soul in search of a thread, a hope, a mercy. I felt the tears welling in my own eyes, and I reached out to take his hand in mine. He let me. Then his head dropped onto my shoulder, and he wept.

"What happened, Mickey?" I asked again sometime later after he'd composed himself. "Who did this to you?"

He shook his head slowly and mumbled that he didn't know.

"You mean a stranger beat you up?"

He shrugged. Was that a yes, a no, or a maybe?

"What did the police say?"

"I didn't tell the police."

"Why not? You should call the police."

"I can't call the police," he said.

"Then I will." I rose from the bed and crossed over to the desk to pick up the receiver.

"Don't!" he yelled. "Don't call the police."

I stopped and regarded him closely. He sat listing to one side, shoulders sagging like a pair of old stockings. His beautiful nose was swollen and scarlet. A rivulet of fresh blood had sprung from his right nostril and run to the top of his bruised upper lip. Under his red eyes, two bluish rings had begun to ripen, promising a double shiner come morning. His cheeks were flushed as if he'd been out on a chilly wintery evening. I replaced the receiver in the cradle and rejoined him on the bed.

"Did you get a look at the person who attacked you?" I asked.

"It doesn't matter," he said, miserable. "There's nothing you can do."

"But the police?"

He turned to face me, anger, not panic, in his eyes. "Who do you think did this to me?"

I choked. "The police? But why?"

"For fun," he said, turning away.

He fell silent after that. I wiped his face clean with warm water and a hand towel, got him out of his wet clothes and into my robe, and laid him down on the bed. I stretched his trousers and blue-and-tan panel shirt onto the radiator to dry. Then I settled into the chair at the desk where I watched him. He stared at the wall for some time, sniffling, dabbing his eyes, and sighing, drowning in his private grief. I switched off the light, but he immediately asked me to leave it on. I flicked the switch again. We stayed that way for hours, him lying on his side on the bed, me sitting at the desk puzzling over why the police would have beaten up poor Mickey Harper. And then I decided I couldn't protect Tony any longer. As Mickey slept, I wrote a long article on the disappearance of hometown hero Tony Eberle.

MONDAY, FEBRUARY 12, 1962

In the morning, I slipped out to visit Marty downstairs in the lobby. I sent him off to fetch some eggs and bacon and coffee. By the time he knocked on my door twenty minutes later, Mickey had crawled off to the bathroom. I was careful to block the bellhop's view of my visitor's clothing on the radiator, grabbing the paper bag from him instead, and tipping him a quarter.

Once he'd put some food into his stomach, Mickey looked less green. Still black and blue, but he seemed stronger.

"Thanks," he said at length. "For letting me stay."

I tried to coax information out of him, starting with innocuous small talk. The weather. Wet. The Lakers? Mickey didn't know what they were. *Franny and Zooey*? Mickey didn't know them either. I told him they were a novel by J. D. Salinger, and it was a best seller.

"I don't read," he said.

"All right, if you don't want to discuss sports or books, let's try talking about you."

"I don't want to talk about me. How about you instead?"

I considered it. "Okay. Here's something interesting. I live in a small town in upstate New York."

No reaction.

"I work for a newspaper, as I told you."

He blinked slowly.

"It's a place called New Holland."

"I know. You already told me you were from Tony's hometown. Actually, this isn't very interesting."

"But it is. It's remarkable because you're from the same little town, aren't you, Mickey?"

That got his attention. He tried to deny it for several minutes, but I told him I knew everything.

"Sorry, but you're wrong," he said, shaking his head. "I don't know where you got such an idea."

I drew a sigh. Why was this kid intent on lying to me? "Fine, we'll put that to one side for the moment. Let's talk about something else."

"Sure," he said without conviction.

I reached into the desk drawer where I'd stashed my Tony Eberle research materials and retrieved a book.

"I like looking at pictures," I said, flipping through the pages until I found what I'd been looking for. "Let's talk about how your name and photograph happen to appear in this yearbook from New Holland's Walter T. Finch High School."

There, sandwiched between Margaret Halvey and Mark Haver, Michael C. Harper, dull and uninspired though strikingly beautiful, stared out of the black-and-white recesses of another rotten senior portrait. Beneath his name, his future plans read "Learn to fly." There were no activities listed except one: *Stage Crew, Drama Club.*

I handed him the yearbook and showed him the page. He set the book on his knees and, hunched over, seemed to be reading it. His eyes ranged over the faces he'd left behind in New Holland, and I wondered what was going on inside his head. Was he reminiscing? Looking back over his past with dread? Refreshing his memory that Anthony Duchessi had been the center on the basketball squad? Or perhaps Mickey had never seen the yearbook before? He did strike me as a loner. A misanthrope, even. No big man on campus he. Despite his singular beauty, I knew in my heart that Mickey Harper had never been popular in school. Surely he'd had few friends besides Tony Eberle. And I realized in that moment that I'd never seen Mickey smile.

"That's you," I said. "You can't very well deny it."

Mickey looked up and closed the yearbook.

"Why won't you tell me the truth?" I asked. "Just once, trust me, Mickey."

"I trust you," he said. Then he thought about it. "But not with everything."

"What do you trust me with?"

"Not to murder me in my sleep. Or to poison me with breakfast."

I rolled my eyes. In other words, Mickey Harper was happy to sleep in my bed and accept my charity. But he wouldn't even tell me his height and weight if he thought I might learn something about him.

"Have you been in touch with Tony?" I asked.

"If I say I have, you'll tell the cops."

"You really think I'll turn you in to the police? You just spent the night in my bed. If I'd wanted to call the cops on you, I would have done it for you making me spend the night in a chair."

He shrugged. "I just know that I'm supposed to deny I know anything about Tony. As soon as I admit I know where he is, we're both in hot water."

"What about April?" I asked, changing tack. "Can you tell me where she is?"

"I don't know. I don't even know her full name."

My patience exhausted, I snapped at Mickey. "Oh, for God's sake. It's April Kincaid, 1402 North Edgemont Street, apartment two-B. She drives an old Rambler wagon and ran off to her family's broken-down ranch house in Barstow with Tony in tow. I went out there day before yesterday and convinced her to come back to Los Angeles. She's holed up with some people I know to keep her safe from whoever killed Bertram Wallis."

Mickey gaped at me, surely taken aback by the violence of my outburst. For the first time, he appeared unsure of what to say to me.

"Did she contact you yesterday?" I asked a touch friendlier.

He cast his eyes downward and picked at his fingernails before finally nodding. "She told me Tony was on his own. She lost him in Barstow."

I drew a sigh. "Did she tell you where she was?"

He nodded again.

"Damn it. Now I'm going to have to move her again. I don't know why I'm bothering to help you people. All you do is lie to me. You, April, and—I'm sure—Tony would too, if I could find him. What is going on with you three?"

"We're not lying to you," he said, though his heart wasn't in it.

I choked out a sarcastic laugh. "Really? You told me you didn't know April's full name, where she lived, or what her car looked like. You said you didn't see Tony Monday night or Tuesday morning. You told me you didn't drive up Nichols Canyon Road last Wednesday night." I paused for breath. "You said you'd only known Tony a short while and you weren't from New Holland. Have I forgotten anything?"

"I tell you what I have to," he said in his defense. "It's not lying."

"Can you tell me one thing truthfully?" I asked. "Was Tony mixed up in Bertram Wallis's death?"

Mickey perked up at the question. "No, he wasn't. See? I didn't lie to you about that. I told you that the first time you asked me. He didn't have anything to do with that."

"What about the witnesses who saw him at Wallis's place Monday night?"

Mickey shook his head. "Maybe he was there, and maybe he yelled at Bertie, but he didn't kill him."

"How can you be sure? You told me you were at a party with friends Monday night and didn't know where Tony spent the night."

"I said what I had to."

I considered myself a patient soul, not prone to outbursts or fits of temper, but Mickey Harper was testing me. His constant lying was making me work twice or thrice as hard to get answers to simple questions. Questions that might have actually helped him and Tony out of the mess they'd got themselves into. Mickey and Tony were fast friends, looking out for each other, that much was clear. Their ties went back years to a small mill town in upstate New York, and I doubted my recent acquaintance was compelling enough to challenge the loyalties they felt for each other. And April made the pair a trio. I couldn't guess at the nature of the threesome's covenant, but the underpinnings clearly stood on devotion, secrecy, and trust. I was unwelcome but determined to break through. My story depended on it. Tony's career might well have depended on it too.

I waited for Mickey to step into the shower before phoning Charlie Reese to dictate the story I'd written in the small hours of the morning. In contrast to the mysterious tone I'd woven into the article with Gene, I told a more straightforward tale of a young man everyone back home already knew. I related the facts. How Tony Eberle had stood on the edge of realizing his dreams, only to see them vanish before his eyes in an instant. Pulling no punches at this late date, I gave the facts: Tony had disappeared the day after producer Bertram Wallis was murdered at his Hollywood Hills home. I wrote that he'd been fired from the picture and that local police and studio representatives all wanted to speak to him. I left Mickey's name out of the article, naming him only as an anonymous friend. To have included him would have set off a firestorm of gossip and speculation back home, and, besides, I'd promised him I wouldn't.

I felt some measure of guilt for my hand in destroying a young man's reputation. Of course I knew that the blame was Tony's alone. But I still regretted it had come to this. I knew my story would cause a sensation in New Holland, but there was no more time to put it off. If I didn't act soon, someone else would scoop me on the story. It was my job to report the news. And this was news. Big news for the New Holland faithful. I was sure I was doing the right thing, even if it didn't feel that way. The only doubt in my mind was how long the hometown fans would stand behind Tony. Heroes can become pariahs overnight. The public is fickle and hard to please, ever ready to abandon a fallen star for the new flavor of the month.

"Kind of a sad tale," I said. "And it's not over yet. It might well get worse before it gets better."

Charlie asked if I had any photographs I could send. He said he could arrange things with the *Times* or the AP.

"I've got everything you need to tell the story. Shots of the studio, Tony's apartment building, and the scene of the murder. Everything except the star himself."

"Good. We've got lots of pictures of him on file. And I'll ask Norma to get a photo of this Wallis guy from the wire service."

We discussed what I would do next. I told him I'd nearly bagged Tony two days before, only to lose him in the mud of Barstow, California. But I had his girlfriend, April, stashed in a safe place. I still had hopes of getting my hands on Tony soon.

"I'll send you a wire in an hour with details on where to drop off the photos for transmission," he said. "Make sure you check back with your hotel. In the meantime, keep punching, Ellie."

"What about George Walsh?" I asked before he could hang up. "Is Short sending him out here?"

Charlie was quiet. I asked again.

"I'll let you know for sure tomorrow," he said finally. "Artie says George is going, but I'm still trying to talk him out of it."

Thanks to April's phone call to Mickey, I felt it necessary to move her from the safety of Nelson and Lucia's guesthouse. Where to I wasn't exactly sure. Before setting out for the Blanchards' place, I stopped at Thelan's and dropped off all the film I'd shot. The clerk assured me it would be ready in four hours. Then I stopped at a nearby bank and cashed some traveler's checks.

I arrived at the top of Astral Drive a little past nine thirty, flush with cash but already flagging from my sleepless night. The rain had slowed to an intermittent drizzle, which pleased me to no end. I'd applauded the weather report that came over the radio on my drive up Nichols Canyon. No rain in the forecast for Tuesday.

Nelson Blanchard met me in the driveway, still in his dressing gown, ascot, and leather slippers. I wouldn't swear to it, but I would have wagered a bundle that he was wearing nothing else underneath the robe.

"Come in, Ellie dear," he said, waving me into the foyer. "I'm afraid I've got bad news."

"Don't tell me she's gone."

"Vanished. Lucia heard a car this morning about six. She saw headlights through the window and peeked out. Your friend April dashed out of the guesthouse and climbed into a car before Lucia could put on her robe. We sleep in the nude, you see."

The last detail was neither a surprising nor germane. I ignored it and asked if Lucia had at least gotten a look at the car.

"Light color. A station wagon. That's all she could tell me."

"Where is she now? Can I speak to her?"

Nelson shook his head. "She's in her bath." Then an idea came to him. "Unless you don't mind talking to a naked lady."

I reminded Nelson that I had already seen Lucia in the altogether the previous summer in the Adirondacks. It had been an unsettling encounter, standing before such a beautiful creature who was wearing nothing but a smile. As much as I wanted to ask for her version of the events, I did not feel the need to repeat the experience.

≈

I had an idea that Tony had made his way back to Los Angeles in the night and recovered April's car from where I'd parked it on Edgemont. He must have hitchhiked from Barstow, as I was sure he had no money for bus fare. But how had April reached him to tell him where she was? Mickey. That was the only possibility I could see. I wondered if that beautiful little boy had engineered the entire visit to my hotel room to provide cover while his friends made good April's escape.

My only option was to find her again. I pulled away from the Blanchards' place, intending to check April's then Mickey and Tony's apartments for any sign of life. I wanted to wring Mickey's neck for his duplicity, but I stepped on the brakes instead. Below me on Solar Drive, a group of reporters had gathered outside Bertram Wallis's house. I thought I could see Gene and Andy in the mix, so I parked the car and went to investigate.

"What's up, boys?" I asked, rousing them both from near sleep.

Andy's face lit up like a Roman candle. Gene puffed on a cigarette.

"Millard's going to give the press a tour of the house in a half hour," said Andy. "You won't want to miss this."

"I've lost April," I told Gene. He straightened up. "The studio was looking for her and sure to find her, so I stashed her with some friends of mine. She lit out, and now I don't know where she's gone."

"A lot of trouble we went to to get her out of Barstow," said Gene, and he tossed his cigarette to the ground where it drowned in a puddle. "Where do you think she'll go?"

"I'm going to cover the bases. Her place, Tony's place. But who knows if they have other friends here in Los Angeles? Or they could be in Nevada by now."

Gene shrugged. "That'll teach you to help folks who don't want helping."

"Here comes Millard," said Andy, grabbing his tripod and heading toward the driveway. Gene and I followed.

The last thing I wanted to do was face Sergeant John Millard, but there was no avoiding it. I joined the crush of reporters that was tightening the cordon around him. Remembering his aversion to crowds, I stayed back, waiting to gauge his reaction. As a result, he didn't see me at first. But I noticed the backside of a walrus I thought I recognized. It was Harvey Dunnolt's amorphous mass displacing three other reporters at the center of the congregation. I'd been in Los Angeles for a week and had almost nothing to show for my time. And now the competition from the *Schenectady Gazette* had arrived. With the speed and stealth of a slug, perhaps, but he was there, ahead of me in line to tour the murder house. I knew I had to act.

"Okay, boys. Get your press cards out," said Millard in his officious tone. "You're going to show them to Officer Phillips here or you're not getting inside for the fun and games." He threw a thumb over his shoulder to indicate a very large and intimidating man in uniform behind him. "Let's go. One at a time."

The reporters lined up and shuffled past the tall Colored officer, flashing their credentials for his inspection as they did. I joined the procession but got shoved to the back. I was the last reporter to approach the gatekeeper.

"No sightseers today, miss," said the officer in a rich bass voice. "Reporters only."

I shrank before him.

"It's all right, Phillips," said Millard, who'd finally seen me.

"Hello, John." I nearly choked on the name.

"I didn't know we were on such friendly terms," he said. "After the other night, I mean."

I had to defuse the situation quickly or be left on the wrong side of Officer Phillips, who was aiming a menacing squint at me. Playing the only card I had in my hand, I thanked Millard for the pleasant evening we'd spent together.

He smirked. "Funny. I don't remember it that way."

"I'd like to go inside to view the crime scene."

"Go ahead," he said after staring me down for a moment. "Provided Officer Phillips here says it's okay."

I pushed past him, pausing to flash my press card to Officer Phillips. He glared at me, and, for a moment, I thought he would turn me away. But then his scowl softened into a smile, and he broke into a thunderous laugh.

"I'm just having fun with you, miss. Go on in."

CHAPTER NINETEEN

Bertram Wallis's house was one of those modern boxes perched on the edge of a ravine, one half clinging stubbornly to the hill by its fingernails, the other standing like a stork on stilts. Enormous. Probably five thousand square feet. Blond wood floors, glass and steel, and dramatic vistas. Views of Los Angeles as well as the canyon below. The place must have set Wallis back eighty or ninety thousand at least.

Beyond the entrance, the ground floor of the house was one huge room, divided into three different sitting areas, each with sofas, chairs, and end tables of different colors. All modern and expensive-looking. There was a bar on one side, a dining table for twelve on the other. A swinging door behind the table must have led to the kitchen. The south- and east-facing walls were floor-to-ceiling glass that provided the view. In the middle of each, a pair of sliding doors opened to the terrace outside. A staircase ran along the north wall, leading up to the second floor.

I joined the group of reporters who'd been herded into the dining area. Harvey Dunnolt was writing something in his pad and still hadn't seen me. Maybe he wouldn't have recognized me anyway. I'd become used to that kind of thing. Most newspapermen look right past a girl reporter. Even when they're leering at her. I slipped behind Andy and waited for Millard to start the show.

"How about a cup of coffee later?" Andy whispered to me.

"If you don't mind a quick one," I said. "I've got some errands after this."

"All right, boys and girl," said Millard, arriving in the room. He'd made a point of looking directly at me as he said it.

I risked a glance in Harvey Dunnolt's direction. Still unaware of my presence, he was standing there, listless, staring at Millard, his mouth hanging open and his eyes half-shut. I wanted to toss a spitball at him.

"You fellas are in for a treat," began Millard. "We're going to show you what we think happened, and you can take pictures and notes for your stories. Any questions before we start?"

Harvey Dunnolt raised his hand.

"You're raising your hand?" sneered Millard. "This isn't school, big boy. Here we shout out our questions."

"Sorry. I only just arrived in Los Angeles last night," said Harvey, blushing from the dressing down. "I was wondering if you have any idea of where Tony Eberle is and if he is a suspect in this murder."

The room erupted into chaos, with the boys of the press wanting to know if Millard had been holding out on them. Who was this Tony Eberle? Was he a suspect? And who was this rotund man asking the question? Millard was on his heels, trying to calm the group with raised hands and voice. At length, he managed to restore order with the promise that he'd explain everything to their satisfaction.

Gene Duerson and I exchanged a quick glance. I could read his face. Any advantage we might have held over the others had just evaporated.

Millard cleared his throat. "Tony Eberle—E-B-E-R-L-E—is an actor in the movie Mr. Wallis was producing," he said, wiping his face with a handkerchief as he did. "We would like to question Mr. Eberle about what he might know about Mr. Wallis's death."

"So you're saying he's a suspect in the murder?" shouted one of the reporters from the back of the scrum.

"I'm not saying that," snapped Millard. "I said we want to question him. He's one of several people who were present at the party Wallis threw the night he died."

"Why haven't you questioned him yet?" asked another reporter.

Millard pursed his lips and shook his head. He clearly hadn't intended to talk about Tony Eberle with the press this day.

"We haven't talked to him yet because we can't locate him."

More rumbling from the peanut gallery, and someone asked if the phone number in Wallis's pocket had been Eberle's. Gene and I again shared a look. I, for one, was glad I'd posted my story with Charlie just an hour before. For his sake, I hoped Gene had something ready to go as well.

"I'm not confirming or denying that," said Millard, for all intents and purposes confirming it.

I was sure the entire press corps of Los Angeles was going to descend on Tony's apartment as soon as the tour of the murder scene ended. I made a note to call Mickey to warn him as soon as I could find a phone.

"So you don't know where this Eberle guy is?" someone asked.

"No."

"Do you have any other suspects?"

"Not at this time."

There was a brief pause in the questioning. Then someone asked how well Bertram Wallis knew Tony Eberle. Were they "intimates"? Oh, no, I thought. Was this where the innuendo would start?

Millard didn't know. All he could say was that Tony had a fairly large role in Wallis's movie.

"Or I should say he used to have a role in the picture. He got fired when he didn't show up for filming on Tuesday morning."

Millard fielded some more questions about Tony. Address, general information on his acting career, and so on. The sergeant answered some and claimed ignorance of others. It was nothing the boys couldn't discover on their own. Then good ol' Harvey Dunnolt decided to share Tony's provenance with the entire room.

"He's from a small town in upstate New York," he said. "New Holland. This was going to be his film debut."

"How do you spell that?" asked the reporter next to him. "Like it sounds?"

Harvey nodded then explained that he was from nearby Schenectady. If he'd been hoping to impress the fellow, he failed.

At length, the questions died down, but not the energy. I could sense that every reporter in the room was itching to run to his car, find a phone, and call in the new information to his editor. But for now they were stuck. The tour was equally important to their stories. Millard led the way to the sliding doors.

"The cleaning lady came out to the terrace Thursday morning when she heard the dog barking. It seems the dog, a pug named Leon"—he paused to throw a look my way—"got shut outside sometime after the party Tuesday morning. We now believe that little Leon might have slipped through the door when the assailant was throwing Wallis's body over the railing. Then the dog got locked out when the assailant closed the door again."

"Why do you think the murderer let him out?" asked a reporter in a long coat and fedora.

"The cleaning lady says the dog lives for sneaking outside. Wallis thought the dog might slip through the bars of the railing, so he never let him out there. He was fanatical about it, she says."

"Can we talk to the cleaning lady?" I asked.

"She's here on Mondays, Thursdays, and Saturdays. Or whenever Wallis throws a party."

My brethren didn't appear to be interested in the cleaning lady, but I liked to cover all the bases. If she worked Wallis's parties, she might have seen or heard something relevant. Or maybe she could fill me in on Bertram Wallis himself. I was sure there was lots to learn about him.

Millard made his way through the glass door onto the terrace, which stretched out over the ravine about twenty feet in a semicircle of white tile. Modern and unremarkable except for the arresting views. We shuffled over to the railing where Millard pointed down into the void for anyone who cared to look.

"As you know already, the body was discovered Thursday morning down there. We measured it: two hundred and eighty-three feet below."

Several photographers, including Andy and me, leaned over the railing and fired off dozens of shots of the scene. The longest lens I had was a 90mm, but it would have to do.

"Has the coroner given any further details?" I asked. "Was Wallis dead before he went over the railing?"

"We figure so. Or at least he was unconscious. No way a person could throw him over otherwise. He was a round gent. A little like you," he said to Harvey. "Only not quite so."

"Any drugs in his system?"

"Don't know. But he didn't die from drugs."

The others were champing at the bit, wanting to leave to pursue the Tony Eberle angle. But I asked if we could see the upstairs.

"What for?" asked Millard. "All the action happened down here."

"We don't know what's upstairs unless we look. For instance, are there only bedrooms? A study? A velvet swing? This is a big house. There might be something worth reporting up there."

Millard shrugged and asked if anyone else wanted to look upstairs. A few others were game, including Harvey Dunnolt. He'd just noticed me.

"You're that Stone girl from New Holland, aren't you?" he asked as we climbed the stairs behind Millard. I couldn't very well deny it. "I thought I recognized you. Didn't think Artie Short would spend the money to send someone all the way out here."

"Mr. Short is a good businessman and a fine publisher," I said, defending the home team. "Why would you think that?"

"No offense, but he throws nickels around like manhole covers."

"He flew me out here first class," I lied. "And put me up at the Beverly Hilton. Where are you staying?"

"Just some place in Hollywood. The Gilbert Hotel on Wilcox."

"Nice place, is it?"

"I think I got bitten by something last night," he said, scratching his side.

"This is Wallis's bedroom suite," announced Millard, interrupting my tête-à-tête with Harvey.

Eleven reporters filed inside. The bedroom occupied part of the space directly above the big room on the first floor and shared the same spectacular views. Hollywood, then Los Angeles beyond, spread out as far as the eye could see. The sky was still gray, even if the rain had stopped. I stared out the windows imagining how much more beautiful the vista was at night with the city illuminated below. I thought it would be a nice place to have drinks.

The floor was covered with a plush white carpet, nearly wall-to-wall. Not quite my taste, but, as my father used to say, "*De gustibus non disputandum est.*" The bed was a monstrosity. Circular and covered with what appeared to be a polar bearskin rug and black satin sheets. The balance of the furniture consisted of a couple of plush chairs and some erotic artwork on the walls. I glanced up at the ceiling and got an eyeful of my head. A great circular mirror, centered over the bed, provided a view of the action below for those who got a kick out of watching while doing. And the final pieces to the tableau were the three tripods: an eight-millimeter movie camera mounted on one, a thirty-five millimeter Heiland Pentax on another, and a spotlight on the third. I noted a variety of lenses and other cameras on the chest nearby. Apparently Bertram Wallis liked to direct as much as produce.

"You can see Wallis liked to document his, ahem, nocturnal activities," said Millard with a grin. Humor was not his long suit. "But you boys know the rules. We don't print that kind of thing, right? At least check with the studio before you even think about it." He turned to Harvey and me. "You two can print whatever you like. No one's going to read it." Again, humor not his long suit.

"Was there any film in the cameras?" I asked.

Millard shook his head. "No. That would've been too easy. In fact, we haven't found much in the way of photographs in the house. Just some artsy black-and-white nudie pics. Nothing you can't find in a photography annual."

There were two other bedrooms and a study on the second floor. After we'd glanced inside them all, Millard announced that the tour was over. I asked if we could have a look at the desk and shelves in the study.

"Just a quick look-see. And no one touches anything."

"May we take pictures?" I asked.

He thought about it and, after a few beats, said okay.

The desk was a glass-top affair, consistent with Wallis's modern tastes. The IBM Selectric sitting front and center made me jealous. Since August of the previous year, the new typewriter had been the talk of the newsroom back in New Holland. But Georgie Porgie was the only reporter who got one. And that was a waste. He could barely type his name with one finger. I'd exacted my revenge on several occasions, though, through subtle and not-so-subtle means. Whereas in the past I'd had to pry the green plastic letter covers off the different keys and switch them around to create confusion, the Selectric's "golf ball" type element meant I could simply remove it and hide it. Or drop it from the fifth-floor window into the street to see how high it would bounce. Other tricks included switching the American type ball for a German one that had come with the machine. It usually took George a paragraph or two before he realized ßomething was öff.

Besides the Selectric on Wallis's desk, there were papers, pencils, and pens, a calendar, and some ledgers of some kind. On the bookshelf I saw dozens of bound scripts, each with its title written by hand along the spine. I figured these were projects Wallis was considering for possible movies. I snapped a photo of the desk and the shelves before we were all hustled downstairs and out the door. I rejoined Andy and Gene in the driveway to review the latest turn of events.

"Your local boy just torpedoed our exclusive," said Gene, lighting up a cigarette.

"At least we still have a head start. They've got to do the same research we've already done."

He nodded. "I'm going over to the *Times* to sell them our story now. Are you okay with that?"

I gave it some thought. What would Artie Short say if he found out I'd written an article for another newspaper? What would Charlie do? I knew very well what they'd do. Fire me on the spot and probably demand

I repay them for the cost of my trip. How I wanted that credit on the story Gene and I had written. I wanted to see my name in the byline. Damn it, I wanted a big-city readership and to have my story picked up by the wire services. Yes, I wanted all that.

"So are you okay with it, Ellie?" he repeated.

I looked him in the eye. We stood there in the chilly, gray morning atop Nichols Canyon, staring at each other.

"Just put your name," I said, turning away.

I walked to my car, and only once I was safely inside did I allow myself to pound the dashboard with both fists.

✺

I drove off down the hill, heading back to Hollywood to collect my film. Swerving down the winding road, I cursed myself for working for a louse like Artie Short. He hated me and took every opportunity to remind me how incompetent he thought I was. All the plum assignments went to Georgie Porgie; the best company cars were reserved for drunken associate publishers who drove them into lakes after bad days at the races; and even when he had to send me to Los Angeles to cover the Tony Eberle story, his hand was itching to pull the trigger and dispatch his son-in-law to take it away from me. And, still, I'd defended him to Harvey Dunnolt. Still, I'd refused to attach my name to the article I'd written with Gene Duerson, all because of a misguided sense of loyalty.

I swore under my breath as I took a curve a mite too fast, and I nearly ran over a lady taking in her trash cans from the side of the road. Slamming on the brakes, I pulled over to the shoulder and jumped out.

"Are you all right?" I called.

"You should be more careful," said the lady. "I almost fell in the mud."

Dressed in a housecoat and slippers, she looked to be in her sixties. Her hair was wrapped around curlers under a hair dryer bonnet. The air tube hung past her shoulder. I apologized and made sure she wasn't injured. Offering to help her back inside her house, I took her elbow and guided her past the trash cans. She scowled at me.

"You people drive so fast down the canyon. Don't you know how tight these turns are?"

"You're right," I said. "It was very careless of me."

"Just last week some idiot smashed my trash cans driving rashly down the road. And it's not the first time. I can't afford to keep buying new ones."

We arrived at her door, and I went back to the street to retrieve the two trash cans. The lady seemed to warm to me after that. She patted her bonnet and smoothed her housecoat.

"You're all shook up," she said, looking me over. "It's okay. You didn't hit me. Come inside, and I'll fix you a cup of tea."

I wanted to decline. Many stops to make. I turned to point to my car, intending to tell her I couldn't, that I needed to be somewhere else, and that was when I noticed the house up the hill a short distance away. It was Bertram Wallis's place. Over the lady's shoulder, I could see another home a little higher up: the Blanchards'.

"Are you . . ." I searched my memory for the name. "Are you Mrs. Hirshland?"

She cocked her head, perhaps wondering how I knew that. Then she nodded.

"Yes, I'm Trudy Hirshland. Are you here to serve a summons?"

"No, nothing like that," I said. "But I'd like that cup of tea, if it's not too much trouble."

CHAPTER TWENTY

I suspected that nothing in Trudy Hirshland's home, built perhaps twenty years before, had ever been moved or changed. From its curling linoleum kitchen floor to the worn wooden planks of her parlor to the faded drapes and braided rugs, the house oozed an air of resignation. It wasn't that the place was dirty or unkempt. It was just tired, as if the occupants had made maximum use of its rooms and walls and floors to squeeze every penny of value out of their investment of a lifetime.

Trudy showed me to the small kitchen where she indicated a chair at the white-and-gold Formica table for my comfort. An old electric stove heated the teakettle, and my hostess offered me some Gerber's teething biscuits. Odd choice, I thought. But not bad tasting. She didn't have milk for the tea, but I hadn't come for the refreshments. I wanted a look into her parlor.

Trudy settled into a chair opposite me, plugged the air tube into a portable hair dryer, and switched it on. A low buzzing noise filled the room as her bonnet inflated.

"It's okay, hon. I can hear you," she said.

"How long have you lived here?" I asked in my normal voice, testing her statement.

"Since thirty-six," she said. "My late husband, Bob, built this place with money he made working in the Inglewood oil fields."

"I was born in thirty-six," I said, trying to put her at ease.

"How is it you know my name?" she asked, apparently uninterested in my life's story.

"I know the Blanchards, Lucia and Nelson. They mentioned you when I saw them a few days ago."

"Why would you three be discussing me?"

"Let me start at the beginning. I'm a reporter from a small town in New York. New Holland. I came out to Los Angeles to profile a local boy from home who'd landed a good part in a movie."

Trudy watched me, teething biscuit hovering over her steaming cup of tea, waiting for me to get to the part involving her.

"The day I went to see my young actor," I continued, "he'd gone missing and hasn't been seen since."

"So where do I come into it?" asked Trudy, finally taking the plunge with her biscuit. She dipped it into her tea and bit off a small piece.

"Your neighbor, Bertram Wallis, was the producer of the picture my actor was in. In fact, Wallis handpicked him for the role."

Trudy's eyes grew, and a smile spread across her face. She dipped her biscuit again and took a larger bite. "Now I see. Your boy is one of those."

"One of those?"

"A homo. One of Bertram Wallis's stable of beautiful young men."

I choked on my tea.

"I know everything that goes on in his house," she continued, relishing the reaction she'd provoked. "Well, not everything, but whatever can be seen through those big windows or on that terrace of his."

I must have looked skeptical because Trudy proceeded to assure me that she'd seen things that "nature never intended."

"Don't get me wrong," she said. "I don't judge. I enjoy it, actually. But that man gave more physicals to naked young men than a doctor at the selective service. And they put on shows; Wallis took pictures and made movies. Rich stuff."

Trudy was on a roll. It was as if I'd opened a spigot and released a gushing stream of ribaldry. This was one randy old gal. Smiling from ear to ear, she catalogued some of the more debauched things she'd witnessed.

"Have you ever met Wallis?" I asked, trying to distract her from the details.

"Many times. He tried to buy my house so he could raze it to the ground," she said with a cackle. "Thought it was an eyesore that ruined his view and lowered the value of his property. I refused to sell, of course."

"Were there ever any complaints from the other neighbors?"

"About my place? Never."

"I meant about his parties."

"All the time. You can hear everything in the canyon. The sound bounces off the walls and gets trapped in here. Sometimes people would call the cops. It doesn't bother me, of course. Those wild parties your handsome young actor attended are my entertainment. I don't have a television. No reception in this part of the canyon."

"But surely you're not saying that Tony Eberle did those things with Wallis and his young men," I said, returning to her earlier pronouncement.

"Who's Tony Eberle? Your actor?"

"Yes."

"Never heard of him. Are you sure he's an actor?"

"New to Hollywood. Was supposed to be in Wallis's latest picture. *Twistin' on the Beach*."

"*Twistin' on the Beach*? Isn't Bobby Renfro in that?"

"Yes."

She harrumphed and grinned some more. "Now him I've seen at Wallis's place. I was surprised the first time I spotted him there. But he was always with a young lovely."

"So Bobby Renfro's not one of Wallis's boys?"

"God, no. That Bobby Renfro is as normal as they come."

"Are you sure about that?"

"Positive. I can tell. I see him all the time through the telescope. And I ran into him twice on the road. He stopped and signed an autograph for me. I'll show it to you."

"That won't be necessary," I said.

We fell quiet for a long moment as I reflected on the scandalous information Trudy was dishing out. The activities she'd described went so far beyond what I'd ever heard or experienced about sex. In my mind, fornication was a game for two. I didn't think of it as an activity requiring enough players for a basketball game. And while I had no qualms about certain acts in the bedroom, the thought of a sixty-something-year-old lady settling in behind her telescope to enjoy the show just made everything sound dirtier.

I shook my head in woe. What kind of story was I going to be able to write for the *New Holland Republic*?

"And you're sure of what you saw?" I asked, reluctant to take another sip of tea for fear of spitting it back in her face when she revealed some new juicy detail of the perversions that went on chez Bertram.

"Come with me," she said, switching off the hair dryer and disconnecting the air tube. "I'll show you something."

We passed from the kitchen down a dim hallway into Trudy's parlor. There, against a bank of large picture windows facing northeast, a telescope stood on a tripod. On the small table nearby were two pairs of military-looking binoculars, one of them short, the other long. I peered through the windows. Not a hundred yards away, Bertram Wallis's modern steel-and-glass Sodom and Gomorrah loomed in the mist of the canyon. I feared I would turn into a pillar of salt just looking at it. And I was no angel.

"Were you watching last Monday night?" I asked.

"I watch every night. What else is there to do up here?"

"Read a book, maybe?"

"That's no fun. I enjoy the show. And, by the way, your friends Lucia and Nelson, bless their hearts, they try their best to accommodate me. But the angles aren't right. I can't see them unless they're pressed up against the glass." She looked off into the distance, eyes a-twinkle, in appreciation of her neighbors. "Truth be told, I'd much rather watch them than Wallis's orgies. Lucia is a beauty. She gives me thrills, that one."

No, no, no. I didn't want to hear this.

"Did you notice anything at Wallis's place last Monday?" I asked. "I understand that the party went quite late and there were lots of guests."

She mugged ignorance. "No hanky-panky going on that night. Just drinking and laughing and dancing."

"Nothing else? Nothing out of the ordinary?"

She shook her head. Okay, I'd heard enough. Nothing more to learn from Trudy Hirshland. I had to pick up my film and wire it back to Charlie in New Holland. And I had to check on Mickey. I prayed he'd had the sense to disappear again. The press would be mounting a frontal assault on his door by now.

"I'll be going," I said. "Thank you for the tea and the . . . conversation."

"Wait. There was that car."

"Car?"

"The car that knocked over my garbage cans," she said. "Son of a gun ran over both of them and just drove off down the hill. I heard the tires squealing and the cans rolling."

"When was that?"

"Maybe three thirty. Quarter to four? I was in bed. Had to get up and go out into the road to pick up the trash."

I examined the trash cans on my way out to my car. Both had been dented badly, then kicked back into some semblance of their original shape, presumably by Trudy Hirshland. Too bad the license plate hadn't fallen off in the collision. Maybe it was nothing, but I would have liked to talk to the driver.

By two I'd collected my telegram from Charlie at the hotel and my film from Thelan's. Following the wire's instructions, I drove to the AP office on First Street downtown, not far from city hall, and delivered the prints to a man named Washburn. He assured me he'd received the order to send the photos to Charlie Reese at the *Republic*.

"Do you know Charlie?" I asked.

The balding man in a short-sleeved shirt stubbed out his cigarette and stared me down. "Now how would I know Charlie?" he asked. "I don't know anybody in Holland."

"No, it's New Holland. In New York State," I corrected. "Please don't send these photos to Holland."

As I'd feared, Harvey Dunnolt's indelicate question to Sergeant Millard had the unintended result of siccing the boys of the press on Tony Eberle. I doubted they'd find Tony anywhere near his apartment, but I wasn't so sure about Mickey. As I pulled to a stop in front of 1859 Wilton Place, a crowd of reporters was jamming the door, stoop, and sidewalk in front of the building. Evelyn Maynard was defending the entrance like a hockey goalie, brandishing a baseball bat in case any of the reporters came too close.

I pushed my way through the throng and came face-to-face with her. I think she was relieved to see me, if whewing and wiping one's perspired brow meant what I thought it did. She lifted her bat like a drawbridge to allow me past, and the men roared their displeasure. Once behind Evelyn in the doorway, I turned to face the angry mob. I spotted Harvey Dunnolt squashed somewhere in the middle. Andy, too, was there.

"Tony Eberle isn't here," I yelled. "He disappeared a week ago and hasn't been back since."

"No offense, sister, but you're a little too cozy with the cops and Stan Musial, here," said one of the guys in front.

Evelyn seemed to appreciate the Stan Musial crack.

"Don't believe me then," I said. "I notice one of you from earlier today is missing."

A chorus of "Who?" followed.

"Duerson," said Andy from the edge of the crowd. "Where's Gene?"

I couldn't have asked for a better cue. Maybe Andy was sharper than I'd thought.

"Gene Duerson is smart enough not to hang around here," I said.

"So where is he?" asked a couple of the men.

I exchanged a glance with Andy, whose lips betrayed the slightest of smiles. Oh, God. If I went ahead with this, I'd end up a pariah with these reporters. Figuring it was the best way to give Gene a fighting chance of selling his story to the *Times* or a wire service, I screwed up my nerve and plunged in headfirst.

"Tony Eberle's got a girlfriend," I said. "She has a place here in town, but she's run back to Barstow where she's from. Eberle is with her."

A general brouhaha erupted among the reporters. Some wanted to drive to Barstow right away. Others remained skeptical.

"What's the girl's name?" asked the man in front.

"Kincaid," I said, wondering if I was mad, putting April in jeopardy, or pulling off the perfect distraction. "I don't know the address."

First, several men at the back of the crush peeled off and made for their cars at a run. Then more took the hint. Finally, the last holdouts jumped into their cars and drove off. The only reporter left was Andy. Even Harvey Dunnolt had swallowed the bait.

Evelyn smiled. "Nice work, Ellie."

"Don't forget Andy, here," I said. "You should be an actor," I told him.

He grinned and waved a hand at me. "I kind of figured you'd want to help Gene, so I played along."

I explained to Evelyn how our friend Gene needed a little head start if he hoped to sell his story.

"And Barstow?" she asked.

"It's true that Tony's girlfriend has a place in Barstow. But they won't be there. That should give Gene six hours at least with the exclusive."

"Tony has a girlfriend?" asked Evelyn. "You're kidding, right?"

I didn't know what to believe. First Trudy Hirshland had suggested Tony was queer—though, in fairness, she didn't even know who he was—and now Evelyn was maintaining the same thing.

"It's just something you know," she said, puffing on a cigarette at the end of her long holder. Andy and I were in her apartment, enjoying a cup of tea as we discussed the near riot she'd fended off out on the stoop. "You just know who is and isn't one of us."

"That would hardly stand up in court," I said.

Evelyn shrugged. "Doesn't have to, does it? It only matters to people who are *this way*."

"It gives me the heebie-jeebies," said Andy with a frisson. I fired a glare at him. "Sorry, but that's how I was raised back in Iowa. It's not natural doing those things with another man. Or two women. It's a disease, isn't it? That's what they say."

"Andy, would you please shut it?"

"It's okay, Ellie," said Evelyn. "I hear that kind of talk all the time. It may seem unnatural to you, Andy. But, the funny thing is, it's the only thing that feels natural to me."

Andy mumbled a lukewarm apology—one of those "sorry if your feelings were hurt," ostensibly laying the blame for her offense at her feet.

Evelyn was magnanimous under the circumstances. We were in her apartment, after all, drinking her tea. But I saw her jaw tighten as she clenched the tip of the cigarette holder between her teeth. Even the clueless Andy took notice, and a couple of minutes later, he predictably remembered an appointment.

"Do you want to have that coffee now, Ellie?" he asked. "I've got a couple of minutes."

I begged off, saying the tea would do for now. And, I told him pointedly, I wanted to visit with Evelyn for a bit. After a pathetic sigh that won him no points, Andy made his excuses and dragged himself out the door.

"I have a favor to ask," I said to Evelyn once we were alone. "It's a lot to ask."

"What is it?"

"I'd like to have a look inside Tony and Mickey's apartment."

It didn't take much convincing to get Evelyn to unlock the door. She told me Mickey had complained about a dripping faucet a week earlier. This was as good a time as any to fix it.

"What are you looking for anyway?" she asked.

"I've got to find out where they've gone. I'm hoping there's some clue, a friend's phone number, something. Anything to point me in the right direction."

"Why do you even care? You've got your story, don't you?"

"Not really. There's a big payoff at the end of this mess, I'm sure of it. It would mean a lot for my career if I could find Tony."

"What if it turns out he's guilty?"

"I always let the chips fall where they may. If he killed Bertram Wallis, I'll turn him in myself."

Evelyn opened up apartment 101. This was my second visit, but this time was different. I was going to search the place. What I was doing might have been illegal, but I didn't think it was wrong. My intention was to find Tony in order to help him. I'd believed Mickey when he told me that Tony had nothing to do with Wallis's murder. Even if Mickey and April had done nothing but lie to me from the moment I'd met them. How I might help Tony once I found him was another question altogether. Did I really think I could get him his job back?

Evelyn monkeyed with the faucet while I went to work rifling through Tony's meager possessions. Starting with the large chest against the wall, I found some clothes, both Tony's and Mickey's, in different drawers. In the top drawer I flipped through some papers, bills, and scripts that Tony must have studied or auditioned for. There were some of his headshots, too, and a telephone directory, but little else that might point to where the trio had fled. I searched the rollaway and lowered the Murphy bed on the off chance he'd dropped a postcard or an address in his haste to leave. There was nothing. A shoebox under the sink was filled with some old snapshots. Photos from Tony's childhood, and not germane to my search.

"Almost done?" asked Evelyn, who seemed to have fixed the drip.

"I suppose so. Those two boys sure know how to vanish without a trace."

My search had left my hands feeling dusty, so I washed them in the small kitchen sink.

"You'd think they'd leave some clue about their lives," I said to Evelyn. "But, no."

I reached for the washcloth hanging next to the sink but, on closer inspection, thought better of it. I dried my hands on my skirt instead.

Evelyn worked a new cigarette into her holder. "I left my lighter across the hall," she said. "Hand me those matches, will you, angel?"

On the shelf above the hotplate, I spied a yellow book of matches. I grabbed it and passed it to Evelyn. She struck a light and tossed the book back to me. That was when I turned it over and saw the cover:

The Wind Up
5151½ Melrose Ave. LA 38
HO2 4841

"Do you know this place?" I asked, holding the matches out for her inspection.

She smiled. "Sure. And that just goes to prove I was right about these two."

"How do you mean?"

"It's a gay bar. What your friend Andy would call a fairy bar."

CHAPTER
TWENTY-ONE

Evelyn said she couldn't take me to the Wind Up because unaccompanied women were not welcome there.

"But don't you all stick together?" I asked.

"Not really. Mostly the boys have their places, and the girls have theirs. The Wind Up is one of theirs."

"How can I get inside, then?"

Evelyn shrugged. "Do you know any queers?"

I told her I might know one. She said that things wouldn't get interesting until after nine. Ten would be even better. And she warned me to dress conservatively. I asked what that meant. She looked me up and down, puffing on her cigarette, and finally said to dress the way I always did.

"It's kind of a rough neighborhood. You don't want to be mistaken for a lady of loose morals. Plus, that place tries to maintain an air of normalcy," she explained. "The owner's a grandmother, I hear. One of your kind. But she enjoys the company of her gay boys. The one thing she doesn't go for is swishing, flitting. The obvious fairies. Thinks that'll attract the cops."

"The cops?"

"Vice squad. They get their kicks harassing and beating up queers."

Before I could visit my first gay bar, I had work to do. It was only just after four when I left Evelyn Maynard to return to the hotel. I wanted a nap after my sleepless night, but there really wasn't time for that. I also needed something to eat. Marty fetched me an egg salad sandwich from Hody's, and I tipped him a quarter.

To get inside the Wind Up, I'd need a suitable escort. I made a phone call and, lucky for me, succeeded in finding a willing victim. Once I'd made the arrangements, I worked on a follow-up article for Charlie, this time concentrating on the Barstow angle. Still no Tony in my story, of course, but it showed a trail that the police and press were now following. And I figured it might still Artie Short's trigger finger for another day. The last thing I needed was George Walsh underfoot.

I had nearly dozed off on my bed when the telephone rang. It was Mr. Cromartie from the reception desk downstairs. He told me I had a call and patched it through.

"Miss Stone?" came the voice from the other end. "Is this Ellie?"

"Dot," I said, though it felt awkward.

"I need to see you. It's urgent."

Dorothy Fetterman asked me to come to her apartment on Rossmore Avenue in a neighborhood called Hancock Park, not far from the studio. I got the impression she wanted to keep our talk a secret from the people at Paramount.

I arrived at the address she'd given me a little past six. The El Royale was a soaring white-stone structure, with palm trees outside, high-arched entryway, marble floors, and a magnificent vaulted ceiling in the lobby. The building's only sour note was the huge green neon sign on the roof that would have looked more at home above a motel. Nevertheless, I had to stifle the urge to gasp when I entered Dorothy's apartment on the fifth floor. I'd assumed Dorothy was an important employee at the studio, but now I realized I'd underestimated just how important. She had to be pulling down a large salary to afford such luxury.

She met me at the door, still in her work attire, and led me through the foyer into a large parlor with multicolored tiled floors, dotted with several Oriental rugs of varying designs, sizes, and colors. The furniture consisted of mismatched pieces. I was no expert but thought they were Scandinavian modern. Chairs and sofas made of wood, some functional with neat cushions and others oddly shaped in bright colors, had prob- ably been acquired in different places at different times. Everything looked expensive. And there were exactly three paintings on the walls: small, colorful abstract futurist pieces featuring airplanes. I should have been able to hazard a better guess given my late mother's expertise as an art dealer, but I'd always been more an observer than a student of art.

"Have a seat, Ellie," said Dorothy. "May I offer you a cocktail?"

"Whatever you're having."

"I believe you drink Scotch whiskey. Dewar's White Label."

How did she know that? I felt a twinge of embarrassment; surely Dorothy Fetterman was used to better drink than my humble and gentle Dewar's.

"Don't fret about it," she said, handing me a tumbler of Scotch and ice. "A host should serve guests what they enjoy."

She poured herself some pastis and added a splash of water. Then she settled into a green chair opposite me. We sipped our drinks in silence for a long moment. Dorothy may have liked to serve her guests what they liked, but she was also damn good at making them feel ill at ease.

"Was there something you wanted to discuss?" I asked finally.

She smiled softly, took another sip of the milky-yellow pastis, and moistened her lips to speak.

"We've come to a crucial point." She paused, and I thought she was searching for the right words to say. "I need your help. I'm asking for your help."

"I don't understand."

"My job is to make problems disappear. I've defused crises for the studio, for actors, directors, executives, bigwigs. I've done it for years, often and well."

She took another tiny sip of her pastis, stared at the floor, and permitted herself a private smile. "Yes, I've done it well," she said. "But now I'm facing the prospect of failure for the first time in my career."

Dorothy fixed me with her gaze. Her eyes were dry, but I sensed a roiling under the placid surface. She just stared at me. Stared for thirty seconds, piercing me, reaching into my soul, it seemed. I wondered if she were reading my mind or trying to hypnotize me. Or begging for my help.

"I work for a powerful man," she continued. "He demands results. He doesn't care a lick if I've done well in the past. If last week I saved him a million dollars and public embarrassment for the studio." She finished off her pastis and placed the empty glass on the Lucite and chrome table to the right of her chair. "What he cares about is today. The newest assignment, the latest trash to dispose of. The moment I cannot deliver, I become PNG."

"PNG?" I asked.

"Persona non grata."

"But this apartment . . ."

"At the pleasure of the king. My position affords me many advantages, Ellie. But there's no security beyond today. Oh, I have savings, but not enough to maintain this kind of life. Not for long, at any rate. I have to achieve results or I become unnecessary to my employer."

"Sounds dire," I said. "Where do I come in?"

"Of course I'd love to offer you a job, but let's not get ahead of ourselves."

"I wasn't aware I'd asked for a job. I want to know how I'm supposed to help you."

"I need to find Tony Eberle."

"But you said he was a nobody. Why?"

Dorothy rose and crossed to the bar, where she poured herself another glass of pastis and water. Then she grabbed another tumbler, dispensed some whiskey and ice into it, and handed it to me.

"We believe Tony stole a script from Bertram Wallis's house," she said, retaking her seat. "We need that script."

"I know where you can get it."

Her right eyebrow arched. "You do?"

"If you want the script, I can show you where it is. But that's all you'll get. A script."

"What do you mean by that?"

"I don't think that's what you're after. And to prove it, I'll tell you right now where the script is. At the Writers Guild."

"What?"

"Bertram Wallis registered his last script with the Writers Guild. They have a copy on file. So your job is safe, don't you see?"

Dorothy pursed her lips and looked away. She reached into a silver box on the table and pulled out a cigarette.

"All right," she said, lighting it and taking a short puff. "It's not a script I'm looking for. What I really need is Tony Eberle."

"But why?"

"Because he has what I am actually looking for."

"Tell me what it is. I might be able to help."

"You wouldn't believe me if I did."

"Then you're on your own for finding him."

Dorothy took another puff of her cigarette. "If I tell you what it is I'm looking for, can you keep it in strictest confidence?"

"I'm not sure. I don't know what you're going to tell me."

"You can't print this in the paper, even in your little New Holland, New York."

"If it's something scandalous, you have nothing to worry about," I said, thinking her insistence on absolute secrecy could only point to some shocking revelation or salacious gossip. "My paper doesn't print that kind of thing."

"Then we have an agreement? You won't print or repeat any of what I tell you? My job and others' reputations are at risk if you do."

I sipped my drink and stared at her. I didn't respond. I'd already told her I wouldn't print anything scandalous and didn't want to appear to be begging. She read the answer in my eyes.

"There were photographs in Bertie Wallis's home," she said. "They've gone missing."

"Photographs of what?"

"Surely you can figure it out, Miss Stone." We were back to formality. "The photographs disappeared late Monday night or Tuesday morning. At least that's our best guess."

"So some of Wallis's personal photographs were taken from his house the night he was murdered. And you suspect it was Tony Eberle who stole them. Why not call the police?"

"We can't involve the police in this. The pictures are pornographic. We need to find Tony Eberle immediately."

"How do you know they're pornographic?"

"Because we recovered the negatives. Those have already been destroyed, along with all the other dangerous pictures. But there are some prints missing."

"And there are faces in the photographs you'd like to protect," I said, wondering how she'd managed to "recover" the negatives and prints from Wallis's home.

"Precisely. And since you seem to have some kind of direct line to Tony Eberle, I am counting on you to tell me where he is."

"But you suspect him of having something to do with Bertram Wallis's murder. Why would he hand over the pictures to you?"

"Because if he agrees, he's going to appear in a major new picture next year."

"You would cast a murderer in one of your movies?"

"Only if he's innocent, of course."

"Who's in the photos?" I asked, taking her by surprise. "It must be someone important to the studio if your job is at stake."

"Don't ask me that. I can't tell you. But, yes, there is someone in the photos whose reputation as a ladies' man we must protect at all costs."

"It's not Raymond Burr, is it?" I asked to break the tension.

A short laugh escaped her perfectly painted lips. "If only," she said. "I wish my problem were as simple as Ray." Then she turned serious again. "I'm willing to pay you for your help. But you must find Tony Eberle for me quickly."

"I have a job. I'm paid by my paper."

"I'm sure the figure I have in mind is more than you earn in a year."

I gulped. "But what if he didn't palm the pictures? What if it was someone else?"

"The offer is for the photographs. All of them. I don't care how you get them."

⁂

One of those long, sleek Jaguars pulled up at the curb outside the McCadden Hotel at the appointed hour of 9:45 p.m. I skipped down the stairs in a sensible navy shirtdress gathered at the waist by a white belt.

"How lovely you look," said Nelson Blanchard as I climbed into his car. "Hot date?"

"You should know. You're it. And I know you're pulling my leg. I was told to dress down for this place."

He glanced at me, his eyes taking me in. "In that case you've succeeded. You look like a librarian."

"Good."

We made our way east along Hollywood Boulevard, turning south at Cahuenga, chatting as we went.

"I'm really grateful you agreed to do this," I said.

"It sounded like fun. How could I refuse?"

"Have you ever been to a gay bar?"

"Oh, yes. Many times. Lucia and I play in many different sandboxes. We're broadminded, as you know."

"And she doesn't mind?"

He turned his attention from the road to me and flashed his horsey grin. "She quite enjoys palling around with queers. Finds them more entertaining than most of our straight acquaintances."

"She doesn't object to your squiring me about tonight?"

"Of course not," he said, watching the road again. "She insisted, especially since she couldn't make it. She has her usual acting recital this evening. And she suggested I bring you home later for a nightcap."

"Let's see how the evening goes. I don't want to hate myself in the morning."

Nelson chuckled. "You are a clever girl, Ellie. A shame you're as straitlaced as a librarian."

The Wind Up was a bit of a hole in the wall on Melrose Avenue, near the corner of Wilton. Not far from Tony and Mickey's apartment, I noted. Nelson almost missed the place, as the front windows were painted over, and the only evidence of a business inside was a small neon sign over the darkened door. A vagrant was camped out in the entrance of the café next door, drinking from a bottle wrapped in a paper bag. Across the street, another bum sprawled in the entry of a wig shop. Judging by the empty bottle next to his head, I figured his evening was over. We parked in the filling station next to the one-story storefront and entered by the side door.

A long bar, packed with well-dressed men between twenty-five and fifty. Dark wood paneling, quite old-fashioned, and several chairs and round tables against the wall. There was a small pool table where four young men were engaged in a game of eight ball. A short, square, silver-haired woman behind the bar looked us over with suspicion.

"Are you folks sure you have the right place?" she asked. "You look lost."

"Oh, no," said Nelson with a confidence that defused some, but not all, of the woman's doubts. "I'm a friend of Henry Dornan's. He's a regular, I believe."

She nodded. "Sure. I know Henry. Nice fellow." She scrutinized us for a long moment then asked if Nelson was a cop.

"Heavens, no," he said. "Just a modest movie producer out for a little drink and fun."

"What's your name?"

"Nelson Blanchard, ASC."

She nodded again. "And who's your little friend?"

"This is my date for the evening. Ellie's an actress, trying to break into the movies."

The bartender looked me over then said I was pretty but not Hollywood pretty. I nearly stormed out the door.

"Yes, I know. But she's a wonderful actress. I was thinking she could play the librarian or perhaps the mentally deranged sister. A blind girl. They're usually plain, aren't they?" He turned to me. "You could play a blind girl, couldn't you, Ellie?"

The bartender wiped her hands on a rag and asked what we'd have. Then she called out to other patrons and asked them to welcome Nelson and Ellie. Everyone turned and greeted us.

A few moments later, a table opened up, and we sat down with our drinks. I pulled out a cigarette, and Nelson extended his lighter.

"That was pretty good back there," I said. "I thought she was going to ask us to leave."

Nelson waved a hand to dismiss my praise. "Nothing to it. If you're a stranger, they're naturally suspicious. It helps if you know someone."

"Who is Henry Dornan? Is he really a friend of yours?"

"I've met him, but we're not friends. He's a set designer over at Paramount. And he's a terrific swisher. I figured he must be an *habitué*."

"Good guess," I said, finding his pronunciation a tad precious. "And what's ASC?"

"American Society of Cinematographers."

"You're a member?"

He blushed. "Strictly speaking, no. Quite difficult to get in. But she doesn't know that."

We cheered each other, and then Nelson asked me about my plan of attack. What did I hope to accomplish with my first visit to a gay bar?

"There was a book of matches from this place in Tony Eberle's apartment. I want to find out if anyone here knows him. Then, if I'm truly lucky, I might be able to track him down."

Nelson weighed the merits of my plan. After a suitable period of reflection, he said he didn't see how I'd be able to gain the confidence of the patrons.

"You saw how careful the innkeeper was. These boys will be even more skeptical. It's their daily routine, after all, to be careful with their secret."

"How would you approach it?" I asked.

He thought a moment, took a swig of his drink—Bourbon—then glanced around the bar. I couldn't say what he was thinking, but he was in deep study of the men in the room. At length, he turned back to me and smiled.

"Perhaps I could ask around. I'm a producer, after all."

"And a member of ASC," I added.

He laughed. "Clever you. Let's enjoy our drink for a few minutes. Then we'll order another. We don't want to appear eager."

The clientele was well behaved. And, if you weren't paying close attention, you might never guess you were in a gay bar. The men all appeared to be "normal." Straight. No swishing, as Nelson had said, and no open displays of affection. In fact, most of the patrons strutted around the place as if the hair on their chests was itching, and the scratch they were searching for would be wearing a skirt and heels.

We sat at our little table, nose to nose, trying to appear to ignore the other patrons, for the better part of an hour and two drinks. I was enjoying Nelson Blanchard's company, which surprised me, especially in light of our introduction the previous summer in the Adirondacks. At the time, I'd suspected the Blanchards of adultery, sex with a minor male, and double murder, all in the same week. As things turned out, I'd been mistaken about the double murder. And now I found myself delighting in pleasant and engaging conversation with the middle-aged man who'd wanted to share me with his voracious, omnisexual wife. She'd once told me that his bark was worse than his bite. I doubted that. I'd seen his teeth. And, given half the chance, Nelson Blanchard, ASC, would have performed perversions on my person to make Caligula blush and look away. But sitting in a gay bar in a dodgy part of Los Angeles, I realized that even degenerates like Nelson Blanchard had their charm. My affection for him was growing. Like a fungus, perhaps. But it was growing all the same.

"It's time," he said, eyeing one of the older gentlemen at the bar.

The man was dressed in a dark suit, tie loosened below his square jaw. I figured he was about forty-five. Athletic, with a full head of black hair and some gray at the temples, he reminded me of a younger Charlie Reese. I probably shouldn't tell my editor that.

Nelson stood and made his way over to the bar, where he leaned in to order another drink. Then he turned his head and engaged the man beside him in a conversation. I couldn't hear from my vantage point, of course, but the two seemed chummy if smiles were any indication. Nelson's new drink arrived, but he hadn't finished. Ten minutes passed before he returned to join me at the table.

"Well?" I asked. "Any luck?"

"What? Oh, no. Sorry, he's never heard of Tony Eberle."

"Then what were you talking about for nearly fifteen minutes?"

"This and that. It turns out we share the same dry cleaner. I've invited him up to the house next week for dinner. Lucia will adore him."

I rolled my eyes and stood up.

"Where are you going?" he asked.

"To talk to the lady bartender," I said.

It was past eleven thirty, and the crowd had settled in. Everyone had a drink in hand, so I took advantage of the lull and asked the lady if she knew a young fellow named Tony Eberle. Her expression soured, and I was sure she didn't appreciate being asked about her patrons.

"As a matter of fact, no," she said. "But I keep my boys' names and business private. Why are you asking?"

"Because he disappeared a week ago, and no one has been able to locate him."

"Who's he to you?"

I cast my eyes downward and summoned a gulp. "He's my younger brother."

The lady patted my hand and refilled my drink. "There, there, honey. Take a little sip and you'll feel better."

"I didn't come out here to be an actress," I said, building on my lie. "My parents sent me to find out what happened to Tony. We're all worried sick about him."

"And your friend over there?" she asked. "What's his story?"

I glanced over at Nelson, who was watching two young men play pool a few feet away. "My uncle," I said. "Mother's brother. He's the black sheep of the family for obvious reasons."

She nodded. "Poor guy. If families would only realize that these boys are the way they are through no fault of their own. A little more understanding and maybe they wouldn't spend quite so much time in places like this looking for Mr. Right."

"But wouldn't that hurt your business?"

"Sure. But I never thought I'd be as successful as I am doing this. I love these fellows. They're my boys. But I'd rather see them happy with their families than looking for a tiny bit of acceptance in here."

"This is my brother," I said, wiping a feigned tear from my eye as I handed her Tony's photo.

She held it at arm's length and studied it for a moment. She shook her head. "No, never seen him before. Are you sure he came here?"

"No. But I found one of your matchbooks among his things. I just thought I'd chance it."

"Hold on a sec," she said. "Hey, boys. Any of you ever seen this fellow?"

She held up the photo for public inspection. Several young men approached the bar and took a look. They passed the photograph around, and a few raised eyebrows in appreciation of Tony's good looks.

"I don't know him," said one. "But I wouldn't mind an introduction."

"None of that, Danny," said the bartender. "This boy's missing, and his sister here is worried sick about him."

Danny assumed a suitably sheepish expression and offered an apology. Then one of the men at the other end of the bar chimed in.

"I've never seen him in here, but I met him once. He was with another fellow who used to come here. You threw him out, Helen. Remember? A small kid, really beautiful eyes and striking face."

Helen, the bartender, frowned and retrieved the photograph. She handed it back to me and suggested I should leave.

"Why?" I asked, doing my best to summon a real tear. No luck.

"Because your brother was associating with a person who's not welcome here. I don't want trouble like that in my place."

"But Tony's never even been in here."

"So much the better. I'm sorry for your troubles, honey. But I can't have young men meeting rich fellows for money in my bar."

"May I at least speak to the man who knew Tony's friend?"

She thought it over for a second and agreed. "Make it quick."

I made my way over to the handsome young man who'd claimed he'd seen Tony. He was slim, dressed in a pair of gray wool trousers and a dark-blue V-neck sweater. His brown hair was relaxed, wavy, and, had I met him anywhere else, I would have pegged him for a Harvard or Yale undergraduate heading to a mixer.

"My name is Ellie," I said. "Ellie Eberle."

He waited to hear what I wanted.

"The man in the photograph is my missing brother, Tony."

"Oh," he said simply. "Sorry. My name's Phillip. Phillip Lowrie."

"I was hoping you could tell me where you saw Tony."

He glanced around the room, cleared his throat, then stammered for a few beats. "I don't remember where exactly. It was a party. I'm sure of that."

"Was he with Mickey Harper?"

"Yeah. That was his name. I'd forgotten it, but now that you mention it . . . I met Mickey a few times in here." He diverted his eyes and coughed. "And at some other places. I think we have a mutual friend or two."

"And was the party by any chance somewhere in Nichols Canyon?"

He shook his head. "No, I've never been to a party up there. It was somewhere in Santa Monica, I think."

"May I call you tomorrow to see if you can remember anything else? Maybe you could contact a friend or two who might have been there too?"

He turned white, looked cornered.

"I wouldn't ask, but we're worried that something terrible has happened to Tony. Please, won't you help me?"

"If you must. I work during the day. You can meet me at my place at six."

He wrote down the address in a Wind Up matchbook and handed it to me just as the front door burst open. Four uniformed policemen and a plainclothes detective strode in like Elliot Ness and the Untouchables raiding a speakeasy. But they were actually there to bully and intimidate a bunch of "fairies" and a silver-haired grandmother. A few quick-thinking men, including Phillip Lowrie, got out the side door before the cops blocked it. Everyone else was trapped. The plainclothes detective, a stocky man in a pinstriped suit and short tie, swaggered around the room, calling patrons various ugly names. Faggot, pansy, fairy, and homo. Then he noticed me, the only female in the place besides the bartender, Helen.

"What do we have here?" he said, sidling up to me and hitching up his pants. "You must be lost, miss. This here is one of those fairy bars. The only folks allowed in here are perverts, pederasts, and inverts. Are you one of those?"

"She came in here by mistake," said Helen. "With her boyfriend over there." She pointed to Nelson.

I didn't know what to say. If I kept quiet, the police would surely let me and Nelson go. It felt cowardly to take the get-out-of-jail-free pass. I wanted to stand up to the bullies and say I was there as a free citizen, as were the other patrons. But that would put poor Nelson in peril. He was only there, of course, because I'd cajoled him into escorting me. I couldn't very well send him off to jail.

"All right," said the cop, wiping his sweaty brush cut with a handkerchief. "You and Mr. Ed over there, get going before we drag you downtown with these Girl Scouts."

"These people aren't doing anything wrong," I said. "They're just enjoying a few drinks and some pool. They haven't broken the law."

"Get out already," said Helen. Then to the cop, "I was just telling them to get lost when you boys broke my door down."

Nelson took me by the elbow and urged me toward the side door. I looked back just as one of the uniformed cops slugged one of the patrons on the jaw with no provocation. The man—little more than a skinny boy really—crumpled to the floor like a boxer down for the count. Then I heard the detective asking the older gentleman Nelson had spoken to at the bar where he worked.

"Come, Ellie," said Nelson, tugging on my arm. "Before that brute changes his mind."

"Where do you work, Mary?" the detective repeated, punctuating his question with a punch in the ribs. The man doubled over, and the last thing I remember was the roar of laughter from the cops.

Nelson floored it. The Jaguar sprang from a standstill and out of the gas station like a thoroughbred from the starting gate. He glanced in the rearview to see if the police were following us.

"That was a close call," he said, glancing at me. Then he pulled over to the side of the road and yanked the handbrake. "Ellie, my dear. Are you all right?"

I couldn't answer him for the better part of a minute. I was struggling for air and sobbing into my hands.

My breakdown surprised me as much as it worried Nelson Blanchard. I could barely breathe for the tightness in my chest and throat, and for a few moments, Nelson thought I was suffering a heart attack. He tried to soothe me, reassure me, hold my heaving shoulders in an awkward, comforting hug. But I needed the fit to pass in its own time. Afterward I reflected on the powerful emotions that had provoked the intense weeping. Escaping a potentially disastrous arrest, complicated by the guilt and genuine sorrow I felt for the men caught in the dragnet, had certainly fueled my outburst. But it was also the fury exploding from inside my chest. Anger at the injustice, disbelief at the inhumanity of it, and maddening helplessness at having been unable to do anything to stop it. They'd punched those two defenseless men for no reason. All of it swirled in my head, clogged my lungs, and summoned my bile. My throat was tingling, my eyes raw red by the time I'd settled down enough to tell Nelson he could stop stroking my head and whispering "there, there" in my ear. I was okay.

"What happened back there?" I asked as we sat idling curbside.

"Alas, it's something that occurs all too frequently," he said. "The police break in every so often to remind the poor fellows that they are perverts and degenerates. They bust a few heads, take names, and sometimes arrest them. And, of course, they extract bribes. Why do you think they booted us out of there so happily? They didn't want any witnesses who weren't trying to protect their own secrecy."

"I can't believe this goes on in this day and age." I was about to ask where were the police when you needed them, but then I realized the irony. I opted for the ACLU instead.

"I seem to recall the ACLU fighting against this kind of thing several years ago," said Nelson. "But the police still carry out the raids. Who's going to risk his job and reputation to accuse the cops of breaking the law? This kind of law."

"How do you mean?" I asked, dabbing my nose with a handkerchief from my purse.

"Did you hear that policeman asking that fellow where he worked?"

I nodded.

"Well, that's because he's going to inform the man's employer of his subversive activities. He'll be out of work tomorrow if he doesn't pony up a hefty bribe."

I felt like crying all over again.

"The boys have to put up with the harassment unless they're brave enough to come clean publicly about their 'disease.'"

"Do you believe it's a disease? Being that way?"

He stared long into my eyes before answering with a sad smile. "No, my dear. I believe it's just the way they are. And I wish people could accept that, but I'm no babe in the woods. We're nowhere near that point. Not for a hundred years. If ever."

"Who are they hurting?" I asked. "Even if you don't understand it or don't like it. Why search them out just to harass them?"

Nelson shrugged. "Some people are obsessed by perversion. I know Lucia and I enjoy it very much. But in a healthy, participatory manner." He winked at me. "Those bullies back there only find joy in attacking what they don't understand. Or maybe they experience those queer feelings from time to time and are repulsed. So they beat up some poor 'fairies' to prove to themselves and their pals that they're not that way."

"You and Lucia have the right approach," I said.

"Any time you'd like to join us, perversion awaits."

I sat up straight in my seat, wiped my eyes, and blew my nose. I patted Nelson on the arm and promised him that if ever I decided to try it, they would be first in line.

CHAPTER
TWENTY-TWO

TUESDAY, FEBRUARY 13, 1962

The streets were dry for the first time in a week. I gazed out the window for a moment before checking the door for the paper. I retrieved the *Times*, yawned, and flipped open the paper. There on the lower left of the front page was the headline, "Producer Murder Suspect on the Run."

It was the story Gene and I had written. A knot tightened in my chest. I read on. And there it was. The byline.

"Eugene Duerson and E. Stone."

He'd shared the credit even though I'd asked him not to. Sure, he'd left out my first name. But no one was going to be fooled by that. If anyone back in New Holland got wind of it, my time at the *Republic* would be finished.

I climbed back into bed and piled a pillow over my head. Darkness and silence. I slept hard for hours, waking up several times but willing myself back to sleep. On cold, gray days like that one, I wanted nothing but soft warmth and quiet. I wanted to be alone, no food, no drink, and no dead bodies. I put my responsibilities second to my comfort. I wallowed, lazed, snoozed, and dreamt. But I didn't cry.

~

I washed out some unmentionables and hung them to dry in the bathroom. Then I asked Marty to take some clothes to the dry cleaners for me. I tipped him a quarter.

My laundry out of the way, I dressed and headed down to my car. It was already past three when I reached Santa Monica. I had no prospects or appointments until six that evening, when I planned on visiting Phillip Lowrie. I felt different that day. A little frightened and insecure after the police raid and my breakdown in Nelson's car. I'd lost all direction, and my subject had succeeded in avoiding me for an entire week. For the first time, I began to think I'd blown it. Lost the trail that might lead to Tony Eberle. Or at least to Mickey Harper. And without either of them, I had no hope of finishing what I'd started. And that would probably mean my job.

I stood barefoot in the wet sand of the beach in Santa Monica. My first glimpse of the Pacific Ocean, if you didn't count the plane's approach a week earlier that had taken us out over the sea for a moment before landing. This was the edge of the continent, I thought as I dipped my toes into the cold water. My trip to sunny California was a bust. No Tony, no story, no sunshine. Then I thought that China was possibly the next landmass in my line of sight, albeit around several curves of the earth's surface. Unless Hawaii happened to be on my course. I smiled at the thought. Maybe Hawaii was cold and gray, too. Why not visit the fiftieth state?

I knew why not. Because I had to find Tony Eberle and finish my story. I needed to talk to Mickey in order to do that. And that meant Phillip Lowrie at six. I knew I had to do all those things, because I wanted to know what had happened and I wanted to know why. I wanted to ask all three of them what it was like to be that way. The pain of being that way. The way they were. Shunned, ridiculed, pitied, hated, and bullied. Shamed and ashamed. I wanted to know if my own brother, Elijah, had felt that anguish before he died. Because what I'd suspected for many years about my dear, late brother was that he, like the men I'd seen at the Wind Up the night before—like Mickey Harper and possibly even Tony Eberle—like Bertram Wallis and Evelyn Maynard; like all of those, he, too, had been that way.

The boxy building on North Martel Avenue was only a couple of years old. Surrounded by modest family homes, it was the only apartment building on the street. I lit a cigarette from the matchbook Phillip Lowrie had given me at the Wind Up, just before the brownshirts broke in to raid the bar. Rereading the address, written in a stylized hand, I confirmed I'd reached my destination. I waited, smoking as the chilly air filtered through the open window of my car. After about five minutes, a thin young man in an overcoat appeared carrying a briefcase. He turned into the walkway and retrieved his keys from his pocket. I stubbed out my cigarette in the ashtray, jumped out of my car, and joined him before he'd opened the gate.

"My God, you frightened me," he said.

"We met last night, remember? I'm Tony Eberle's sister, Ellie."

"I'd rather forget about last night."

"You managed to get out. It was lucky you were close to the door."

He frowned but said nothing.

"I don't blame you for running. No one would. The cops let me and my friend go, too. I felt terribly guilty about it."

"Yeah, guilt is one thing I feel." He stared at me for a long moment before inviting me inside.

"The humiliation is bad enough," he said, once we were seated on a sofa in his apartment. He'd poured us each a glass of Chianti. "But the threats and insults are just too much. All I want is to be normal. Normal like anybody else."

"But don't you . . . enjoy being who you are?"

"You must be kidding. Nobody wants to be like this. It's a nightmare."

"My friend from last night, he says he likes who he is."

"He's respectable," said Phillip. "I saw him. Rich, and he likes women besides. He can pass."

"But you can pass," I said before realizing. "I mean you don't seem . . ."

"No, I'm not a swish. It would be professional suicide, for one thing. And I don't need the harassment from construction workers as I sashay down the street."

"You said you wished you were normal. But haven't you found friends like you? What about the people at the bar?"

He sighed and admitted that helped. But it was no substitute for family, a wife and children.

"My parents don't know about me," he said. "I can't tell them. They'd be so ashamed."

"I'm sorry." I couldn't find anything else to say.

After a second glass of wine and some canapés he'd warmed in the oven, Phillip switched on the radio: Sam Cooke. "When a Boy Falls in Love." He relaxed.

"Can you tell me about Tony's friend?" I asked tentatively.

"I couldn't say anything last night, but I remember Mickey very well. We were chummy for a while last summer. Nice kid. And beautiful. Boy, did the older men go for him."

"What older men?"

Phillip shifted in his seat and took a sip of wine. His lips had gone purple. "I work in an advertising agency," he said. "I've been there six months now. It's a good job. The boss likes me. Doesn't know what I am, of course, or I'd be out on my duff."

"Is your boss one of the older men who liked Mickey?"

"God, no. Mr. Reynolds is a nice, ordinary, normal guy. I envy him his regularness."

"Then what's he got to do with Mickey?"

"I don't want to go back to doing that," he said. He was on the verge of tears. "It was a mistake and the worst thing I could have ever done to myself."

I moved closer to this man I barely knew and put a warm arm around him. He struggled with his emotions for a minute before getting a grip. He apologized but continued to say he could never go back to that.

"Go back to what?" I asked. "Did it have anything to do with Mickey Harper?"

He stared me in the eye, blinked slowly, then looked away. "I took money for . . . Money from men."

I considered my words carefully. I wanted to comfort him, but I couldn't shake the image of my host buggering or—let's face it—more likely being buggered by some rich old man. A man who was probably respectable and wealthy, married with children, possibly even famous. This was Hollywood, after all. I couldn't deny the sense of shock in the pit of my stomach. I pitied the man. So respectable on the surface, but tortured by past sins just under the skin. He was miserable.

"And you knew Mickey from those days?" I asked as gently as I knew how.

Phillip nodded, sniffled, and wiped his nose with a napkin. "I met a man. A nice enough fellow, handsome and really charming. Skip Barnes. A former sailor. I was on the skids at that time. No job, few friends, and far from my family who had no idea what kind of things I was up to. They're Methodists. Illinois. God, they'd disown me if they knew."

"And this Skip fellow said he could help you?"

"He helped lots of fellows like me. Young homophiles in need of funds. And girls, too. Anyone who was willing to do things for money. But only young and good-looking people, he said. That's why he does so much business with actors and actresses."

"Who are his clients?"

"He has connections with rich folks. Mostly people in the movie business. A lot of actors. Really famous people. You wouldn't believe some of the names."

"And Mickey was one of the young boys in need of funds?"

Phillip nodded slowly. "Poor kid. Totally broke. No education, not very bright, and no prospects. At least I have a college degree. But Mickey was beautiful and nothing else. All he had was a cherubic face and one other remarkable attribute. . . . Well, you can guess."

Phillip blushed, and I probably did too.

"We never did anything together," he said, as if that were the worst thing he'd told me so far. "Not with each other. We were just friendly for a couple months last summer."

"So Mickey found a way to make some cash?"

"Skip got him lots of dates with powerful men. Mickey was popular. Some guys like to dominate the skinny effeminate queers like Mickey. It makes them feel like big shots. And the straights take out their own homo shame on the weaker ones. Sometimes they beat them up or just screw them so hard they have to go to the hospital."

He apologized for his language.

"My God, that's awful. And Tony?"

"I met him with Mickey for lunch once. And we had coffee another time. But mostly, it was just Mickey telling me about him. Tony was going to be a star, he used to say. Tony was so handsome. Tony was his oldest friend in the world."

"And he was in love with Tony?"

Phillip thought about it a moment. "You don't mind talking about your brother this way?"

I'd nearly forgotten my lie. My detachment must have seemed strange to Phillip. "It's okay. I've always suspected he was that way."

"I asked Mickey once if Tony was queer, and he said no. He was adamant about it. But I thought he might have been protecting him. Yes, I think he was in love with your brother."

"So Mickey was supporting Tony until he could get his first big break?"

"That's how I figured things were. It was kind of sad for Mickey. If Tony was interested in Mickey, he sure didn't show it in public."

We digested that thought for a long while, sipping wine and smoking. The radio was playing rubbish, and Phillip switched it off.

"Did Mickey have any other friends?" I asked at length. "Anyone else in Los Angeles?"

"There was a guy he met through Skip. Always smoking marijuana. Very handsome. His name was Bo something. I don't know his last name. Another struggling actor. I assume he's still struggling since I haven't seen him in any movies."

I somehow convinced a drunk Phillip Lowrie to call Skip Barnes and ask for Bo's number. At first he didn't want to open that door again. He wanted to forget he'd ever met Skip, but I told him some good might come of his mistake if he could help me find my brother. Yes, I felt like a wretch for lying to Phillip about that, but I was in too deep to tell him the truth now. If Skip gave him Bo's number, I might find Mickey and Tony yet.

"What excuse can I give Skip for asking?" Phillip wanted to know.

"Tell him you met a producer who's looking for an actor, and Bo would fit the role to a T."

Phillip dialed the number and listened. A woman's voice came on the line. Answering service. He left a message for Skip to call him back.

CHAPTER
TWENTY-THREE

WEDNESDAY, FEBRUARY 14, 1962

St. Valentine's Day. I was spending it alone with no chocolates or flowers. As I stepped into my skirt and buttoned it around my waist, the phone rang.

"Got it," came the voice over the phone.

"Who is this?" I asked.

"It's Phillip," he said, sounding injured. "Phillip Lowrie. And by the way, the hotel has you under a different name. Stone. Why's that?"

"I'm married," I lied. "Well, not anymore. That is I'm a widow."

"Oh. Sorry to hear that."

"Did you say you'd got it?" I asked, moving on from my loss.

"The address. I got Bo Hanson's address. The actor I told you about last night."

❧

The address Phillip Lowrie provided me was in Malibu, at a place called Paradise Cove. I drove into what appeared to be an improvised fishing village made up of all manner of trailers and makeshift homes. The one Phillip had directed me to was at the far end of the court, moored near the embankment leading to Pacific Coast Highway above. The trailer was an old Airstream job from the thirties or forties, its aluminum finish dull and scratched from years of use and abuse. I circled my car around on the access road and parked it where I could observe the trailer unseen. I watched for several minutes, waiting to see if there was any activity inside. The radio kept me company as I smoked a cigarette. "The Lion Sleeps Tonight."

A car pulled into the compound and stopped on the grass near the Airstream trailer. One of those VW station wagons that look like a box. There was a surfboard strapped to the roof. The man who climbed out of the little blue bus was tall and blond, with shaggy hair all windblown. From a distance, he gave the impression of a Tab Hunter stunt double, but as I stared more closely, I could see that he was rougher around the edges than Tab Hunter. More like a young Randolph Scott.

He grabbed some supplies from the back of the VW—groceries in paper bags—and trudged off toward the trailer. I popped the door and followed.

My knocking prompted an immediate response. The trailer was only about twenty-two or twenty-five feet long, after all. The sandy-haired beach bum stood in the arched doorway and looked down at me.

"Hello, baby doll," he said, giving me the once-over. Twice, actually.

"Are you Bo Hanson?"

"Last time I checked."

I tried to see past him, but his broad shoulders filled the doorway.

"May I come in?"

"That depends. What is it you want?"

"I'm from Paramount Studios," I said. "Since you don't have a telephone, I'm here to talk to you about a role that's come up. We think you might just do for the part."

His face lit up like Yucca Flat on a Saturday night. He grinned all his teeth at me and asked if I was funning him.

"Why would I drive all the way out here to pull your leg?"

"Come on in. I'll fix you some tea. Or would you rather have a beer? Some reefer, maybe?"

"Mr. Hanson, you should know that the studio frowns on that kind of behavior. We won't hire you if you're on grass. You're no Bob Mitchum."

Bo turned white and insisted he'd been joking. He had tea, just the normal kind—the kind from China or India or wherever they made the stuff. Would I like an Orange Crush instead?

I climbed the steps and entered the close quarters. The first thing that hit me was the thick odor of marijuana. Not recent, either. The smell had been baked into the upholstery, probably over the course of years. My second impression was the general disorder and grime of the place. The hot plate in the kitchenette was encrusted with the blackened remains of boiled-over beans or canned chili. No amount of steel wool and elbow grease was going to help the discolored countertop, pockmarked with burns and permanent stains. The floor was warped from floodings, courtesy of the tiny clogged sink and the leaning countertop. I smelled mildew. The rest of chez Bo followed the same predictable pattern: ripe odors and willful neglect of any housekeeping. And it wasn't that the place was too large to clean. Little more than twenty feet from stem to stern, yet every inch presented new horrors.

On one end of the trailer, two twin beds, rumpled and piled with discarded clothes, had been wedged into the space wall-to-wall. There were two pillows on the bed closer to me, one pillow on the far one. At the opposite end of the trailer, a small, ratty sofa sat cockeyed against the wall. Another pillow, a wool blanket, and a shirt had been balled up in a heap on one of the cushions. The kitchen held dominion over the center of the trailer, although there was nothing more than the small hot plate, the drinking-glass-sized sink, and the pair of moldy cabinets hanging on the wall above. Somewhere a toilet lurked. I knew it was there because I could smell it.

"Tell me about the part," said Bo, handing me a chipped mug stained black from too many tea parties. I resolved to let it sit un-drunk.

"We're looking for an athletic, swimmer type."

"I'm athletic. And I swim like a banshee."

"Do banshees actually swim?" I asked.

"I don't know. Maybe I should've said like a dog."

I squinted at him. "How about like a fish or an otter? Maybe a dolphin?"

"But dogs can swim, too."

"Can you act, Bo?"

"I sure can," he said. "I can act like a banshee."

"Do you have anything stronger than tea?"

A half hour later, we were making progress. Bo had calmed down, especially after I'd told him to go ahead and blast the weed.

"So what's the movie?" he asked through a curtain of smoke.

"*Twistin' on the Beach*," I said.

Bo choked on his spliff. "You got to be kidding me. My agent told me *Twistin'* 's been canceled."

Oops. I hadn't heard of that development.

"He said the studio pulled the plug after the producer got knocked off. And the second actor disappeared, too. Is that the role you're talking about?"

I fidgeted. "Sorry, I misspoke. We had a meeting about that movie this morning, and the name stuck in my head."

"Then what's the picture?"

"I've been asked not to mention the title just yet." What a terrible lie. "But Mr. Stemple will provide those details when you meet him. I've come here to ask you to have your agent contact him tomorrow."

"Sure," he said. "Say, what's your name again?"

I glanced away. "Fetterman. Dorothy Fetterman."

"What do you do at the studio? Script girl?"

"Yes, I'm a script girl," I said, envying Dot her glamorous job. It must have been a thrill to have such responsibility. And respect. "You mentioned the actor who was going to play the second lead in *Twistin' on the Beach*. Do you know him by any chance?"

"No, afraid not."

"I thought all struggling actors knew each other."

"Not me. I spend most of my time out here, especially when the surf's up. This winter the waves have been cooking."

"So you don't know Tony Eberle?" I repeated. "You must compete for the same parts. You've never run into him at a casting call?"

He shook his head. "Sorry."

"Well, I should be getting back to the studio," I said, rising to leave.

"Are you sure you have to go so soon?" he asked, his right eye twinkling at me. "Maybe we could spend the afternoon together."

I smiled. "In here? What about your roommates?"

"What roommates?"

"The clothes on the beds," I said. "It looks like you've got company. And more than one."

Bo waved a hand to dismiss my concern. "They crash here now and then. I don't expect them back anytime soon."

"Are your friends surfers?"

My questions were making him suspicious. His friendly demeanor faded, and his eyes narrowed. "Just some buddies of mine," he said.

"That's a girl's jumper over there on the bed," I pointed out. "You like to entertain girls and boys?"

"Buddies, like I said. Maybe you should get back to the studio, Dorothy. I just remembered I have to prepare for an audition."

"Do you want this job, Bo?" I asked, making no move to vacate the trailer.

He hesitated. "Well, sure. Of course I do. Who wouldn't?"

"Then do me a favor. Tell me where Mickey is."

"What?"

"Mickey Harper. He's a friend of yours, isn't he? And the owner of that balled-up shirt on the sofa. The blue-and-tan panel shirt."

Bo threw a glance at the bed then turned back to me. He insisted that it was his shirt and he didn't know anyone named Mickey Harper.

"You couldn't fit into that shirt if you greased yourself up like a banshee."

Bo gaped at me but said nothing.

"Okay. I believe you, Bo. But Mr. Stemple is a tougher sell. Maybe you're not quite right for the role after all."

"What? No, I'm perfect for it. Come on. Give me a chance."

Bo stared at me, his pupils dilated like a couple of saucers, and not from the low light inside the trailer. I couldn't be sure what thoughts were coursing through his head, but he might well have been weighing his friendship with Mickey against a potential meaty role in an Archie Stemple film. I didn't know exactly what Mickey, Tony, April, and Bo were up to in that smelly Airstream trailer, but make no mistake, that was Mickey's shirt on the sofa. I knew because I'd stretched it out to dry on my radiator just three nights before.

"You're not really a script girl, are you?" he asked.

I shook my head and treated him to a sly smile. He wiped his brow and—so it seemed—searched for an escape hatch from his own trailer. I was well aware of just how wholeheartedly I'd embraced my Dorothy Fetterman role. I relished it. What a heady sensation. And, I realized, it was more than a bit creepy on my part.

"You're some kind of big shot, aren't you?" said Bo, studying me in the close air of the dark trailer. "Kind of young. But maybe you know how to get ahead."

"Is that how you hope to impress me, Bo? By impugning my reputation?"

"Look, Dorothy, Miss . . ."

"Fetterman."

Now that he thought I was something more than a script girl, Bo Hanson changed his tune. Like a batter who'd just been called out on strikes, he realized too late that he'd blown it. He set about begging for my forgiveness with a phony ardor only a hack actor like him could muster. I thought that if I'd actually been Dorothy Fetterman, this guy never would have landed a role in one of our pictures. Yet his fawning only made me feel more like Dorothy. For the first time in my professional life, I was on the receiving end of the respect that had always been reserved for people wearing trousers. I urged myself to rein in my zeal for the farce I was playing. I wasn't Dorothy Fetterman, no matter what Bo Hanson believed.

Once he'd run through his repertoire of sad, rueful, and contrite expressions, he returned to my question about Mickey.

"Miss Fetterman, I don't know why you're interested in Mickey Harper, but..."

"Don't forget Tony Eberle," I interrupted. "And April Kincaid. I assume that's her jumper over there."

"I don't know why you're interested in them, but I don't know where they are."

As his words faded in the trailer, the door latch moved. Before he could wipe the oh-damn-it look off his face, the door swung open and Mickey Harper stepped inside. Bo slapped himself on the forehead. There went his movie career. I was going to see to that.

"What are you doing here?" Mickey asked me from behind two black eyes and a bandaged nose, mementos of the recent beating he'd endured.

"I need your help. Tony needs your help."

"I don't know where Tony is," he said, turning away just as April arrived behind him with a bag of groceries of her own.

"My God," she whispered. "How did she find us?"

"Is Tony with you?" I said.

"Dorothy, this isn't what it looks like," said Bo. "Do I still have a chance for that role?"

"Dorothy?" sneered April. "Who's Dorothy?"

"Her," said Bo, indicating me with a jog of his head.

"No she's not. Her name is Ellie Stone. She's been lying to you."

"Where is Tony, April?" I asked. "If he's innocent as you say, I can help him. Dorothy Fetterman promised me a new role for him."

"I thought you were Dorothy Fetterman," said Bo.

"Tony's not here," hissed April. "You're not going to find him. He knows the cops want to hang this murder on him, and he's not taking any chances."

"But I'm on his side."

"You're on your own side. You don't even know him. You just want to sell newspapers."

"Newspapers?" asked Bo. "I thought you worked at the studio."

"We saw your article in the *Times*," she continued. "You plastered his name all over the newspaper. Practically accused him of murdering that awful man."

"He's long gone," said Mickey softly. "Gone someplace where the police won't find him."

"Please, Mickey. Unless he murdered Bertram Wallis, Tony can still salvage his career. He can make it in the movies. Dorothy Fetterman promised me he would have a good role in a major motion picture next year. A major motion picture. Not some beach bum surfer movie."

"I thought I was getting a role in a picture," said Bo.

"Tell me where he is."

"I want that role!"

"You'll never find him."

"For God's sake," said Bo, trying to wrest my attention away from the others. "Tony's on his way to Ensenada."

CHAPTER
TWENTY-FOUR

With Bo Hanson's declaration, the veil of secrecy was torn away. April wailed . . . well, like a banshee at the idiot who'd just given away Tony's whereabouts. At the end of a stream of insults and profanity, she also finally succeeded in convincing Bo that I was not Dorothy Fetterman, I did not work at Paramount Studios, and there was no juicy role waiting for him. He exhibited all the civility of a petulant rhinoceros that had just been kicked in the rump. He clearly regretted the false apologies he'd issued a few moments before, if threatening my well-being and calling me a very, very bad word meant what I thought it did.

In the interests of safety, I stepped outside the trailer to put some distance between him and me. Mickey followed.

"What are you going to do now?" he asked. "Rat out Tony to the cops?"

I lit a cigarette and stared at the gray Pacific below as it stretched to the horizon. To my right, I could see Point Dume. A cool breeze ran up the hill from the ocean. I stood there and shivered, wondering how to answer him.

"Without Tony, I really don't have much of a story. And without a story, I suppose I'm finished. Unless . . ."

I took a drag on my cigarette and exhaled toward the ocean. The wind blew back the smoke and scattered it behind me.

"Unless what?"

"Unless you can tell me about the photographs."

Mickey said he didn't know what I was talking about. I explained about the photos missing from Wallis's house.

"Tony doesn't know anything about that," he said.

"What about April? And you?"

"I didn't steal any photographs."

"I thought you weren't even there."

"Right. That's why I didn't take them. I wasn't there. I've never been there."

I turned back to watch the ocean. A squadron of ten or twelve brown pelicans wheeled into view over the water and headed west for a few hundred yards. Then, as if on command, they began plunging headfirst into the ocean one by one. They'd dropped in on a school of fish, and the feast was on.

"Why must you always lie, Mickey?"

"I'm not lying."

"Yes, you are. You've been to Wallis's place several times, including the night of the party."

"No, it's not true."

"Didn't you get your bruises that night? Your split lip?"

"No, I fell."

I decided to tack in a different direction. "Phillip Lowrie."

His eyes grew, but he gained control over his reaction in short order. Assuming a nonchalant air, he asked me to repeat myself.

"Phillip Lowrie," I said.

"Who's that?"

"Skip Barnes."

That one hit the target. Mickey uttered a short gasp and took a step back. He glared at me with some kind of combination of surprise and hatred. Or maybe it was dread. After all, I knew a lot that he'd tried to conceal.

"Why don't you tell me where Skip Barnes fits into your life?" I continued. "How he fits into your bruises and finances and late-night parties. Tell me about how you got kicked out of the Wind Up."

Mickey's horror dissolved into a breakdown. He began to cry right there in the grass of the trailer court overlooking the Pacific. I wanted to comfort him, but his lying had exhausted my patience and sympathy. I wanted him to unburden himself and finally spit out the truth. A warm hug and a pat on the back weren't going to encourage him to talk. So I waited. Then I realized he was just buying time, hatching yet another lie for me. The tears were all an act.

"I know Phil," he sobbed. "But no one named Skip. Phil's lying about him."

"I didn't say Phillip told me about Skip. I didn't mention any connection at all between them."

Mickey wailed louder as he worked on his next attempt. But nothing was forthcoming. April and Bo emerged from the trailer and demanded to know what I'd done to Mickey to make him cry.

"I just asked him about some people he knows," I said.

"Who?" demanded April.

"Someone Bo knows as well. Skip Barnes."

Bo actually took a step toward me and drew back his fist. His face had gone purple, and his strong, white teeth shone all the more brightly for it. April stepped between us and saved me from a punch in the face.

"Who is this chick, anyway?" he roared at April. "Why did she come out here lying about who she is? And I don't know any Skip Barnes. I'm no pillow biter!"

"Who said anything about pillow biters?" I asked.

If it were possible, Bo's fury intensified, and I wondered if he would kill me with his bare hands or kill himself with a stroke. Perhaps he feared I'd expose him to the world as "a pillow biter." Or maybe he just hated reporters. Whatever the reason for his anger, he'd confirmed to me that he knew very well who Skip Barnes was.

April pushed him back as he threatened me some more. He let fly the foulest words he had in his quiver and at top volume. An elderly couple from a nearby trailer appeared to investigate the noise. Then two more men and another woman arrived at a run. Finally, a burly man with hairy arms and a big, friendly smile skidded to a stop on one of those Italian motorbikes. Bo noticed him and immediately clammed up.

"What's going on here, Bo?" asked the man.

This time the surfer's apology sounded genuine. "Sorry, Papa Joe," he said, holding up his hands. "Real sorry."

Then he nodded an apology to the other neighbors and disappeared back inside his trailer. April and I managed to convince the onlookers and Papa Joe that everything was under control. Bo had received some bad news and was upset. We would take care of him. The crowd dispersed.

In the meantime, Mickey had stopped his weeping. He might have thought he'd escaped my questions and, if so, didn't know me very well. I asked him again about Skip Barnes. April interrupted and suggested we find someplace quiet to talk.

We strolled down to the wharf below the village and leaned against the railing at the very end, April next to me and Mickey sulking a few feet away.

"Who's Skip Barnes?" she asked.

I tossed a glance over at Mickey, who was staring down into the water. "Maybe Mickey should explain."

"I don't know any Skip Barnes," he mumbled. "Never heard of him."

"Why did Bo get so angry when you mentioned his name?"

I looked to Mickey again, wishing he would come clean. I didn't want to be the one to say it. But he closed his eyes and ignored me.

"Bo went ape because Skip Barnes is a well-known panderer who arranges homosexual encounters for rich men—famous actors and directors—with handsome young newcomers."

"Bo Hanson? A queer? I don't believe it. Look at him. He's all man, that one," said April.

"Which is why he reacted so violently. Look, he denied being a homosexual when I mentioned Skip Barnes. How did he know that 'pillow biters' were Barnes's stock-in-trade?"

April still couldn't believe it. And she insisted that Mickey didn't have anything to do with Skip Barnes. "He lives with Tony. Don't you think we'd know it if he was a fairy?"

"I think you do know," I said. "I think the three of you know everything about each other. You close ranks when an outsider gets close, and you work together to deceive any and all comers. Not even Bo qualifies for your exclusive club. He's just a convenient stop in your game of hide-and-seek. Bo and Mickey both know Skip Barnes, make no mistake."

"You can't prove it, and it's not true besides."

"I'll tell you what else I think. I think Tony got into some hot water last Monday night at Bertram Wallis's party. And I don't believe he was invited."

Through the corner of my eye, I saw Mickey perk up. I had his attention.

"This is nonsense," said April. "You don't know anything."

"I know that Mickey was the one invited to Wallis's party that night. He was going to meet someone. Someone who'd paid Skip Barnes to arrange the encounter. Isn't that true, Mickey?"

"Lies. None of it is true."

"Weren't you working with Skip Barnes because you and Tony needed money? And you didn't want Tony to have to do those things? He was going to be a big star, after all."

"No."

"And the phone number in Wallis's pocket. I assumed he had it to call Tony. But I was wrong. It was *you* he was calling, wasn't it?"

"I don't know anything about that."

"Where did you get the rent money last week?" I asked.

April told me to lay off.

"And what about you?" I asked her.

"What?"

"How well do you know Skip Barnes?"

"I just asked you who he was. I don't know him. And, in case you haven't noticed, I'm not a homosexual. Not even a lesbian."

"Skip Barnes is a procurer of boys and girls. He'll broker a deal for anyone who wants sex."

"Are you calling me a whore?" she demanded.

"I'm asking if you know a man named Skip Barnes."

April seethed, struggling to control her rage.

"What if you looked for the person who actually murdered Wallis instead of accusing us of prostitution?"

"Can I believe you that Tony had nothing to do with Wallis's murder?"

"Yes."

"And what about you and Mickey? Did you have any reason to want Wallis dead?"

"Are you going to tell the cops Tony's running to Mexico?" she asked, ignoring my question.

"Why would I do that?"

"Because you're a nosy reporter who wants to get her story no matter who you hurt in the process. You'll print it in your paper, and the police will know where he is."

"I don't print anything without corroboration," I said. "And I'm not so sure Tony is on his way to Mexico anyway."

She took Mickey by the hand and began leading him back to shore. "Tony is innocent," she said over her shoulder as they went. "And so are Mickey and me."

"Then tell me who you think killed Bertram Wallis."

She stopped and turned around to face me, staring me down for a long moment before responding. "Anyone who ever met him."

I watched them go until they disappeared behind some trailers. Mickey didn't look back, didn't say good-bye. I couldn't really blame him. I'd accused him of turning tricks with men, after all. And, with April's help, he'd succeeded once more in avoiding my questions with his lies and silence.

Driving back to Hollywood, I gave myself plenty of grief for worrying about Tony Eberle's career. What did I care if he'd mucked things up for himself by hobnobbing with "inverts and perverts"? Why did I feel the desire to protect him from his own poor choices? Was he guilty of murder? Things certainly looked bad for the handsome young actor, but somehow I believed Mickey's professions of Tony's innocence. Maybe I wanted a happy ending for the story I'd been sent to write. Or maybe I just didn't want to be the one to deliver New Holland its punch in the gut, deserved or otherwise. It was Tony Eberle, after all, who'd taken a powder, not me.

My priority was to bring home the story of what had happened to the golden boy. And if he was a murderer, too bad for him and his loved ones. I didn't script these things. I only reported them.

I dragged myself into the lobby of the McCadden Hotel a little after five and headed up to my room. A voice called to me from across the lobby as I mounted the stairs.

"You're a hard gal to find."

CHAPTER
TWENTY-FIVE

I turned to see Dorothy Fetterman standing there in a smartly tailored green suit. A frisson of shame tripped over my shoulders and down my spine. What if she'd found out about my impersonation of her with Bo Hanson? Surely it couldn't have gotten back to her so quickly. But if it had, what would I say to her? How would I explain?

Calm down, I urged myself, drawing a breath. *She can't possibly find out.* How long had she been waiting for me, anyway? I couldn't say. But, as always, she was impeccably turned out, her face made up and not a hair out of place.

"Where have you been all day?" she asked.

"Trying to find your Tony Eberle for you."

"So now he's mine?"

"You're very keen on locating him, after all."

"I thought you were looking for him as well."

"Yes," I said. "But my motivations are different from yours."

She smirked at me. "You're not going to tell me that your intentions are purely altruistic, are you? I think you're as self-motivated as I."

I noticed Mr. Cromartie at the front desk. With nothing else to distract himself, he appeared to be listening in on our conversation. I motioned to Dorothy to follow me up to my room. Once safely away from eager ears, I ditched my handbag on the bed and reached for the bottle of Scotch.

"Will you join me?" I asked.

"It's been one of those days," she said. "I won't say no."

I poured her a stiff drink, and she took it.

"So have you made any progress?"

"Not exactly," I said. "Tony's spooked. He doesn't want to be found."

Dorothy wasn't happy with the news. "What about his friends?"

"His friends do nothing but lie to me."

Dorothy drew a short sigh. Despite the protestations I'd made to myself, I did want to impress her. There seemed to be a rout on my stock, so I decided to challenge her. She was asking me for my help, after all, not the other way around.

"Why are you relying on me to find him? You don't know me. Maybe I'm not up to the task."

"I'm not putting all my eggs in your basket. I've got my own people looking for him as well. You haven't forgotten our little visit to Barstow, have you?"

"Any luck?"

"We have some leads to follow. But since you have a connection to him, I'm expecting you to produce results."

I thought this was the moment to play a new card. I told her that Tony's friends were claiming he'd run off to Mexico.

"Mexico?"

"For what it's worth, I don't believe he's gone anywhere."

She stared at me for a long moment, took a sip of her drink, then smoothed her skirt over her knees as I'd seen her do before.

"What makes you think he hasn't gone to Mexico?"

"No money. No means to get there."

"Let's hope not," she said, as if it had been my job to make sure Tony Eberle didn't leave the country. "What about my photographs?" she continued. "I don't suppose you've made any progress in locating those."

I shook my head. "Nothing yet. I'm hoping Tony will be able to help on that score."

Dorothy frowned. I pegged her for one of those executives who offered you one chance to prove your worth, then gave up on you with disappointed resignation if you didn't deliver right out of the chute. But in this case, her frustration was unwarranted, at least to my mind. I'd managed to track down Tony's slippery friends while her men could not, drawing a line, not from A to B, but from A to D. The fact that I hadn't put my hands on Tony's shoulder and brought him back to Dorothy was too bad, but not something I could solve in that moment. Still, she had a knack of making me feel like a failure.

"The roommate swears Tony didn't steal any photographs from Wallis's place."

"Then all is right with the world," said Dorothy with a sneer. "No need to worry because some pretty boy assured you that his sticky-fingered roommate is a paragon of virtue. I feel quite let down by you, Ellie. I pegged you for a competent girl. One I might like to hire to work for me."

She reached into her purse to retrieve a cigarette. She lit up, inhaled deeply, and exhaled the smoke in my direction, almost as if she were trying to make me disappear in the fog.

"There's no avoiding it," she said, waving her cigarette at me. "You'll simply have to go to Mexico to retrieve the pictures."

"I'm not going to Mexico."

"I beg your pardon?"

"I said I'm not going to Mexico. I don't work for you."

A long moment of silence ensued. Dorothy was a guest in my room, after all, and she must have realized for the first time that she couldn't exactly dictate terms. She needed me more than I needed her. Her expression softened a touch, and I thought I might just have found the right tack. She clearly disliked doormats.

"Of course you're right," she said, tapping her ash into a nearby tray. "Where do you think he is?"

With the exception of Nelson Blanchard, I hadn't met anyone in Hollywood I could trust. Not Archie Stemple, Sergeant John Millard, Andy Blaine, or even Gene Duerson. Sure, Gene had been fair and generous with the shared credit on our story, but he was out for himself just like everybody else. April Kincaid hoarded the truth as if it were gold, and I was sure Mickey Harper could lie his way past a troll guarding a bridge better than any billy goat. But Dorothy Fetterman surpassed them all when it came to raising my doubts. She figured at the very top of my list of double-dealers.

Tony Eberle hadn't run to Mexico, I was certain. How would he have managed it? He had no money, and neither did his friends. Another thing I knew for sure was that four people had slept in Bo Hanson's trailer the previous night. Three in the two beds and one on the sofa across the room. The number of pillows. Four in all. And despite Bo's convincing betrayal of Tony's whereabouts, I was confident Tony was still flopping in the Malibu trailer. After more than a week of tracking him, I thought I just might be able to catch him unawares. His friends probably felt safe after feeding me the lie about Mexico. If Tony was going to surface, this would be the night.

So I asked myself if I could trust Dorothy with the information about the Malibu hideout. And could she be of any use to me? Perhaps. If she were true to her word and gave Tony Eberle a juicy role in a big picture the next year, that could only help my career. Was that enough reason to let her in on my hunch? I couldn't say, but it was better than going back to New Holland with nothing more than a golden-boy-craps-out-and-goes-to-jail story. Yes, I wanted Tony to make it big. And Dorothy could help me with that.

But, at the same time, I also realized that if I told Dorothy my suspicions, she'd have a gang of Teamsters lifting Bo Hanson's trailer off the ground and shaking out its contents like pennies from a piggy bank in no time flat. I couldn't risk it. I needed to take Dorothy into my confidence, but couldn't let her know where we were going until we got there.

"Where do you think he is?" she repeated.

"I won't tell you," I said. "But I'll show you."

⁂

Dorothy dialed her service to retrieve messages. Then she asked if I'd mind if she called Archie Stemple. It was urgent. I nodded.

Suspecting she might pull some kind of trick, I stayed close at hand as she spoke to Stemple, making sure she knew I could hear every word. She listened for a bit, then sighed and rubbed the bridge of her nose.

"Yes, Archie, I know all about it and will take care of it in a couple of hours." She paused and listened some more. "Yes, I promise. Just follow the instructions I gave you, and this will all blow over."

"Trouble?" I asked once she'd hung up the receiver.

"What else?"

"Care to share your woes?"

"You know I can't do that. It's a confidential matter."

⁂

"Tell me about yourself," said Dorothy as we motored west on Sunset Boulevard. "Why are you playing at this reporter game? Why aren't you married?"

"I'm not playing at being a reporter. It's my job. And I'm pretty good at it."

"You still haven't managed to find Tony Eberle," she said.

"Have your men found him? It seems that I've made more progress than they have."

That quieted her for a moment, but she refused to admit defeat.

"Where are we going?" she asked. "You can tell me now that I have no access to a telephone."

"Malibu."

"Nighttime surfing?"

"If you like. But I'm taking you to Tony Eberle."

With my eyes on the road, I couldn't gauge her reaction, but she probably hadn't moved a muscle. She was calculating, though. Considering scenarios and options as I drove. Formulating new strategies and contingencies.

Then she repeated her earlier question. Why wasn't I married?

"For starters, no one's asked. And for seconds, I haven't met anyone I'd like to marry. What about you?"

"Turn here," she said. "Take La Cienega to Wilshire then turn right."

"But I plotted our course using the Thomas guide, like a proper Angelino."

"That's fine, but I know which streets are busy and which are not. Turn left then right on Wilshire. We'll make it to Santa Monica in no time on San Vicente."

I flicked on the turn signal and followed orders. New Yorkers didn't drive this way. It was all avenues and perpendicular streets, north, south, east, and west. Easy. And it was always a cabbie making the decisions.

"You didn't answer my question," I said.

"Of course I didn't answer your question."

"Why not?"

"I'm not discussing my life with you," she said, and just as dismissive as it sounds.

I pulled to a stop at a red light and stared at her. She was looking straight through the windshield, her eyes impassive, inscrutable. I watched her for a long moment. If she'd meant to discourage my curiosity with her curt answer, she'd failed. Why wasn't she married? What had made Dorothy Fetterman the powerful, intimidating woman she'd become? Was she happy? Had she wished for something different in life? Or had she become exactly what she'd wanted to be?

"The light's changed," she said.

I turned my attention back to the road and drove off, resigned to make the rest of the trip to Malibu without another word. But Dorothy resumed our conversation as if nothing had happened.

"How did you track down Tony's friends when my boys couldn't?" she asked.

"Maybe I worked twice as hard as they did. Or I'm twice as smart."

"Maybe. But how did you find them?"

"I found a matchbook in Tony's apartment."

"You got into his apartment?" she asked. This was the first real surprise I'd managed to provoke in her. "How?"

"A girl has to have some secrets," I said.

"Fine. Tell me about this matchbook."

"It was from a small place called the Wind Up. On Melrose near Wilton."

"But . . . that's a queer bar, isn't it?"

"A gay bar, yes."

"But Tony's not queer. Why would he have a matchbook from such a place?"

"His roommate, Mickey Harper," I said. "He used to frequent the place until they threw him out. They claimed he was soliciting."

"So how did the gay bar lead you to Malibu?"

"I met a man there who knew Mickey. He put me in touch with another man—an actor—who was mixed up in the same racket as Mickey. And he's in Malibu."

Dorothy seemed to be putting the information in order in her head. Her mien darkened as she considered what I'd just told her.

"What's the name of this actor?" she asked.

Perhaps she was worried it was one of Paramount's young up-and-comers involved in a potential sex scandal. I knew that wasn't the case. Bo Hanson had a dim future in the movies, so I gave her his name.

"Never heard of him." She seemed relieved. One problem she wouldn't have to fix.

"He's heard of you," I said. "And he wants a part in one of Archie Stemple's pictures."

"*Twistin' on the Beach* was canned yesterday. It was cursed. Once Bertie died, it was just a matter of time."

"Really? That's too bad," I said, feigning surprise. I hesitated before telling her a slightly modified version of my meeting with the surfer. "And I might have told Bo Hanson that I worked for you when I saw him this morning."

"Bo Hanson?" she asked. "I think I know him after all. Is he that muscle-head beach bum? Blond, good-looking, but oh so dumb?"

"That's him. Straight out of central casting."

"Don't say that. Nobody says 'central casting.' Still, I suppose I must congratulate you on getting as far as you have. My boys turned up a boarding house where Tony stayed last year and a couple of unpaid dry-cleaning bills. Nothing helpful. And for what I pay them . . ."

"Tony's girlfriend, April, and his roommate, Mickey, both spent last night with this Bo Hanson in Malibu," I explained, relishing my little victory. "I believe Tony slept there as well."

"Have you considered that maybe this Mickey met a rich old man and scraped together some pocket change? Enough to get Tony to Mexico?"

Not with a broken nose and two black eyes. I thought it more likely that the trio was waiting for the dust to clear so they could slip away somewhere safe.

"If you think I'm wrong, I can turn around and take you back," I said, dusting off some bravado.

She told me to carry on. But as I drove into the heart of Beverly Hills, doubts began to eat into my confidence. I tried to disguise my concerns from Dorothy, but she wasn't watching me anyway. She simply stared out the windshield and plotted her silent machinations. What if I was wrong and Tony was in Ensenada at that very moment working his way down to the worm at the bottom of a tequila bottle? In my professional life, I'd always found it better to brag about being right only once you'd proven it.

We made our way through Westwood and onto San Vicente Boulevard in silence, except when Dorothy gave me directions. Once we reached Santa Monica, she asked me if I didn't want to listen to the radio to pass the time. Emboldened by the success achieved when I'd stood my ground, I told her I preferred silence or conversation to the disposable music of Rockin' Johnny Bristol.

"You know he had a small part in *Twistin' on the Beach*," she said with just a touch of amusement in her voice. "Before we pulled the plug, that is."

"Yes, I know. I had a long chat with him and Bobby Renfro the other day."

"You met Bobby Renfro?" she asked.

I explained that both Bobby Renfro and Rockin' Johnny had been helpful. "Bobby told me he'd been to a party with Tony in the hills. I thought that was a coincidence. But he also lied to me about how many times he'd been to Wallis's house."

"I'm going to ask you to tread carefully," said Dorothy.

I'd come to understand that in all her dealings with me, she'd stuck to a strategy that aimed to sap my self-assurance. She'd gained and maintained the upper hand that way. The confrontational, dismissive tone she'd been employing to keep me off-balance—the one that questioned my competence and cleverness—had vanished, replaced now by a warning.

"Bobby Renfro may not be the brightest star in the galaxy," she continued, "but we have plans for him. I don't want to have to squelch some filthy gossip about him. And I will squelch it. Make no mistake."

"I believe you. But I'm not interested in Bobby Renfro. Unless he's mixed up somehow in this whole thing."

"Then we understand each other?"

"Provided our interests don't conflict."

I turned onto Pacific Coast Highway and pointed the car toward Malibu. Traffic was light.

"You know, Ellie," said Dorothy after a short pause, "you have an uncanny knack of sneaking into places where you don't belong, and gaining access to people you have no business talking to. It's annoying."

"I'll take that as a compliment."

"Being a nuisance is hardly a virtue."

Fifteen minutes later, I eased into the left lane, pumped the brakes twice, and turned off the highway.

"Paradise Cove?" asked Dorothy. "I might have guessed. Your Bo Hanson is a surfer, after all."

I parked a safe distance from Bo's Airstream trailer. It was just seven thirty, and I didn't want to alert Tony—assuming he was there—with blazing headlights through the parlor window. I switched off the engine, and all went silent except for the tumbling surf on the beach below.

"Shall we?" said Dorothy, popping open her door.

We trudged up the path and wound around a couple of trailers before reaching Bo's place. Cars rushed by on the highway above, their tires humming different notes against the asphalt as they passed. There was a light inside the trailer, and some Miles Davis playing loud enough for us to hear. As my guest, Dorothy deferred to me for the green light. This was my moment, after all. I nodded, and we approached the door in lockstep.

I rapped on the aluminum. No response. I knocked again, this time producing the desired results. The door opened, and Bo Hanson appeared, smiling broadly with a bottle of beer in his hand. The distinct order of marijuana wafted past him on the night breeze. His eyes focused on me, then on Dorothy. A short moment passed before he recognized me. I doubt he had any clue of who Dorothy might be, but his first instinct upon finding his wits was to slam the door in our faces. A commotion ensued inside, and the trailer rocked on its moorings. A phonograph needle screeched across Miles Davis, and the night went quiet. Dorothy took charge, stepping up to the trailer and tapping three polite knocks. Her calm stood in contrast to the panic taking place on the other side of the door. Frantic whispering, clattering, and scrambling. It sounded like a rodeo going on inside a tin can. I counted at least three voices—though I was betting there were four. There was no exit, save through the door Dorothy and I were blocking, unless the occupants were willing to stuff themselves through a porthole in the rear. Dorothy knocked again.

The tumult inside abruptly ceased, and, after a hushed exchange that we could hear but not quite make out, the door cracked open again. This time it was April. She slipped through the opening, pausing on the top step, and closed the door again behind her.

"What do you want now?" she asked me.

"I want to speak to Tony," I said. "I know he's here."

April seemed to gauge the plausibility of a denial as her gaze shifted from me to Dorothy and back. Sure, she could insist he wasn't there, but we all knew that the best proof of that would be to open up and let us have a peek inside. And she wasn't about to do that.

"Who's she?" she asked, nodding to my companion.

"She's the woman who can save Tony's career," I said.

"My name is Dorothy Fetterman. Open the door and tell Tony to come out. I want to speak to him."

April stood her ground for another moment until the door moved behind her. She tried to hold it closed, but the person on the other side had the advantage. April nearly tumbled headfirst off the steps, but managed a safe landing in the mud before us just as the door swung open. There in the doorframe, unshaven, hair mussed, with an expression wavering between hopeful uncertainty and terrified resignation, stood Tony Eberle.

"Hello, Tony," said Dorothy.

He practically swallowed his tongue. "Hello, Dot."

CHAPTER TWENTY-SIX

Dorothy wanted to speak to Tony alone, but that hadn't been part of our deal. I insisted on keeping them on a short leash. With a sigh, she acceded, and the three of us took a stroll through the salt air down to the wharf. No one spoke until we'd reached the very end. Dorothy, head bowed, tented her fingers, touching them to her perfectly painted lips as she considered how to open the conversation with the handsome young actor she'd all but denied even knowing, the man who somehow knew her as "Dot." At length, perhaps realizing there was no escaping me, she threw a vexed glance in my direction then began.

"How did you get yourself into this mess, Tony?"

He exhaled two lungfuls of air and hung his head. He mumbled something about everything was ruined. Everything was over.

Tony and I hadn't been formally introduced, but he must have known who I was. April and Mickey had surely warned him about the nosy girl reporter from New Holland who'd been making their lives miserable for the past week. I wasn't sure if he'd speak to me, but I hadn't come this far just to admire a moody seascape on a cool February evening.

"Did you kill Bertram Wallis?" I asked, dragging him out of his self-pity and gloom and back into the moment.

He stared at me, bemused, in the pale light of a waxing moon. Maybe he didn't know who I was after all. But then he spoke.

"You're going to write terrible things about me, aren't you?"

His eyes sparkled in the dark, not from tears but from the glassy clarity, the clean, fresh youth of God-given beauty. I'd seen many photographs of the would-be heartthrob. His yearbook portrait, candid shots from his high school acting performances, and even his headshot. The one with Irv Greenberg's phone number on the back. But now I gazed at him for a long moment, taking the time to consider the living, breathing Tony Eberle. Gone was the artifice, the practiced poses, and the coiffed hair. No more makeup, beauty dishes, or touch-ups. This was the real McCoy standing before me. A man in crisis, at a turning point in his career and his life. He was disheveled, shirt untucked, with his hair blowing wildly in the wind. And he was just about the handsomest man I'd ever seen.

"I'm trying to help you, Tony," I said. "But I can't do that if you don't tell me the truth about what happened. Mickey and April have done nothing but lie to me from the start. I need you to be straight with me. Did you have anything to do with Bertram Wallis's death?"

"How can you help me? Why would you help me?"

"Our interests are the same. You need a happy ending, and so do I. If I report that you shoved Wallis over the railing, we both lose. You go to jail, and I'm the reporter who took down the local hero and broke a town's heart. But if you become a star . . ."

"I didn't push Bertie off that terrace," said Tony. Then he repeated it—with feeling—to Dorothy, as if auditioning for a part. In a way, I suppose he was doing just that.

Dorothy took a step forward, settling in front of him, just inches from his chest, her nose on a level with his chin. She gazed up into his eyes and willed him to be calm. The silent, almost magnetic harmony of their postures betrayed an intimacy that was impossible to ignore. I studied the two standing before me, hoping to gain some insight into the bond they shared. Tony appeared distressed, but that was due to the situation, not any discomfort with Dorothy. For her part, Dorothy was solicitous, gentle, and kinder than I'd ever seen her. They didn't speak for nearly a minute, and I had to scold myself for fluttering like an adolescent girl who'd just stumbled upon some juicy gossip. Twenty-four-year-old Tony Eberle and forty-something Dorothy Fetterman shared a tender secret. They were lovers. There was no doubt in my mind.

I wondered how much April knew about the relationship between Tony and the powerful studio executive. Was Tony just playing the game? Making friends with a woman who could help him advance his career? Or was there something more? And what about Dorothy? Should I begrudge her a little harmless naughtiness with a handsome young actor? They were both adults, after all. I didn't care what they did where or with whom; I lived by the same code in my own life. But then I reconsidered. Perhaps Dorothy's behavior wasn't as harmless as all that. Maybe she made a habit of extracting favors from the stable of ambitious young actors at her disposition. How was that any different from what Bertram Wallis and countless casting directors had been doing?

"I swear he was alive when I left him," Tony said to Dorothy.

She held his hands and soothed him, whispering in his ear. I felt extraneous to the proceedings, but they seemed to have forgotten that I was there. At length, Tony drew back and sighed deeply as he contemplated the night sky.

"Did you remove anything from Bertie's place?" asked Dorothy so softly I barely heard her.

Tony shook his head. "What would I take?"

"Photographs."

"Of course not," he said. "I argued with him at the party, and some of his friends threw me out. Then I went back there after two, had a shouting match with Bertie, and I slugged him. Decked him. Right there, flat on his back on the floor, he wiped his bloody lip and told me I was fired from the picture."

"And that's it?"

Tony rubbed his head. "No. I was so mad I wanted to kill him, Dot. I really did. But that annoying dog of his was barking and running back and forth, confusing me. I tried to kick him real hard, but I missed and knocked myself down."

"Oh, Tony," whispered Dorothy.

I pictured Tony, whiffing completely on his swing at the pug, hoisting himself off the ground with the acquired momentum of his pendulating right leg before falling back to earth on his duff. Equilibrium, if not dignity, restored.

"Then I left," continued Tony. "Bertie was swearing and frothing at the mouth. He was drunk and couldn't pick his fat self up off the floor. He actually called to me to give him a hand just before he threw up on himself."

Now I had to contend with the image of a rabid Bertram Wallis spewing—rather barfing—orders at Tony. I turned away to hide my snorting laughter. Dorothy glared at me in disapproval.

"Were you two alone?" she asked Tony. "Were there any witnesses?"

He frowned and shook his head, his expression troubled by some memory. "I didn't see anyone, but . . . But Bertie said there was someone in the next room. He said they were discussing business. His next picture, I think."

"And you're sure you didn't see anyone? No one saw you?"

"Just the dog, yapping."

My fit of laughter had passed.

"Why did you hit Wallis?" I asked. "Why were you two arguing?"

Tony reeled around as if I'd surprised the two of them kissing, as if I hadn't been there all along.

"Tony," said Dorothy. "Remember she's a reporter."

"I didn't kill him. I wanted to but I didn't. April can back me up. I just knocked him down."

"You said there were no witnesses. But April was there?"

"Yes," he admitted. "No one else."

"Why did you knock him down?" I asked again. "Why did you want to kill him?"

Tony looked to Dorothy for advice. She just held his hand and gazed at him, perhaps wanting to know the answer as well.

"Because of what he did to Mickey," he said, his voice trembling.

Tony dropped Dorothy's hand, punched his leg, and turned away from us both. He struggled to speak, the words catching in his throat, choking him until he finally managed to spit them out.

"Mickey. My friend Mickey. He used him for his perversions, humiliated him. He did unspeakable things to him, then shared him with his friends. His rich, disgusting friends. And one of those bastards beat him up just to show what a tough guy he was. To prove he wasn't a queer even though he'd just . . . Even though he was a damn faggot. Yeah, I wanted to kill Bertie, all right. Him and all his sick, perverted friends." He paused in his rant, heaving for breath, his cheeks wet with tears. "But I didn't. April stopped me."

Dorothy said nothing. She just rubbed Tony's arm up and down, soothing him as a mother might. He wiped his eyes and his face and stared out at the black sea beyond the end of the wharf. After a while, he strolled partway back to shore and leaned against a pile where he continued his miserable contemplation of the night.

"Do you think he was telling the truth about the photographs?" I asked Dorothy.

She shrugged and glanced over at Tony. "Why wouldn't he lie?"

"But I saw you two. Surely you . . ."

"I'll believe him once my boys have finished searching the trailer," she announced.

I gaped at her. She looked back at me, impatient. "They followed us out here. You didn't think I'd entrust something this important to a girl reporter from the back of beyond, did you?"

"The phone call to Archie Stemple," I said, feeling gutted and betrayed. "From my room at the hotel."

"Only it wasn't Archie on the line. Don't feel bad. I never would have found Tony without you."

I wandered back toward the beach. She called after me, but I ignored her. Instead, I hooked an arm through Tony's as I passed him and tugged him gently along with me. He was startled but came along without protest.

"She's searching the trailer now," I told him as we walked. "She lied to me. I'm sorry, Tony. This is all my fault."

CHAPTER TWENTY-SEVEN

"Nothing," said the bruiser whose back was turned to me. Something about him was familiar. He stood there in a suit, tall, athletic, towering over Dorothy about ten yards from Bo Hanson's trailer. The voice rang a bell, too. Then the moonlight caught on his gold wristwatch, and I knew. He turned his head, showing me his face. I felt a kick in the gut and must have gasped. He glanced over at me for half a second, no more, before looking away. What a fool I'd been.

Chuck Porter, the music executive who'd tried to pick me up at Musso and Frank. The one who'd helped me reach Bobby Renfro through Rockin' Johnny Bristol. Now, in the dark of a Malibu evening in February, he studiously refused to make eye contact with me.

"That can't be," said Dorothy to him. "Have your boys check again. Turn that tin can inside out."

"We've done that already, Miss Fetterman. We found the dirty magazines the beach bum had squirreled away under the floor, and his stash of marijuana. Quite an impressive amount, by the way. Of both. What do you want me to do with the weed?"

"Smoke it. Sell it. I don't care. I want the photographs."

"Sorry," he said.

Dorothy leaned against the fender of my car, rubbing the bridge of her nose. Tony, April, Mickey, and Bo Hanson stood nearby, surveying the jetsam that Chuck Porter's boys had thrown from the trailer during their search. With the exception of Bo, who looked as if he'd just stumbled away from a plane crash, the others seemed resigned to clean up the mess, happy that no one had been beaten up or arrested.

I, on the other hand, wasn't happy about any of this. I set out after Chuck Porter as he headed toward a dark sedan parked a short distance away. He didn't respond when I called out to him to wait, but I caught up with him just as he reached the car.

"You work for Dorothy Fetterman," I said to accuse. "You're just a stooge."

He stood there trapped against the door, frowning down at me. I couldn't say in the dark which bothered him more, my presence or the insult I'd hurled at him, but he stared at me for a long moment searching for a rejoinder. Finally he spoke.

"I had a job to do and I did it."

"You lied to me. From the moment you sidled up to me at the bar, you were just playing me for a chump." He didn't deny it. "I should have realized it when I met you at the hotel. You knew Tony Eberle's name that day, didn't you? Even though I'd never mentioned it to you. And the meeting with Bobby Renfro and Johnny Bristol? That was Dorothy pulling strings, wasn't it?"

He blinked at me but remained otherwise as still as a statue. Why was I bothering to confront this man whom I barely knew? He'd done nothing but try to seduce me. He hadn't befriended me. Hadn't taken me to dinner or asked me about my family. I'd met him exactly twice. Why did I care? He was just one of Dorothy Fetterman's minions. A henchman. Hired muscle. Not a music producer as he'd said. I thought what a pathetic specimen he was. Yet, somehow, he'd duped me. I prided myself on being sharper than my competition, whether it was on a story, a crossword puzzle, or a game of charades. And Chuck Porter—Alden—was the flesh-and-blood proof that I was a fraud. He and Dorothy had outsmarted me. I wanted to slap him but knew if I did I would collapse right there in a heap of shame and defeat. Instead I stared him in the eye until he had to look away.

"I know where the photographs are," I said.

He gazed at me, eyes narrowing, but still he said nothing. My lie was nothing more than an attempt to win the battle after having lost the war. He'd report to Dorothy, and that would be my revenge: her coveting the pictures that I would refuse to give her.

Chuck climbed into his car, turned the ignition, and drove off. I trudged back to the others.

Poor Bo Hanson was reeling. I felt sorry for him, despite the threats he'd made against me earlier in the day. He was swimming against considerable disadvantages in life, after all. Sure, he was tall and handsome in an obvious way. But he was dim, with no spirit beyond a love for the surf and reefer. Now, stepping over his belongings strewn on the mud outside his

Airstream trailer, Bo approached Dorothy as if she were an unexploded shell to be defused.

"Excuse me, ma'am."

"What is it?" she asked, nearly turning him to stone.

"I was wondering, well . . . I'd like to get my tobacco back."

She stared at him for a full ten seconds before speaking. "Tobacco? Do you mean your marijuana?"

He nodded.

"No," she said simply, and Bo—in defeat—shuffled back to his trailer like a condemned man to the gallows.

"Was that necessary?" I asked.

She didn't answer me. Just pushed off the fender and said she wanted to go. I told her to find her own way home.

"Don't be a child. Let's go."

"Ask Mr. Alden for a ride," I said.

"You know very well that he just left."

I shrugged. "Then perhaps Bo Hanson will give you a lift."

⁂

Their sojourn at the beach at an end, Tony, April, and Mickey wanted to return to LA. April told me she was taking Tony in her car, which had been hidden under a tarpaulin behind the garbage cans not far away. She asked me to drive Mickey back to his place. I wondered what poor Bo was going to do all by himself in his smelly trailer. As we drove off, Papa Joe, the man on the motorbike I'd seen earlier, was helping him pick up his scattered possessions.

CHAPTER
TWENTY-EIGHT

THURSDAY, FEBRUARY 15, 1962

I stepped out into the rain and made my way to Hody's, wondering how I was going to wrap up the Bertram Wallis murder. I'd found Tony, but that hadn't cleared up anything. I still had nothing more than the story of how Tony Eberle had blown his big chance. I labored over my notes, working on a new article to dictate to Charlie Reese. With nothing else to report, I wrote that Tony had been traced to a trailer park in Malibu and that he'd denied any involvement in Wallis's death. It was thin. Poor work on my part, and I knew it. I was debating whether to scrap it and wait until I had something more substantial, when a figure slipped into the seat opposite me in the booth.

"Good morning, Ellie." It was Dorothy Fetterman.

The waitress arrived, and Dorothy ordered a cup of black coffee.

"I see you made it home last night," I said.

"Yes. Bo Hanson was only too happy to oblige me once I promised him a role in an upcoming picture." She paused. "And I gave him back his marijuana."

"Then everything worked out," I said, damning her silently for her ability to bribe people with promises of a job.

"I want the photographs."

"I don't have them."

"You told Mr. Alden that you did."

I shook my head. "I told him I knew where they were."

"Stop splitting hairs. I want you to tell me where they are."

I stared her down, and she received the message loud and clear. I was the one holding the cards, and there was nothing she could do about it. Except perhaps to throw money at me, which was her next gambit.

"How much do you want?"

"For the photos? I'm sorry if you misunderstood. They're not for sale," I said, folding my papers as I prepared to leave.

Dorothy's nostrils flared, but her face betrayed no other signs of anger. Then she attempted a friendlier tack.

"Let's start over, shall we? Perhaps have dinner this evening? We can discuss your future at Paramount. I have some ideas."

"No thanks."

"I don't know what I did to offend you, Ellie, but I apologize."

I shrugged. "Come back and see me once you've figured it out."

There was no sign of Tony or April at her North Edgemont apartment. No one answered the bell, and her car was gone, too. I figured the two of them were tooling around town, burning through the high test I'd pumped into her tank in Barstow. Mickey was nowhere to be found on Wilton Place where I'd dropped him the night before. Evelyn Maynard answered my knock.

"Haven't seen you in a couple of days," she said, inviting me in.

"I've been on Tony Eberle's heels. Caught up with him last night in Malibu."

"Congrats, angel. That's good news."

"Not entirely. He's disappeared again."

"When are you going to forget about him and let yourself go with me?"

I laughed. And Evelyn did too. Then I caught myself and worried that I'd insulted her again. But, no. She'd been kidding.

"Let's plan an evening out when this thing is over," I said. "I'd like to thank you for your help."

Evelyn smiled weakly and puffed on her cigarette holder.

"Sure thing," she said. "I'm all yours, Ellie darling."

I gulped. And I scolded myself. And I felt like a fraud.

I was out of ideas. Whatever my next move was, it was eluding me. I returned to the hotel to call Charlie with the uninspired story I'd put together. He agreed that we should wait until something brighter emerged. At least give Tony a chance to resurrect his career before pronouncing it over.

"I've hit a dead end with the principals," I said. "I'm going to take a step back and speak to Wallis's cleaning lady. She might have some information on his enemies."

Charlie agreed it was as good a place as any to start.

I reached down to pet the small Chinese pug that had met me at the door. He took a sniff of my hand, found nothing that piqued his interest, and waddled away to sit leaning against the sofa leg.

Patricia Gormley lived on the second floor in a one-bedroom apartment on Lexington Avenue. The place was loud—traffic noise from the nearby freeway through open windows—and smelled of wet leaves and mud from the rain. My heels clacked on the old tile floors of the darkened corridors, echoing off the high-gloss paint of the walls and ceiling. The lights were either switched off or broken. I reached her door and knocked. A small dog inside barked like a doorbell.

"Thank you for agreeing to speak to me," I said, once she'd let me inside.

I reached down to pet the small Chinese pug that had met me at the door. He took a sniff of my hand, found nothing that piqued his interest, and waddled away to sit leaning against the sofa leg.

"That's Leon," said Mrs. Gormley, a tall, thin woman in her fifties. Her inflections, occasional odd turns of phrase, and rolled Rs betrayed a stubborn Irish accent. "Mr. Wallis's dog. I took him in when Mr. Wallis died."

"That was good of you. He looks like a nice little fellow."

She shrugged. "He's all right. I live here with my daughter and my grandson. She's workin'. He's at school."

The apartment was small and crowded with furniture and boxes of belongings piled against the walls. The moist air had permeated the cardboard, creating a musty smell that dominated the room.

"As I told you over the phone, I'd like to ask you a few questions about Mr. Wallis and what happened that night."

"He always asked me to work parties, to pass the trays of food and drink and clean up after. He liked having me around to serve the guests.

Said he didn't want no Coloreds or Spanish. Didn't give the right impression, he said."

"What time did you leave that night?" I asked, thinking what an odious man he must have been.

She didn't need to search her memory. "I left at two thirty after I did the washing up in the kitchen and hauled the rubbish out to the bins. I rang for a taxicab. Mr. Wallis always paid for carfare when I stayed late."

"Did you see anyone in the house after the guests left?" I asked.

"A man showed up while I was mopping the kitchen floor. Mr. Wallis took him into the study."

"Did you recognize him?"

"I didn't see him, did I? But I heard voices in the hall."

"Anything else?" I asked.

"Just the couple that showed as I was getting into my cab. Pulled up real fast in a station wagon and nearly ran into the dustbins."

"Did you get a look at them?"

"Sure. And I told the police, too. A young couple. A man and a girl. They legged it inside. I was worried something was off, so I told the driver to wait. But he said to find another taxi if I wanted to admire the view."

"Did you recognize either of them?"

She nodded smartly. "I didn't know their names, but I've seen both of them there at Mr. Wallis's parties. The boy was tall and handsome. An actor, I think. And the girl was pretty. I told the cops, and they showed me photographs to identify them."

The description was enough to convince me. "Did the police say what their names were?"

She shook her head. "They didn't tell me nothing. They just thanked me and sent me home."

"You said you'd seen the girl before. Are you sure?"

"She was fairly regular at Mr. Wallis's parties. Always with a different gentleman." She pursed her lips. "A shame when a young girl like that goes wrong."

I'd had my doubts about April, but she'd denied ever having attended Bertram Wallis's parties. I remembered the man in the diner in Barstow. The one who'd told me that April would do anything to get what she wanted. And I knew that Tony had decked Wallis during the confrontation that took place shortly after he and April stormed the house. He'd told me as much. But what was April's involvement? Tony claimed she'd stopped him from beating Wallis, perhaps even saved his life. Or were the lovers covering for each other? Had Tony perhaps rushed outside while April shoved the drunken man over the railing and down the ravine? All were possible scenarios, but I had already known of their presence in the house after the party. What I wanted to dig into was the identity of the man in Wallis's study. Might he have emerged from the other room to finish the job Tony had started? Or, if he was an innocent bystander, he could have seen or heard something to corroborate or debunk Tony and April's shared alibi. But Mrs. Gormley insisted she neither saw nor heard anything that might identify the man.

"Can you tell me what you found on Thursday morning when you arrived at the house?"

"A holy mess. Not like I left it Monday night after the party. Overturned chairs, vomit and blood on the carpet, and the bedroom was turned upside down, like someone tore it apart looking for something."

"The bedroom? Not the study?"

She shrugged. "The study was like always. It was the bedroom."

"What else did you see?"

"Little Leon was locked out on the terrace in the pouring rain."

"How do you suppose he got out there?"

"He was always trying to slip out that door. Learnt his lesson, I'll wager. He won't be trying to escape no more."

"But who would have left him out there?" I asked.

She opined that whoever pushed Mr. Wallis over the railing would have had no qualms about leaving a dog out in the cold for two days and nights.

"Surely not," I agreed. "But why risk a barking dog where the neighbors might hear him?"

"It's a mystery to me."

As it was after four, Mrs. Gormley announced tea and biscuits and disappeared into the kitchen to put the kettle on to boil. I waited in the cluttered parlor staring at little Leon, who was still sitting against the sofa leg, panting as if he'd just broken a four-minute mile. I thought about him trapped on the terrace with Wallis dead three hundred feet below. Poor thing. No food, and it had been quite chilly, at least at night. And I asked myself again why anyone—even a confirmed dog hater—would leave a dog outside where his barking might attract attention. As things turned out, Leon didn't summon anyone with his barking. But the murderer wouldn't have known that. And I could only conclude that Leon had slipped out onto the terrace while the murderer was dragging Wallis to the railing. Whoever that was must not have noticed the dog had escaped. Then, the deed done, he—or she—probably slid the door closed again with the little pug on the other side.

Mrs. Gormley returned with a tray. Leon perked up and shadowed her across the room. "You'll have some tea?" she asked me.

"Thank you," I said.

I'd noticed a bottle of Irish whisky on the sideboard that would have been more to my liking, but I behaved myself, sipping the tea and nibbling on a digestive biscuit. Little Leon waited at my ankle, eyes fixed on my right hand, following its every move, especially when a biscuit was in play.

"Could you tell if anything was missing from the bedroom?" I asked.

"Can't say for certain. But there was books and papers everywhere. Pulled off the shelves and strewn about."

"Did you see any photographs?"

"There were plenty on the floor. I picked them up and put them back in their boxes."

I felt awkward asking her the next question, but there was no avoiding it. Were they dirty photographs? Mrs. Gormley regarded me down her long nose.

"Artistic photos, they were. I was used to seeing such things at Mr. Wallis's place."

"Nothing pornographic?"

She shifted in her seat, then sipped her tea. "Like I said, they were artistic photos. Some of them might have been a little naughty. Nudes. But that's the way it is with art, isn't it?"

"Did you recognize anyone in the photos? Anyone famous?"

She shook her head. "You could barely see anyone's face. All dark and shadowy. Very . . . well, artistic."

"Were you able to tell if any were missing?"

"I'm not in the habit of looking at Mr. Wallis's things. Sure, I've seen some of those photos from time to time because he kept them around. But I can't say if anything was taken. And I told that lady from the studio the same."

I felt a jab in my right temple.

"She's been here?" I asked. "Miss Fetterman?"

"Nice Miss Fetterman, yes. She came by to check on me. Offered me a job, I'm happy to say. I start next week at the studio." She beamed. "Wardrobe department."

Damn that Dorothy.

"What about Mr. Wallis's movie scripts?" I asked. "Did you notice any of them in the study?"

"Sure. The place was full of them. He was always reading new movie scripts. He was a producer after all. Sometimes he'd throw them away when he was finished, but usually he put them up on a shelf in the study."

"Did you happen to notice one called *The Colonel's Widow*?"

"I didn't read the titles."

Patricia Gormley turned out to be a dead end. The only bit I'd learned from her was that Dorothy Fetterman continued to be a step ahead of me. That was about to change.

CHAPTER
TWENTY-NINE

"Miss Stone," called Mr. Cromartie from behind the front desk. "You had a call from someone named..." He read from a scrap of paper. "...Blanchard. Dr. Nelson Blanchard, ASC. Don't know what that means," he mumbled. "He left his number. Said it was urgent."

I took the scrap of paper from the clerk.

"And there's a gentleman waiting for you over there." He indicated one of the armchairs across the lobby.

In the low light, my eyes couldn't quite make out who the large figure was. Then it hit me. Harvey Dunnolt, the reporter from the Schenectady paper. How had he found me? I'd told him I was staying at the Beverly Hilton, after all. Seeing no escape, I approached Harvey and took a seat opposite him, realizing too late that the dullard had been asleep. I could have skirted around him quietly, but my arrival roused him.

He coughed a few times, rubbed his eyes, and straightened himself in the chair.

"There you are," he said, smoothing his walrus mustache. "I've been wanting to talk to you about the show you put on the other day. Sending us all on that wild goose chase to Barstow. The boys were hopping mad. They wanted to find you and teach you a lesson. Not very gentlemanly of them. But what you did wasn't nice either."

"What do you want, Harvey?"

"Some information. After your little trick, I think you owe me a favor."

"What kind of favor?"

"I want you to tell me where Tony Eberle is."

"Why would I do that?"

"Maybe because you don't want Artie Short to know about your moonlighting."

"Moonlighting?" I choked.

"I saw that piece you and Eugene Duerson wrote for the *LA Times*. Highly irregular to write for two newspapers at the same time, isn't it?"

"That was a different E. Stone," I said in a pathetic attempt to wriggle out of the corner where he had me trapped.

He chuckled, shaking like a bowl of Jell-O in his chair. "Yeah, Artie Short'll believe that. . . ."

"I'm not sharing anything with you," I said.

"Suit yourself. Maybe I'll phone Short collect just to make him even angrier."

He had me. But I thought I might be able to hold him off for a few more hours, maybe longer if I was lucky. I put on a good show of conceding defeat and told him Tony was hiding out in Malibu in a trailer near the beach. Harvey would investigate, and, provided my name didn't come up, Bo Hanson would tell him that Tony had indeed been there but was now gone. There was a chance Harvey might be satisfied and resist the urge to rat me out to Artie Short.

"If this is a trick . . ." he said as a warning.

"I saw him there last night. Spoke to him. I swear."

"All right, Eleonora. If this checks out, I'll keep my mouth shut." He smiled at me. "See you around."

I watched him waddle out the door and down to the street. Was I wrong to be disappointed that he didn't trip and fall down the stairs?

I telephoned Nelson Blanchard. He sounded out of breath.

"Did I interrupt your dinner?" I asked, consulting my watch. It was just past seven.

"Not at all," he panted. "Lucia and I were just working on our *Kama Sutra*. Nearly broke my back, but we managed the Bridge. Lucia is *tout à fait épuisée*. By the way, you're welcome to join us anytime for a reprise. But I must warn you, there's a toll to pay on my bridge."

"Is that what was so urgent?" I asked, furiously scrubbing the image of a wheezing Nelson Blanchard and his twisted sexual positions out of my head.

"Actually, no," he said. "A strange thing happened this afternoon. It's probably nothing, but I thought you should know. I saw that friend of yours."

"Which friend?"

"That girl who stayed here. What was her name? April."

"You saw April? Where?"

"Here. At the house. She was skulking around. Lucia spotted her through the window and let me know. I went out and called to her, but she jumped into a car and drove away."

"What do you suppose she was doing there?" I asked. "Did she leave anything behind when she disappeared on Monday?"

"I doubt it. The cottage was cleaned after she left. Our girl didn't mention anything."

"I'd like to have a look around, if you don't mind."

"Why don't you pop up for a bite to eat? We've finished our exertions for the evening, so you needn't worry about your virtue. I'm preparing a cheese soufflé for a chilly wet evening. And wine, of course."

It sounded tempting. Especially the wine. And I wanted to get to the bottom of April's mysterious visit. Why would she return to the Blanchards' place? The draw was too much. I stepped into a black wool skirt, wrestled myself into a turtleneck sweater, and put on my face.

※

"Ellie, *ma chère*," said Nelson Blanchard at the door. Pablito had followed him to investigate the visitor. He sniffed my wet shoe, looked up at me, perhaps deciding if he recognized me, then wandered back into the big room and his place in front of the hearth. I am a constant source of indifference to dogs. "Please come in and give me your coat," said Nelson.

I complied, and he asked if there was any other clothing I'd like to remove. I flashed an indulgent smile.

"You're relentless. I'll say that for you."

Lucia emerged from the bedroom in a black silk kimono. Her hair was wrapped in a turban, also black. Not exactly Japanese, but she was stunning as always.

"How beautiful you look," I said.

"You must be admiring the glow in my cheeks," she cooed, fluttering her long eyelashes at me. "Nelson and I were just enjoying some intimacy before you arrived."

"That's lovely," I said, wincing through my discomfort.

Nelson stood by grinning, without even the decency to look abashed.

"May I mix you something to drink?" he asked.

"Whiskey is fine," I said, and he set about dispatching the task. "Tell me about April."

"Nothing more to tell. Lucia spotted her out the window, and I went to investigate. Scared her off. Ice?"

"Yes, please. I've been asking myself, what would prompt a person to return to a place where she spent one night while on the run?"

"And what did you conclude?"

"There's only one possible explanation. She left something here and came back for it."

"But our girl's been through the cottage with a broom and mop. She would have mentioned it if there'd been anything left behind."

"Unless April didn't want her to find it."

"Are you saying she hid something in the bungalow?"

I shrugged. "It's possible."

"Let's have a look," said Nelson.

"There's time, *mi amor*," called Lucia from the divan where she'd taken a seat. Assumed a pose reminiscent of Olympia was more like it, except that Lucia was wearing the aforementioned kimono. But unlike Manet's model, I doubted she would have bothered to cover her . . . pulchritude had she been nude. "This is the cocktail hour," she continued. "I'm sure Ellie would like to enjoy her drink."

After drinks and an airy soufflé, Nelson popped open a large umbrella and led me down a pebbled pathway to the guest cottage. Lucia was still weak-kneed from her bridge crossing and begged off, opting to wait for us in front of a roaring fire in the hearth.

The guest cottage was a cozy, single-story bungalow that looked to have been there for decades. Nelson explained as he rattled the keys in the lock that the cottage had been on the lot when he purchased the place ten years earlier.

"I thought it might come in handy as a study or a guesthouse," he said, throwing open the door. He stepped inside and switched on the light. "It took me two years to build the house, so I stayed here for a while back then. Now, we almost never use it."

I surveyed the place. Adorable if tiny. A small galley kitchen at the entrance, then the parlor and shoebox bedroom beyond. There was a fireplace that looked inviting, especially on a cold, rainy night like this one. I laughed at myself. After ten days in Los Angeles, did I really consider fifty degrees cold? I crossed into the parlor, whose wooden plank floors creaked under my feet. Nelson explained that he'd renovated the cottage after he'd moved into the new house.

"I opted for a genteel-backwoods decor," he said. "Nothing modern about this look. I thought it would be fun to create an anachronistic contrast with the main house."

"You've succeeded. It's terrifically romantic. A quaint little love nest."

"Cheep, cheep," he said, his grinning lips revealing his long teeth.

"Not just after dinner, Nelson. You'll get a stitch."

I set about looking for April's hiding spot. The parlor was clean. The bedroom, too. And nothing in the kitchen. Nelson and I rummaged through drawers, end tables, and books on shelves. We knelt down to peer under the sofa, chairs, rugs, and the bed. We threw open every cabinet in the house, stuck our heads inside the icebox, the oven, and up the flue in the fireplace.

"Looks like you've got a leak," I said, pointing to a spreading wet spot on the ceiling in the kitchen.

Nelson inspected the affected area and pronounced himself stumped. "I put in a new roof seven years ago. Workmanship isn't what it used to be."

"Does everything else seem in order to you?"

"Nothing out of place," he said, shrugging. "Let's get ourselves another drink."

Back in the main house, Nelson mixed up a sampler of South Seas rum cocktails, including a Babalu, a Tahitian Pearl, and a Wahine. I broke my rule of never mixing liquors and sampled them all. A little too sweet for my tastes, but Nelson took such joy in preparing them—like a mad chemist—that I couldn't refuse him. He looked crestfallen when I declined a refill of a Shark's Tooth, and I said I had better go.

He pouted. "But I just made a pitcherful."

"I really can't. It was delicious, though," I added to be polite.

"Then I'll give you a thermos to take with you for a nightcap back at the hotel."

Nelson embarked on a mission to locate a thermos in the kitchen. After a few minutes he returned empty-handed and asked Lucia if she'd seen it.

"You're always lending things to people, *mi amor*," she said. "I think you gave it to that April girl the other night."

Nelson snapped his fingers. "That's right. I made her some Irish coffee to keep her warm. I'll just go fetch it from the guesthouse."

"Don't bother," I said.

"Ellie, darling, I can't send you home empty-handed."

"No, I meant don't bother going out in the rain. There was no thermos in the bungalow."

"Are you sure?"

"I checked every cabinet in the place," I said. "There's no thermos."

"This is why you shouldn't take in stray cats. No matter how pretty. They steal."

"I'll have that Shark's Tooth, after all," I said, sensing a familiar itch that told me something was off.

Nelson filled our glasses then put some soft music on the hi-fi. The opening strains were a rhythmic strumming of guitar, followed by a deep, sensuous Brazilian voice.

"*¡Dios mío!*" said Lucia, laughing. "João Gilberto? Bossa nova? You're never going to seduce Ellie, *mi amor*. Give up!"

Nelson put up a flimsy defense that he'd merely played what was already on the turntable, but I think Lucia knew every ploy in Nelson's bag of tricks. We sat quietly for another half hour, listening to the music and sipping our Shark's Teeth.

I was bothered about the thermos. Why would April steal something so banal? Why not take something more useful or valuable? Like a cigarette lighter, silverware, or wine? And what had she wanted with the guesthouse if there was nothing inside to recover? Nothing that we could find, at any rate.

I asked Nelson where exactly he'd spotted her outside.

"She was near the porch. Just a few feet from the cottage. Why?"

"I don't know. Let's go see what might have interested her."

Under the protection of Nelson's giant umbrella, we stood there in the rain staring at the guest bungalow. It was just a cottage with a wooden porch attached. The rain plopped on the canopy of our umbrella in heavy drops, and we considered the view in silence. Finally, Nelson asked me how much longer I needed.

"That's enough," I said. "It's time for me to go."

I lay awake in bed, wrestling with the riddle—if that was what it had been—of April Kincaid's odd reappearance chez Blanchard. There had to be an explanation for her visit, three days after she'd decamped from the safe haven I'd so carefully arranged for her.

The rain was steady, not heavy. At one, still unable to sleep, I rose and lifted the shade to peer out the window. The same brick wall with its Selma Hardware sign greeted me. I found comfort in the contemplation of the city under the cover of night. It reminded me of the hours I'd spent gazing out the window of my childhood apartment in Greenwich Village. I used to count the cars as they passed, uptown and downtown along lower Fifth Avenue. The traffic ran in both directions back then. And I listened to the honking horns and roaring buses, at least in the years after the war. Everything was quieter and darker during the war. Blackouts and gasoline rationing.

I lowered the shade again and returned to bed, wondering why I was thinking back to my childhood. Sometimes the mind takes its own route and steers your thoughts where it will. Recollections of my youth and growing up in the throes of world war continued to trouble my sleep. I recalled listening to the radio, lying on the floor, sketching pictures of cats with a pencil on paper as my father fiddled with the dial. Sometimes it was an FDR fireside chat or a baseball game or a quiz show. Serials were my favorites. Occasionally my father would allow broadcast music to enter the house. And that was when I grew to appreciate the big bands, Benny Goodman especially. I think my father secretly enjoyed it, as well, though it was not an appreciation he was about to concede.

I pulled the covers tighter around my neck, savoring the warmth of my Hollywood hotel room, and willed myself into a comforting dream of my youth. But my mind drifted back to the war, to my mother and father sorting through ration cards as they prioritized how to feed Elijah and me, to air raid drills in the basement of our building, to our small victory garden on the window sill next to the drainpipe. Concrete memories dissolved into an eddy of riddles about wayward girls and missing boys. I thrashed in my bed, butting up against the impasses of my investigation while groping at strategies that might lead me to a solution.

I sat up in bed wondering for a short moment exactly where I was. In Hollywood, of course, hopelessly marooned at a stubborn dead end. Only I wasn't. The jumbled memories, dreams, and nightmares had cleared a path for one idea—one sudden inspiration. This was a triumph. I jumped from bed and climbed back into the clothes I'd removed a couple of hours earlier.

Mr. Cromartie was snoring away in one of the lobby armchairs. I breezed past him and out the door into the rain. Minutes later, I was roaring west on a deserted Hollywood Boulevard before turning up Nichols Canyon Road.

The main house was dark, except for some lights outside. I'd parked far enough away so as not to wake the Blanchards. Sheltered by my umbrella with the fractured ribs, I slipped past one of the plate glass windows, praying I wouldn't rouse Pablito on the other side, and found the pebble path to the guesthouse. I stood before the small bungalow, considering it from the same angle Nelson and I had done several hours before. Nothing had changed, but this time I knew what I was looking for.

CHAPTER THIRTY

The rain continued to fall, soaking the roof, before collecting in the drainpipe mounted under the eaves that routed it safely to the ground. Only the drainpipe wasn't dispatching its duties. A leak had formed above the kitchen ceiling, and studying the scene more carefully now, I could see why. Runoff water was bubbling atop the vertical drain. The pipe was blocked and overflowing.

Using a broken stick I found nearby, I snaked the drain from the bottom, soaking my coat, skirt, stockings, and shoes in the process. But I needed barely ten seconds to clear the clog. A small object flushed out of the tube and dropped into the puddle on the ground. A gush of water from above followed. I should have expected it, of course, but my mind had been otherwise occupied. I recoiled, leapt backward, before losing my footing and landing with a splat on my rear end in the mud.

Cursing April Kincaid, I righted myself and wiped my muddied hands on the only thing I had handy: the front of my wool skirt. Then I grabbed the object—a small thermos bottle—and sloshed back to my car.

My hands trembled as I shook the thermos to confirm my suspicions. There was no Irish coffee inside; I was sure of that much. In fact, there was no liquid at all. But something jounced lightly back and forth within. I pried off the cap, unscrewed the stopper, and upended the vessel to dislodge its contents. A cylinder slipped out into my muddy lap. It was paper, rolled tightly together and bound with cellophane tape. Photo paper. When I opened it, I knew why Dorothy Fetterman had been so desperate to get her hands on the photographs. If I'd had a mouthful of Coca-Cola, I would have spat it out against the windshield and called my eyes liars.

I confess that the photographs, seven in all, unsettled me. I'm no prude and understand people have their peccadilloes and secrets, but here was a Hollywood star kissing another man on the lips. A big kiss. A wet one.

An extremely famous, talented, and sexy leading man. A manly man, to echo Andy's words from the first day I met him. And there he was kissing a handsome young man full on the lips in three shots. And more in the other four, including two where his kissing partner had dropped his trousers and drawers as if for an army physical. And the leading man was holding said other man's . . . penis in his hand, mugging for the camera, as two other men looked on and laughed. The very last photo took the fun and games one giant step further. There was no mistaking what was being done and by whom. If ever the photographs surfaced, they would end the actor's career and probably get him arrested for sodomy as well.

Yes, I was shocked. And I felt a knot in my stomach. It shook me hard, and my discomfort was compounded by my disappointment in myself for thinking that way, for wanting that famous actor to be "normal." Straight. Not queer. Not the way I suspected my own brother had been.

I loved my brother, Elijah. And his death nearly five years earlier still harrowed my soul with a violence that could take my breath away. I had worried and fretted for him, even as I felt I might be able to accept him. But at the same time, I had agonized over the revulsion and shame and suffering he would either heap upon himself or have heaped on him by the outside world. The abandonment, or perhaps downright disowning, by my father would have crushed him. I'd experienced heavy doses of that medicine from my father for years, and I certainly would not have wished it on my beloved brother.

I caught myself and drew several restorative breaths. I shook thoughts of Elijah from my head and asked myself, why? Why had the pictures upset me so? Would I have preferred it if the man in the photographs had been performing the same acts on a woman? I'd seen a couple of dirty magazines in my day, even watched a stag film with fifteen other undergrads at a drunken party in college. But those actors had been anonymous, and it was impossible to discern their faces in the gritty, poorly focused movie. I didn't enjoy the dirty magazines, though I found them informative. And the blue film was awful, even if we all laughed in attempts to cover our discomfort.

I managed to reel in the scandalized panic I was feeling. Self-analysis, like looking into a mirror, had always helped me to tame my most frightening doubts and loathing. I'd been able to talk myself into measured responses and reactions. And so I did as I sat on my hotel room bed staring at amateur pornographic pictures of an actor I'd once lusted after. Him. The one who'd looked so sexy in the torn T-shirt. The manly man who'd invaded so many of my erotic dreams. That one. He wasn't who I thought he was. But why should he have been? I certainly didn't live my life to suit others. Why should he?

Putting my shock to one side, I considered the implications of the photographs in April Kincaid's possession. While it was possible that Tony had given her the scandalous pictures, I thought it was unlikely. More probably, April had grabbed them from Bertram Wallis's bedroom at some point when she was inside the house with Tony. And that pointed to a terrible possibility, perhaps even a likelihood. That April had killed Wallis herself. Again I recalled the man from the Charlie Horse Diner in Barstow. He'd said April would do anything to get what she wanted. I wondered what she might have wanted from Wallis. Perhaps simply to protect Tony. Wallis had just fired him from the picture, after all. And what about her own wicked behavior? According to Mrs. Gormley, April had been a regular at the parties, always on the arm of a different rich man. I asked myself if I believed April capable of such an act. Of murder. And my answer was yes.

The photographs in my possession frightened me more than anything I'd ever laid my hands on. Too many people wanted them. Too many people would suffer if they ever surfaced. I lay awake in bed, hoping the lock and the flimsy door could withstand the efforts of an intruder bent on getting inside. I rose several times to investigate a noise in the corridor or voices in the alleyway below my window. Instead of counting sheep, I found myself counting the cast of desperate people who wanted the photographs enough to take them from me. And if I stood in their way, how much were the pornographic pictures worth to them? Enough to kill me to get them?

First in line was April. She'd already stolen them once, and I doubted she would hesitate to grab them again. And I had no reason to trust Tony Eberle or Mickey Harper. The sum total of my experience with Mickey consisted of trying to work around his lies. And I'd only met Tony once.

Dorothy Fetterman, and by extension the studio, wanted the photographs. She'd kept me close for more than a week in the hopes that I'd lead her to them. And that meant any of her henchmen might kick down my door at any moment, even that snake Chuck Porter. Or Archie Stemple. He'd disliked me from our first meeting. And he'd shown a violent streak, even in public settings, that made me nervous.

Cops, reporters, blackmailers. The list grew as the minutes passed. And what of the matinee idol in the photographs? I could picture him, sweaty muscles flexing as he snapped my neck in order to recover the evidence that could—in the wrong hands—kill his career.

At four, I rose from bed again, slipped into my robe, and pushed the dresser against the door. I doubted that would save me from a determined burglar, but it might give me enough time to jump from my second-floor window into the trash cans in the alley below.

Now I was truly paranoid and losing my cool. I checked on the photographs once again, ensuring they were still in the thermos. They were, of course, but in my sleep-deprived, frightened state, I needed to see them to be convinced. I wanted to hide them better. My suitcase was no Fort Knox and would be one of the first places someone would search. Then I remembered Ray Milland in *The Lost Weekend*. His alcoholic character found devilishly clever spots in his apartment to hide bottles of liquor from his brother. Everywhere from dangling from a string out the window to stashing one behind a grate in the bathroom to stuffing another inside the vacuum cleaner bag. I had no vacuum, no string, and no heater grates at my disposal, but there was the ceiling light fixture. Ray Milland had squirreled one up there as well. Feeling that was my best option, I dragged the chair to the middle of the room and clambered up with the thermos in my hand. Too short, I couldn't reach. The bed was only inches higher, and I was still several inches too low to slip the thermos into the frosted-glass shade.

I slumped on the bed and considered my options. There was Marty the bellhop. He was tall. But I couldn't risk adding a coconspirator to this plan. The photographs were too toxic to share with anyone. I was alone until 9:00 a.m. when I planned to run to a bank and take a safe deposit box to secure the pictures.

But what to do until morning? Despite my own efforts to convince myself that it was only paranoia, I had a terrible premonition that someone was coming for the photographs. Hadn't I told Chuck Porter that I had them? Or knew where they were? And he'd told Dorothy, who'd already approached me for them. Why had I lied? I looked at my watch then at the door. It was half past four.

I pulled the thermos out of my bag and shook the photographs out onto the bed. After removing the tape again, I flattened them as best I could on the desk. These were three-and-a-half-by-fives. I scanned the room, searching for someplace to hide them. Then my gaze fell on the door. On the hotel rates posted on the door, to be precise. I made my way across the room and considered the small picture frame. Holding one of the photographs up against it, I saw that it was just about the right size. I took down the frame and went to work. A few minutes later, I'd replaced the rate card on the door with the explosive pictures hidden inside. They were invisible. But then I had a thought. Again remembering Ray Milland in *The Lost Weekend*, I decided I needed a decoy. I undid my recent work, removing one print from the bunch. One that showed the actor kissing the younger man full on the mouth. I rolled it and wrapped it with tape, then slipped it back inside the thermos. The other photographs stayed in the frame, which I rehung on the door.

I stashed the thermos in my suitcase under the bed and switched off the light. It was nearly five, but I felt safer. Safe enough to doze off sometime later. I slept. I slept hard. Until a banging on the door roused me.

CHAPTER THIRTY-ONE

FRIDAY, FEBRUARY 16, 1962

Waking from a deep sleep, I fumbled for my watch on the bedside table, knocking it to the floor in the dark. The door banged again, prompting me to bolt from the bed and grab my robe to cover myself. A voice growled from the corridor, demanding I open up. I dashed to the window and yanked open the curtains, letting in some light. More banging at the door and a furious rattling of the knob.

"Who is it?" I shouted.

"Police," came the answer.

I pulled the dresser back from the door and unlocked it just before it burst open, knocking me backward onto the bed. Chuck Porter and two men in wet overcoats stepped inside.

"Police?" I shrieked.

He stood above me, face calm, and he motioned to his thugs to search the room.

"I'm calling the police," I said, pushing myself off the bed.

But Chuck blocked my way, placing a firm hand on my right shoulder and maneuvering me back into a sitting position on the bed. "I can't let you do that."

"What you're doing is criminal. This is breaking and entering. And impersonating a police officer."

"Yeah, sorry about that," he said, turning to check on his goons.

Chuck Porter's two men looked vaguely familiar, and I was pretty sure they were the same gorillas who'd emptied Bo Hanson's trailer onto the muddy ground two nights before. Now, as I watched them rifling through the chest of drawers and the desk, I struggled to control my alarm. They were going to find the photographs.

"Okay, fellas," said Porter. "Under the bed. And be quick about it."

Chuck Porter and his two thugs decamped shortly after pulling the thermos from my suitcase beneath the bed. They performed a few more perfunctory look-sees before deciding there was nothing else to find. The last thing I remember of their visit was Chuck gazing back at me from the door as he closed it on his way out. His eyes fixed on mine for a fleeting moment, before looking away in shame.

With the most damning photographs secure in a safe deposit box at the Metropolitan Bank on Vine Street, and the key to the box hidden between the film and the shutter inside my Leica, I returned to the hotel to pack my bags. I felt unsafe there. As I passed through the lobby, Mr. Cromartie and Marty the bellhop avoided my gaze, both trying to melt into the upholstery and the heavy curtains.

"He paid you off, didn't he?" I said, stopping to confront them. "You took the money and turned a blind eye as they broke into my room."

They said nothing. Cromartie coughed, and Marty just stared back at me as he fiddled with the buttons on his wrinkled tunic. On my way out the door twenty minutes later, the old man behind the desk made a feeble attempt to stop me. Something about settling the bill. I told him he'd already been paid.

I dragged my bag to the car in the nearby lot and threw it into the trunk. As I climbed into the driver's seat, a voice called my name from the sidewalk. It was Mickey Harper.

"They've arrested Tony."

"Get in," I said, and we drove off.

CHAPTER THIRTY-TWO

"What happened?" Mickey asked as I headed east on Hollywood. "I decided I didn't like the hotel."

I was still wondering how the three of them—Mickey, Tony, and April—fit together. Were they acting as a team, taking turns deceiving and distracting me? Or were there secrets they kept even from each other? That was one of the reasons I didn't tell Mickey about the raid on my hotel room. I didn't trust him.

"Where are you going to stay?" he asked as I turned onto Wilcox.

"I'll find another hotel, I suppose."

We sat in silence for almost a minute. Then Mickey said I could stay with him. "That is if you don't mind sharing a room with a man."

"Why would you invite me to stay with you? You don't even like me."

"I like you very much, Ellie. More than you know. You took me in when those cops beat me up."

"Your affection's not always evident," I said.

"It's hard for me to trust people."

"Do you trust me?"

He shrugged. "I don't have any choice in the matter. I have to trust you now. But that's no reason not to like you."

"You don't need to have anything to do with me."

"I need you for Tony."

"Tony has you," I pointed out. "And April."

My eyes were fixed on the road. I didn't see Mickey sigh, but I heard him. It was a subtle lament with a hint of frustration. Or was it annoyance?

"Something about her you don't like?" I asked.

"I hate April. I always have."

"He's got a lawyer," said my old pal Sergeant Millard.

He'd agreed to meet me despite the unpleasant end to our date. We were seated a couple of feet apart on a bench in a corridor of the Wilcox Avenue police station in Hollywood. "A good one, too. Your boy'll be back on the street by tomorrow."

"Where does a penniless actor find the funds to engage a top-notch lawyer?"

Millard shrugged. "Beats me. So what do you want?"

A few officers passed by, heels clicking on the floor as they went. I waited until they were out of earshot.

"I'd like to speak to him," I said, leaning in to keep our conversation private. "Tony Eberle, not the lawyer."

"And why should I let you do that?"

"Because you were a gentleman about our date, and I'm sorry for how I behaved."

God, that was hard to say, but I felt it was my only option. Appeal to his better nature, apologize for my rudeness, and hope for the best. He hadn't been expecting that, I could tell.

"Funny how people dish out apologies when they need something."

A cop escorting a sad-looking man in handcuffs neared us. The prisoner looked like a middle-aged accountant who'd propositioned the wrong street-walker and discovered a vice squad officer beneath the makeup. The policeman acknowledged Millard with a nod and continued down the hallway.

"I don't think his lawyer would approve of me letting a reporter in to talk to his client," Millard said at length.

"You're right, of course. Even if he trusts me and might tell me something that could be of use to you."

"Nice try."

"No, I mean it. His phone number was in Wallis's pocket. The two argued. Tony knocked him down, watched him vomit all over himself on the floor. Obviously you suspect him, or he wouldn't be here. A smart Jewish lawyer's going to get him off, and you won't get that promotion you've been wanting. Maybe he'll tell me something you can use."

"First of all, I didn't say the lawyer was Jewish," said Millard. "And, by the way, he isn't. And second of all, you've got a lot to learn if you think things work that way in the big city."

"It's not a crime to let me talk to him, is it?"

"So you're going to be a jailhouse snitch, is that it? I thought you were on this Tony Eberle's side."

He was right, of course. I had no argument for that. Millard was a tougher nut to crack than the police back in New Holland.

"You know, it kind of hit me like a slap when you jumped out of my car that night," he said as he stood to show me out. "Maybe I came on a little strong. Can't blame a guy for that. But if I'm saying no to you today it's not because you gave me the air. It's just not done that way, is all."

I nodded and thanked him just the same.

"Tell you what," he said. "I'll let you know when we release him."

"I left the hotel."

"Where can I find you, then?"

"I'm staying at Tony Eberle's apartment."

"I got to hand it to you," he said with a chuckle. "You got a knack for putting yourself in the middle of things."

Outside the station, I ran into April Kincaid, who was approaching from the direction of my parked car, where Mickey was waiting for me. She huddled in her jacket in the light, misty rain, eyes on the wet sidewalk, and didn't see me until I called her name.

"What are you doing here?" she asked.

"I tried to get in to see Tony."

"So you can write more lies about him?"

"I haven't written any lies. And I'm not going to try to explain to you what a reporter does."

"You have no business here."

"Mickey asked me to come."

"What's that little fairy got to do with this?"

"Look, April. I came to help Tony."

"He doesn't need your help," she snapped. "And he doesn't need Mickey, either. I'm taking care of things."

"So you're the one who got him the expensive lawyer?"

She seemed vexed that I knew that, as if she'd wanted to spring the news on me herself.

"I arranged it," she said.

"How did you manage that? With the ten dollars I gave you in Barstow?"

She smirked. "Funny. But I've got something that's worth a lot of money to some people. And they were only too happy to help me out in exchange."

"Must be something really special," I said.

"It is. And don't bother asking, because I'm not telling."

"Is it bigger than a breadbox?"

"What?"

"Or as small as a thermos?"

The color drained from April's already fair cheeks. "What? What are you talking about?"

"The thing you're exchanging for Tony's pricey lawyer. It wouldn't be something in a thermos bottle, would it?"

"Clever. Too bad you'll never find it."

"Already did," I said.

CHAPTER
THIRTY-THREE

After picking up some provisions—ground beef, potatoes, bread, milk, and eggs at the Hollywood Ranch Market—I dropped Mickey and my suitcase at his place. I was grateful for his offer to take me in, but I still didn't feel ready to open up completely to him. And I was feeling desperate to talk to someone about what had happened to me that morning. The weight of my questions and doubts was crushing me. I needed someone who wouldn't lie to me. Someone who would listen. Gene Duerson was glad to hear from me.

"I owe you a drink or two for those bets," he said over the phone. "And some money."

"What money?"

"For the *Times* article. Half of it is yours."

A drink sounded grand. There were only a few drops left in the bottle in my suitcase. But remembering how he'd been struggling to make ends meet, and knowing that my share would not mean a great deal to me, I suggested he stand me to a simple dinner instead, and we agreed I'd pick him up at his apartment.

"A word of warning," he said. "My place isn't fancy. I'm not as rich as I look."

❦

Gene lived on the second floor of a five-story building southeast of Hollywood. He apologized for the state of the place, which, in truth, looked as though he'd given it a quick brushup before my arrival. Books and newspapers everywhere, but stacked in piles. Secondhand furniture, a telephone on one end of the kitchen table, a boxy Motorola portable television set on the other, and a couple of exotic landscapes in frames on the papered walls. Two closed doors off the main room must have led to the bathroom and the bedroom. I couldn't tell which was which. There were two windows that opened to the alleyway that ran between Third and Fourth Streets below. That was where Gene had told me to park behind the beaten-up blue De Soto. He hadn't been kidding. The car was a mess. A tarpaulin stretched over half of it. Dents and scratches, a mangled front bumper, and oil all over the floor of his parking space.

Gene invited me to have a seat on the small, lumpy sofa.

"Is everything okay with you? You look worried," he said, offering a glass of whiskey from a freshly opened bottle of White Label. I was sure he'd run out to buy it just after he'd hung up the phone.

"That's why I called you. I need to talk to someone I can trust. Just talk, even if it's just for a while."

"Sounds like fun. Tell me what happened?"

I recounted how my room had been invaded by three men looking for evidence. For the moment, I left out the part about what the evidence was.

"I have a terrible secret, Gene. It's burning a hole in my chest. I've just got to talk about it with someone."

"Go on."

"Do you know who Dorothy Fetterman is?" I asked.

"Sure. You told me about what happened in Barstow."

"But did you know who she was before I told you?"

"No. But as a matter of fact, she contacted me a couple of days ago. She wanted to know about the party at Wallis's place. I was there that night, after all."

"And let me guess. She offered you a job."

He nodded.

"And in exchange, you'd help her find something?"

"Not exactly. She wanted me to spy on you. To get something from you. Maybe it was your terrible secret."

I gulped, and it wasn't the Scotch.

"I turned her down, of course," he said. "I need money, but I'm not a rat."

I barely knew Gene, of course. If he'd wanted to, he certainly could have betrayed me to Dorothy Fetterman for the cash he so desperately needed. But I hadn't heard from him in days, so I doubted he was spying on me. And Dorothy already knew I had the photographs. Those had been her goons in my hotel room, after all. So I thought I could trust him with my secret.

But at the same time, a different doubt crossed my mind. Was Dorothy, by chance, onto my ruse? Had she realized that Chuck Porter only recovered one fairly innocuous photograph? An image that might well be explained away as a famous movie star horsing around at a drunken party with friends. Not that anyone involved would have wanted it to be seen, but it wouldn't have spelled the end to said heartthrob's career either. Dorothy had been a step ahead of me from the start, so the odds were good that she'd figured it out.

"Hello," said Gene, interrupting my internal ramblings.

"Sorry. Just worried about things."

"I won't betray your confidence, Ellie. I'll keep whatever secrets you tell me."

My intentions were good. I certainly didn't want to splash such offensive pictures on the front page of the *New Holland Republic* or any other newspaper, for that matter. What I truly wanted was my story back. I wanted to see Tony Eberle doing the twist on a sandy beach in a real Hollywood picture. My fondest wish was for a young man I'd met only once to become a movie star. Because that would work out for me, too. I knew I intended to use those photographs to achieve my goal. Safely locked away in a bank, they represented my insurance. Dorothy Fetterman wouldn't dare harm me, physically or otherwise, as long as I had the dangerous evidence in my possession. And she knew I had the goods. So I told Gene. I told him the entire story, even the name of the actor, which prompted him to show the most emotion I'd witnessed from him to date. A raised eyebrow and a short sniff.

"Well, I'll be blowed," he said with his characteristic phlegm.

"What should I do?" I asked, refusing to give him the satisfaction of laughing at his bawdy humor.

"About what? Do you want to convert him back to women?"

"Don't joke, Gene. I mean about the photographs."

He thought a moment. "Where are they now?"

"In a safe place. No one can touch them but me."

"You're sure?"

I nodded. "So what should I do?"

"There's always the cops."

I didn't see the utility in that. That would only result in blackening the name of a famous man and ruining his career.

"I wanted to ask you if it would be wrong to use them for my own ends."

"Like getting them framed and hanging them in your parlor?"

Okay, that made me laugh. "Come on, Gene. Enough. I need your advice. Would it be wrong?"

"That depends. What did you have in mind?"

"Would it be wrong to use the photographs to convince Dorothy Fetterman to give Tony Eberle another role in a major movie?"

"Sounds like blackmail."

"I was thinking quid pro quo."

"Paramount would take him back?"

"She promised me, yes."

"Then why do you need the photographs?"

"Because I don't trust her. The pictures are his ticket to stardom. What would you do, Gene? What if you were holding the photographs? What if they could fetch you enough money to live off of for the rest of your life? Would you use them for your own ends?"

"In a heartbeat," he said, reaching for my empty glass. "Let me get you a refill."

Gene returned a few moments later with my drink and a glass of his own. We talked about other things. Everything but Bertram Wallis, Dorothy Fetterman, or photographs of famous actors caught in flagrante. We reviewed the weather. When was the ceaseless rain going to stop? He said he didn't worry about things he couldn't change. We discussed the Cuban embargo and the Space Needle being erected in Seattle. And books, classics and current best sellers. It was all a relief to sweep the dark clouds and pornographic pictures from my mind.

When Gene got up to refresh our drinks a third time, I felt cheered enough to stand up and stretch my legs. I wandered across the room to his desk. A typewriter, newspapers, stacks of documents, phone directories, reference books, and dictionaries. I glanced at the top of one of the piles of paper. It was the article he and I had written together. I smiled, happy for him. Maybe it would lead to other assignments.

He reentered the room and joined me at the desk.

"Are these your scripts?" I asked, pointing to the shelf above the desk.

"Yes," he said, taking one down. It looked to be about a hundred type-written pages held together by a couple of brass fasteners. "I've written seven of them. This one is a western. *Caissons across the Prairie*. And this is a biography of Anatole France." He chuckled as he flipped through the pages. "I got paid to write it, but they never made the movie. Is it any wonder? Anatole France. They've never made any of these into movies, as a matter of fact."

"Keep at it, Gene. You're a smart fellow. You'll break through."

He shrugged and replaced the Anatole France on the shelf with great care. An almost loving gesture.

"Tell me about . . . *Twilight in the Summer Capital*," I said, reading the title of the last script in the row.

"It's a coming-of-age tale. End of an era, and all that. Set in India during the war. Another that'll never get made. Here, look at this one. It's a war picture set in Burma, called *Jungle Battalion*. The story of a small corps of American and British soldiers in the jungle fighting the Japs."

He reached for the script just as a knock came on the door.

"I'll show you later," he said and went to answer.

"Andy," I heard him say from the entry.

"Geno," said Andy. "I was in the neighborhood and thought you might like some company, you old loser."

I could tell he'd been drinking. Gene showed him inside, reluctantly it seemed. Andy stopped in his tracks when he spotted me by the desk.

"Ellie?" he asked with a grin. Then he looked back at Gene. "What's going on here? Am I interrupting something?"

"Not at all," said Gene. "We were just having the drink I owe Ellie."

Andy sauntered in. He was carrying a wet paper bag under his arm.

"I owe her a drink, too," he said, producing four bottles of Lucky Lager. "But it looks like you two already have things figured out."

Gene sighed. "Yes, we polished off a banquet, drained a barrel of wine, and made a couple of large deposits in the vomitorium before you showed up. And you missed the orgy. Sorry."

"Still, you could have invited me."

"You're welcome to join us for dinner," said Gene. "It's my treat. We got paid by the *Times* for our piece."

Andy turned sullen. "No thanks. I had some tamales on the way over. And a few beers."

"Suit yourself."

"We were just talking about Gene's movie scripts," I said brightly.

"But not about using my pictures in your *Times* piece."

"Come on," said Gene. "I already told you. There wasn't any time, and you didn't have the pictures we needed anyway."

"It's okay," he mumbled, but I sensed that it wasn't. "You and Ellie have your own little thing going. I understand."

"That's out of line," said Gene before I had a chance to respond.

"Sorry," repeated Andy. "Forget it. Let's have a drink."

We settled in, Gene and I on the sofa, Andy slumping in the armchair. He started out nice enough, but after a few minutes he was grousing about everything from the weather to the state of his apartment, which was disgraceful. After he'd cracked open his second beer, he was complaining about how there were too many Negroes and Mexicans in Los Angeles.

"But you eat half your meals at taco stands," said Gene as he puffed on a cigarette.

Andy shrugged. "They make good food, but there are too many of them. We don't have any beaners in Davenport, and I say that's a good thing. Some of the coons are okay. The ones who know their place."

"Maybe you've had enough, Andy," I said.

"Enough of beaners and coons? Sure." And he laughed.

"And I've had enough of that," I said. "I won't sit here and listen to such awful talk."

"Take it easy, Ellie. I'm sorry. Sorry. Sorry."

We sat for a long moment, all of us uncomfortable with the exception of Andy, who was grinning like a sot and muttering under his breath. Finally he broke the silence.

"Sorry," he repeated in a messy slur. "It's not like I said anything about the kikes." And he laughed again.

He stopped laughing when my drink hit his face. And it was a full glass, ice and all. He sat there in his chair, stunned, Scotch dripping down his cheeks and chin. Then he started to cry. Gene hustled him out the door before I could throttle him.

CHAPTER THIRTY-FOUR

"**A**ndy's drunk. And an ass," said Gene, handing me a fresh drink. "If I say something wrong, you can throw this in my face. Just wait till the ice melts before you do it."

Suddenly I felt sick. I took a sip of my drink and experienced a remarkable sensation. I swallowed the Scotch, and a familiar, spreading warmth washed down my throat. I felt I'd found an old friend. The comfort startled me, if two such opposing actions and reactions can coexist. And though I realized in that moment that the palliative of the whiskey might have been nothing more than a rationalization for my love of the stuff, I gave myself over to soaking up as much of it as I liked, because it felt like a miracle cure.

❧

Our dinner plans went down the drain, replaced by a couple of whiskeys and some pork cracklings that Gene produced from the cupboard. He avoided the topic of Andy and his bigotry—I avoided the cracklings—and we discussed our losses instead. Gene lent a patient ear as I shared the sorry tales of my brother, mother, and father's recent deaths. He comforted me, questioned me with the skill of a seasoned reporter, and made me laugh just when I was on the edge of tears. And he told me how he'd buried his own father after the harvester accident. Just fifteen, Gene quit school and went to work in a rendering plant to support his mother and sisters.

"You'd think I'd have lost my taste for pork," he said, popping a rind into his mouth.

"Those things make me want to keep kosher."

"My daddy used to eat these. We all did. Momma would fry up a mess of 'em on Sunday, and we'd eat 'em throughout the week. She never made any after Daddy died. Said she never much cared for them."

"Did you eat anything?" Mickey asked.

I admitted that I'd eaten nothing, if you didn't count half a pork crackling. Mickey boiled an egg and toasted some bread. He'd made up the Murphy bed for me and served me the meager repast that tasted like a feast. Afterward, we sat and talked as Mickey washed the plate and glass. I sipped the last of my Dewar's on the Murphy bed.

"You drink too much," he said.

"It's my medicine."

"Don't joke. Between your whiskey and your cigarettes, I worry about you."

"Thanks. I worry about you, too."

It was almost eleven. I was tired, but I sensed Mickey wanted to talk.

"You said you hated April. I saw her at the police station today."

"What did she say?"

"That Tony didn't need my help. Or yours. She was taking care of everything."

Mickey scoffed at that. "She thinks she can do anything. But she can't change the past or the present. Never mind the future."

"What do you mean?"

He frowned. "She thinks Tony is her ticket to the top. But she's just an average nobody like the others. Maybe less than average. She tied herself to Tony's star and wants to ride it like a rocket to the moon. She's a girl from nowhere with no prospects. No matter how many . . ." He caught himself and shut up. "Forget it."

"I want to believe you, Mickey," I said, after I'd let his words hang in the air for a moment. "I like you. I want to be friends."

"What's your point?"

"I want all those things. But I can't accept any of them if you don't level with me. You've got to treat me like a friend, or else I'm just someone who took you in on a rainy night."

He stared at me long enough to make me uncomfortable. Finally he told me that he wanted the same thing. Didn't I think he wanted to trust someone? Didn't I know that he'd had enough of lying to people? To me?

"You have no idea how lonely lying makes you feel," he said. "To have to hide what you are."

"Explain it to me. I want to know."

"Really? You want me to tell you what it's like to be a degenerate? A pervert?"

"You're not those things, Mickey. You're a sweet boy."

"I'm twenty-four years old," he said. "And I'm a faggot."

I froze on the bed. The misery on his face broke my heart. I wasn't sure which he regretted more, having shared his pronouncement or the fact that he was what he said he was. Either way, I didn't know how to respond. He spared me the embarrassment of untangling my tongue.

"Does that shock you?" he asked. "I can't help it, you know. I can't make myself be different. And no psychiatrist is going to cure me. I've tried."

I shook my head, still unable to summon a response.

"I don't know," he said. "Even with the humiliation, the mocking, the cruelty, and the regrets—my God, the regrets . . ."

He never completed his thought, pivoting in a new direction.

"Tony's not like me. He can't accept the humiliation. He can't live without the adoration. He craves it. And he knows it would disappear if people thought he was a queer."

"Is he?"

Mickey folded his hands and looked away. "I didn't say that."

"I don't understand."

"April's no better than me," said Mickey, ignoring my comment. "She's a whore just like me," he added with a shrug, as if it weren't perfectly obvious.

"Are you sure?" I asked.

"Who do you think introduced Tony to Bertram Wallis? How do you think she survives? She'll give it up to anyone who might help her get ahead. That's the one difference between us. She does it for herself. I did it for Tony."

CHAPTER THIRTY-FIVE

SATURDAY, FEBRUARY 17, 1962

Light usually wakes me, but Mickey had drawn the shades. I slept soundly and late, lying in the Murphy bed—in proper pajamas for a change—and dreaming of a lazy morning with nothing more momentous to worry about than the crossword puzzle. I dreamt of nothing in particular. Just thoughts of pillows and blankets. Nothing could be safer or more comfortable. The world could continue spinning through the heavens, but I was catching another few winks as it did. Then I heard the metallic click of a key turning in a lock. I sat bolt upright in the bed, expecting to see Chuck Porter and his cat burglars in tow, just as the door opened. But it wasn't Chuck. Nor was it my second choice: Dorothy Fetterman. In the framed light of the doorway, I distinguished a solitary figure. Tall and slim and holding a bag, he switched on the light. It was Tony Eberle.

"What are you doing here?" he asked, alarmed. "Where's Mickey?"

"He must have gone out. He said I could stay. I left my hotel."

Tony closed the door behind him and entered the room tentatively, as if each step might trip a landmine. He circled around the bed, glaring at me the whole time, and approached the dresser.

"I'm glad to see that you're out," I said, trying to ingratiate myself.

Fat chance of that. I was a reporter from his hometown with more dirt on him than he would ever be able to scrub off. And now I was sleeping in his bed and chumming around with his best friend, who knew every secret I did and then some.

"I turned myself in, you know," he said, reaching into the middle drawer and scooping out an armful of clothing. He stuffed the lot into the bag and reached for more.

"That's not why they let you go."

"Nope. I got a fancy lawyer to work his magic. Now, thanks to you,

I've got to get out of here before Dot finds out April can't give her what she promised."

"The thermos?"

He stopped emptying the drawer for a moment and turned to regard me. It seemed an idea had come to him.

"Wait a minute," he said. "You've got the pictures. So you can give them to me, I'll give them to Dot, and everything's square again."

"Except I'm not going to give them to you."

"What if I just take them?"

"Do you really think I've got them with me?"

Tony made a feeble attempt to intimidate me, taking a menacing step in my direction with clenched fists. Perhaps he'd learned that in acting class. But I wasn't biting. Tony wasn't a tough guy. He was a pretty boy.

"Where are you going?" I asked once he'd abandoned his threatening posture and turned his attention back to the dresser.

"Why should I spoil your fun? You'll find me anyway."

"Are you and April running off?"

"I'm getting as far from Hollywood as I can."

"What about Mickey?"

Tony stopped stuffing again and, holding several pairs of briefs in his mitts, stared back at me. "What about him?"

"You're just going to leave him behind?"

"He's a big boy now."

"He's your oldest friend, isn't he? And maybe more than that."

Tony threw the underwear to the floor in anger, and, despite the tension of the situation, I had to resist the urge to snigger at the spectacle.

"I'm not queer!" he roared at me. "I have a girlfriend. And Dot. And there've been plenty of other girls, believe me."

I said nothing. Just watched him from the bed.

"Do I look like a fairy to you?" he continued once the silence in the room had grown too loud. "Do I mince around like a pansy? Do I?"

"Of course not. Neither does Rock Hudson or—" God, I'd nearly said the name of the actor in the photographs. But then I realized that Tony must have known already. April had stolen the pictures, after all. So I said the name, and Tony didn't flinch.

"I'm not queer, I'm not queer, I'm not queer," he repeated over and over, turning away from me.

"Okay, Tony. But won't you reconsider? What will become of Mickey if you abandon him?"

"I don't know. I don't even know what I'm going to do."

"I can get you back in pictures," I said. "Dorothy wants the photographs so badly that she'll arrange things."

Tony faced me again. "Do you really think Dot will do anything she doesn't want to?"

"But I've got the photographs."

"And as soon as you give them to her, I'm out again. Besides, do I want to make it by blackmailing my way into movies?"

"I can give her the photos and reason with her."

"You don't know the first thing about Dot. She lies; she's ruthless. And she always wins. Everything's ruined for me. My career's over. I've got to get away from here. Away from Dot and Bertie Wallis and Skip Barnes and all the rest of them. Pathetic, disgusting people who've spoiled everything and everyone."

"What about April? She has her own ambitions."

"She loves me and will give up her dreams for me. We'll disappear. Find some place decent to live. And we'll never look back at what happened in this cesspool."

Tony sat on one of the two wooden chairs and hung his head. He fell silent. I slipped out of bed and approached him with caution. Deep in his misery, he may not have noticed me at all until I put a hand on his shoulder. He began sobbing, and there was nothing I could do to comfort him. I just stood there, hand resting on his shoulder, until he grabbed it and held it to his cheek.

"Don't tell them how you found me," he said, pleading with me. "Don't say you saw me like this." He gazed up at me with the most beautiful, shining eyes I'd ever fallen into. "Please."

CHAPTER THIRTY-SIX

Dry. I hardly recognized Los Angeles without the rain.

I looked up at the tall white building as I stepped from my car. This was a different world from the one Gene Duerson inhabited. Miles from the life Tony Eberle and April Kincaid led. A different reality from Mickey Harper's. And mine, too, for that matter. I could see a light in the fifth-floor corner apartment. She was in. The doorman buzzed her and announced me, and moments later Dorothy Fetterman opened the door.

"Ellie," she said simply, and stood to one side, a signal for me to enter.

She was dressed casually, in a manner of speaking. An oversized, loose-fitting wool sweater and simple white capris. She managed to look elegant even when lounging around the house. Ever the proper hostess, she offered me a drink, and we sat down for a chat.

"No date on a Saturday night?" she asked.

"I guess we're both washing our hair this evening."

She coughed a phony little chuckle. "I wasn't expecting you."

"I want to talk to you about Tony Eberle."

"Have you seen him?"

I wasn't about to tell her I had. She surely felt double-crossed by April and was itching to get her hands around her skinny neck.

"No. But I wanted to revisit our discussion of a new role for Tony. Remember you promised me you'd arrange it."

"I said I'd put him in a picture if you got me what I wanted. And if he wasn't involved in any way in Bertie Wallis's murder. Neither of those conditions has been met."

"You didn't recover a certain photograph stuffed inside a thermos?" I asked, feeling her out. Though I was fairly sure she knew I'd outwitted her hunting dogs with the decoy photo, I wanted to hear it from her. She obliged me.

"We're beyond the point of being coy, aren't we? I know you let my boys find that thermos. You knew they wouldn't realize there was more hidden somewhere else. Quite clever of you." She paused to reflect. "And sloppy of Mr. Alden."

"Then you believe I have the photographs?"

"Yes, I do. It surprised me. I had assumed you were bluffing. I thought Tony's little girlfriend had taken them from you. She swore to me she had them. Described them in great detail. But now I see. April didn't take them from you. You took them from her."

"Something like that."

Dorothy sipped her aperitif. Perhaps she thought she was nearing the end of her quest to retrieve the photographs. What would I want with them, after all? I'd hand them over to her for a reasonable sum, a promise to put Tony back into a picture, or a job. That was her first offer.

"Let's make a deal," she began. "That's why you've come, after all."

I was listening.

"You know how important it is for me to have and destroy those photographs. You've done a remarkable job in finding them. Succeeded where I couldn't. In fact, you've overcome my earlier doubts and convinced me that I want you on my staff."

"Will I be working with Mrs. Gormley?" I asked, batting my eyes and smiling eagerly. "Or Bo Hanson and Gene Duerson?"

"I'm offering you an important position," she said, a touch flustered. People didn't usually mock her and her generous offers, I was sure. "You'll assist me on delicate matters that require a woman's touch. You've proven to be a very capable investigator. You're smart. You have imagination. Why wouldn't you accept the job?"

"Because I don't trust you, Miss Fetterman."

"Please, call me Dot."

"Miss Fetterman," I repeated. "I don't believe you'll deliver what you promise. Or you'll fire me as soon as you have what you want. Or you'll ask me to do things I can't, in good conscience, do."

"What makes you think that?"

"Tony Eberle."

Dorothy stiffened in her seat. Then she reached for a cigarette from the box on the table.

"So you tricked me. You said you hadn't seen him."

"And you tricked me when you sicced Mr. Alden on me at Musso and Frank."

Dorothy expressed true surprise. "That's what's upsetting you? Miffed because a handsome man flirted with you only because I paid him to do it? Not the fact that three gorillas tore apart your room?" She twittered. "Really, I thought you were made of sterner stuff."

My nostrils flared. It had felt great to toss my drink on Andy Blaine the night before, but I needed finesse to work this situation. And I'd only taken a first sip; I wasn't going to waste a good glass of whiskey on Dorothy Fetterman's sweater.

"You're right," I said. "Mr. Alden should have tried to charm the photographs out of me yesterday. Then perhaps you'd have them in your manicured mitts now."

She didn't like that. Her mirth vanished.

"All right. Tell me what you want."

"I've told you. Tony gets a contract for a real picture. Signed and iron-clad. Then you'll get your photos."

"That's it?" she asked. "Nothing for the clever little girl from the back of beyond?"

"The price just went up to two movies," I said. "One more smart remark and Tony's going to be starring in those pictures."

She tapped her cigarette into the ashtray. "I've got to know that the photographs are safe. Please tell me no one can get at them before you hand them over to me."

"No one."

"How can I believe you?"

"You can't. But Mr. Alden couldn't find them. You'll just have to trust me."

She held up both hands in surrender. "All right, Miss Stone. Tony will get his contract. A second male lead in two upcoming pictures. We'll start with *The Colonel's Widow*. There's a nice role for a young cavalry officer."

"Bertram Wallis's movie?"

"Yes. Mr. Balaban is determined to make it, even more so now that Bertie's gone. We'll have to change that title, of course. It's awful. I'll have our legal department draw up the contracts and send them over to his agent. What was his name again?"

"Irving Greenberg."

"Oh, God. That old geezer? I thought he was dead."

Mickey was waiting when I returned to the Wilton Place apartment with a bag of potato chips and a fifth of whiskey under my arm.

"Where've you been?" he asked.

"Saving Tony's career."

"Don't tell me you've been talking to Dot."

"I was. She agreed to draw up a contract, ironclad, to guarantee Tony two pictures. Good roles, including one as a cavalry officer in the film Wallis wanted to make. *The Colonel's Widow*."

"Why would she do that?"

Despite my gratitude and growing affection for Mickey, I couldn't quite bring myself to share the details of the photos with him. I still wasn't sure how much I could trust him, whether he would betray everything I said to Tony and April, whom I didn't trust either. After all, if they ever discovered the key inside my camera, all they would need to get into the safe deposit box was the address of the bank and my driver's license. April was close enough to the height and weight described on my license to pass for me in front of a bank clerk who hated his job and couldn't care less who fiddled around with the safe deposit boxes inside the vault.

I cracked open the bottle and poured myself a drink. I sensed Mickey disapproved.

"I appealed to Dorothy's better nature," I said, returning to his question.

Mickey scoffed at me. "You know they were sleeping together, don't you?"

"That seemed obvious."

We talked for a couple of hours. We even laughed. But the conversation turned serious when I asked Mickey about his childhood.

"You must have had a tough time."

"I used to pray to God that I'd change. I didn't want to be a fairy. Nobody does. At least not when they first realize it."

"Can I ask you something?" I said, gathering my courage. I wasn't sure I wanted to know the answer to my question.

"Go ahead."

"Do you have any brothers and sisters?"

"A younger sister. Donna. Why?"

I weighed my words carefully. Did I truly want to know the answer? And would it resolve anything in my heart? Would it amount to a comfort? Or simply confuse me? But the pull was too strong. I wanted to know, so I asked.

"Did Donna know? Did she suspect?"

He drew a deep breath as he considered his answer. "Of course. After a while, at least. Everyone else did. My mother, my father, the kids at school. They made my life miserable with the taunting. Everyone except Tony."

"He didn't tease you?"

"A little, maybe," said Mickey with a sad smile. "But we were so close. I forgave him."

"And your sister?" I prompted. "How did she know?"

He shook his head wistfully. "Kids are dumb, you know. They don't have the experience. The only thing they know is what they've got. So Donna was my little sister. I was her brother. She loved me. She hated me sometimes. And later, when she understood, she was embarrassed by me. It must have been hard on her."

I wanted to pursue the matter, but Mickey said he didn't want to discuss it.

"Hey, let's invite Evelyn over," I said to change the mood.

Mickey shrugged. "I hardly know her. But if you're looking for love . . ."

Evelyn Maynard answered the door in a housecoat, her head wrapped in a red kerchief, like Rosie the Riveter. She brandished her cigarette holder as if it were . . . well, a rivet gun.

"Ellie. The answer to my dreams. What are you doing here, angel?"

"Staying across the hall for the time being. Mickey was gracious enough to take me in last night. Join us for a pajama party?"

"Thanks for fixing the sink," said Mickey once Evelyn had settled in on the corner of the Murphy bed. There were only two chairs in the place.

"Don't mention it. I heard the cops got Tony. Too bad."

"He's out," I said. "Got a good lawyer. Probably far from here by now."

Evelyn glanced at Mickey, surely wondering how he was going to manage the rent without his friend. She took a drag on her cigarette and asked if I was moving in. Mickey wrinkled his nose at the smoke but kept quiet.

"Afraid not," I said. "I'm holding out hope Tony will come back. I still think he's going to be a star."

The three of us chatted into the small hours, getting to know each other better. I felt more and more comfortable with them. At some point late in the evening, I even confessed that I had a crush on Paul Drake. They both laughed.

Evelyn was funny in a wicked way. A remarkable mimic with a wide range, she imitated singers like Connie Francis and Brenda Lee with uncanny skill. I could have done without her spot-on version of Frankie Lymon and the Teenagers' "I Want You to be My Girl." She was every bit as annoying and creepy as little Frankie. And with Mickey singing backup, I nearly ran from the room.

Evelyn said she had something called Jiffy Pop in her apartment, and she dashed across the hall to get it. Ten minutes later we were coughing up smoke and eating burnt popcorn. More fun to make than eat. We discussed the release of Francis Gary Powers by the Russians and Jacqueline Kennedy's televised tour of the White House, which both Mickey and I had missed. Evelyn had enjoyed it, though. We played charades, but that fizzled out. Awkward with three people. Evelyn suggested we play spin the bottle. That was my cue to go to bed.

"I'll take a rain check on the spin the bottle," said Evelyn at the door. "Thanks for the fun."

"She really digs you. You know that, right?" asked Mickey once we'd closed the door.

"She's harmless. It's just a game. I don't mind."

"Don't lead her on, Ellie."

"Was I doing that? I'll be more careful."

"Have you ever kissed a girl?" he asked.

"Don't be silly."

"Neither have I," he said.

SUNDAY, FEBRUARY 18, 1962

A lazy Sunday morning. It was a little after eleven, and Mickey and I were sipping our coffee and crunching some toast when a knock came at the door.

"I'll get it, dear," he said, making me smile.

Now that we were roommates, I was seeing a new side to him. He was an adorable sweetheart when he wasn't lying to your face. Poor thing. He'd had such a hard time of it. All his life.

He rose from the table and shuffled to answer the door.

"Hi. Is Ellie in?"

"Bobby Renfro?" said Mickey.

"The one and only. No autographs. Is Ellie in?"

"What are you doing here?" I asked, appearing behind Mickey.

"I came to find you," he said, trying to look past my little friend who stood between us. "I haven't been able to get you out of my mind since I met you." Then he addressed Mickey. "Do you mind?"

Mickey retreated into the room.

"How did you find me?"

Bobby mugged confusion, as if I should simply be thrilled that he'd chosen me out of all the girls in the world to fall for. Then he smiled, and I could see why he was a movie star, even if he no longer passed for a teenager. He had real charm when he decided to flip the switch.

"I ran into Tony, and he said you were staying here for a few days. Nice guy, that Tony."

"Where did you see him?"

"At the Richfield station on Van Ness. Yesterday. Around noon."

"What do you want, Bobby?"

"You treated me and Rockin' Johnny to drinks and burgers. I thought I could return the favor. A fancy dinner and night on the town. Not Barney's Beanery."

"Is Rockin' Johnny coming along?"

Bobby chuckled. "No. Just you and me."

I glanced at Mickey. "I'm not sure I'm free."

"Just say yes," he said from across the room. "If you don't go, I will."

I telephoned Charlie Reese collect. His wife answered and was about to refuse the charges. Good thing Charlie overheard and grabbed the receiver.

"You've been hard to find," he said. "I called the hotel. They said you checked out. What's going on?"

"I'm getting close, Charlie."

"Close to figuring out who killed the producer?"

"No. But I think I'm going to make Tony Eberle a movie star again. Bigger than before."

"That would be a happy ending. The readers would like that."

"Everything's in place except for Tony's approval."

"He's not onboard?"

"Not yet. Says he's finished with this town and wants to get as far away as fast as he can."

"Try to convince him. That would be a great story for us."

We moved on to discuss the progress on the murder case, and I confessed I was stumped.

"I have suspicions, of course. There are a few people who seem ruthless enough to kill for the right reason. That woman from the studio, Dorothy Fetterman, for one. And she has no shortage of henchmen at her beck and call who would do it if she crooked her finger."

"Who else?"

"I shouldn't say, but Tony's girlfriend is desperate and rash enough to do it. She's ambitious for herself and Tony. Wallis had plenty of enemies, though. Maybe someone I haven't come across. Maybe even the director, Archie Stemple. He's a real hothead. Or Bobby Renfro."

"Bobby Renfro? The actor?"

"Why not? He's been cagey about the night he lit out of a party at Wallis's house about a month ago. And he was there again the night Wallis died. A witness saw him there."

"Maybe you should follow up on that," said Charlie.

"Bobby Renfro is taking me out this evening. I'll let you know."

"Wow. Are you going to abandon us and marry some movie star?"

"Hardly," I said, thinking I'd rather bag a job like Dorothy Fetterman's than a matinee idol like Bobby Renfro for a husband.

"What about Tony?"

"He gave himself up to the cops the other day. But they've released him for now."

"You sure he's not mixed up in this?"

I glanced over at Mickey who was reading a movie magazine on the bed. "Mostly sure. But I don't know him well enough to eliminate him."

"And the roommate?"

"Same," I said, throwing another look in Mickey's direction. He didn't appear to be listening. "I doubt it, but who knows?"

Charlie asked me for my new hotel information. I was pretty sure I was crossing some invisible journalistic line by staying in the apartment of the person I'd been sent to profile. I didn't want to lie to him, so I didn't. I told him I was staying with friends, hoping he'd let it go at that. He did. But he wanted the phone number in case he needed to reach me.

"One last bit of news from my end," said Charlie. "Now that you've located Eberle, Artie has decided to send George out to LA. He's arriving tomorrow afternoon."

"Now he's sending him?"

"He's frustrated with the waiting."

"Good luck to George finding Tony. He's lit out again."

Charlie sympathized with me but insisted that it would certainly work out in my favor. "Any time you go head to head with George, you come out on top. It won't be any different this time."

I had bigger headaches than George Walsh, including the possibility that Harvey Dunnolt would rat me out to my boss. I knew that even Charlie would fire me if he found out I'd written a piece for another paper.

"Why did you leave the hotel anyway?" he asked before hanging up.

"Bed bugs," I said. And that was a lie, pure and simple.

Bobby Renfro drove a red-and-white Corvette convertible. He beeped the horn from outside on Wilton. I peered through the curtains to see him primping in the rearview mirror. If he thought I was going to answer a car horn, he'd be waiting a long time for dinner. After two more tries, he found the manners to climb out of the car and come to the door.

"Didn't you hear me blowing the horn?" he asked.

"I sure did."

"Then why didn't you come out?"

"A gentleman comes to the door to collect his date."

He gaped at me. "Really? I always just blow the horn."

In the car, Bobby informed me that he was taking me to the Beverly Hills Hotel. I said that was rather presumptuous.

"Oh, no. Not like that," he said as we turned onto Sunset Boulevard. "We're going to eat there. Have you heard of the Polo Lounge?"

"I suppose so. Wasn't it in some movie or other?"

"Probably. Not my usual speed. Generally I go for less fancy places."

"Then why are you taking me there? I treated you to Barney's, after all."

"Never mind that," he said. "I wanted to show you a nice time."

Bobby roared down Sunset in the Vette, and I confess it was a sweet little ride. Not very practical for grocery shopping or family vacations, but a wonderful lure for attracting and hooking young lovelies.

"Nice car," I said. He grinned. "Is it practical in the rain?"

"It doesn't rain in Southern California."

"In my experience, it does nothing but rain here."

"This year's a little unusual," he granted.

Our date was off to a great start. We were talking about the weather. I tried to make more small talk and told him I thought it was too bad the studio had pulled the plug on *Twistin' on the Beach*.

"There'll be other pictures. I've got a contract."

"You were in three or four of Bertram Wallis's movies. Do you think they might put you in the next one?"

"That widow movie? I heard about it on the lot the other day. Not really my kind of thing. Horses and India and all that. Plus I can't do an English accent to save my life."

"Bobby," I said, stiffening in my seat. I clenched the door handle.

"What is it?" he asked, looking over at me. "Are you sick? You're as white as a ghost."

"Take me back to Tony's place. Right away, please."

"What's going on, Ellie? Did I say something wrong?"

"No, Bobby. You said something just right. But I can't go to dinner with you tonight."

I didn't know why it hadn't struck me earlier. It had taken Bobby Renfro's commentary on his own acting abilities to jostle the thoughts in my head, and when he said he wouldn't be right for a role in *The Colonel's Widow*, everything rushed into focus. I knew who had killed Bertram Wallis.

CHAPTER THIRTY-SEVEN

"What are you doing back so soon?" asked Mickey.

"I can't talk right now," I said. "I have to phone the police."

Millard didn't believe me once I managed to reach him, but he said he'd stop by to hear me out. I hung up the phone and excused myself from Mickey and slipped into the bathroom, my suitcase in tow.

Once safely alone, I popped open the latches and dug into my belongings. It didn't take long to locate what I was looking for. A photograph of Bertram Wallis's study. I needed to look through a loupe to confirm my suspicions. But the proof was there in black and white.

Millard took me to a Mexican restaurant, El Coyote on Beverly, where we sat in a booth to talk. I didn't want to discuss this in front of Mickey or anyone else. Over a drink, I told him he needed to get a search warrant for the Writers Guild.

"It's Sunday night," he whined. "Where am I going to get a warrant?"

"Tomorrow morning," I said.

"What are we looking for?"

"A script."

"Really?" He sounded skeptical. I nodded. "You say you know who killed Wallis. Why don't you just tell me, and I'll go talk to the guy. People usually like to confess once they're cornered."

"There's no reason for an arrest until we see the script. Trust me for twelve hours. By ten tomorrow morning you'll have your murderer. And your promotion."

Millard dropped me back at Mickey's a little after ten. I had to speak to Gene. I dialed his number. No answer. My heart was in my throat. I called Andy on the off chance Gene was with him. He wasn't. Our conversation felt awkward after what had happened the previous night. He offered an apology, said he shouldn't drink because it made him angry. I didn't answer.

"I know where I can find him," he said.

"Have him meet me at Tony Eberle's apartment. It's urgent."

"Okay, Ellie," said Mickey once I'd hung up the phone. "You called off a date with Bobby Renfro, then you ran out for a mysterious meeting with a cop. And now you're begging some reporter to get over here right away. What's going on?"

I couldn't tell Mickey. I couldn't tell anyone. The only person I could talk to was Gene. I apologized to Mickey and lied that Millard had ordered me not to say anything to anyone until the next day.

"And, by the way, that was no date with Bobby Renfro," I said. "That was Dorothy Fetterman trying to trip me up, I'm sure. She must have had me followed, since I doubt Bobby saw Tony at the gas station. Dorothy arranged the whole thing in the hopes that I'd fall for Bobby and tell him everything."

"Tell him what?" asked Mickey, almost pleading.

"You really don't know?"

"Know what?"

"When was the last time you saw April and Tony?"

Mickey tried to recall. "It was the night in Malibu. They left me there with you and went to her place on Edgemont."

He was convincing, but I just couldn't take the chance and tell him about the photographs. Certainly never tell him the actor's name. He was a sweet kid, after all, but damaged and unstable. I didn't know whom he might tell if I shared the information. Or even if he'd smother me in my sleep on orders from April and steal the safe deposit box key. I wasn't yet sure whose side he was on, so I lied again.

"Dorothy wants to know what happened to the script for Bertram Wallis's next film. I know where to find it."

It wasn't entirely false. I did know where to find the script. It was collecting dust among the Writers Guild's inventory.

I had a drink to steady my nerves as I arranged my thoughts and waited for Gene to show up. An hour ticked by. Still no knock at the door. I phoned him again, but there was no answer. Same result at Andy's number. Mickey dozed off on his bed. I dimmed the lights and poured myself another drink.

It was past eleven thirty when I heard someone climb the stoop outside and enter the hallway. A moment later there was a soft rap at the door. I rushed to open and found Andy Blaine standing there.

CHAPTER
THIRTY-EIGHT

"Andy. What are you doing here? I was expecting Gene."

"Aren't you glad to see me?" he slurred.

"Where's Gene?"

Andy shrugged and tried to push his way inside. I held him back with a hand against his chest.

"Where's Gene?" I repeated.

"Who cares about him? I'm all you need."

"You're drunk," I said. "I think you should go home and sleep it off."

"No, I want to come in." He proceeded to do just that.

"Andy, no. You have to leave now."

"Come on. How about a kiss?"

"No."

"Come on. You can't leave me hanging like this."

And he was on me in an instant, pushing me back into the wooden chairs and onto the floor. Roused by the rumble, Mickey called out. I couldn't see him, but he was yelling for Andy to stop. Andy had me pinned on the floor like a wrestler. His hands held mine over my head, and he'd forced his legs between mine. His unshaven face pressed against my cheek in an attempt to immobilize my head, which I was thrashing back and forth to resist him. I could smell the beer and tamale sauce on his breath, and I wanted to vomit on him. He was heavy, and he used his size to hold me in place. Then I felt the wallop of more weight on my body, nearly knocking the wind out of me. Where was the referee to call piling on? Another of those odd thoughts that occur so unexpectedly in life-threatening moments. And, indeed, someone had piled on. Mickey. I caught a glimpse of him—tiny little Mickey—on Andy's back, riding him like a bucking bronco. He screamed, spat, and pulled at him, grabbing him by the chin as he tried to pry him off me. Andy was screaming something incoherent about teaching me a lesson, and despite Mickey's bravest efforts, it looked as if he might succeed. Then Mickey's delicate hands found Andy's eyes. My aggressor roared and reared up like a wounded beast, shaking Mickey off his back. Andy stumbled to his feet and turned his attention to my overmatched champion. Mickey had fallen into a jumble on the floor near the kitchen sink. Andy lunged at him, throttled him with both hands, and lifted him up by the throat.

"I'm going to kill you, you little faggot!"

I righted myself, intending to rescue Mickey. I didn't know how I'd manage it, but I was going to do it. Only I never got the chance. The clap of a baseball bat, colliding with the back of Andy's head, put an end to his plans for Mickey. On the other end of the bat, Evelyn Maynard's sturdy hands gripped the handle. She stood there in her nightgown, a gladiatrix towering over her flattened foe. And her long, ebony cigarette holder, clenched between her teeth, jutted upward to the ceiling in victory.

"Hollywood Girls Softball League," she said in a hoarse whisper.

MONDAY, FEBRUARY 19, 1962

The rain returned with a vengeance. I was sore and tired after my late night. Wrestling with a deranged photographer and then making a statement to the police afterward. But I had an appointment with Millard and didn't intend to miss it.

"I heard you had some trouble last night," said Millard as I climbed into his unmarked car.

"Not exactly an evening with Ozzie and Harriet."

"You're a magnet for trouble, you know that?"

"Did you get the warrant?"

Millard patted his left breast pocket and threw the car into gear. "It's a little irregular for me to let you come along," he said. "But the warrant kind of clued us in to what we're looking for. If you're right, that was pretty clever of you. So as a reward, I convinced my captain to let you be there for the search. You can't say or touch anything, but you can stand a few feet away and watch."

"Thank you, Sergeant."

"You're welcome, Miss Stone."

The nice folks at the Writers Guild choked when Millard and two patrolmen presented them with the warrant at 10:15 on a Monday morning. Truth be told, they probably would have been happy to show the police what they wanted to see without a warrant. But the writ made things official. Blanche, the same woman who'd assisted me nearly two weeks earlier, showed the two patrolmen through a door behind the front desk. The three of them returned five minutes later with a couple of parcels. Millard took possession and placed them on a desk. Each parcel, wrapped in brown paper and bound with string, measured eight and a half by eleven inches.

Millard flashed the woman a big smile. "Would you be kind enough to identify these two items?"

Perplexed, she gaped at him through her horn-rimmed glasses and asked if he knew how to read. Millard's smile dimmed, and he told her a little less politely to read the labels.

"This one says *The Colonel's Widow*, and it's registered to Bertram Wallis," she said.

"What's the date on it?"

"November fourteenth, 1961."

"And the other one?"

"It says *Twilight in the Summer Capital* by Eugene Duerson. Dated February ninth, 1962. Oh, it's a new one." She smiled.

"Thank you, ma'am."

Then he turned to one of the patrolmen and instructed him to open both parcels.

"Neatly," he said. "No ripping. This isn't Christmas Day."

Once the scripts had been opened, Millard shuffled through them, glancing back and forth between them for about a minute. At length he held out some pages from the middle of both piles for the two officers to see. One of them drew a sharp whistle.

"Yeah," said Millard with a knowing nod. "Except for the titles, they're identical to the last word."

He ordered the men to rewrap the scripts and take them in as evidence. Then he told them to radio the precinct to send a couple of black-and-whites to pick up Gene Duerson.

☙

"That was some fine guesswork, Miss Stone," said Millard, extending a hand in congratulations.

I must have blushed.

"What tipped you off?"

"It was Bobby Renfro."

"Bobby Renfro? The lousy actor Bobby Renfro?"

"Yes, him," I said, realizing I was impugning poor Bobby's career. It was one of those when-did-you-stop-beating-your-wife questions. "He mentioned Wallis's next film. The script you just saw. *The Colonel's Widow.*"

"What of it?"

"It got me thinking. Actually, it hit me like a bolt from the blue. I remembered something I'd read in Wallis's biographical sketch, right here at the Writers Guild. It said he came from a distinguished military family. His grandfather was a colonel in the British Army and served on the personal staff of the viceroy of India after that."

"I don't get it."

"Somehow I never connected the dots of his next film, *The Colonel's Widow.* But during the war, British children were shipped off to the colonies, Canada, Australia, and even India, to keep them safe from the Blitz. Bertram Wallis's family sent him to India to stay with his grandmother, the colonel's widow, in a place called Simla."

"You've lost me. How does that connect Wallis's movie to Duerson's?"

"I studied history in college. And one course I particularly enjoyed was on the decline of British colonialism."

"And?"

"And I remembered one chapter about the British administration in India that sounded so romantic to me. Each year, they would pack up everything—offices, families, horses, everything—and move from Delhi to a summer capital in the foothills of the Himalayas to escape the heat."

"Let me guess," said Millard. "It was that place you just mentioned. Simla."

"The summer capital. Where Bertram Wallis spent the war years with his grandmother."

"The colonel's widow."

We sat in one of the meeting rooms for several minutes more, discussing the development. Thanks to Andy Blaine's photographs and Gene's own admission to me, we knew Gene had been outside Wallis's house the night of the murder. It was a short step from there to conclude that Gene might well have been the man in the other room whom Mrs. Gormley had described to me. What was missing was a motive. But with the appearance of identical scripts under both men's names, a powerful motive was coming into focus.

"So what do you think?" asked Millard. "Duerson wanted the script and stole it from Wallis? Killed him to get it?"

"No," I said. "I think Gene Duerson wrote the script and Wallis stole it from him."

"How do you figure?"

"I believe Wallis hired Duerson to write this script then stiffed him or refused to give him writing credit or something along those lines. Gene once told me that the lowest thing you can do to a writer is steal his work. He had a very strong opinion about it. And once he called Wallis a plagiarist, though he gave no explanation. I think Gene considered it his property, even if it was Wallis's grandmother's story."

"How can you be sure? Wallis made quite a few pictures. Duerson hasn't made one."

"Take a look at this," I said, retrieving the photo I'd dug out of my suitcase the night before.

Millard squinted but couldn't see it. I handed him my loupe and pointed to the bookshelf in the photo. He scanned the image closely for several seconds before he saw it.

"'*Twilight in the Summer Capital*,'" he read. "Duerson's script. It's right there on his shelf."

"I'm glad you let us take pictures of the study."

"Me too."

"Wallis made silly teen romps. Now suddenly he pulls a brilliant art film out of his hat? No. That's Gene Duerson's work."

"Sounds like you and Duerson are friendly. Don't you feel bad about turning him in?"

"Of course I do," I said, thinking of how he'd comforted me two nights before.

One of the patrolmen knocked on the door and entered.

"Just talked to the captain," he told Millard. "Told him about Duerson."

"And?"

"The captain said thanks, but no need. Duerson turned himself in twenty minutes ago. Strolled into the station and said he wanted to make a confession."

CHAPTER THIRTY-NINE

Monday afternoon I tried to visit Gene at the Wilcox station. He sent word through his public defender that he didn't want to see anyone except his youngest sister, who was on her way from Texas on a bus.

"He hates me, doesn't he?" I asked the lawyer, a young man who looked as if he'd just passed the bar that morning.

"Why? He turned himself in and confessed, didn't he? Made my job a little easier doing that. Not as much fun, though." He tucked his briefcase under his arm and walked off down the corridor.

Millard showed up with a cup of coffee for me.

"How's he doing?" I asked.

"Not too bad. Probably feels better now that he's got it off his chest. That's the way it is with most killers. At least the amateurs like him. Now Andrew Blaine is another story. Not a big fan of yours right now. But don't worry. He won't be bothering you anytime soon."

Mickey, Evelyn, and I had all signed sworn statements detailing Andy's attack. The police thought I might have to return to California at the time of the trial to testify.

"And how's he doing?"

"He'll live. He'll be in the hospital for a while, though. That dyke clubbed him good with the bat. Nearly killed him. She should bat cleanup for the Dodgers."

"Did Gene say why he did it?" I asked, ignoring Millard's musings on Evelyn's baseball prowess.

"He said he went there to talk things over with Wallis. He hadn't heard from him in weeks about the script he wrote. He was waiting for Wallis in the study when there was a ruckus in the next room."

"Tony beating up Wallis?"

"That's right. Duerson saw Tony and his girl running from the place. Wallis was on the floor, covered in his own blood and vomit. Duerson helped him up, gave him a drink. Then he brought up the script. The chat turned ugly, and they argued. Wallis said it was his idea. Said he paid Duerson to write the script and now it was his. He was going to make the picture, and Duerson sure as hell wasn't getting his name on it."

"And that's when Gene lost his temper and killed him?"

"You'd think so, but no. He said he was about to drag his sorry self out of there. Go home and lick his wounds when all of a sudden Wallis offered him a new deal to write another script. And this time he'd let him keep the writing credit."

"And? He didn't take the offer?"

"No. Something snapped. Your boy went ape. He says he knew Wallis would just take advantage of him again, so he slugged him. It felt good, so he slugged him again. Then he kept punching him even after he fell to the floor. When he regained his wits, he thought he killed him. Must have hit him hard or banged his head on the floor, because he was sure he was dead."

"And that's when he tossed him over the railing?"

Millard nodded. "Locked the dog out on the terrace by accident, I figure. He never even noticed him. Then he jumped into his car and drove off."

"By any chance, did he knock over a neighbor's garbage cans?" I asked.

Millard wasn't sure. I guessed it didn't matter, but that might have explained Gene's twisted bumper and Trudy Hirshland's dented trash cans.

We talked a few minutes more, and I realized my opinion about Sergeant John Millard had changed. He was coarse, possibly on the take, but a damn good cop. And deep down inside there was a grain of decency in his soul. Our brief acquaintance was at an end. We might see each other again if I returned to Los Angeles for Andy's trial, but who knew? Fiddling with my crippled umbrella—the same one I'd borrowed from Marty the bellhop—I apologized again for the way I'd treated him on our dinner date. He shrugged but said nothing. Then I thanked him for his help, and he thanked me for mine.

"You be more careful in the future," he said before I took my leave. "There are a lot of bad guys out there. They're not all sweethearts like me."

I spent the rest of Monday evening writing three new articles on the Bertram Wallis murder, one focusing on the victim and his history, another on the murder itself, and a third on my friend Gene Duerson. Tony more or less faded into the background of those stories since he'd ended up a mere footnote, a temporary suspect who'd been cleared.

I phoned Charlie Reese in the middle of the night, his time, and got his wife, Edith, again on the line. She screeched at me until Charlie wrestled the phone away from her. I apologized for the late hour and told him the big news. He was giddy, promising he would serve up some humble pie for Artie Short in the morning. I dictated my stories to him, and he congratulated me on my fine work.

"I never doubted you, Ellie," he said.

I'd learned to resist the urge to rub men's noses in their own mistakes, so I didn't contradict him. Charlie was a good egg, after all. He'd hired me when no one else would, and had shielded me from Artie Short's wrath on many occasions. Probably saved my job just as many times. But I knew that my reputation at the *New Holland Republic* was only as strong as my most recent day of work. That was the price I paid for wearing a skirt in a man's job.

TUESDAY, FEBRUARY 20, 1962

"Do you have an appointment?" asked the guard at the Bronson Gate.

"No, but I'm sure she'll want to see me."

He picked up the phone and dialed three numbers. After a moment he announced that Miss Eleonora Stone was there to see her.

"She says she doesn't have an appointment." He listened for a moment then nodded. "Yes, Miss Fetterman. I'll drive her over right away."

The guard invited me to sit in a small motorized car, and he took the wheel.

"Are we going golfing?" I asked.

"Funny," he said and drove off.

Dorothy met me in the alleyway below her office bungalow. She'd thrown her coat over her shoulders and waited in the light misty rain with no umbrella.

"Thank you, Thomas," she said to the guard.

She didn't say a word to me until we were seated opposite each other in her office. "I understand the police have arrested Gene Duerson for Bertie's murder."

I nodded.

"And you figured it out. Have you come to gloat? Or have you reconsidered my offer of a position?"

"No, I haven't come for a job."

She pursed her perfectly painted lips. "Then it's to gloat."

I reached into my purse, retrieved a sealed brown envelope, and placed it on the desk between us. She eyed it with ill-concealed avidity.

"What's that?" she asked.

"Open it."

"You don't want Tony's contracts before I take it?"

I shrugged my indifference. "Tony's gone. He might come back, but I doubt it."

Dorothy stared at me for a long moment. I fancied she was trying to look into my soul again. I was sure she couldn't fathom why I would fold my hand when I held all the best cards.

"You know I've already sent the signed contracts to his agent," she said, perhaps trying to score points on some invisible integrity meter. Perhaps she was trying to prove something to me. "The deal is his if he wants it. I can't rescind the offer."

"Good luck and congratulations to him," I said.

Dorothy sliced the envelope open with a painted fingernail and reached inside. She retrieved six three-and-a-half-by-five photographs.

"Oh, God," she said after the briefest peek, and slipped them back into the envelope, which she closed with some tape. Then she scrawled her signature over the seal and drew a cleansing breath.

"Thank you, Miss Stone. Some very important people will be pleased that this has been resolved at last."

"I'll be going then."

She watched me closely as I rose from the chair.

"It hasn't been easy, you know," she said.

"I beg your pardon."

"You asked me once why I never married, and I didn't answer you. It hasn't been easy."

Purse in hand, ready to leave, I stood there above her and stared.

"I made a decision long ago," she continued. "I chose the life I wanted, and I've stuck with my choice. For better or worse. And I've been happy for the most part."

She paused, and I waited. I wasn't going to interrupt her.

"You think me heartless," she said. "Ruthless, especially where someone like Tony is concerned. But you're wrong. I have feelings, you know. Feelings for Tony. More than you know. And there've been others besides him. Such beautiful men. Young and talented with great futures before them and absolutely no interest in falling in love with me. I know my talents and my limitations. Yes, I'm sure they enjoy the wicked secrecy of a clandestine affair with an older woman. What young man wouldn't? A little adventure they'll recall fondly, deliciously perhaps, as they grow older. But not one of them ever considered me anything more than a lark." She snickered with a hint of melancholy. "And that includes Tony. I was a pleasant stop on his journey to manhood. Perhaps I taught him something about love or about himself."

"Why are you telling me this?" I asked. "I'm not judging you."

"I think I've wanted to tell someone for a long time. Just tell someone. I have no close friends, Miss Stone. Just young men for brief, exhilarating periods at a time. Oh, I'm not looking for pity. As I said, I chose this life and I like it. It has its many perks." She managed a weak smile. Then it faded on her lips. "But it hasn't been easy. That's what I wanted to tell you."

"Thank you for answering my question," I said and turned to reach for the doorknob. I looked back at her. "Good-bye, Miss Fetterman."

Dorothy's confession inspired me to right one last wrong. I was still in possession of an object that did not rightly belong to me. So to expunge any possible recrimination one might lay at my feet, I returned to the McCadden Hotel to give back the crippled umbrella.

Mr. Cromartie nearly fell off his chair when he saw me enter the lobby. But I approached him without hostility. I laid Marty's umbrella on the desk and told him we were square. In truth, I don't believe he remembered the tattered old thing or what I was talking about. But I felt noble, self-righteous at having settled my debt. Of course I was aware that I hadn't paid the bill, but that was technically a problem for Artie Short's conscience, not mine. I wished the old man good day, turned on my heel, and walked out into the street with head held high.

As I stood on the stoop, pulling my gloves onto my hands, a taxi rolled to a stop at the curb. My old pal Marty the bellhop sprang into action. He avoided my eyes as he yanked open the rear passenger door and welcomed the arriving guest. A man struggled to extricate from the cab, spilling a jumble of papers into the gutter as he did.

"Let me help you with that, sir," said Marty, bending over to gather the wayward documents.

A man in his forties wearing a Hawaiian shirt climbed out of the taxi. No overcoat or umbrella for the wintry California weather. Greenhorn, I thought. Then my heart skipped with joy. It was George Walsh. He'd arrived just in time to close the barn door after the horse had run off.

EPILOGUE

Andy Blaine copped a plea for a lesser sentence, thereby sparing me a return trip to sunny California. The judge took pity on him, as it was his first offense, but ordered him to stay away from Mickey Harper and Evelyn Maynard. And me.

Gene Duerson took a deal on a manslaughter charge and was sentenced to twenty years, according to Millard. He'd kept me apprised of the situation after I left California. And Gene wrote to me years later to say he was sorry for what he'd done. That he'd never intended to kill Wallis. And that he'd written a novel, *The Wrong Side of Luck*. I don't believe he ever found a publisher, which, I suppose, could have been predicted by the book's title.

I did see Mickey again down the line in much different circumstances. But that's a story for another day.

Tony Eberle never returned to Hollywood. At least not that I ever knew. He never appeared in any movies, that much is certain. New Holland's golden boy must have boarded that train for oblivion, the depot Gene Duerson had written was reserved for broken dreams.

Upon my return to New Holland, Charlie insisted I close the chapter on Tony Eberle. We had to publish something about what had happened, he reasoned. So I wrote a brief summary of his decision to leave the movie business once *Twistin' on the Beach* was shelved.

"Local Actor Walks Away from Hollywood" was the headline of my two-paragraph story. No, I didn't tell the hometown folks how I'd found him. I gave him a break to make up in a small way for the break he'd thrown away. I debated whether to write about the offer he'd refused, the one for a two-picture deal that Dorothy Fetterman had extended to him like a farewell kiss. In the end, I decided to leave it out. It would only have invited more gossip and recrimination against him among the local populace. As it was, I tried to make his departure sound almost heroic in my piece. But, in truth, I failed. I gave so few details, no quotes, no description of Tony's life or state of mind—respecting his last plea to me—that his "brave" decision to leave the dirty world of Hollywood rang false, as if I'd tacked it onto the story.

And, in fact, New Holland did not react well to Tony's downfall. He was mocked, ridiculed, and pilloried for having embarrassed himself and the town. Harvey Dunnolt, who never did report my moonlighting to Artie Short, wrote a scathing article on Tony in the *Gazette* two days after mine appeared, holding back nothing. He characterized Tony as a fickle, weak-willed failure who'd pushed away a chance at success with both hands. Many in his hometown agreed. One evening a month after I'd returned home, I overheard a bar full of drinkers and diners at Tedesco's reveling in their contempt and derision of the once-adored local boy. Some even joked that he'd run off with a rich fairy who made him earn his supper the hard way every evening. They used a cruder term.

"Hey!" yelled the proprietor, Jimmy Tedesco, to silence the talk. "Watch your language. There's a lady here."

But long before all the unhappy endings—Tony's, Gene's, and even Andy's—had played out, I still had one last evening left in Los Angeles, and I spent it with my friends Mickey, Evelyn, Nelson, and Lucia. They wanted to take me someplace special, if for one night only. I insisted on dinner at Musso and Frank, and reluctantly they agreed. We drank and gorged ourselves on what I hoped would be Artie Short's dime. Perhaps not, but I intended to submit the bill as an expense just the same. As things turned out, Nelson Blanchard sneaked away from the table at a certain point and settled the bill without my knowledge. I told him he still wasn't getting me into bed.

After three hours, a steak Diane, and several glasses of whiskey, I told my friends that it was time to push off home. I was tired.

"You might want to wait one minute," said Evelyn, grinning like a thief at something over my shoulder.

"Why?" I asked, turning to see what she was smiling at. But there was a large man in a checkered jacket standing directly behind me blocking my view. "Excuse me, sir, but would you mind—"

I swallowed my words and choked. The man in the checkered coat was William Hopper, Paul Drake in the flesh. And he was smiling at me.

"Hiya, beautiful," he said with a wink. Then he walked out of my life forever.

We nearly laughed ourselves out of our chairs.

"How? Who? When?" I stammered.

"It was Evelyn," said Mickey. "She saw him at the bar and begged him to come over. She even told him what to say."

I melted and actually shed tears of happiness. After an emotional, waterlogged two weeks in Los Angeles, during which practically everything had gone wrong, I threw my arms around Evelyn and hugged her tight. She had given me the greatest parting gift I could have hoped for. And it wasn't Paul Drake.

ACKNOWLEDGMENTS

As always, I'm indebted to my editor, Dan Mayer, and my agent, William Reiss. Thank you to Mary Ziskin, Jennifer Ziskin, Dr. Hilbert, and Dr. Kunda for their feedback and advice; as well as to Jeffrey Curry for his keen eye in editing this book. A special thanks to Paul D. Marks for his generous assistance and expertise.

ABOUT THE AUTHOR

James W. Ziskin is the Edgar, Anthony, Barry, and Lefty Award–nominated author of the Ellie Stone mysteries. He lives in the Hollywood Hills.